Victoria Corby was .... in England. She travelled and worked in Australia and Hong Kong before returning to London to work in advertising and PR. She now lives in south-west France with her husband and three daughters. *Something Stupid* is her first novel. Her second, *Seven Week Itch*, is also available from Headline.

Something Stupid

Victoria Corby

First published in 1999
by HEADLINE BOOK PUBLISHING

First published in paperback in 2000
by HEADLINE BOOK PUBLISHING

10 9 8 7 6 5 4 3 2

ISBN 0 7472 6336 1

Typeset by
Letterpart Limited, Reigate, Surrey

Printed and bound in Great Britain by
Mackays of Chatham PLC, Chatham, Kent

HEADLINE BOOK PUBLISHING
A division of the Hodder Headline Group
338 Euston Road
London NW1 3BH

www.headline.co.uk
www.hodderheadline.com

For Roshnara, Diana and Christina

CHAPTER 1

So I should never have accepted that lift from Hugo Parry-Smith. Though he seemed quite respectable, which I know doesn't mean anything – Crippen probably looked as if he was kind to children, animals and wives – but Hugo didn't stink of alcohol (which was more than could be said for a lot of the people at that party), and he was related in some way to the hostess so he wasn't just someone who'd heard music and wandered in off the street. The truth is that by then I was so teed off with my boyfriend Daniel that I would have happily accepted a lift from someone who had 'if found please return to the asylum' stamped on his forehead, if it meant I could leave with dignity, with a man, and not looking like some poor abandoned sad act. Daniel, after taking me to this party given by his friends, had abandoned me after five minutes to huddle in a corner with a well-endowed blonde (top and bottom) and was still there two hours later, gazing down her cleavage. I'd have stormed out ages before (tottering would have been more like it in four-inch heels) if I'd had some way of getting home, but I didn't have the cash for a taxi and as for walking, forget it. It would have

1

been asking for trouble. With a skirt that short, on a freezing January night we're talking hypothermia. So there were loads of good reasons why I accepted Hugo's offer like a shot.

But I discovered before the first set of traffic lights that he was what my mother calls NSIT: not safe in taxis. In fact he wasn't safe *anywhere*. Most men have the decency to delay making a dive for your boobs until they've known you longer than five minutes – especially if they're driving at the same time. This man was *seriously* over-sexed. I superglued my knees together and crossed my arms defensively; he still got at the waistband of my skirt and, considering how tight it was, that took some doing. I've been around men before who are completely unable to understand that I haven't been bowled over immediately by their charms, but Hugo was in another category altogether. It wasn't that he was one of those who thinks 'No' or 'Stop that!' mean 'Perhaps' and 'Persuade me that I want to' – negatives weren't in his vocabulary at all. I reckoned I was safe enough for the moment. Rape's got to be difficult in a low-slung sports car, with a large and no doubt deeply symbolic gear stick between you, but if I let this piece of rampant slime take me home I really would be asking for trouble. Unfortunately I no longer shared a flat with two members of the university rowing team and I couldn't see that Hugo would be deterred much by the presence of Liv, my current flatmate. Since she's blonde and willowy he'd probably have a go at her too. Besides I didn't want him knowing where I lived. Hell, I didn't even want him to know what *part* of London I lived in. I began going over my options. I could try jumping out of the car when we slowed down at traffic lights, but given that my legs were sticking almost straight out in front of me and my skirt allowed about as much movement as a plaster of Paris mould it would be more of a slow wriggle than a jump. And if he were so inclined he'd be able to catch me in about three seconds, no doubt humming 'Let's Do It in the Road' at the same time.

Abruptly he swung the car into a space at the end of a road and, engine still running, leaned over and made another grab at me. I recoiled as far as I could, but still not far enough to evade his fingers completely. 'Wouldn't this be more comfortable at home?' I ventured nervously, trying to restrain a shudder. 'It's only a couple of minutes away.'

To my intense relief his hand withdrew to its proper place. 'I wasn't sure you were going to ask me in,' he said, looking at me with glazed eyes. So he was helping himself in advance, just in case. 'But I thought you said you lived in Clapham? That's more than a couple of minutes away.'

I cleared my throat. 'Well, it's Clapham borders, sort of.'

He nodded, his mind probably too fogged with lust to notice that the edge of Putney can in no way be described as two minutes from 'Clapham borders'. 'Where exactly do you live?'

I licked my lips. What the hell was I to do now? The road sign just outside my window caught my eye. 'London Borough of Wandsworth.' I swallowed hard. Could I? I hate having to admit that I've made a fool of myself, and I'd never live it down . . . But it was marginally preferable to claiming I lived next door to the police station and going in and throwing myself on the protection of a no doubt spotty constable, younger than myself, which was the only other thing I could think of at short notice.

My heart was thumping so loudly I was almost sure he could hear it as I said, 'It's not far. Half a mile down here. Take the first left and . . .'

It was the wrong direction. I smiled apologetically at him and said with a nervous laugh, 'I've only just moved, I still don't know the way in the dark.'

'So *that*'s why you think you're still living in Clapham,' he said, hand roaming sideways again.

'Er, yes.' I squirmed away a bit. 'Up there,' I said as we turned on to a short row of Georgian cottages. 'That one.' Thank God there was a light shining out through the half-moon fanlight above the door. I could only pray there was someone in and it hadn't just been left on as a burglar deterrent.

I had my hand on the door handle and my legs tensed ready for flight as Hugo slowed the car, looking for a parking space. Someone drew out halfway up the road and he backed into the space. I wriggled out at high speed before he had a chance to do more than reach for the ignition keys. Dammit! I was never going to be able to move fast in these shoes. With extreme reluctance I took them off and, jiggling from side to side from the shock of the icy tarmac under the soles of my feet, poked my head back in through the car window. 'Thanks for the lift, Hugo. Actually I think it's a bit late for you to come in for that cup of coffee. My husband's a light sleeper.'

And before he could say anything I dodged around the back of the car and bolted across the road to the house opposite, stumbling up two shallow steps and banging the lion's head knocker loudly on the door. The noise seemed to fill the silent street. It wasn't just going to be my putative husband who was woken up at this rate, I thought, glancing over my shoulder to see what Hugo was doing. He sat motionless in his car, watching me, looking distinctly put out. I smiled nervously. 'Silly me! I forgot my keys.' Oh, God, if James wasn't there, what was I going to do? I wasn't going to have to cope with a merely randy weirdo, but a seriously pissed off randy weirdo.

Just as I was beginning to despair I heard a voice saying grumpily, 'Hold your horses, I'm coming!' and the door was flung open with a bad-tempered crash. 'What the—' exclaimed the tall brown-haired man in the doorway, eyes narrowed under straight brows as he glared at me.

I flung my arms around his neck in a hug. 'Darling, I'm so sorry to disturb you!' I exclaimed loudly enough to be heard over the road. The body beneath my embracing arms was unflatteringly stiff and unwelcoming. 'Did I get you out of bed?'

There was a startled pause. 'Of course you didn't, you idiot!' His tone was distinctly frosty. 'If this is another example of your oddball sense of humour . . .'

'Shush!' I murmured. He was one step above me so I had to go up on tiptoe to speak against his ear. 'I'm sorry about this, James. I couldn't risk going any further with that man over there.'

He sighed heavily. 'Oh, come on, Laura! What is this?' he demanded. 'Had a row with the boyfriend?' He definitely wasn't in a receptive mood.

5

'No! It's not Daniel. Someone else. I think he'd have raped me in the car if he'd been able to get over the gear stick! He's a *maniac*!'

James went rigid under my arms. 'What did he *do*?' he said, stepping back, eyes scanning me for damage. 'Did he hurt you?'

I shook my head. 'Only ripped off a few buttons! But he was still in warm-up mode. He frightened me.' To my annoyance I could hear a bit of a tremor in my voice.

James opened his mouth, no doubt with some elder brotherly remark pouring scorn on my complete lack of common sense in even contemplating getting into a car with a male younger than my grandfather (I've heard them before), then must have thought better of it. (He's heard my reaction.) He sighed. 'You'd better come in until he's gone.'

I've had more welcoming invitations, but frankly I was too glad that I was going to be on the right side of his door to care. My murmured thanks were lost as a voice called from inside the house, 'James, darling! What *is* going on?' My heart plummeted. Brilliant timing, Laura! My apologies to James for disturbing him were going to have to be even more humiliatingly grovelling now. And, I realised with a further sinking of the heart, as he'd got someone here he wasn't going to be able to give me a lift back to my flat as I'd hoped. Not only was I going to have to sit around and play gooseberry with him and his girlfriend while we waited for a taxi, but I was going to have to borrow the fare off him as well.

He called back, 'Just a minute! Why don't you go in, Laura?' and glanced over my shoulder. 'I'll just go and advise Sonny Boy to move on if he knows what's good for him.'

His tone was so grim that I grabbed his sleeve as he went past. 'James, you won't *do* anything, will you?'

His teeth gleamed very white as he smiled. 'I'm fond of you, Laura,' he said with something of an effort, 'but that affection doesn't run to risking a black eye!'

This last was certainly true. I doubted strongly if James would risk getting a black eye, or any sort of injury, for anyone. As he advanced across the street like the Sheriff in *High Noon* Hugo started his engine and began to reverse out of the parking space with an alacrity that spoke of long practice at dodging annoyed protective males. He wasn't quick enough. Short of actually running James over he had to listen to whatever it was that was being said to him through the open window of his car. Try as I might I couldn't hear what it was, but it didn't sound conciliatory. Good. James straightened up and turned around, strolling back with his hands in his pockets while Hugo revved the engine and crunched the gears at least twice as he sped away.

'He won't bother you again,' James said with a note of satisfaction. My curiosity mounted. What *had* he said? For though tall, he just doesn't look like one of those men who could punch you out at a moment's notice. Well, he certainly doesn't to me. He doesn't bulge with muscles from work-outs at the gym for one thing. 'But I didn't realise we'd got married,' he added mildly as he reached me at the top of the steps. 'I know it's traditional for the bridegroom to get absolutely plastered, but I think I would have remembered *something* about the ceremony.

Unfortunately your young man appears to have a thing about married women.'

'He's not my young man!' I interrupted crossly.

James ignored me. 'He likes to fill in for the inadequacies of their husbands.' His tone was frosty. 'I assured him you had no inadequacies at all to complain about so far as I'm concerned!' He sighed in deep exasperation, his long mouth tight with disapproval. 'Honestly, Laura, the men you get yourself tied up with! You must have the worst taste of any woman I know! But this one really was the pits. Couldn't you see that?'

'All right! All right!' I interrupted crossly. 'There's no need to bang on about it!'

I glared with displeasure at my stepbrother; or ex-stepbrother to be accurate since my mother and his father divorced five years ago. James had a highly annoying tendency to become very elder brotherish at times, especially about my boyfriends, presumably on the grounds that as he had behaved so badly himself he knew exactly what the male species could get up to. I, on the other hand, had never been prepared to accept him in the role of fraternal mentor, especially now that I was twenty-six. (It didn't stop him trying, though.)

'James! Really, *what* is going on?' demanded the same voice, with a definitely petulant ring to it. It was vaguely familiar. Trying to place it, I caught my foot on the doorstep. My arms windmilled ridiculously for a moment as James stepped smartly backwards to avoid the shoes which flew out of my hand like spiky missiles. I twisted to one side to avoid impaling myself on the contents of a china umbrella stand and ended up measuring my length on the floor. As I lay swearing, nose deep in about three inches of Axminster carpet, I heard her say in horrified tones, 'God! Who's that?'

I levered and twisted myself into a sitting position and saw an expensive blonde, framed decoratively in the doorway to the sitting room, staring at me in appalled surprise. My heart plummeted even further. This was all I needed. She carelessly tossed a hundred quid's worth of expertly casual styling and blow drying back over her shoulders and then her eyes, exactly the same blue as her slim satin slip dress, widened in incredulous recognition. 'Laura! Laura Moreton! I would hardly have known you.'

'Since I had pigtails and a straw boater on my head the last time you saw me it's not surprising!' I muttered, wanting to bury my face in James's carpet again. What a perfect ending to what was rapidly turning out to be one of the worst days of my entire life. It was bad enough having to bear comparison to someone like Serena Slater at the best of times, but when you've just done a prat fall in front of her, can feel that your skirt has rucked up to knicker level and you've got a hole in the knee of your tights, and that's just for starters, it counts as complete and utter humiliation.

I scrambled on to my feet with difficulty; rising elegantly from a prone position has never been one of my accomplishments, especially when trying to stop my tummy button showing from beneath my skirt. James put out a hand to help me up, then looked from me to Serena with curiosity. 'Serena was my form captain,' I said woodenly. She had also been the cleverest in the class, the only one who didn't get podgy or spotty or both, a prefect and all-round superstar. Luckily for natural justice the loveliness of her face hadn't been matched by a commensurate beauty of disposition so I could quite legitimately dislike her without being guilty of jealousy. (Though naturally I was that too.) The abuse of her form captain's powers (she had set me, as a new girl, to do the worst job in the form-room cleaning rota) still rankled thirteen years afterwards.

James was quite well versed enough in the way of women to have noted the complete absence of enthusiastic cries of 'How *are* you?' 'What have you been doing since I last saw you?' etc. He studied both of us with a glint of amusement and said, 'You must have a lot of catching up to do. Are you both about to indulge in reminiscences of how you won the third-form hockey match against St Cuthbert's?'

Considering I was usually the one who inadvertently scored an own goal and won the match for the other side, this was highly unlikely. I could see from Serena's expression that what she wanted to catch up on most of all was the exact terms I was on with James. How come I felt able to ring his bell at midnight? And hug him? She looked at me and then at him as if checking to see if he was wearing a strange colour of lipstick on his neck. Unwittingly he muddied the waters a bit more by absently rubbing his chin as if he could be wiping off telltale traces as he said, 'Laura was having a problem with some over-sexed ape who was taking her home.'

'Bit more than a problem,' I interrupted. 'More like a full-blown attack on my virtue.'

Serena let her eyes drift up and down me with an expression that implied I should seize *any* such threat with both hands. If James hadn't been there she would probably have said it out loud. 'So you came to James for help. How *wise* of you,' she purred. 'And how marvellous to know that someone is such a good friend they won't mind your coming to them, no matter what time it is.'

From James's slightly complacent smile he'd taken this remark absolutely at face value. 'But how did this happen?' she went on in her caring tone. 'When did you meet this horrible man?'

Oh, hell! I could hardly say about ten minutes before I got into his car, could I? If we'd been on our own I could just about have coped with James telling me I'd been a bloody fool (which was a certainty), but in front of Serena . . . I sort of mumbled into my chest about being stranded at a party and accepting a lift from the hostess's cousin. True as far as it went, but I could see from James's narrowed eyes it didn't work as a full explanation.

Serena threw him a speaking glance. 'We all make mistakes sometimes,' she said kindly, as if I had the mental acuity of a six year old. 'But personally I *never* accept lifts from people I don't know really well. I always take a taxi, never leave home without ten pounds in case of emergencies.'

James was nodding agreement.

'Neither do I,' I lied through gritted teeth. 'But before I realised my lift had fallen through, I blew it on two lines of cocaine.'

Serena dropped the sugary sweet act incredulously. No doubt the next issue of the school mag would have all the hot goss about how Laura Moreton was now a raving drug addict, but I was too pleased at having shut her up to care.

'More like two lines of talcum powder at that price,' said James, eyeing me coldly.

'Maybe it was. I thought it was a bit smelly,' I agreed affably. 'But you'd know, wouldn't you?'

That earned me another cold stare. Justified too. I shrugged apologetically. 'I'm sorry. James doesn't know anything about drugs,' I said to Serena, 'he wouldn't have a clue what cocaine costs. At least, I'm sure he doesn't. I mean, he's got *loads* of vices, but drugs have never been—'

'Laura, will you just *shut up*?' he interrupted in an exasperated voice.

'Glad to,' I murmured. I was beginning to feel very odd. My head was swimming and the walls of the little hallway appeared to be moving in and out in the most alarming way. My knees were sagging as if they were made of over-stretched knicker elastic. 'Can I sit down, please?' I gasped. 'I don't feel very well.'

'Catch her, James! She's about to fall on that vase!' shrieked Serena.

He's certainly a fast mover. He scooped me up and sat me down on a Regency hall chair before I had time to do anything more than a mild sway. He's stronger than his wiry frame looks too. I'm not exactly fat but I'm certainly no lightweight.

A none too gentle hand pushed my head down between my knees. 'Serena, get a glass of brandy from the decanter in the sitting room. Now!' he added.

She took her time and his hand stayed heavily on the back of my head so I had plenty of opportunity to observe the floor beneath the chair. It was spotlessly clean. His daily dusted and polished in the places you couldn't see as well as the surfaces, a rare treasure these days. At long last I was allowed back upright and a very small measure in a very large glass was thrust ungraciously at me.

'I don't like brandy,' I said.

'Drink it. It's good for shock,' James said firmly, standing over me and looking as if he was about to hold my nose and force it down if necessary. I knew he was quite capable of doing exactly that, so I decided it wasn't worth saying that my faintness was more likely to be due to my not eating anything all day so that I'd be able to do up my skirt. I drank it. It was such a minute amount that it went down quite quickly. I have to admit that once I'd finished choking I did feel a bit better. The cold pit in my stomach had been replaced by a nice warm furnace.

'Good, you've got some colour back in your face,' said James with satisfaction.

'That's all the broken blood vessels due to being held upside down,' I answered sourly.

He laughed, unruffled. 'Rubbish! Maybe you ought to have another one for good measure.'

I shook my head firmly. I could cope with one brandy on an empty stomach; two and I might have embarrassing difficulty in negotiating a straight line in those heels. 'I'll ring for a taxi for you,' he said, running his fingers through his already untidy brown hair absent-mindedly. 'And as it might be a few minutes you'd better come and sit by the fire while you wait,' he added with all the enthusiasm of someone asked to sign for an unwanted parcel. Given the circumstances I couldn't really blame him.

'She can't! She's bleeding all over the carpet!' exclaimed Serena in disgust, pointing one perfectly manicured fingernail at my foot.

I looked down. She was right. Somewhere along the way, presumably when I tripped over the doorstep, I must have stubbed my big toe which was bleeding liberally. Now that Serena had kindly pointed it out to me it hurt like hell, as did the graze down my leg and the carpet burn on my knee which I felt for the first time. The soles of my feet hadn't been improved by my barefoot dash across the road either. To my horror I could see a trail of footprints and ominous gouts of blood leading from the door to my chair. I couldn't think why I hadn't noticed them before – too preoccupied, I suppose – they stood out beautifully on the pale carpet. It looked brand new too.

'James, I'm sorry!' I pulled a nearly clean tissue out of my coat pocket and began dabbing at the biggest of the bloodstains.

'Leave it! You're only rubbing it into the carpet!' he snapped. I left it and got up, intending to hop down the passage to the loo to wash my foot. James looked as if he might explode. 'For God's sake, sit down! I don't want even more bloody footprints over my carpet.'

I subsided like an obedient Labrador and put the injured foot up in the air, hoping the blood would run backwards to be soaked up by my tights. 'I'll get carpet cleaners in tomorrow . . .' I mumbled.

'Forget it!' He seized an old newspaper from a pile in the corner and shoved it under my foot. 'Stay there and don't move until I get back with something to clean that up with. Understood?'

I nodded meekly, muttering, '*Ja wohl, mein Führer!*'

He glared at me down his nose. He's got a good nose for that, long and straight like a Norman knight's on a tomb, perfect for annihilatingly supercilious looks. I returned it with a smile and, muttering something, he disappeared in the direction of the kitchen.

Serena leaned back against the doorframe, fingering a single diamond on a chain around her neck, her eyes following him as he went. Goodness, she seemed to have it bad. I was vaguely surprised. I wouldn't have thought a mere antiques dealer would be rich and rare enough for her. By any standards James is attractive. With those indecently long eyelashes he'd be doing OK even without being tall, fairly dark and laid back. But even when she was fifteen her boyfriends tended to have daddies with yachts and spent a month at a time skiing in St Moritz, and she certainly hadn't yet got to the age of fading looks where she had to grab any male who was single, solvent and straight (maybe even ignoring the first two). She turned her head and stared at me in unfriendly silence. I tried my snottiest expression back, but without her inner conviction of being so superior to the opposition I couldn't carry it off properly. Luckily, before my eyes had begun to cross with the effort, James came back with a bowl of water and a sinister brown bottle that looked as if whatever was in it was going to hurt like hell. 'You'll have to take off those tights before I can start,' he said absently, putting down the bowl and fishing a packet of plasters out of his pocket.

He looked up to see me sitting there motionless. 'Come on, Laura! I don't want to take all night.'

'Perhaps the bathroom . . .' I ventured.

He sighed heavily and gestured at my toe, still leaking gore. I could see his point. 'Look, I've seen you wearing a lot less often enough for you to know your modesty's in no danger from me!'

More's the pity, I thought gloomily. When I was fifteen I'd paraded myself in my skimpiest swimsuit dozens of times in front of James and he'd barely bothered to raise his eyes. It had taken me years to get over the subsequent grudge. But I didn't care any longer if he was about to go weak at the knees at the sight of my unclothed legs (admittedly unlikely), it was simply that too close an acquaintance with packets of chocolate Hobnobs had meant that, even after a day's starvation, I had hardly been able to do up the zip of my skirt this evening. Now I was absolutely damned if I was going to struggle out of a pair of extra strong tummy firmer tights under Serena's unblinking gaze. She had far too much self-control even to contemplate comfort eating. Besides, no man would *dare* leave her hanging over the telephone for a week waiting for him to call.

Eventually, seeing that I wasn't going to whip off the wretched things (wriggle, push and heave in truth), James, with considerable ill grace, fetched a pair of nail scissors and cut them off halfway to the knees. Given his mood he was surprisingly competent in tending to my wounds, but I was absolutely right about what was in that brown bottle. To take my mind off the red hot pokers being driven into my foot and to stop myself from uttering the sort of words I believe are usually only associated with women in the throes of childbirth, I stared at the scenery, most of which consisted of Serena who had taken up position against the door again. I couldn't think why she didn't just go and sit down somewhere comfortable until James had finished, she obviously had no intention of either helping or offering me a bit of sympathy. Perhaps she was worried that without her restraining presence I might, overcome by lust, grapple James to the ground and have my wicked way with him.

She was certainly looking at him as if she'd like to do just that herself. If anyone that cool could be said to smoulder, Serena's coals were glowing. Why hadn't it occurred to me before that it was unlikely they'd been sitting decorously at either end of the sofa sipping coffee when I started thumping on the door? Any observant eye could see that Serena's perfection was ruffled and blurred around the edges; the top of her dress wasn't sitting quite right, as if her bosom had been put back in a hurry, and James's half-untucked shirt was probably due to more than his usual indifference to dress. I giggled in appalled horror. I have put my foot in it at times, but I don't think ever quite so royally as this. And when I thought about my crack on the doorstep asking if I'd got him out of bed . . . No wonder he'd been so unwelcoming!

He looked up curiously. I adjusted my expression quickly. It would be wiser to pretend I hadn't noticed. 'Were you out at something very grand tonight?' I asked. 'You're both looking terribly smart.'

'A City dinner,' said Serena importantly. 'Some of my clients were attending and naturally it's essential that our company has a presence at affairs like that.'

Well, of course. 'How glamorous. You must have enjoyed it, James?'

He looked at me suspiciously. He knew that I knew his opinion of City types. It couldn't have changed that much. 'Long speeches, indifferent food, and drink that tasted as if it had just come out of the cat. And only a glass and a half of that – in *three* hours,' he said bitterly. 'Serena's boss was wise not to go.'

'So you deputised for him? How terribly high-powered!' I gushed. That earned me another suspicious look from James. 'And what do you do now, Serena?'

'After university,' so she hadn't gone to Oxford or Cambridge or she would have mentioned them by name, 'I joined one of the major players in banking in the City. I'm executive assistant to one of the directors.'

I heroically restrained myself from asking if that was another title for a secretary and made some vague fulsome comment about how exciting that must be. She looked as if she was receiving only her due and barely that, and then, with palpable lack of interest asked, 'Did you ever manage to find a job in publishing like you wanted? It's such a hard field to break into that most people fail.'

I regretted my self-restraint. 'I decided there wasn't enough money in it,' I said grandly, as if the decision had been mine and not forced on me. 'I'm with a public relations agency.' No mention that there wasn't a lot of money in that either, at least not at my level.

I did have the satisfaction of seeing her eyes narrow

slightly. To those not in the know PR sounds incredibly glamorous, but she rallied after a moment. 'How *interesting*,' she cooed. Her bright blue eyes slithered over me. 'But not in fashion PR, I presume?'

The cow! Goaded, I glared back at her. 'How long have you and James been going out, Serena? Not very long by the look of it.' My gaze rested pointedly on her disordered top.

James gripped my foot painfully hard. 'Not another word, Laura!' he said in a menacingly low tone. 'Understood?'

Green eyes glared gimlet-like into mine. That brown bottle was still open. I touched an imaginary forelock. 'Yes, boss.' The look he shot me made me decide to behave. After all, it wasn't his fault if his latest flight of fancy happened to be the person in the world most likely to put my hackles up, and he'd been quite decent about my bursting in, presumably just as things were really beginning to hot up. A minute or two later and he might not have been in a fit state to answer the door. So it wasn't just to defuse the situation that I obeyed the rare prompting of finer feelings and said, 'Thank you,' as he put on the last two plasters. 'I don't know what I would have done if you hadn't been here.'

He sat back on his heels and stared at me. 'Do you know Laura, that's the first nice thing you've said to me in about ten years.'

I stopped saying nice things to James when he failed to notice how well I could fill a B-cup. Man-like, this reasoning had completely escaped his notice but I was hardly going to tell him now, was I?

'Surely not?' I said with a nervous laugh. 'Anyway I mean it, thank you. And for the doctoring too. You've got a very well-stocked medicine cabinet.'

James stood up, brushing carpet fluff off his knees, and grinned. 'It's left over from the last time Harry's dog, Barker, was staying with me and I had to do some running repairs after he got entangled with the ginger tom down the road.'

I craned my head trying to read the labelling on the bottle. Did that red line really read 'for animal use only'? I shrugged slightly. Even if it did, I was sure James would only use the best on his brother's beloved dog. It was unlikely I was going to grow paws.

Serena shifted restlessly. 'Laura looks absolutely exhausted, and no wonder after that terrible experience,' she emoted. 'She doesn't want to hang around chatting. She needs to get straight home and into bed with a warm drink as soon as possible.'

You couldn't speak much plainer than that. Actually I quite agreed with her. Bed, my pig-shaped hot water bottle and the company of my cat – though that was a doubtful luxury – seemed the pinnacle of bliss just at that moment.

James flashed her a smile for her kind thoughtfulness and Serena sort of glowed. But to do him credit, for he too must have been dying to see the back of me, he said, 'Perhaps Laura should recover by the fire for a bit and have another drink?' I have to admit he didn't sound terribly enthusiastic about the idea.

'That's very kind of you,' I said, standing up gingerly. Serena sent both of us a venomous look. I didn't have the energy to tease her any further. 'But what I'd really like would be to clean myself up and then go home. Could you call me that taxi, James?'

'Of course,' he said quickly and with inhospitable relief. 'Use the bathroom upstairs, it's warmer than the one down here.'

I took a cautious step, putting my weight down slowly on the balls of my feet. It wasn't quite like walking on broken glass but near enough to make me realise that for the immediate future I was going to be waddling along on my heels like a duck. Great.

All things considered it was pretty decent and restrained of Serena not to put 'wash' at the beginning of her list of what I should do. I couldn't understand how the face that stared back at me out of the gilt-framed mirror had managed to get so dirty. It had been clean enough when I'd left the party. At least I hoped it had. Surely contact with James's carpet couldn't have done that much damage? I thought, peering at the liberal quantities of grime adorning my nose. Perhaps his daily wasn't such a treasure after all. As for my hair . . . I had put it up in a fashionably loose knot, I love it when the latest styles allow me to indulge my natural messiness, but now bits of it had fallen out to create a windswept style *au naturel* that was the complete antithesis of Serena's pomaded, blow-dried, backcombed and extremely expensive designer hairdresser version. Actually nothing short of a very pricey wig was ever going to make my hair look like hers so I might as well stop thinking about it. After five minutes of brushing and polishing I was nearly back to looking human again –

though a complete makeover would have helped. Unfortunately any improvement was severely marred by the effect of a red velvet mini skirt worn over a pair of torn off tights, looking for all the world like the latest in grunge footless leggings. I thought about displaying the glory of my luminously blue-white legs in their entirety – perfect for a washing powder advertisement. But if I took the tights off Serena and James would be able to see that the skirt wasn't just snug but a positive danger to my circulation so, as the lesser of two evils, they stayed put.

I'd only been to this house a couple of times before, and never upstairs, so being nosy I was keen to see what it was like. I opened the bathroom door quietly and tiptoed as softly as possible to the middle of the landing, satisfying my slightly uneasy conscience by pointing out to it I wasn't actually going *into* any of the rooms, I was simply looking through any doors that happened to be left conveniently open. I stopped guiltily at the rumble of voices carrying up the stairwell. There was a laugh as if at some shared joke, then Serena said with the resonance of someone who was taught to speak to the back of the hall (our drama mistress fancied she had a bunch of budding thespians), 'Really, James, you must be a complete innocent! How likely is it that Laura's potential ravisher just happened to be driving her home this way? As you said yourself, it's not on any direct route to her flat.' It is actually if the driver keeps on missing turnings because he's too busy trying to put a hand up your skirt. 'Even Laura knows that the quickest way to get to a man is to look fragile and appeal for his help!'

What a bitch! Even at the height of my infatuation

(sixteen and a half) I had never contemplated a scenario quite like this one in an attempt to get James to notice me. Seething, I crept silently over to the banisters, unable to resist the temptation to hear more ill of myself.

'Do you think so?' There was a chuckle then a pause while he chewed the notion over. I gripped the banister rail hard in annoyance. Then, after much too long for my liking, he said, 'No, I don't believe it. Laura really had the wind up about that bastard. And quite right too, I've met his type before. All that surprises me is that for once she had the sense to realise there are worse things than loss of face.'

Serena's answer was an exasperated sigh. I leaned forward as she began to speak and a board creaked under my weight. She was peremptorily shushed. Cursing softly to myself, I clumped down the stairs with an ostentatious amount of noise as if I had never been doing anything so underhand as skulking around eavesdropping. When I limped into the little sitting room Serena was draped along a Chesterfield, looking sulky, while James sat several feet away in a chair next to the fire. It was too much to hope that he'd gone off her because she'd been spiteful about me. He certainly wouldn't feel he owed me that kind of loyalty, especially not when it would mean spurning someone as gorgeous as her. In fact he was probably only avoiding sitting next to her in case he was tempted to return to activities more properly left until I was safely off the premises.

They turned to look at me. I was still in two minds about whether to pick a fight with James about his daring even to consider that I'd been staging a stunt, but his wintery expression convinced me it wouldn't be a good idea. In fact I got the impression he was in a state of such barely controlled irritation, arising from acute frustration most likely, that if I so much as put one sore foot wrong I'd quickly find myself standing on the doorstep in the cold. The silence seemed to stretch into eternity. 'This really is a lovely house, James. You were clever to find it. The mirror on the landing is super. What is it? Georgian? Did it come from the shop?' I burbled in a vague attempt to raise the temperature half a degree or so. 'And you've done so much decorating everywhere. I love the paper in the hall . . .' My voice trailed off guiltily as I remembered the state the hall carpet was in.

This vapid outpouring was greeted with the silent contempt it deserved from Serena. She barely bothered to glance at me before her eyes resumed studying the flames flickering up the chimney. My conversational gambit didn't appear to strike James as particularly scintillating either, though he did have the manners to smile briefly in response. 'Yes, the mirror's nice, isn't it?' He leaned forward. 'I've rung for a taxi but they say it'll take at least half an hour to come at this time of night so I think I'd better drive you home myself.'

Serena's arm tensed slightly. So that was why the atmosphere was so frosty. She didn't want him leaving her. She probably thought a nice walk would do me good, though I was sure she was too wise to say so.

'Are you certain it's OK? I mean, won't you be over the limit?' I asked dubiously. There was a half-full glass of whisky on the table by his chair and if he'd really had such a boring evening earlier I'd be very surprised if it was his first.

He shrugged. 'You sound like my mother.' I gathered he probably was, but had summed up the risk versus the benefits and decided it was worth it. Not particularly flattering, but understandable. 'I don't want to rush you,' he added, getting to his feet before I could venture another step into the room, 'but we might as well start.'

He turned around and picked something off the coffee table, holding up a pair of novelty slippers in the shape of huskies, complete with ears and tail. 'These were left behind by one of the cousins when she was staying. I thought with your sore feet you'd find them more comfortable than your own shoes.'

Vanity battled against comfort for a long moment, then I decided that even husky slippers couldn't make torn-off tights and too compact a skirt look much worse than they already did. I put them on. They were blissfully comfortable, like wrapping my feet in cotton wool, but definitely not glamorous. I didn't need a long mirror to guess exactly what sort of prize prat I looked, but at least they didn't bark when I walked. Thank heavens for small mercies.

''Bye, Serena. Nice to have met you again,' I said with radiant insincerity. She was in such a filthy mood she didn't even look at me while she addressed an equally mendacious reply to the back of the fireplace, so missed the full glory of my get up. James was so eager to be rid of me that he was already in the hall rooting for his car keys in a Chinese bowl that seemed to be a general dumping ground for everything. I couldn't resist putting my head back around the door and saying cheerily, 'Don't worry, I won't keep him long. And you won't miss out. He's got lots of stamina. Believe me, I know!'

James gave me a very old-fashioned look as I joined him on the doorstep, sending my guilty conscience into overdrive. Had he overheard? But he just looked at the shoes dangling from my hand and said, 'Can I ask why you were careering around in bare feet on a winter's night?'

'I can't run in them, and I thought I might have to.'

His eyebrows rose disdainfully as he pulled the door to. 'In future it might be more sensible to wear something you can walk in rather than hooker's shoes.'

'They aren't hooker's shoes!' I protested. 'They're much too expensive!'

He made a noise that sounded very rude and opened the door of a red Renault Clio. 'A skirt you can walk in would be useful too. Or any skirt at all!'

He banged the door shut before I could answer. He got in and, gunning the engine, slammed into first gear and we careered off down the road in a manner certain to gain the attention of the traffic police for miles around. 'In fact,' he said, 'if you've got to go around looking as if you're hoping to get laid, it'd be wiser not to get into a car with a man who has a problem keeping his flies buttoned!'

'I didn't know that at the time, did I?' I said. I was trying to be understanding. If I hadn't completely wrecked James's evening I'd put a considerable damper on it, and unpleasant stains all over his new carpet too. 'I think I should be able to accept a lift without being molested by some creep who keeps his brains between his legs!'

'Of course you should. Just as much right as I'd have to walk into a Catholic pub in Belfast and say I don't think much of the Pope. Free speech and all that! It's just that if I'm not a complete moron, I might care to consider the consequences first!' I clutched the handle on the door for protection as he jammed his foot down on the accelerator to emphasise his point and the G-force pushed me back into my seat. He glanced at me, daring me to answer back so he could give vent to the bad temper he was barely keeping in check. I didn't.

I have never made the journey back to Clapham quite so quickly. I doubt anyone has. I stared stonily out of my window watching the darkened houses flash by, annoyance fuelled by the knowledge that even if James was completely out of order in coming the heavy like this, he wasn't entirely wrong. If I hadn't been in such a snit I would have seen that Hugo was a completely slimy git and wouldn't have gone so far as the other side of the room with him. I gestured silently for James to turn down a side road and then at the block where I share a flat. He stopped, double parking, and I got out with as much dignity as I could manage. 'Goodbye, James. Thank you very much for all you've done. I'm really sorry to have interrupted your evening like this,' I said, determined to show that I, at least, knew how to behave. Then temptation got the better of me, and I spoiled it by adding, 'I hope you'll be able to pick up where you had to leave off. Or should I say take off what you had to put back on?'

He glared at me poisonously. I shut the door smartly and retreated into the safety of the entrance to the flats. But more eager to return to Serena than for vengeance, he was already halfway down the road. I watched the tail lights of his car disappear and turned around to go inside. My foot brushed something and I looked down, heart sinking. Oh, hell! I'd forgotten the husky slippers. I was going to have to return them, wasn't I? Maybe I could put them in the post, or leave it for a week or so. He might have calmed down by then.

CHAPTER 2

I was being suffocated. He was pinning me down, his arm across my chest, weight driving the air out of my body, his foul breath eddying across my mouth and cheeks. I thrashed around, trying to scream, but no sound came out. My heart felt like it was about to burst out of my chest. A waft of old fish drifted past my nose.

Fish? With difficulty I opened my eyes. A pair of green eyes stared balefully at me. The large shape sitting on my chest opened its mouth and yawned widely, giving me a second chance to savour what had been found in next door's dustbin. At least he hadn't been along to the Indian restaurant at the end of the street. I struggled up and pushed Horatio's considerable weight off me. I *would* be the only person in London to own a cat addicted to curry.

To my surprise it was nearly eight o'clock. It didn't seem that I had slept at all. When I'd got in last night Liv had just got back from her job as a theatre lighting technician. Unlike most theatrical folk Liv's in work pretty well constantly so due to our wildly different working hours and her habit of dashing off after last performance on Saturday to visit her farmer boyfriend in

Wiltshire we usually pass like ships in the night, only pausing to leave notes or borrow essentials like hair-dryers. We tend to seize every opportunity when we're both in, alone and reasonably compos, to have a mega gossip and catch up. Or otherwise if Liv isn't particularly busy at work she'll ring me on her mobile. This happens more often than you'd expect; her company is very forward-thinking and likes to experiment with new techniques. The play before last had a long sequence where the actors donned night vision glasses and all the lights were turned off. Something to do with not allowing sight to interfere with the spoken word. This particular session, due to my news, hot off the press, naturally lasted well into the small hours, despite Liv having finished off our last bottle of wine with two of her workmates a couple of nights before, so we'd had to make do with coffee. Not that it mattered. Neither of us needs alcoholic stimulation to get talking. Liv has a particularly lurid imagination (she's very fond of Stephen King), and her increasingly wild speculations about what might have happened had I been crazy enough to invite Hugo in for a cup of coffee as a thank you for the lift were quite enough to keep me awake for ages dwelling uneasily on all sorts of horrid 'might haves'. My eyes felt gritty and I had a low head-ache niggling away behind my forehead that for once I knew really was due to lack of sleep and not an excuse for a little too much, or much too much, the night before. Not even the most alcohol-sensitive person in the world could have a hangover on Serena's minuscule measure.

I got stiffly out of bed, feeling about ninety years old, and shuffled along to the kitchen, not helped by Horatio weaving in and out of my legs. Much to his loudly expressed annoyance I picked up the coffee machine for an urgently needed caffeine fix before heading for the tin of cat food. Horatio started life as an alley cat and he's never forgotten that there was a time when he didn't know where the next meal was coming from. He always makes sure he's got at least two in hand tucked under his capacious waistline, and in between official mealtimes he goes and visits neighbours for a snack. Considering how tight his somewhat moth-eaten fur is stretched around his stomach it always amazes me that he can con people into thinking he needs to be fed, but his acting abilities seem to be limitless.

I ladled out some Kittykins, or whatever he was on that week, into his dish and put it down for him. It smelled almost as bad as his breath. But the smell was easily compensated for by the silence. I poured my coffee and got the milk out of the fridge. Before the raucous caterwaul could slice through my head again I hastily gave him his saucer of milk. I've tried explaining to Horatio that experts say cats don't like milk but he doesn't believe me.

The coffee didn't do much in terms of bringing me back to something approaching life. I had a feeling nothing would bar a thunderbolt. The idea of choosing what to wear for work seemed as impossible as scaling Everest in a bikini. I contemplated taking the day off; even though my boss could fairly be said to lack most, if not all, of the finer human feelings, surely even she might agree that under the circumstances I deserved a bit of cosseting? On the other hand, Darian Mumford, Senior

Account Director at Manly Field Public Relations, didn't consider anything short of hospitalisation (and preferably that should be arranged for the weekends or taken as holiday) an excuse for one of her staff not being in the office, on time, bright as a button, neat as a pin, smart as a bandbox and ready to put her best foot forward. For someone who considers herself so right on Darian has a remarkable fondness for antiquated truisms and clichés. Add to that the odd phrase which had been wafted around in my hearing recently such as 'Perhaps better suited for something else', or the more frank 'Useless', and I decided the wiser course of action would be to go into the office. After working with Darian for a bit you tend to pick up her speech patterns.

'Laura! You're late! Again. I've already had to warn you at least twice about your time-keeping. And,' pause for her voice to rise an indignant octave, 'what on *earth* do you think you look like! Have you forgotten what I said to everyone about standards in dress last week?'

Honestly, the woman must have X-ray vision. I had barely set one sore foot in the office and I'd swear she hadn't come out of hers. Either she could see through the wall or she had set up a system of mirrors so she could spy on the menials in the main room. I'd have to warn the others. She swept out of her doorway, the sharp tip of her nose going rather pink as she stopped dead and looked her junior account trainee up and down with mounting disbelief and rage. It was a new low even for me.

I have to admit I wasn't looking my best. The problem had started at the opposite end from usual, with my damned foot. The only reasonably respectable shoes I could get on over my heavily plastered and now swollen toe were a pair of strappy yellow sandals which were great for wafting around in on a balmy June evening but quite out of the question for a foggy January morning. So I'd ended up by borrowing Liv's pair of seventeen-hole DMs which can happily accommodate bad toes since her feet are a size larger than mine. I do agree that their like are rarely seen in top public relations agencies – not the ones that have clients with a mental age of more than seventeen anyway. Then, since wearing them with one of the smart little suits that Darian insists make up my normal working wardrobe would have convinced any impartial observer that I was at the very least bizarre, if not downright certifiable, I'd put on an ankle-length denim skirt and a leather bomber jacket. I thought I looked pretty funky, but chic I wasn't. Darian prefers chic.

At last she spoke. 'Have you forgotten we have a meeting with Rainbow Cosmetics this afternoon?' she demanded in throbbing tones.

My expression must have clearly shown that I had. Not only was I dressed unsuitably, but before leaving last night I had been given firm instructions to come in fully decked out in warpaint from Rainbow's latest spring collection (Spring Rain colours – very original). Darian has a fond belief that our clients note and approve of such dedicated professionalism. Personally I'm pretty sure most of the marketing men we deal with wouldn't recognise their own product on the hoof, so to speak, if it leaped up and bit them.

I was about to give her my perfectly reasonable explanation as to why my cheeks were bare of Rosy Rust Blush and my lips weren't gleaming with Rosy Light Stayput Shimmer Lipstick but she didn't give me the chance. I got the full spiel about my irresponsibility and inattention to detail, how my mind was taken up with my useless boyfriend, how I should spend less time thinking what I was doing that night and more on writing my copy.

She finally stopped in mid-rant long enough for me to get my own word in edgeways. Since listening to Darian carpeting someone is one of the office sports a major proportion of the staff had already found something to do in our office so there was quite an impressive audience hanging around in corners to listen to my story. It sounded properly dramatic the second time around. I didn't exactly exaggerate or make things up, I was just determined Darian wasn't going to do a Serena on me and accuse me of having the hots for my stepbrother. The audience liked it, especially the part where I had to defend myself and my honour with nothing more than my door keys.

Darian was looking pretty grim by the time I'd finished. I don't think she was very happy about rushing in to slate me off like that before she'd heard what I had to say. It didn't make her look too supportive towards the sisterhood, but that wasn't my fault. Not really. It's very difficult to stop Darian once she gets going, and it wasn't my intention to show her up. Not my primary intention anyway. No doubt I'd get the blame eventually. Darian is never in the wrong. To believe in the rightness of your every action was one of the key things she'd learned on her assertiveness course. Though personally I think Darian needed assertiveness training like your average Pit

Bull needs a shot of testosterone. She muttered something about my foolishness in accepting lifts from men I didn't know (now where had I heard that before?) and then switched into caring mode. 'But at least you weren't hurt. That's such a relief,' she cooed. 'Do you need to go home and rest?'

I shook my head. 'I'm better off with something to do,' I said truthfully. My imagination was still dwelling unpleasantly on what might have happened. Even work was better than thinking about Hugo's wandering hands.

'Well, perhaps Rainbow . . .' She looked at me thoughtfully, no doubt weighing up the pros and cons of taking me with her looking (in her view) like a tramp, against the potential advantage of a brave little PR executive being seen to overcome personal trauma to attend important briefing meeting on promotional campaign in teenage magazines. Much to my relief the tramp factor won. I quite liked the people at Rainbow but going with Darian meant I was relegated to the role of note-taker; needless to say if they didn't like her ideas afterwards it was always because I had taken down the instructions wrong. 'You'd better catch up with the skin-care advice letters this morning. It's pretty straightforward, you won't need my help, and it would be nice to see you up to date with your work for once.'

I didn't point out she had never offered me any help on the Cathy Ashby skin-care letters. They didn't pay a large enough retainer for a big cheese like her to get involved, which was why I ended up doing them. Every box for the Morning Dew range of skin preparations carried an invitation to write to Cathy for her personal advice on all your skin-care problems. Much to my amazement she got about twenty letters a week, many of them from teenagers whom you would have thought could find some hipper way of getting skin-care info. Cathy was a bit long in the tooth, she had been dishing out her words of wisdom since the thirties and, frankly, both the products and the packaging looked like it too. Still the letters kept on coming. Nearly all my replies were stock letters under headings such as 'Teenager – spots', '30s – combination skin', 'wrinkles', etc, and included shatteringly novel recommendations such as 'be sure to cleanse your skin morning and night with a proprietary product' (Morning Dew naturally) or 'to help prevent the signs of ageing use a moisturiser morning and night' (such as Morning Dew intensive care lotion). The customers seemed astonishingly grateful for such bog standard advice and surprisingly often I got letters from those who thought that if I could help with basic skin care then perhaps I was an expert on other matters, such as how to lose a stone in ten days (wish I knew), where to meet a good-looking, unattached, non-psychotic millionaire (ditto), and whether it was a matter for concern when your husband liked silk underwear. (On whom?)

I had barely sat down at my desk and got out my 'to be answered' file – it was bulging a little more than I had thought, a lot more in fact – when Emma who sits on the other side of the office materialised by my side. 'Hey, Laura!' she hissed, casting a quick look at Darian's slightly open door. 'Did all that really happen?'

I opened my mouth to assure her that every word was

true then saw her looking at me with a beady eye. She knows me too well. 'Most of it,' I said, then added more truthfully, 'Well, some.'

'But what happened? I thought you were going to a party with Daniel.'

'I was. I did,' I hissed, metaphorical steam coming out of my ears.

'So?' she demanded urgently. 'How come you missed a chance to get your hands on him later? Have you broken up or something?' There was a bit too much eagerness in her voice for my peace of mind.

'Will you two stop talking and get on with your work!' came a clarion-like command from inside Darian's office. We were practically whispering. Either she has preternatural hearing or she's got the place bugged. Emma blew a silent raspberry towards the door and went back to her desk.

We worked in obedient silence for all of two minutes and then Emma said in a loud voice, 'Bother! I've got to go and check the files for Dento.' She headed for the dark hole that acts as our general storeroom, library of cuttings, file and photocopier/fax room. It's also the only place on that floor where we're allowed to smoke. Darian is a fanatical anti-smoker. As David, the actual owner of the agency, likes a cigarette or twenty himself even she doesn't feel she can ban smoking entirely, so she's compromised by making it as difficult as possible for the dedicated smokers amongst us to indulge.

Needless to say the photocopying room is the communications centre for the whole office. Since cigarettes have much the same effect on Darian as garlic on a vampire, it's the only room in the whole building besides the men's loos where she never sets foot. Naturally she wouldn't dream of sending her own faxes or finding a file. On certain days when she is being more than usually impossible the main office is deserted while the photocopier is obscured under a thick pall of smoke. I sometimes wonder if she ever speculates why she appears to be the only manager in the building to have a team apparently made up entirely of smokers.

A minute after Emma went I discovered there was something vital I needed to look up for the Cathy Ashby letters. I was glad to see Emma had prepared for a really extended session with two cups of inky coffee from the machine and some biscuits. I eyed the biscuits virtuously, knowing that I was going to have the strength to refuse them even if they were chocolate digestives. The shame of nearly having to reveal my buttressed tights to Serena last night was still too strong in my memory. 'So what happened with Daniel? Tell all!' commanded Emma a bit indistinctly through a mouthful of chocolate digestive.

I took a swig of coffee, shuddered as stewed caffeine hit my taste buds and absently broke off a corner of a biscuit while I framed my answer. 'He was enjoying himself and I wanted to go home, so I accepted a lift from our hostess's cousin.'

Emma wasn't buying that one. She fixed me with a deeply sceptical eye. 'He was ignoring you and you took off in a justifiable snit,' she proclaimed eventually. She's not too keen on Daniel. I'm embarrassed to say she's witnessed him doing something not dissimilar on another occasion, but then it was in a wine bar with a fellow writer (male), so it was nothing like so bad as last night.

I broke off another bit of biscuit. The calories don't count if you take them in tiny amounts. You use up more by chewing than you gain by swallowing, or something like that, I'm sure I read it somewhere. 'Not exactly,' I hedged. Emma's look became even more cynical. 'Well, maybe just a bit like that,' I admitted at last, though I immediately added defensively, 'There's probably a perfectly good reason. She might have been asking him to tutor a writing course or something. He's very dedicated to his work.'

Emma snorted inelegantly but to my relief didn't pooh-pooh my weak excuse straight away. Luckily for me her butterfly mind had alighted on another, to her, more interesting subject. 'You weren't very forthcoming about the reaction of the man you knocked up,' she said as she leaned back against the photocopier and blew a smoke ring into the air. 'Was he chuffed to be able to aid a damsel in distress?'

'Um, not really. Not at all, in fact.' I thought of James's irritated expression as he opened the door. 'You see, he was about to do some knocking up of his own when I turned up.'

White smoke streamed out of Emma's nose as she choked. 'You didn't get him in mid . . .' she exclaimed, and had to stop to cough a bit more.

'Well into the warm-up stage,' I said with a giggle. 'Considering how long it took James to get to the door it must have been a re-dressing job. Lucky I didn't arrive a minute or two later, then he'd have been in a *really* bad mood.'

'You know him?' That was one of the elements I'd skated over. I was sure Darian would have withheld all her muted sympathy if she'd twigged it hadn't been a complete stranger I'd burst in on. Besides it made for a better story. 'James ... James?' Emma mused. 'Good God! It wasn't your *stepbrother* James, was it? The one you dislike so much?'

It was my turn to look at her in surprise, then the fog of mystification in my brain blew away to leave an embarrassing clarity. Oh, God! One inebriated evening I'd waxed loquacious about coming back from school the summer I was fifteen to my new stepfather's house. The first thing I'd seen was James, in a pair of cut off shorts and nothing else, mowing the lawn. I'd abruptly lost interest in ponies, film stars and D'Artagnan and taken to mooching around in too much eye make up while reading romantic novels. That was when I wasn't creating fantasies where some improbable situation occurred and James was forced to look at me properly for the first time. He would then breathe huskily, 'I had no idea you were so beautiful, Laura.' I didn't have a terribly original imagination in those days. I even tried drowning in the swimming pool in front of him, but instead of diving in to save me he just told me to stop splashing about, I was making his book wet. But since Emma wasn't nudging me suggestively or winking she must have drunk even more than me and could only remember the bits where I'd gone on about how impossibly bossy he can be.

'Yes, that James, but even he wouldn't put me back on the street to be pounced on by a sex maniac just because I get on his goat sometimes,' I said airily. 'And it gave him an excuse to lecture me about how stupid I'd been,' I added darkly.

'From what you say he'd have happily given up the opportunity to lecture you just this once!' We looked at each other and then spluttered with laughter, holding our hands over our mouths and glancing towards the door in case of a stentorian demand to know exactly what we were up to.

Luckily the muffled snorts and grunts went unnoticed for though Darian seems blissfully unaware of the real use to which the file room is put, even she can twig that filing is normally no laughing matter. By the time I'd finished telling all to Emma, who being a kindred spirit can easily understand that there are fates worse than death but not many fates worse than being shown up in front of some-one like Serena, the plate of biscuits between us was empty. I looked at it, wondering who had eaten them, and sucked a bit of chocolate off my teeth.

Emma cocked her head. 'I think I can hear the dulcet tones of our leader calling you.'

So could I, unfortunately. I grabbed a fat file at random and walked out, smiling sweetly at Darian as I passed her and asking innocently, 'Did you want me for something?' I sat down at my desk. 'Sorry I've been so long, it took ages to find this, it was buried right at the back.' I opened the file ostentatiously and picked up a piece of scrap paper as if I was about to start making notes.

Darian glared at me suspiciously but must have decided it wouldn't be politic to nag me today. She smiled at me with all the synthetic sweetness of artificial sugar but fortunately didn't follow it up by coming over and offering to help me with what I was doing. She might have wondered exactly why I needed the report on consumer reaction to three new flavours of soft drink that had been commissioned in the 1970s to aid me in answering a query about how to avoid bags under the eyes. (Get more sleep.)

The news of my adventure had spread like wildfire through the agency, and like Chinese whispers gained quite a lot and changed direction slightly in the re-telling each time. I had a constant stream of visitors with supposed queries, but really just wanting to know if it was true I had fought off a man and a Rottweiler, KO'd him with a karate kick, if he had dragged me down a side street, and was it really the case that he had been in the middle of slicing my clothes off with a knife when a car had slewed to a halt and my rescuer had leaped out, etc, etc. They were quite an eye opener about the sort of occurrence people thought was par for the course for London and made me miserably aware that I hadn't paid enough attention at self-defence classes – I had *no* idea how to do Thai kick boxing, but then I don't suppose Thai kick boxing is much use in a sports car. Darian's resolve to be nice to me because I'd had a Traumatic Experience was pretty tried by the end of the morning. As it is she thinks I talk too much and don't have a serious enough attitude to my work without adding disrupting the work of the whole agency to my list of sins. I tried to tell her that everyone was coming to me and I'd prefer to be left in peace; she said things like that only happened to me, which isn't quite fair.

Luckily for her blood pressure she was at Rainbow in

the afternoon so she wasn't there to witness how everyone came back a second time to confirm the details. Emma was researching how many mentions our competitors were getting (reading the papers) and I was passing her desk when a photograph of a pretty blonde on the gossip page caught my eye. I stopped, sure I recognised her from somewhere. It was Cressida Wynne, who had been christened 'the loveliest girl in England' by a besotted gossip columnist, and the sobriquet had stuck. I had never met her, but I'd seen her photo so many times that her face was instantly familiar. I'd also often seen her pictured with James as she had once been his girlfriend. His very serious girlfriend according to family gossip that had been buzzing backwards and forwards like a swarm of bees. It had been rumoured that Cressida had been seen going around the General Trading Company with a wedding list look in her eyes and that any minute she would be shyly, but proudly, showing off a large diamond on her left hand.

Then at a charity ball she was introduced to one of the sponsors, Count Stefano Buonotti, an Italian businessman (of, as the family excitedly whispered later, very dubious reputation) some twenty-five years older than her. He was very rich, apparently very charming, and after the death of his wife the year before was looking for a new one.

Three months later Cressida wafted down the aisle of the Brompton Oratory in a cloud of antique lace as the new Contessa Cressida Buonotti and departed to live in a *castello* near Milan, leaving James with egg on his face and a broken heart (according to his aunt who is of a sentimental nature). A lot of people doubted that James had a heart to break, but it was certainly true he hadn't had a serious girlfriend since.

I put my hand on the page to stop Emma turning it over, to her indignation, and leaned across to her to read the story. 'Milan society is about to lose one of its brightest stars – for part of the year at least. The beautiful Countess Cressida Buonotti has told us that she and her husband Stefano have bought stately Hurstwood House in Derbyshire so Cressida can see more of her family, though they will be catching the summer sun in Italy. It suits Count Stefano too. He has the major share in a consortium that is converting several town houses in Kensington into what we hear will be the largest and most luxurious "country-style" hotel in London. Word is that it's going to be called The Hurstwood.'

I wondered if James had seen this, and what he felt about having Cressida back in the country again, then realised she must have been back lots of times already. Someone as rich as that was bound to have a flat in London. He might even have been round to have drinks or dinner just to show they could all be civilised and still good friends.

Emma was huffing rather crossly about having her research material hi-jacked so I told her who Cressida was. She grabbed the paper back, stared at it, and whistled softly. 'Your stepbrother must certainly know how to pull the birds! Was that Serena last night as gorgeous as this?'

I looked at Cressida's picture. Even grainy newsprint couldn't disguise the fact that she knocked most, if not all, of us for six. 'Serena's pretty stunning, but she doesn't quite match up to this.'

'Cor! What's your James got to get girlfriends like that? And how come you've never tried to get your hands on him?'

Thank heavens for the amnesiac effects of alcohol.

'You say he isn't particularly rich, or stonkingly good-looking, which are usually prerequisites for really classy women like that,' Emma flicked a finger at the paper, 'so I suppose he must be really good in bed. In my experience that's the only thing that can reconcile a rich woman to love in a hovel.'

I thought of James's little house and how very cross he would be to hear it described as a hovel. Besides Emma's experience is nothing like so great as she likes to pretend sometimes, so I took the rest of what she had to say with a mega pinch of salt. Though I have to admit I had speculated myself sometimes . . .

'Actually he is quite attractive. Very attractive, I suppose,' I amended in a mood of large-minded fairness. 'But nothing like as good-looking as Daniel.'

'Who could be?' asked Emma in a disparaging voice. She thinks Daniel trades on his good looks to get away with the sort of inconsiderate behaviour not allowed to us less-favoured mortals. I have tried to point out this isn't fair. Daniel doesn't *ask* me to clear up after him, it's just that he takes being a writer very seriously so he tends to ignore things other people find important. I'm not that fussy, but I was brought up with certain standards of hygiene. I prefer to know how long the thing I'm treading on has been there and what it might have been originally.

Of course when Emma kindly offered to drive me home, thus making herself late for a hot date, I couldn't very well ask if she would mind detouring by an extra twenty minutes so I could see if Daniel was at home to proffer an explanation about last night. There are limits beyond which friendship will not stretch, and jeopardising a chance at six foot two of good looks with a loaded wallet is one of them. My flat felt depressingly empty. Liv had already left for the evening performance. Judging by the trail of discarded possessions that led from her bedroom to the front door she'd been in a tearing hurry too. I picked them up and returned them to her room before Horatio, the oldest kitty in town, could decide that they were playthings and rip them to pieces. Even Liv, who is the only person I know who pretends to enjoy sharing living space with Horatio, can get a bit ratty when he's been playing 'kill the hedgehog' with her wooden-handled hairbrush. We were never supposed to be permanent residents here anyway; I hardly knew Liv except as the girlfriend of my then boyfriend's brother when she offered me her spare room for a couple of months while I was waiting for another flat. We got on so well that I never moved out, even after I split up rather acrimoniously with my boyfriend and out of excessive fraternal loyalty hers told her I'd have to go or he wouldn't take her out any more. He shouldn't have been so confident about which choice she'd make.

It's the first time she's shared with anyone who isn't connected with the theatre in some way and I think she finds it a great relief to have a tenant who isn't frequently 'resting' and consequently using that as an excuse not to come up with the rent. And since I don't go on tour with the company I look after the flat for her while she's away and make sure nothing vital gets cut off (which used to happen quite frequently). We're in complete accord about the housework too. As neither of us is asthmatic the dust doesn't matter.

I looked without much hope at the answering machine (Daniel doesn't like them), my heart leaping when I saw the red light blinking. But it was my mother ringing from Paris where she lives, just checking, so she said, to see if I was still alive. I felt a pang of the requisite guilt but she'd have to go on savouring fantasies of my imminent or recent demise for a bit longer. My mother is an excellent parent – long-distance variety. She truly adores her two daughters, but she prefers to leave the nitty-gritty of actually dealing with their problems to any responsible and suitable, or irresponsible and unsuitable, body who comes to hand. She's certainly given us a large enough quantity of step relations to perform the function. But it would only take a few minutes of her form of maternal truth drug before I'd be spilling all the beans about last night. The inevitable panic that would follow, for my mother is someone who believes firmly in making a drama out of every crisis, with her ringing my father, stepmother, sister, aunts, ex-stepfathers – God forbid – and probably stepbrothers as well, urging them to *do something* about it, didn't bear thinking about.

I went off and got myself acquainted with a stiff drink and lay on the sofa, with Horatio stretched out heavily on my lap, watching something comfortably mindless on the telly. I couldn't summon up the energy to think about

Daniel, annoyance is very enervating, and for some reason my mind kept drifting to Cressida Buonotti and James. Whatever it was of his that had been hit by her marriage – pride, his heart as a sentimental aunt would have it, or whatever – it had been hit pretty hard. I'd bumped into him a couple of months afterwards and had been struck by his air of guarded self-control that had never been there before, as if it was hiding something deeper. I smiled at myself. I was letting my imagination run away with me. But I prayed that now Cressida was back James wouldn't be tempted to do something stupid to prove he didn't give a toss about her any more. Like proposing to someone else. I was fond of my ex-stepfather and his relations and knew I'd never be able to face another Lovatt family do again if Serena became part of the family.

CHAPTER 3

Sunday morning found me back up James's road, though this time I was in Liv's blessedly comfortable DMs, rather than bare feet. I was looking forward to this encounter with all the enthusiasm I usually reserve for the three weeks' worth of ironing that lurks in the corner of my room. On cool reflection I was just a little bit worried about what Serena might have said to James when he got back to her but I had a duty to perform and almost anything was better than hanging around the flat, staring at the phone and willing it to ring with an apologetic errant boyfriend on the line. Of course *I* wasn't going to be the one to make the first move. I wasn't the one at fault.

This time the door opened almost before I had time to take my finger off the bell and I wondered for a wild moment if I was about to do my second prat fall into James's hallway in under a week. 'You're becoming a positively familiar sight at my door, Laura,' he said in a level voice that didn't give me a clue as to whether he was harbouring murderous thoughts about me. He was in a dark jacket and chinos and on his way out somewhere.

Even I could work that out; he had his car keys in his hand. 'And what can I do for you today?'

I smiled placatingly and held up a carrier bag. 'I brought the slippers back.'

'You shouldn't have bothered. There was no hurry.'

I cleared my throat. 'There's a bit of a problem...' I fished in the bag and held up one slipper. It wasn't a happy sight. The ears were tattered and it now had only half a tail; the other, still in the bag, was in an even worse state. 'I'll buy a new pair if you tell me where I can find them,' I mumbled.

His eyebrows shot upwards. 'What on earth have you been doing? Having dog fights?'

'Cat fights,' I said unhappily. 'Horatio won't stop attacking them. He took exception to them when I first walked in wearing them – probably thought they were replacing him in my affections.'

'So he went all out for revenge? Remind me not to get on the wrong side of your cat. But don't worry about replacing them – Harry's dog has already had a good suck and chew at them so your aggressive feline was just finishing off the job.' He took the bag from me and casually slung it inside the door. 'How's the foot?' he asked, turning back and giving me a critical once over. I got the feeling I didn't pass. At any level.

'Much better,' I said brightly.

'I'm glad *some* part of you is. The rest of you looks like it's just been disinterred!'

'Oh, thank you, James! You're so good for a girl's self-confidence!' I reckoned I looked perfectly reasonable, certainly a lot cleaner and neater than when he last saw me, if run a bit ragged by too little sleep and what there was of it punctuated by bad dreams. If they weren't about giant slugs (slugs? There must be something very weird about my sub-conscious) they were variants on a changing room with hundreds of Serenas all craning their heads as I tried to force myself into a size 10 dress. I didn't know what was worse, waking up with my skin crawling with revulsion, or waking with the crippling humiliation of knowing I had to go on a diet *immediately*. OK, I was a bit pale and there were shadows under my eyes, but what are blusher and concealer cream for if not to use on days like this? It seemed they hadn't worked.

He sighed in the way men do when faced with unreasonable women, took a breath and said, 'Let's start again. To anyone else you look like the normal Laura, pretty, bouncy, a bit tired maybe, but to someone who knows you you're looking stressed into next week.'

Me, pretty? James had called me pretty? He didn't pay me compliments. Long ago I was relegated to that corner of the universe which is occupied by sisters, strangely sexless beings who need protecting from all other predatory men but otherwise don't have any of the normal female characteristics. They certainly aren't ever *looked* at.

And of course I was stressed. The telephone wouldn't ring. But I doubted James would be sympathetic about that. 'Well, perhaps I shouldn't have sat up so often gossiping with Liv,' I said with a fine regard for the spirit if not the letter of the truth. It might be three days since our last session but there had been lots before.

James took this at face value, nodded and reached

behind him to slam the door shut. I can take a hint. 'I won't keep you. I just wanted to drop the slippers in before Horatio destroyed them completely.'

'You didn't think of shutting them away in a cupboard where he couldn't get at them?'

I smote my forehead dramatically with my hand. 'Oh dear! Now why didn't I think of that?' Probably because my cupboard was so full of clothes, most of which I couldn't wear, it wouldn't shut.

'Because it was altogether too practical an idea?' There was a smile in his eyes so I didn't think he was being serious. He looked at his watch, frowned and jiggled the keys in his hand. 'Look, a couple of guys I was at university with are having a private view of their pictures this morning. Why don't you come with me? You might enjoy it.'

It sounded quite fun, I like that sort of thing. 'But I haven't been invited.'

James shrugged. 'I have, and I was told to bring a friend. Besides they'd welcome you with open arms anyway. The more people there, apparently with a view to buy, the more successful they're going to look.'

Another first. James had described me as a bloody nuisance before, several times. A friend, never.

'Aren't you taking Serena?' I ventured. If she was being picked up on the way I really would discover that I couldn't delay attacking the ironing pile.

'No, she's beating the bounds at some family affair in the country.'

That was fine then. 'How long have you two been going out? I haven't heard anything about it.'

James gave me a narrow-eyed look. 'Planning to be the first with the news on the family grapevine?'

'Good God, no!' I said instantly. 'I'd have to explain how I came to find out and I'm certainly not telling any of them why I knocked on your door at midnight! Your lecturing me was bad enough.'

He laughed. 'You deserved it. It worries me sick to think what might have happened.' It looked like he meant it too. 'And to answer your question – not very long, so I'd rather keep aunt-type speculation out of it for the moment.' I couldn't blame him. 'Well, are you coming?'

Why not? It sounded like a pleasant way of whiling away a couple of hours on a Sunday morning. Then the usual female bugbear raised its head. 'I'm not dressed for a private view.' I waved vaguely at the black trousers and cherry-coloured shirt I'd put on after hours of agonising. It had been difficult to choose something that was neither too scruffy nor too smart for returning a pair of chewed slippers nor looked as if I was trying too hard. It might have been Serena who'd answered the door.

'It's hardly a hats and gloves occasion. The Wittle Gallery's not the Royal Academy. And Justin's and Robert's pictures definitely aren't!' James gave me a once over to check if there were any obvious holes or gravy stains. There weren't. 'I expect most of the people there will be dressed much the same. Though if you'd been in the sort of get up you were wearing the other night I'd have had second thoughts about taking you. Justin can get a bit over-excited.'

'I'm hardly likely to wear my party gear on a Sunday morning, am I?' I pointed out.

'Depends if you're on your way home or not,' he retorted. 'And in my opinion you'd be better off not wearing that kind of outfit at any time outside a room with tightly drawn curtains. But what you've got on now is fine. Quite acceptable.'

Talk about back-handed compliments! If it had been any cooler he'd have had icicles dripping off his tongue. 'All right then,' I said a touch ungraciously, and then added as a new and worrying thought hit me, 'So long as I'm not expected to buy anything. My bank balance won't stand it.'

'Neither will mine,' said James frankly. 'Robert and Justin are enthusiastic believers in the idea that you don't get taken seriously unless you put a price tag of several thousand on your work. Given that most people only buy pictures like theirs if they're spending someone else's money Rob and Justin end up giving away a lot as Christmas presents. Look, we'd better get a move on, I have to be somewhere for lunch at one. There's my car, just over the street.'

As we walked to it I asked, 'What happened to that thing you had before? A TVR, wasn't it? Something that looked like a sex aid and was very noisy in tunnels.' It had been the latest in a long line of elderly but fast cars with which James had amused himself to the consternation of his family who were constantly afraid he'd be brought home in several pieces.

His mouth curled slightly. 'It didn't go with the image of the respectable and staid head of an antiques business.'

There was a distinct edge to his voice. I looked at him sharply and said, 'You? Staid? Never! And if you try too hard the effect will be so unbelievable you'll only end up looking shifty!'

He laughed, the hard expression disappearing from his face. 'Thank you for your vote of confidence, Miss Moreton! Some of my more elderly clients thought that a young man who drove an obviously fast car must be a bit of a flash Harry and, more importantly, was also likely to rook them on the price – which of course I regularly do,' he added with a straight face. 'I just prefer them not to realise it! So as there was no point in having a car like that rusting away through only being used once a month, I sold it.'

I smiled in response, but couldn't help wondering if James was finding running the business a strain. Harry as the eldest had been earmarked to take over while James had pursued his passion for pictures, gaining experience in various art galleries, in between chasing women and living a lifestyle that was guaranteed to put white hairs on the heads of all who loved him. Then Harry announced he wanted to be a barrister and Henry Lovatt had a heart attack. James took over the shop on a strictly temporary basis; he was still there five years later. He'd turned out to be unexpectedly good both as a dealer and at managing his father, who saw no reason why he shouldn't continue to dominate the business and everyone involved in it from his sickbed a hundred miles away. According to the jungle drums (which still work remarkably well since at least one person in every family of this extended series of steps and cousins is an inveterate gossip and regards the dissemination of information as far more important than the possibly wounded feelings caused by the odd divorce or two), James finally managed to 'persuade' his father to let him do his work without interference. I gathered that the persuasion involved the sort of discussion that had elderly aunts clucking and saying they knew dear James was finding it difficult but he should still try and be more respectful to his father... Still, he didn't look too unhappy, and it was no bad thing if he'd been steered away from driving lethally fast sports cars. However, thinking of the drive back to my flat the other night, he certainly seemed to have learned how to handle this car like one.

The exhibition was in a gallery on the north side of Hyde Park, not top drawer but still pretty prestigious. 'Justin's uncle owns it,' explained James, 'but even so he's not giving them more than ten days. Hence the private view on a Sunday, they're trying to pack in as much as they can.'

It took me all of ten seconds to see that James had, in thoroughly masculine fashion, completely under-estimated the desire to dress up for a Sunday morning social occasion amongst those who know that they are going to be as much on display as the paintings. Liv's DMs and my French Connection trousers stood out like a hen in a field of golden pheasants among all the little dresses and cashmere twin sets and asymmetrical jackets and suede somethings from Prada and Whistles and Ghost and Edina Ronay. I tried to hide one DM'd foot behind my leg in a vain attempt to conceal how big they were and hoped desperately that everyone there would think that I was into reverse chic.

I was introduced to Justin, all artistic attitudes and

floppy hair, who was still astute enough to sum up almost instantly that I didn't have the sort of bank balance that could make me a potential patron. He smiled vaguely at me, murmured in a very camp manner that he hoped I would enjoy the show, and drifted off in pursuit of hotter prospects. James grinned at me and handed me a glass of white wine which turned out to be several cuts above the usual acidic and lukewarm offering you normally get at gatherings like this. He muttered sardonically that it must be an effort to get the guests paralytic enough to buy several paintings before they left, it was certainly the only way most of this lot was going to get shifted.

'Come on, they aren't so bad,' I protested, looking around, worried in case we were near either of the two maligned artists. 'They aren't *ugly*.'

'No, but they aren't worth five thousand nicker either!'

He had a point there. The pictures seemed to be mainly pastiches of other, more talented artists, like Van Gogh. The ladderback chair with a vase of yellow flowers on the floor alongside it had some particularly familiar elements. But at least none of the canvases included body parts. The policy with the wine seemed to be working too. A surprising number of the paintings had little red dots beneath them, indicating that they'd already been sold. James had been waylaid by a university friend so I was left to wander around looking at the exhibits on my own. Unlike the other night I didn't in the least mind being abandoned as it was the sort of gathering where you can talk to complete strangers because you've got a ready-made subject in common – what was on the walls. It was quite easy once you'd made sure exactly who you were talking to. Fortunately the elderly gentleman who turned out to be Justin's father was deaf or I might have found myself ignominiously turned out on to the street.

After we'd been there about an hour James waved to me from the other side of the room, pointing at his watch to indicate that we'd have to be leaving soon. I nodded and turned my attention back to the plate of spicy little somethings in filo pastry that I was busy getting myself outside. The eats were just as good as the wine. I had another glass of that too. The diet could start tomorrow. James had been absolutely right – in his opinion nothing unusual – to get me to come. There's nothing like a series of pretentious and completely uninformed discussions about modern art to make your own woes seem less pressing. I might have been one of those who woke tomorrow and realised that in an excess of good-will and better wine they'd spent several thousand on one of the series of canvases covered in multicoloured dots entitled 'A Homage to Pointillism'.

'So which of these daubs have you bought?' asked a voice next to me.

A tallish, fair-haired man with a faintly cross-eyed expression that suggested the glass in his hand wasn't his first, or his fifth for that matter, was staring intently at a vague representation of a pontoon bridge over a river. It looked as if he wasn't even sure what it was supposed to be. 'None of them.' I made a face. 'They're a bit beyond my budget.'

'Completely overpriced, you say? I agree with you,' he said in a loud voice. Several people turned around and glared at me as if it was I who had voiced such a heinous opinion. I smiled weakly at a woman I recognised as Robert's sister. She had been quite pleasant to me ten minutes ago. I doubted she would be again.

'I said, I couldn't afford them,' I corrected through gritted teeth.

'No, neither can I.' He stared morosely into his glass, apparently surprised at the magical way it seemed to have emptied itself. 'I can't afford much these days – it all goes to the wife, or most of it. And it was only a one-night stand. So what if it was one of her friends? And I suppose I shouldn't have done it in our spare bed – at least it wasn't ours! – but all the same, it was quite unreasonable of her to throw me out . . .' I smiled politely and started to edge away before he got on to the *really* embarrassing reminiscences. However, with that sixth sense that drunks seem to have he grabbed my wrist and held me fast. 'I was meeting my sister but she hasn't turned up, so as you're alone why don't we go out and have some lunch? My car's just around the corner.'

This time I didn't need my guardian angel prompting me to refuse this particular offer of a ride in a car. I was well on the case already. 'But I did come with someone. Sorry, I can't.'

'He's been neglecting you so he's not going to mind just this once,' the drunk slurred, fingers tightening on my wrist. 'We could have some fun.' And went on to make a suggestion of such inventive depravity that it took me a few stunned seconds even to register what he'd actually said. When I had I was torn between swooning from outraged modesty and letting him know at full volume what I thought of his proposition, thus causing a ruckus not usually seen at respectable private views. He was watching me with a satisfied expression that made me wonder if he actually got his kicks from shocking the pop socks off women he had never met before and in fact had no real intention of performing the acts he had just suggested. I hoped he didn't. Especially not with *those* props. But I didn't have the bottle to ask.

'Er, my boyfriend's a really jealous type,' I said quite untruthfully. 'He'd never let me go out with anyone else.' In fact I don't think it ever occurred to Daniel even to wonder what I did when I wasn't with him, which was most nights of the week. Sometimes I saw this as an utter lack of passion for me which depressed me enormously; other times I wondered if it was because he had a low sex drive. I didn't know which was worse.

The man still showed no signs of letting me go. I didn't particularly mind staying where I was. I could still reach for my glass with my other hand and could see that rescue was near. James was making his way over to our side of the room, though his progress was slow as he appeared to know virtually everyone and kept on stopping to talk.

'Oh, is that your sister?' I asked brightly, seeing a woman I was sure I recognised, with the same distinctively coloured dark gold hair as my captor who looked as if she had just arrived. She was wearing a white coat of the sort only those who can afford continual dry cleaning bills even contemplate. It also hung from her shoulders in the elegant folds that come from meticulous hand stitching in some designer workshop, I noted enviously. 'So you'll be able to go out to lunch with her after all. I wouldn't dream of butting in on a family party, so if you'd just let me go . . .'

He stared at me owlishly. I hoped he was working out how to open his fingers. My hand was beginning to get pins and needles. 'Orlando, I do not believe that the *signorina* is enjoying her capture,' said a middle-aged man with a lot of inky black hair cut uncompromisingly short. He was broad-shouldered and stocky, and wore the English gentleman's uniform of navy blazer and grey wool trousers that screamed good tailoring from somewhere like Savile Row, but even without his marked accent he was palpably foreign. No Englishman looks that polished. Most of them don't smell that good either.

Orlando swayed a bit. The newcomer cleared his throat meaningfully. Orlando blinked and obediently dropped my wrist. I turned to the smartly dressed man and said with genuine gratitude, 'Thank you,' but he wasn't looking at me. Instead he was staring intently into the middle of the room like a terrier that has just spied a rat. I followed the line of his head and all I could see was the fair-haired woman with her arms wrapped around James's waist as she gave him an enthusiastic kiss. It wasn't the air kind either. He returned the kiss with what looked like equal enthusiasm and stepped back slightly – just enough to slip a knife between the pair of them – as she chattered away with a lot of hand movements that showed off how pretty they were.

My rescuer made a noise in his throat rather like that of an enraged bull and said absently, 'It was my pleasure. Excuse me.' If his intention was to break up James and the woman his effort was wasted, for somebody had already tapped her on the back and she turned around to speak to him while James began to ease towards me, nodding without any noticeable degree of warmth at the dark-haired man as he passed him. He reached me and put a hand on my arm. 'Ready to go?' I got the impression he couldn't wait to get the hell out of there. 'Hello, I didn't see you,' he added in a guarded tone as Orlando turned around from slopping wine into his glass.

He looked at James, at his hand, then at me with mounting alarm. 'I'm sorry,' he said to me, enunciating his words with painful difficulty. 'If I'd known it was *James* you were talking about, I wouldn't have said what I did.'

James raised his eyebrows quizzically but before he could ask what it was that Orlando was talking about I said quickly, terrified he might just be drunk enough to spell it out, 'Forget it, I have.'

Orlando smiled gratefully and said in a burst of wine-fuelled bonhomie, 'I'm not surprised you've been keeping this one to yourself, James old boy. She's an absolute cracker. And a sport too,' he added with a sideways glance at me. 'Very understanding.'

James looked a bit startled to hear of our new relationship but rose nobly to the occasion. 'I'm so glad you approve, Orlando. And I quite agree with you Laura is – exciting. Unlike most people she starts at the conclusion and works backwards.' Orlando looked justifiably confused, and probably fearing that James and I were about to have 'words', turned away to glance sorrowfully at the empty bottle beside him. James looked at me with raised brows. 'I take it we're no longer married? I have to say that's a relief, I don't think marriage would suit me. Come on, Laura, I'm afraid we have to go,' he said in a voice that brooked no delay. 'Goodbye, Orlando.'

I nodded and obediently followed him as he pushed his way through the crowd. We stopped by the doors to the street to congratulate the two artists and tell them with the deepest insincerity how much we'd liked their paintings. Attention wandering as the three men exchanged views on some dramatic affair that I knew nothing about, I glanced back over the room and saw Orlando, joined by the fair-haired woman who'd been all over James, pointing me out and saying something with the urgent air of someone passing on a piece of really interesting gossip. Oh, dear, it seemed that he was busy telling the whole world that I was James's latest woman. I grinned and shrugged. It would probably get back to Serena, someone here was bound to know her. But I had no objection to Serena's cage being rattled a little. Her deft removal of my boyfriend of two days when I was seventeen still rankled.

James was unusually quiet for him as he drove me back to my flat, not even demanding to know what I'd been so understanding about, which was most unusual. 'Is that fair-haired man with the original line in chat up a friend of yours?' I asked.

'Did he ask you to come up and see his feelthy pictures?' asked James absently.

'Not see them, act them out!'

That got his attention, momentarily. 'Did he now? Good thing you didn't accept, his wife's got a strong right hook! She always takes him back in the end, poor fool.' He glanced over at me severely. 'I don't know what it is with you, Laura. You seem to attract over-sexed bozos like bees around a honey pot.'

'Come on! That's not fair!' I protested. 'It's only been twice. It just so happens they've both been in the last few days.' James looked deeply sceptical. 'Anyway, Orlando wasn't responding to any attraction of mine. He was so drunk he'd have made advances to a Grecian urn if it was curvy enough!'

James laughed. 'Judging by past history, you aren't far wrong! He's a complete loser. I only know him through Cressy. He's her brother.'

'Oh!' Light dawned belatedly. 'He said he was waiting for his sister. Was that her in the white coat?'

'Yes. I had no idea she'd be there. I've hardly seen her since— She's invited me to go and stay with them at their new house for some ball or other.' Talk about being ultra-civilised! But it was impossible to tell from his tone whether he was looking forward to it or not. No wonder he was looking so thoughtful. Meeting an ex out of the blue was unsettling enough even if the break up had been entirely mutual and amicable, but if you'd been dumped . . . And he didn't even have the consolation of a supermodel girlfriend on his arm to salvage his pride. Oh, God! And now Cressida thought his girlfriend was the very un-supermodel me! Usually I'm an expert at putting my great big size 6's straight into it but this time I had the sense not to say another word. Besides when he appeared with Serena in tow at this party it would just add to his reputation as a lady-killer, and he was a normal enough male not to object to that.

James let me out in front of my flat, mouthing plati-tudes that I was sure he didn't mean, like it would be nice to see me again soon and to give his regards to my mother. I waved him off and reluctantly returned to the pile of now urgent ironing. I whiled away the boredom by speculating on exactly what that expression on his face had meant until I decided there wasn't much point in concerning myself about him or his feelings about Cressida Buonotti, since I was hardly likely to meet her, or probably even see James again, for absolute ages.

You can be really spectacularly wrong, can't you?

CHAPTER 4

I still hadn't heard from Daniel by the middle of the week. You'd think that any normal man would have been at least a *little* curious about why his girlfriend had stalked out of a party without him. With another man too. He was a writer, for God's sake! He was supposed to be interested in motivation. But by now I suspected that Daniel usually found his own motivation infinitely more interesting than those of others, and certainly easier to write about. The worst thing was not being able to talk about it to any of my mates at the office. I knew perfectly well that Emma, fresh from her success with tall, dark and loaded, would say something along the lines of: I'd hear from Daniel as soon as he ran out of clean socks.

Liv was rather more understanding, but then she has to live with me so she knows what'll happen if she's too open in her criticism. The atmosphere in a shared flat can become mighty frigid even if neither party actually lays eyes on the other for days on end. It usually lasts until one of us needs to borrow something. But she's hardly in a position to cast stones, her William isn't exactly a shining example of a New Man either. When he undresses

67

he lobs his shirt vaguely in the direction of the fireplace and just assumes that someone (female) will eventually pick it up. And he's also been known to forget to call her when he said he would because he's too busy communing with his pigs. So I could really have done with boosting my spirits with a couple of in-depth discussions about Daniel's better qualities over cheap red and a pizza. Instead I had to make do with lengthy telephone calls which, while comforting (Liv knows how to say all the right things), just weren't the same. It also infuriated Darian who has an uncanny knack for appearing from her office just as I'm settling into the really juicy bits. You know, where you drop your voice and make it disastrously clear you aren't talking to a client.

In fact, I was doing a pretty good job of getting up Darian's nose generally. Her patience, never her strong suit, was severely tried by the way I jumped like a scared rabbit each time the telephone went and lunged for the receiver, sending papers flying. She doesn't appreciate other people, especially other women, being the centre of attention and my fame for an escape from the man who had grown into the successor to the Boston Strangler had by now spread well beyond the confines of the agency and done the rounds of our clients. When her favourite, a celebrity hairdresser who gave her a discount when having her hair done by one of his minions, asked how 'little Maura' was, she knew exactly where to point the finger of blame. Despite the misnomer, the fact that no one in possession of reasonable eyesight and in their right mind would call me 'little' and that I hadn't spoken to him for a month, I was still accused of putting myself forward in a way that was severely detrimental to the agency's success – quite how wasn't explained – and several of my other failings were candidly outlined at the same time. Having satisfactorily vented her feelings Darian dumped a bulging file of work on my desk with instructions that I'd better get a substantial portion of it finished by that evening if I wanted to stay in PR, then swept out of the door dolled up to the nines in Donna Karan, on her way to a lunchtime meeting at Le Gavroche.

I picked up the file and flicked through its motley collection of chores. God! It was as if she'd been deliberately compiling a punishment file – for months. Number one was to draft a press release for a new brand of panty liner. Number two to think of ideas for a promotion in the trade press of an athlete's foot powder. Time off for good behaviour (unlikely) might mean someone else got to do number six, despatching a sample of mint-flavoured waxed dental floss to everybody who had entered a 'spot the celebrity teeth' competition in a very local, local newspaper. I sighed. And some people thought PR was glamorous! When I'd been offered this job I had imagined exercising my carefully honed prose on slightly more exotic subjects than sticky side panels, comfort bands and embarrassing itching between the toes. In fact I'd been so fired up with enthusiasm that I'd joined a writers' group, thinking it would sharpen my writing skills. It took only one session to realise everyone far preferred to talk about writing rather than actually pick up their pens and get on with it. And that they didn't want any constructive criticism either. No criticism at all, in fact, otherwise there'd be a mass outbreak of artistic temperament. But they were a nice bunch, if a bit odd, and the sessions in the pub afterwards were great fun. Occasionally we got a 'proper' writer, i.e. one who had been published, to come and give us a talk about writing so we'd have a real excuse for yakking and not putting pen to paper. One evening the speaker was Daniel, who paid the rent by taking odd jobs like this while he was waiting for inspiration to strike so he could write his second novel. He was good; quick to sum up this motley bunch of bad poets and aspiring romance writers, and didn't make his talk too intellectual. And there's no doubt that it helps when a 'real' author looks like Lord Byron with two good feet.

I'd like to believe it was the beauty of my brown eyes that made him come and sit next to me in the pub afterwards but I have to be honest and admit there were only two other women under forty in the group, and they were holding hands, so I didn't have much competition. Anyway it was certainly the beauty of *his* brown eyes and all the other bits that bowled me over, though naturally I was interested in his mind too.

I never went back to the writers' group. I couldn't face the knowing looks and speculation about what had happened after I'd left the pub wound around their guest speaker. The most lurid conjectures would have been embarrassingly accurate too. Though there had been absolutely nothing to speculate about for far too long now, I thought sourly, hitting the keyboard with unnecessary but satisfying violence.

It's true what they say in the best songs about the darkest hour; just as I was contemplating whether to go and drown myself in the ladies' Emma called over in a disapproving voice, 'It's him. Give him hell, Laura!'

With a squeak I dived for the phone, sending my pot of pens flying to the floor, and of course I didn't give him hell. I didn't have the chance. Daniel didn't refer to the party, the blonde, or why I'd gone haring off into the night with tall, dark and slimy. Instead he wanted me to share his triumph over the very productive two days he'd had. He'd written three pages and had been able to salvage *two and a half* paragraphs. I was very pleased for him. Daniel is not a fast writer; as he says, writers of quality rarely are, their words are too valuable to come quickly. Perhaps I could come around that evening, he suggested, and he'd show me what he'd done. (Show me being the operative phrase. Daniel doesn't believe that I *understand* what he writes. He's right, I don't.)

I stared at the telephone and wondered, not for the first time, if he and I came from the same planet. Did he have *no* idea that I had reason to be completely fed up with him? Quite possibly, I decided, as in a surprised tone he repeated himself. Normally my yeses came out so fast he didn't have time to finish his sentence. 'That'd be nice,' I said vaguely. Somehow it seemed a bit impolite to mar his pleasure at his impressive work rate with a carping question about how he came to ignore me at a party *he'd* taken me to, given by one of *his* friends. I'd deal with that later.

'About seven-thirty, and will you be able to pick up something for dinner on your way? You're so much better at choosing than I am,' he said beguilingly.

And so much better at cooking it too. Daniel doesn't appear to mind what he eats, but I do. I'm not a fan of

71

Daniel's style of cooking: throw everything that doesn't smell too bad into his one saucepan and boil for twenty minutes. I'm a dab hand at heating up things from Marks and Sparks. I was about to fall in with his every wish when my eye was caught by the menacingly large folder of work sitting in the middle of my desk. Darian's threats seemed to be banded across it in neon letters. I had to tell him there was no way I could take the time to slope off to the shops and that I was going to have to work quite late too. He took the news in remarkably good part, suggesting we meet in a local wine bar instead. Perhaps he did have the vestiges of a conscience, I thought in surprise after he'd rung off.

Normally when I'm going out with Daniel I spend the whole day beforehand in a daydream and a frenzy of preparation, slipping off to the loos every five minutes to do yet another minute adjustment to my make up or hair, but today I settled down straight away to a session of the most astounding virtue. It's amazing how a threat to your livelihood can aid concentration. I even read the whole file on the panty liner people before I started writing the release, not that I actually found anything useful to include which is why I don't usually bother. Michelle, who works for one of the directors on the floor upstairs, took advantage of Darian's absence to come down for a good gossip under the guise of discussing the holiday rota for next July and August. As a rule I'm only too willing to be distracted but seeing my head bent over the keyboard she respected unwritten agency protocol and tiptoed past me with exaggerated care to go and perch on the edge of Emma's desk. I'd about finished what I thought was a fairly reasonable attempt on the first chore, one down, five to go, when Michelle called over.

'Hey, Earth to Satellite! Call for you.'

I looked up vaguely, my mind still on the 'double protection zone'. She was waving a telephone receiver at me. 'Who?' I mouthed.

She shrugged. 'It's taken me so long to touch base with you I've forgotten, if he ever told me.' Belatedly she remembered to put the call on hold and hissed helpfully, 'He's got a really nice voice. It must be the boyfriend. He said it was a personal call.'

Daniel was ringing to cancel, I thought in dismay. I knew it had been unrealistic to think he'd come out and meet me when he was in mid-creative flow. I'd have to make him feel he wanted to do nothing more than meet me in a friendly ambiance, like just around the corner. The trick was to Think Positive. I picked up the phone and prepared to ooze positivity with a dollop of sexy charm thrown in for good measure. 'Darling, how lovely to hear from you again so soon!' I purred. 'I can't wait to see you again. It seems so long. You haven't forgotten where we're meeting, have you? It's Bruce's at eight, just around the corner.'

There was a deafening silence from the other end of the line. I had a nasty feeling that positivity and sexy charm had been a resounding failure. Then I heard a laugh. *'Darling?'*

I wanted to sink through the floor, curl up and die, find a cupboard in a dark corner and hide away my embarrassment. Most of all I wanted to throttle Michelle. Nice voice indeed! Must be a boyfriend! Why the hell was she so idle she couldn't be bothered to take a caller's name? I thought vengefully, glaring at her. She looked back, rather surprised by my expression. I saw her face change as she realised she'd just landed me in it, but instead of doing the decent thing and turning away she prodded Emma in the ribs. They both cocked their heads towards me expectantly and I had the added joy of knowing that they'd be listening to every word of my side of the conversation.

'You know perfectly well I thought you were someone else,' I snarled into the mouthpiece.

'Darling, I presume,' James said with relish.

'What did you think you were doing, ringing up under false pretences?' I squeaked, hearing my voice go higher and higher with rage. 'Saying it was a personal call and refusing to give your name. No wonder I made a mistake like that.'

'Personally, I make it a rule to hold off the endearments until I'm absolutely sure to whom I am talking. I said who I was, but I expect the girl who took the call was too busy gossiping to pay attention. She was deep in a discussion of Chanel nail varnish. She likes deep red but fancies their fuchsia too.' I sent a poison dart look at Michelle. Automatically she pointed towards Emma with an 'it's her fault, not mine' gesture.

'Do you address all your clients in such a friendly manner? It casts a new and interesting light on the meaning of "public relations".'

'I do not!' I snapped, and rolled my eyes upwards, trying to find patience and forbearance somewhere on the ceiling. As usual breathing deeply and counting to ten worked better. After a few seconds I felt I had enough control of myself to be able to speak to him without resorting to yelling. 'What do you want, James? I'm very busy and can't waste time in idle chatter.'

The sounds of inelegant snorting wafted over from the direction of Emma and Michelle. I flicked them a rude sign; it might have been the first time either of them had ever heard me utter such an unlikely thing, but still. 'What a busy bee you are.' It sounded as if he hadn't believed it either. 'Then I won't waste your valuable time. Something's come up which I'd like to discuss with you.'

'What sort of thing? Is it your father? He hasn't had another heart attack, has he?'

'Don't worry, the old codger's absolutely fine, energetically making life absolute hell for all the neighbours as usual,' James said breezily. 'It's another matter. Shall we meet about seven this evening for a drink?'

'I can't,' I said automatically. I don't know why, I don't think I've got any sort of sixth sense. 'What about sometime next week? I've too much to do here to be able to get away until quite late.'

'But somehow you're going to manage to meet Darling at eight. Bruce's. Isn't that the wine bar in Fronton Street? If you're so busy we could meet there at, say . . . seven-thirty. Half an hour should be long enough.'

I stared helplessly at the phone. I couldn't think what James wanted to see me about that was so urgent. A natural antipathy to his assumption that I had plenty of time to spare at short notice warred with curiosity to know what this was all about. Of course curiosity won. Besides he was perfectly capable of turning up anyway –

once Daniel had arrived. 'All right then. If I must.'

He laughed. 'You might at least *pretend* to be pleased at the prospect of seeing me again! Don't be late. Darling might not appreciate it if he arrives to find me still talking sweet somethings with you.'

He rang off before I could think of a suitably crushing reply, which to be truthful would probably have taken me five minutes at least. I put down the phone and settled for an easier target. She was just sneaking out of the room. 'Oh, no, you don't!' I roared in best pantomime fashion. 'Explain how you came to make me make an absolute fool of myself.'

I ignored a comment from Emma along the lines of did I need anyone's help? Michelle turned around and spread her hands in an apologetic gesture. 'I'm sorry. You're always saying what a sexy voice Daniel's got, along with all his many other attributes.' Did I detect a note of sarcasm here? 'And when this man comes on the phone asking for you with the sort of voice that makes my toes curl, I made a very natural mistake. It's easy to confuse the names, they sound very alike.'

'There's no resemblance whatsoever between the way you say James and Daniel!' I said frostily.

Michelle thought for a few seconds. 'They've both got an "a" as a second letter.'

Even Emma found this a really weak excuse, but then turned towards Michelle, eyes dancing. 'You know this is the bloke Laura ran to when she was in danger of a fate worse than who knows what the other night? She never mentioned that he's got a toe-curling voice – the sort that can make *yours* wobble about, Michelle. What do you say to having a drink in Bruce's after we've finished tonight?'

I stared at her in horror, thinking of the last time Emma had happened to drop by to spy on my latest male interest. Not that James was that, of course, but that wasn't the point. In her defence I suppose I have to say she doesn't normally drink that much and I didn't fancy him much anyway. But the office gossip afterwards was really embarrassing. 'No!' I said sharply. 'You keep out!'

There followed a free and frank exchange of opinions in which Emma declared her absolute right to have a drink in whatever wine bar she chose, and I eventually had to concede that right but affirmed mine to kill her if she so much as came over to my side of the room, let alone spoke to my companion. This was eventually agreed to as being quite fair, and the new *entente cordiale* was cemented by a close examination of the fashion pages in the latest edition of *Marie Claire*.

Even with that not-so-brief hiatus, by the evening I had managed to leave an impressive, for me anyway, pile of work on Darian's desk for her to criticise witheringly the next morning. I even had half a report in the computer waiting to be finished. My toe had recovered to the point of being able to wear normal, not too tight shoes and I had one of my better and newer suits on so it didn't look too tired or stretched across the seat. One of the advantages of working for an agency that has a cosmetics company as its client is that there are always loads of samples to nick, so I was completely re-made up and felt that I didn't look too bad. In general I was feeling pretty pleased with myself until as I was going in at the door of Bruce's it suddenly occurred to me that in my hurry to go off and paint my face I'd switched off the computer before I'd saved the report. Oh, God, was I going to have something to explain to Darian tomorrow!

Bruce's was pretty full, most of the tables already occupied by workers celebrating the fact that the end of the week was in view. Well, we'd got halfway. It's just around the corner from the agency so it's the natural place to congregate when we want to unwind or complain about the management. Unwinding usually involves the latter. We started coming here when a down-at-heel pizza restaurant converted itself into Jimmy's Wine Bar, complete with lots of stripped pine, blackboards on the wall listing the latest offerings from the kitchen and cellars, a few large plants and posters of 1930s movie stars. In other words, what can be found to a lesser or greater extent on most suburban high streets. A few months later Jimmy, who was actually Giovanni from the pizza restaurant, was made an offer he couldn't refuse by the health department. The new owner had the bonzer idea of being really original and having an Australian wine bar. We've still got the stripped pine, the plants, the blackboards and posters, but now the posters are of Australian notables such as Dame Edna, Kylie, Crocodile Dundee and a koala, and the blackboards feature Australian wines and beers with names that would bring a blush to your mother's cheeks. They did try an Australian menu as well, but it was discovered that even cosmopolitan London stomachs can't cope with delicacies such as crocodile steaks and Australian pie floaters, so it's returned to standard wine bar food – whatever you like providing it comes with rocket or sun dried tomatoes.

Emma and Michelle were tucked in a corner about as far away from the main action as was possible. I thought it almost certainly wasn't by design but perhaps it showed someone upstairs was making sure things would go my way tonight. James was already seated on the other side of the room, looking unusually formal in a grey suit. I weaved my way towards him and waved at Bruce as he polished glasses behind the bar. He's really called Trevor, but he didn't think that 'Trev's' would have the same ring to it.

James stood up as I approached, he's always had the most meticulous manners, and said, 'Congratulations, Laura!' I couldn't think what he was talking about. He smiled. 'I think this is the first time I've known you be even remotely punctual, you're hardly late at all.'

'Bother! My watch must be running fast.' I was past the age of rising to baits like that one. 'You're looking very sober. Been to see the bank manager?' I asked as I took my coat off and slung it over the back of my chair and sat down.

He made a face. 'Got it in one.' It didn't look as if it had been any more of a pleasant meeting than an appointment with my bank manager would be. Though I deliberately have my account at a branch a hundred miles away so there is no chance I might ever accidentally be seen and called in. James reached out towards an open bottle on the table. Either he was intending to console himself with a whole bottle or he'd just assumed he knew what I wanted to drink. Daniel does that. He's usually wrong.

James's eyes followed mine as they glowered at the bottle. 'I hope you still like white wine? I thought I'd better order while I had the chance, otherwise with this crowd we'd have to wait ages to be served.'

My guns thoroughly spiked, I could hardly now insist on having one of Bruce's exotic and not very nice cocktails. James poured me a glass and pushed it over, saying, 'I haven't seen you in your working gear before. Very smart.' He sniffed the air. 'But smelly. Darling fond of perfume, is he?'

'The bottle slipped,' I muttered. I had been applying some to my pulse points, as recommended in all women's magazines, when I shook a bit too hard. I'd tried to wipe it off but the result was still a saturated bra and the most perfumed cleavage in West London. It was another reason why I was extremely relieved that Emma was safely over on the other side of the room. It was her precious bottle of XS which she keeps secreted at the back of her desk drawer I had filched, and she has an excellent sense of smell.

'It may wear off a bit,' James said in an encouraging voice, but didn't sound too convinced. He was laughing at me! My fingers clenched around my glass but I thought that before I threw it at him I ought at least to have the benefit of one mouthful. It was excellent, much better than the vinegar that purports to be wine which is all we usually allow ourselves. I took a second swig, and decided even I couldn't fantasise about throwing this, it was much too good.

It was also having a beneficial effect on my temper. I could feel myself becoming more mellow with each sip. I smiled at him. 'Thank you for taking me to the private view. I enjoyed it. Did you get any feedback about how they did with selling their pictures?'

James gave me a completely unreadable look. 'I got

plenty of feedback, but not about the pictures.'

Probably about meeting Cressida, I thought, wondering if I'd touched on a sore subject. 'I see,' I muttered vaguely and thought I'd better try to change the subject. 'How's Serena?'

James put his glass on the table with a slight but distinctly terse clink. 'I wouldn't know. When I last saw her – on Sunday evening – she was in a stinking temper. She's given me the push,' he added when I didn't respond.

My immediate reaction was 'Whoopee!' The next, remembering the way she'd virtually devoured him with her eyes in front of me, was astonishment. 'Why?'

He picked up the bottle and started to examine the label with minute attention. 'Because of you,' he said without looking at me.

'Me?' I squeaked. 'I don't believe it! You're having me on?'

He shook his head slowly. 'I'm not.' He continued to examine the label as if his life depended on it. 'We had a ... bit ... of a row when I got back after taking you home. She thought I'd been paying you too much attention,' he said tonelessly.

'Too much attention? Perhaps you could have sent me to sit on the steps and wait for Hugo to come back, but otherwise you couldn't have made it clearer you wanted me out of there as soon as possible.' With extreme generosity I added, 'Although I suppose in the circumstances I can't really blame you for that.'

A faint smile touched the corners of his mouth. 'You're too kind. And I was a bit ... er ... annoyed about her attitude to you. I told her so. She didn't like it,' he added in what must have been a masterpiece of understatement. I would love to have been a fly on the wall for that particular row, I thought gleefully. 'But no sooner had I managed to convince her that your turning up out of the blue at midnight was entirely innocent than you had to go and announce to a roomful of people that you're my girlfriend.'

'I didn't! Orlando just got the wrong end of the stick. It wasn't my fault!'

James's face bore an expression of infuriatingly polite disbelief. 'Needless to say, half the party was straight on the phone afterwards to inform Serena of my despicable two-timing behaviour. And now she assumes that when I said I knew you, I meant it in the biblical sense.'

'She actually believed we were having an affair?'

His eyes were mocking. 'Well, you assured her yourself that we knew each other *very* well.' My hand flew up to my mouth in horror. 'I swore to her I wouldn't *dream* of having an affair with you, but I'm afraid she didn't believe me.'

Bruce swept by, distributing ashtrays. 'Only a whinge-ing pom'd turn down a chance to have a go at Laura,' he said over his shoulder as he passed.

I hid my burning face in my hands as James laughed. 'So the upshot was Serena flounced out saying she wasn't going to waste her time on a man she couldn't trust.' He shook his head in disbelief. 'I'd never have imagined someone so cool could have such a jealous streak. Did you ever see anything of it when you were at school?'

Goodness, he must have it badly if he was cross questioning me for insights into her character. 'I didn't know her that well, we weren't in the same crowd.' I seemed to have done enough damage already without revealing her reputation as a champion sulker. 'She didn't like me very much.'

'Yes, that was obvious.' He grinned. 'But her storming out like that has put me in a bind, and I need you to help me out.'

Help him out? How?

James concentrated on refilling our glasses until they were exactly equal then looked up at me. 'Have you heard about this hotel Cressy's husband is opening?'

I nodded.

'She was telling me all about it at the private view. It's going to be quite something. Loads of chintz, a genuine antique in every room, a Labrador in reception, and still only five minutes from Harrods. It's going to need a lot of furnishing.'

Slowly I began to twig. 'I see! You're hoping they're going to buy things from the shop,' I said brightly, though I was still mystified as to how this could possibly concern me.

James looked pained. He's very proud of the shop and I don't think he appreciated hearing his prize stock described as 'things'. 'A *lot* of things,' he corrected and fiddled with his glass, seeming to choose his next words with care. 'Frankly, Laura, the business isn't doing too well. Before he finally hung up his spy glass Pa bought some fiendishly expensive cabinets for the Far Eastern market which have been near impossible to shift. We've got a fantastic amount of capital locked up in them – they'll go eventually but I can't afford to sell at too much of a loss.' I was leaning forward, intent on every word. It was rare – no, unknown for me – to hear James dropping the casually laidback spin he normally puts on even the worst of events. 'I've just had to pay a fortune for a new lease. Then there's a pension for Pa which is paid out of the business, and as you know he doesn't care for life on the cheap. Maintenance for your mother. She's not cheap either.' I had to nod in agreement. 'If the hotel isn't to make do with reproduction furniture, Stefano's going to need several people searching for good pieces or it'll take years. It's quite common for people buying large houses to give a shopping list to dealers – I make a tidy sum out of doing that sort of thing for clients already.' He paused, his eyes distant. 'But this is a really big job. If I got even part of it I wouldn't have to worry about the business for the next two years or so.'

'James, I'm sorry. I had no idea things were that bad.' I hesitated, afraid of giving offence. 'But why should Stefano even think of you?'

Mercifully he didn't look in the least miffed. 'Basically because Cressy has asked him to and he likes to indulge his wife whenever possible. And so far as my expertise is concerned, that won't be difficult for him. He knew of me before he met Cressy. He's been in the shop several times and bought a lovely little escritoire, so he knows I don't deal in tat – or fakes. I value my skin too highly to try and pass off a ringer on someone like Stefano.'

He drummed his fingers on the table. 'The problem is Cressy.' I nodded sympathetically. It would be a terrible strain for James to have to work in proximity to the woman he'd loved but lost. 'Stefano has what you might call a typically Latin temperament. Boys are allowed to be boys but his wife is for him alone. He's convinced any man has only to set eyes on her to be carried away by desire.'

It didn't say much for Stefano's opinion of her morals then. After all, it takes two to tango. Then I thought of how Cressida had been hurling herself at all the males in the room at the viewing and realised that even less pathologically jealous men might find that a bit difficult to cope with.

'He swiped Cressy off me and I suppose he's afraid I might try to swipe her back.' James didn't look terribly grieved at the thought. 'He's quite extraordinarily jealous and,' he raised his eyes to meet mine, 'he's especially suspicious of me as the last man in her life.' I nodded again. I was nodding so much I was beginning to resemble one of those toy dogs in the back windows of cars.

'So, you see, being the sort of man he is, his suspicions will already have been aroused by Cressy's asking him to give me some business. He certainly won't believe me if I tell him she now leaves me cold since he doesn't believe that's possible.' Well, I couldn't blame Stefano there! I too had my doubts about James's professed reluctance to sweep Cressida into a clinch. 'I reckon the only way I can convince him I won't be whisking her off to country house sales to have my wicked way with her in the back of the viewing tent is to arrive at the hunt ball they're about to hold with a girlfriend who's taken Cressy's place – and one who's halfway credible. That's why Serena's pushing off is such a disaster. I've already said I'm bringing a girl, so you can imagine what'll be going through

Stefano's mind if I turn up alone. If I'm not thrown straight out, he'll be patrolling up and down outside my room all night with a loaded shotgun in case I feel like a bit of corridor creeping!'

He looked at me expectantly. I gaped at him, forgetting to nod. I almost forgot to breathe in my astonishment. 'James, you know I'd help you if I could but I'm the last person who could get Serena back for you. She wouldn't believe anything I had to say on principle.'

I took a much-needed gulp of wine.

'Oh, God, I don't want *Serena* back,' he said impatiently. 'That scene the other night only hastened the end. It's *you* who'll have to come with me now.'

'Me?' I spluttered through a noseful of wine. 'Me?' I repeated when I'd finished coughing. I wiped my eyes and turned around to give my dirtiest glare to the couple at the next table who were killing themselves over my doing the nose trick. It gave me a bit of a chance to get my thoughts back in order. 'I couldn't possibly!'

'Why?'

'Well . . . well . . .' I couldn't think exactly why, but I was sure there must be loads of reasons. At last I came up with one. 'I've already got a boyfriend!' I said triumphantly.

'So what?' he asked blankly. 'I'm not asking you to commit adultery. I merely want you to play a part for a couple of days.'

The part of devoted girlfriend? 'But, James, look at me.' Obligingly he did so. With the sort of glazed unseeing expression people reserve for things that are useful and quite decorative – like a teapot. 'You might have got away with it with Serena, but me . . . Stefano's going to smell a rat the moment he sees me. He's never going to believe you'd prefer to make eyes at me than play footsie under the table with his wife!'

James looked at me with rather more attention, then slowly started to smile. 'You underrate yourself, Laura.' This is turning out to be an evening of surprises, I thought. He's actually about to pay me a compliment. 'He'll have no difficulty in believing it at all. Cressy's very slim and you're quite different—'

'Are you saying I'm fat?' I exclaimed crossly.

He put up his hands, laughing. 'I wouldn't dare! But Stefano, being Italian, is certainly going to understand perfectly well why I'd want to make eyes at that magnificent cleavage,' he finished with a grin.

I felt myself beginning to blush. Even without the miasma of XS wafting around it was undeniably impressive tonight, but that was mainly due to the Wonderbra I kept in my desk drawer for those unexpected calls from Daniel. Sadly nature has blessed my bottom rather than my bosom. 'Even so, you must know loads of other girls who'd be only too delighted to play your girlfriend.'

'I do.' Never one for false modesty, my stepbrother. 'The problem would be convincing them to *stop* playacting after one weekend. Anyway that'd really give Stefano the idea I'm not to be trusted with women. You forget, he's already seen you in your self-appointed role as my latest love.'

'Oh, was he the man who got Orlando to let me go?' I should have realised earlier, but I'd been too busy thinking about Cressida and James to wonder about her husband.

He looked at me expectantly. 'So what do you say?'

I thought about it for a moment. It'd be fun to go somewhere glamorous for the weekend. And I suppose I did owe James one for inadvertently getting rid of his girlfriend ... but if I mucked it up Stefano would be really angry at being tricked and he'd never do business with James again. 'I don't know ...'

James fixed me with a beseeching gaze. '*Please*, Laura.'

Lots of men have 'come to bed' eyes, which in my experience they don't only use for the obvious but to get other things they want, like the washing up done or an afternoon watching cricket rather than going round the sales. Most have a toss on a double bed or a roll in the hay eyes; the more proficient a long slow squeeze on a king size with snowy cotton sheets. James's eyes promised a seduction on a four-poster with satin sheets, a silken tent in the desert heaped with Persian carpets, a thoroughly five-star service in every sense of the word. I've seen him use that look on elderly ladies who have been reduced to a palpitating heap of adoration for this *nice* young man who understands them so well, and on four year olds who conceive an instant passion for 'Uncle James' and obey his, to them incomprehensible, wish that they should go and play quietly elsewhere. I know that look and I'm proof against it. Am I hell! My resolve was melting under his expert manipulation.

'All right,' I said weakly, but my voice was drowned as two young City types loudly discussing the bull market lurched against our table and rocked it violently. James caught the bottle as it toppled sideways but I was too slow to stop what was left in my glass from splashing over my black jersey shirt. So now instead of smelling like a tart's boudoir I was going to smell like a tart after a heavy night, I thought with resignation as I tried to dry myself with paper napkins. There were lots of apologies and offers to buy a new bottle of wine or for us to join them in a drink, both firmly refused.

An alcoholic cold bath did wonders for clearing my head and making me consider one or two vital questions. Such as, to convince Stefano that he didn't have the hots for Cressida any longer was James planning on doing anything more than leering at my cleavage? And if so, exactly what? Were we to be found in a passionate clinch in a corner? Or something more perhaps?

James finally got rid of the two embarrassed young men and turned his attention back to me. 'So you'll do it?'

'I'm sorry. I'd like to help you but I can't,' I said with as much firmness as I could muster.

To my slight surprise he didn't look in the least downhearted. He sighed slightly. 'Oh, well, I tried.' There was a pause then he added reflectively, 'I had to ring your father to get your number at work. I spoke to Imogen and she was so pleased we were back in contact again. She was most intrigued by how we happened to meet up this time.' There was another, longer pause while I waited for what was coming next. 'I'd hate for it to slip out accidentally, but you know how persuasive she can be . . .'

'You wouldn't!' I breathed.

'Only if I have to,' he said absently.

I chewed my lip, but already knew he'd won.

Imogen is my father's third wife and my stepmother. She takes both roles very seriously. She exerts herself ceaselessly for the benefit of others: packs her sons' trunks personally when they are going back to boarding school; never uses frozen food or things from the chiller cabinet; checks the ironing each week in case Mrs Robinson has used spray starch on my father's shirts; and if you come and stay there's always a vase of flowers, picked by her, in your room so you realise what a valued guest you are. Naturally she's also active in charitable works, the head of several committees as she's so good at organising people. Since she stretches herself so thin she can't actually do much of the work, but she is an inspiration and a figurehead. Photographs of her accepting flowers from some terrified child frequently appear in the local papers. In other words Imogen is a thoroughly Good Woman. No one is more aware of this than she herself.

But to be able to continue to do all her many good works it is essential that Imogen has peace of mind. Not that she ever reproaches you directly if you've upset or worried her in some way; she sweetly confides in my father and then *he* gets upset on her behalf, and so the ripples spread, wider and wider, until most of your acquaintances know you've been both unkind and ungrateful enough to wound Imogen's feelings. My life wouldn't be worth living after it became generally known I'd caused her to have sleepless nights by my thoughtless habit of accepting lifts from any available sex maniac who happens to pass by. Since, by one of those weird coincidences that my family delights in, Imogen is James's aunt's oldest friend he knows her modus operandi only too well. He's suffered from it too, from time to time, which only made his threat an even lower trick.

I glared at him in a manner that would have blown my

cover in seconds had it been seen by Stefano. 'You unscrupulous bastard,' I hissed. 'You dirty rotten cheat. You skunk. You louse.' I ran out of epithets, repeatable ones anyway, and gave him my best, most shrivelling look. 'You win, I'll do it, but just this once.' I slapped my hand down on the table so he knew that I meant what I was saying. 'And if you try to pressure me into doing anything more for you, you ... you unspeakable ... I'll tell Imogen you tried to blackmail me into being your *lover*! And I'd really enjoy seeing you extricate yourself from that one!'

'*Touché*,' he said admiringly. 'I'd no idea you had it in you, Laura.' His mouth curled slightly at the corners. 'It would almost be worth doing just that to see what her reaction would be,' he said to my alarm. But not even James would be prepared to risk being reproached by Imogen for months, or maybe longer. She's quite capable of holding on to a wounded feeling for years. He tipped the last of the wine into our glasses. 'Shall we drink to our agreement? It won't be so bad, Laura. You might even enjoy it.'

Oh, well, a chance to see how the *really* rich lived wasn't going to be that much of a hardship. I raised my glass obediently. Might as well get in a bit of practice in my role as his girlfriend. I smiled at him in sultry fashion over the rim.

Before I could work out what his startled reaction meant an indignant voice exclaimed from behind me, 'Laura! There you are. I've been combing the place for you.'

I swivelled around in my seat and squinted up at Daniel, who stood glaring at the pair of us. He looked even more heartrendingly good-looking than normal in a worn leather jacket and denim shirt, his dark hair for once confined neatly in a pony tail instead of flopping all over his face. He'd even shaved. 'Oh, have you?' I said vaguely, my hormones going into overdrive at his very presence and as usual completely removing any power to think rationally.

Out of the corner of my eye I could see two women in expensive suits at a nearby table gazing at him with tongues hanging out. I felt a glow of pride. He often elicited that sort of reaction. One of them looked at me with a faintly surprised air, eyes flickering between me, Daniel and James. There was an almost visible thought bubble above her head. What had someone like me done to get *two* such attractive men? I preened and sent her back a look saying, 'Wouldn't you love to know?'

'You said you were working late and couldn't get here until eight.' Daniel looked pointedly at the empty bottle. 'So as I arrived early I went over and sat with your friends. I've been watching out for you for ages. They didn't seem to know you were here already,' he added accusingly.

'Didn't they?' I'd have Emma for this, I thought vengefully. My heart lurched with guilt for upsetting him. His ego was very fragile and needed a lot of reinforcement. It was mean of me to feel irritated that he'd arrived just when I was practising . . . I craned my face upwards. 'I'm so glad you found me at last. Aren't you going to give me a kiss?'

He did so and stood up quickly, wrinkling his nose and looking at me in rather a puzzled way. 'Are you wearing a new scent? It's a bit . . . strong, isn't it?'

'Eau de Bushwhacker's Creek,' I muttered. As Daniel continued to radiate an aura of offended male, I said quickly, 'Daniel Blackstone, meet James Lovatt.'

The two men stared at one another as if neither was particularly impressed by what they saw. 'What a pleasure to meet you,' James said in a drawl I'd never heard him use before and held out his hand. 'I've heard a lot about you, Daniel.'

'You have?' I queried in surprise as Daniel took it, rather reluctantly it seemed to me. As I'd never mentioned James to him he was at a disadvantage.

'From Laura's sister.' James's smile indicated Katie had been thoroughly indiscreet. 'Why don't you grab that spare chair there? I'll be going in a few minutes.'

As Daniel sat down James said apologetically, 'I'd offer you a drink but unfortunately Laura and I finished it – what didn't go down her front, that is.'

'But she doesn't drink much,' Daniel protested.

'Yes, she does,' James said firmly.

Unlike most people who claim both Irish ancestry and their legendary fluency with words Daniel hardly ever touches alcohol. It interferes with the creative spirit apparently. Since he is never not creating, even if he isn't actually sitting with pencil over lined notebook (word processors are death to creativity too) he's contemplating his next few sentences so he can't afford to allow his wits ever to become befuddled. He's always said he doesn't mind my drinking when he isn't, but I don't like to, especially since he dislikes the smell of alcohol.

I said quickly before the prevailing air of *froideur* could become too pronounced, 'I do sometimes, but not that much.' James raised his eyebrows meaningfully, no doubt remembering one or two occasions which should remain safely buried. Mercifully he remained silent, which might have had something to do with the force with which my foot hit his shin as he opened his mouth.

Instead he said affably, 'I hope I haven't intruded on your evening. It's good to see Laura looking so well after the other night, isn't it?'

Daniel looked at me with a blank expression that made it quite clear he didn't have a clue what James meant. As briefly as I could, I ran through what had happened. He looked at me reproachfully. 'Oh, Laura, all I was doing was talking to a potential new agent. You know I'm not happy with Tony, he doesn't understand me. If only you'd waited for me. You know I was expecting to take you home. I was worried.'

Of course you were, I thought blissfully, and felt a sharp pang of annoyance with James who said nothing but simply sat there with a deeply sceptical expression on his face that spoke volumes. How dare he raise doubts like this within me? He didn't understand creatives and how forgetful they can be.

'I won't intrude on your reunion any longer,' said James with a distinct edge to his voice and pushed his chair back loudly. He leaned forward and, putting a hand on my shoulder, kissed me slowly and deliberately on the mouth. 'I'll give you a ring next weekend. You will bring that sexy nightdress, won't you?'

CHAPTER 5

I'm sure that if James intended anything at all it was only a bit of mischief but it had unexpected results. I discovered to my pleasure that Daniel was by no means as reformed a New Man as I'd presumed. All the old hoary male instincts of 'no one messes with my woman' rose straight to the top of his particular primeval swamp. I had to do quite a bit of explaining. I'm not sure that he totally believed me. It was the best night we'd had for ages. He didn't stop what he was doing and reach over to write in his notebook once.

I decided to forgive James – for the time being.

The next ten days sped away like the Bullet Train. There was a major panic attack when I discovered that even to hire a suitable dress for a grand hunt ball (and one which would pass James's exacting standards) would cost about as much as the National Debt. My bank account hadn't recovered from Christmas (that usually takes until about June which is why I never go on expensive holidays) so I did what I usually do in times of clothing crisis: apply to Liv. She has an enviably extensive wardrobe, particularly in the formal wear department. Her mother was one of the last debutantes to be presented to the Queen at court and though she has long given up her dreams of Liv following in her footsteps as a glittering social success, culminating in a misty and pearly engagement photograph in *Country Life*, she still expects Liv to turn up occasionally at the sort of parties she goes to. She's decent enough to pay for the necessary dresses so naturally enough Liv's quite happy about it.

I dragged her out of bed on Saturday morning, at least two hours before she's used to stumbling around getting ready to turn up for the matinee, and begged a trying on session. Liv likes the fitted effect in the evenings which is a bit unfortunate, since despite the larger feet she's both a bit shorter and a bit slimmer than I am. Eventually we managed to shoehorn me into her second best ball gown, deciding that the seams would probably last long enough for me to avoid being arrested on a charge of gross indecency. Liv stepped back, surveying the frankly startling effect of so much of me on display, and raised her eyebrows. 'I shouldn't worry. Even if you do give an involuntary striptease all that'll happen is that the hunting types will yell "Tally ho!" and give chase. You'd be surprised what an effect riding horses has on the libido.' She grinned. 'And if you're lucky it'll only be men in the pack!'

'Thanks a bunch for the confidence boost!' I muttered, wriggling out of the dress and taking what seemed to be my first full breath for hours.

'There's a pair of shoes that goes with it somewhere,' she muttered, rooting around in the bottom of her wardrobe, and pulled out the most scrumptious pair of black and green satin shoes. My heart flipped with desire. I have a passion for shoes. When you spend a lot of your life feeling challenged in the waist and hip department, shoes are bliss. They never make you look fat. The mirrors in shoe shops always cut you off just above the ankles too, and even in my gloomiest moods I can't really claim there's anything much wrong with my ankles. Luckily my toe was well on the road to recovery, for not even I am so obsessed with the beauty of my footwear that I'm pre- pared to risk not being able to dance because of sore feet. 'These must be a bit tight on you,' I said craftily, turning my foot to one side so I could admire the effect of the spindly heels. It was a good thing James was so tall.

'Even if they are, you aren't having them!' retorted Liv. I took that to mean that though they would continue to reside in her wardrobe the shoes might have a few more outings on my feet. Much like my sheepskin jacket which according to Liv positively enjoys going down to the country each weekend when she goes to see her farmer.

Having provided the dress she felt that she had a duty to make sure the rest of me matched up to it. She knows perfectly well I am never reluctant to think about making myself look better (actually doing anything about it is another matter. That is why diets always start tomorrow) but I was still bombarded with instructions about haircuts, skin foods, skin firmers, the latest shades in eyeshadow and how to make my obstinately straight eyebrows curve into a delicate arch. I had to bow to Liv's expertise; she may harbour dreams about being a farmer's wife but she has every intention of being the kind of farmer's wife who only ever smells of Alliage, never of pig muck.

Realistically speaking I knew that no matter how much I dolled myself up no one was going to bother to look at me much when there was Cressida around but all the same I still obeyed Liv's instructions and used my lunch hours to bolt off round cosmetics counters to look for the latest in magic potions to make me look fresher, dewier, more appealing – just like Juliette Binoche; then off to the hairdresser's for a new cut to do much the same, and round the lingerie departments to look for magical garments to squeeze some of me in and other bits out. To be honest I didn't look much different when I'd finished, if maybe a bit more polished. I had hoped that I'd be thinner at least since I hadn't had time to go out and have lunch with the girls once or even stop inside for a gossip over sandwiches, but it's amazing how many calories you can consume on the hoof and all that walking around trying out new perfumes hadn't made one iota's difference to my hip measurement.

It was doubly frustrating since I was being kept so busy that I didn't even have time for extended chat and biscuit sessions over the photocopier either. Several weeks before I had been attending a meeting in Darian's shadow with a manufacturer of downmarket baby toys and accessories called Freddie French. Quite why this particular client had landed in Darian's lap heaven only knows, unless David, the agency's owner, has a very mischievous sense of humour, for she loathes children even more than W.C. Fields did. The sales director, who likes to believe he has a really *wicked* imagination, was casting around for a really *different* and *interesting* location for the sales conference that would also cleverly reflect the company's image. In my opinion Grantham fitted the ticket perfectly. I didn't suggest it. Instead, as I was idly listening to suggestions about cinema complexes in Brighton, grain warehouses in Tilbury and a converted sixteenth-century dairy near Devizes being turned down, I stopped writing Daniel's name all over my pad and said, 'What about France? Freddie French – France. Geddit?' For my sins, the sales director was ecstatic about the idea. I had been thinking vaguely along the lines of Le Touquet in the late spring: easy to get to from the tunnel and even if the seaside weather was disappointing the food would be better than Brighton. But the sales director was a rugby fanatic and unluckily for all of us his club was playing in the European Cup at Bordeaux and he'd been allocated tickets in the draw. He promptly moved the whole sales shebang to a little conference centre he'd found (charming position on the banks of a river and English spoken) for the week following the match. Darian, who had been keen on the idea of five days sampling the seafood of northern France, looked up the average temperatures and rainfall for south-western France in February and promptly announced she felt it was time I started looking after clients all on my own.

Actually even downmarket baby products became interesting when they were my responsibility and to the dismay of Emma, who said that I was turning into a Darian clone, I took to staying late – well, a bit late, half an hour or so – to work on the presentation for the salesmen to convince them that selling Freddie French baby products was a really *wicked* thing to do. (The sales director was presenting it.) The logistics were proving a nightmare; the sales director had decided he'd done enough in finding the location and had turned all the rest over to his PR agency. I was landed with making the arrangements for twenty-three salesmen and women, partners and assorted hangers on to travel via train and car to France (naturally nobody was prepared to simplify matters by travelling in a group), and issuing directions so they could actually find their accommodation which was in the middle of nowhere, three miles down a road unmarked on all but the largest maps. I was gloomily sure that at least half of them would have lost the photocopies I had sent by the great day. The person responsible for the 'English spoken' claim was definitely over-optimistic about her prowess, certainly so far as the speaking bit was concerned, and since my own French is rudimentary to say the least communication could be fraught at times. But somehow it was all coming together and Darian was being positively benign – for her. She even said that one day I would make quite a useful little account executive – though the implication was that this would be sometime in the far distant future.

I was beginning to think that perhaps for once everything was going right; the job was working, Daniel was being attentive – he'd telephoned three times in the last week despite being on a roll with his writing, I was going to a party in a dress that didn't make me look too fat and I liked the new cut the hairdresser had given me. It just shows that it doesn't do to get overconfident, doesn't it?

When James had said that Stefano and Cressida had bought a Queen Anne house I had envisaged something quite large obviously, for people with that amount of lolly don't buy bijou little residences, but along the lines of the sort of thing you see advertised in *Country Life*: square red brick affairs, two or three storeys high, with pretty little dormer windows in the pitched roof and an indefinable air of cosiness. What I saw when we at last reached the end of about two miles of driveway that meandered through striking but bleak parkland, with an admirable view of the Peak District in the distance (also striking but bleak), was a large grey stone house plonked squarely in the middle of sweeping lawns dotted with a few cedar trees. The flat roof was bounded with a waist-high parapet and there wasn't a dormer window in sight, though light reflected dully off the huge panes in the triple rows of windows, which graduated from full-length at the bottom to half height at the top, on each façade. Impressive it was, cosy or pretty it definitely wasn't. I couldn't think why the marquee erected to one side of the house was necessary, the house looked big enough to accommodate a ball for several thousand. James whistled softly, no doubt happily wondering if Stefano and Cressida were going to need furniture for their house as well as the new hotel, while I experienced a pang of pure panic. How on earth was I going to carry this off? The more that I learned about Stefano Buonotti from odd snippets that came my way, the more I felt like Daniella going into the lions' den. He was reputed to be clever, ruthless and very acute; it was also said that there were areas of his business dealings the authorities would love to inspect more closely but so far they had not come up with a legally enforceable cause. James and I had been supposed to meet to get various story lines straight, like how long we'd actually been going out, but what with one thing and another there simply hadn't been time. On the journey down he seemed preoccupied, frowning and drumming his fingers on the steering wheel, though fortunately he did appear to concentrate at least while overtaking other cars in situations I wouldn't have attempted on an arcade game. I'd tried to ask him once or twice if there was anything I should know and he had replied absently, 'I'm sure you'll do just fine, Laura.' A touching faith in my abilities which he had never shown before.

We parked under an enormous portico big enough to shelter three carriages side by side. Tall double doors were thrown open even before James had switched off the engine. A slight figure came hurtling out and flung herself at him. 'You're here at last! I thought you were never coming. I've been waiting for ages!' We'd said we would arrive around four-thirty, it was actually twenty to five. Cressida stood up on tiptoe, throwing her arms around his neck and kissing him warmly. This was a really clever way to allay the suspicions of a jealous husband, I thought, watching James look warily over her shoulder, then move his head to one side so that her pursed lips hit his cheek rather than his mouth.

He gently disengaged himself and, holding her hands at arm's length, stepped back. 'You look wonderful, Cressy,' he said with a broad smile. 'Marriage certainly agrees with you. And with you too, Stefano, you look very well,' he added to the man standing glowering a couple of feet behind her. Our host barely glanced at me, eyes fixed on the dancing figure of his wife as she clung close to James's side. James motioned me around to his other side with a slight jerk of his head. 'This is Laura Moreton,' he said, putting an arm possessively around my shoulders. It tightened automatically as I tensed in surprise, and the fingers resting apparently lovingly on the top of my arm dug into my skin in warning. Luckily my coat was thick or there would have been a couple of embarrassing bruises to explain later that evening when I appeared in my sleeveless dress.

I relaxed obediently, it was more than my life was worth to do anything else, and Cressida flashed me an enormous smile that lit up the whole of her face, not that anyone as pretty as she needed any extra radiance. The cold grey light of the winter afternoon clearly showed that the stunning photograph of her that had appeared in the papers when she made her so-called fairytale marriage had not been touched up one bit. In fact she looked even better, for newsprint couldn't do justice to the loveliness of such colouring or to the constant play of expressions that passed like quicksilver over her mobile face. 'It's lovely to meet you, Laura,' she breathed, and I had the unnerving sensation that she really meant it. It really wasn't usual for women to greet their ex's (supposed) new girlfriend with such enthusiasm. As well as being too pretty to be true it also appeared she was nice as well.

'Nice' wasn't a word you'd apply to her husband, I thought, looking at him with rather more attention than I had on the previous occasion. His face was harsh and angular with a dark chin that gave the unnerving impression of being made of polished steel. His whole stance looked tough too; he was a solid man, not fat but the breadth of his shoulders, which a tweed jacket did nothing to disguise, made him seem both shorter and broader than he really was. My heart sank. He wasn't the sort to be fooled easily. Now that he appeared to be assured his wife wasn't getting up to anything on the drive with her guest he was examining me with interest. I received a more refined version of the visual once over most Italian men seem to learn in the cradle: first up and down assessing the basics, then the face, then lingering on the important bits that go in and out, finally contemplating what you'd look like with your gear off. I didn't have a clue from his impassive expression whether he thought the prospect an appealing one or not.

He held out his hand. 'I too am delighted to meet you again, Signorina.' His smile didn't reach his dark eyes. I had a nasty feeling that if he didn't actually know, he at least suspected I was a ringer. I wondered if I could invent a sudden crisis in the family so I could leave immediately, but a hard nudge from James reminded me I wasn't likely to receive much co-operation from that quarter.

I took Stefano's hand. His grip was hard. 'Good afternoon . . . Count?' I floundered with an air of helplessness. I'm good at airs of helplessness. Sadly they're usually absolutely genuine.

He responded as I'd hoped, smiling a bit more warmly this time. 'Stefano. That is if I may have the privilege of calling you Laura?'

'Of course,' I said demurely. We were much the same height so I couldn't do the peeping coyly through my eyelashes trick, which I quickly decided was probably a good thing. He was too acute and besides I'm not very good at being coy. I'm too big for one thing and I don't concentrate hard enough and soon forget my maidenly role. The slight soreness at the top of my arm was proof of that.

Cressida had shielded her hands high up the sleeves of a sloppy grey cashmere top that I would have been prepared to kill for and was hopping from foot to foot in the chill wind that seemed to be coming straight down from distant peaks. At least we were protected from the drizzle that was now falling gently. I wondered if the size of the portico had been dictated not by the number of carriages it needed to cover but by the necessity for a permanent giant umbrella. 'Shall we go in?' our hostess asked plaintively. 'Stefano never seems to feel the cold despite his southern blood, but I'm always freezing.'

Both men looked as if they would like to offer to take her tiny frozen hand in theirs immediately. 'Yes, *cara*, take Laura in to have a cup of tea. She will need it after the long journey.' Stefano spoke English as easily as if it were his mother tongue, though his pronunciation had an unmistakably Italian cadence. Cressida told me later that he'd had an English nanny. 'James and I will take the bags. The staff are busy getting everything ready for the ball. '

I was very happy for James to cope with my cases. On the principle that I hadn't really known what to expect I had included most of my wardrobe, all the clean things without holes anyway, as well as six pairs of shoes, boots, trainers and gumboots (you never know what to expect in the country), and most of the contents of Selfridges cosmetics hall. I hastily reminded him to be careful of the dress in its travelling bag and not to crush it, and escaped before he could discover exactly how much it all weighed.

Cressida took me into a cavernous hall dominated by an ornate stone fireplace of quite incredible ugliness which could only have been put in by a Victorian owner who was heavily into gothic, and monumental gothic at that. A meagre fire of about two logs burned sullenly where half a tree wouldn't have been lost. Cressida grimaced as we went past. 'It smokes. I'd like to put in a flame-effect gas fire but Stefano prefers to sacrifice comfort to architectural integrity.' She rolled her eyes to indicate the general unreasonableness of men.

We went into what she called the small sitting room, positively cosy by the standards of the hall since it was merely about twenty-five foot by twenty-five, with a proper fire burning in a Regency fireplace and a huge silver tea tray already laid out on a side table. It was furnished with a medley of elderly furniture that had never been particularly good or particularly bad, just ordinary. The sort of things which are pronounced to be antiques in many shops simply because they're over fifty years old. A pile of artist's sketches of the room and fabric swatches were jumbled amongst copies of *Vogue*, *Elle* and *Interiors* on the glass coffee table. I glanced at them curiously as Cressida pressed a bell in the wall. Presumably this was her own special domain, for the designs, though stunning and looking as if they could easily feature in the pages of *House and Garden*, had a fluffy, fussy feel about them, especially the sheer quantity of proposed ruffles on the sofas. Even on a couple of minutes' acquaintance I was prepared to bet Stefano was anything but fluffy or frilly.

Two different kinds of tea appeared like magic, brought

in by a plump middle-aged woman with a harassed face who said, 'Pleased, I'm sure,' when I was introduced and promptly removed herself. I never did discover what her name was. 'She's worried about leaving the kitchen in case the caterer's assistants pinch the silver,' Cressida said as she poured the tea. 'They aren't local, you see, come from Nottingham.' She made a face. 'And you know the sort of person who comes from *there*.' She sat down, holding out her hands to the fire, and chattered away about how pleased she was that we had come, the other guests who were arriving later, all relations of hers of one sort or the other, and how ridiculous it was that in this huge house they could have so few people to stay as they hadn't yet got around to furnishing all the bedrooms. (I did a swift reckoning. It sounded as if even so they could still manage to accommodate eight guests.) At least they had a decent-sized dining-room table so she was going to be able to have a proper dinner party before the ball.

It was impossible not to like her. Like a puppy she seemed to assume that everyone was going to be captivated by her and it was difficult not to respond. Luckily for me she was so caught up in the excitement of entertaining properly for the first time in her new house that she merely skated over some potentially awkward subjects, such as how long had James and I been going out and whether she and I had ever met as my face seemed familiar . . .

James seemed to be moving a bit stiffly when he came in, as if he had strained his back. Discreetly I did not enquire. 'Is your room all right?' asked Cressida with another of her beaming smiles.

'It's perfect,' he said in a slightly strangled tone, giving me a quick look. 'I should think the view in daylight is wonderful.'

'Yes,' she said without any marked enthusiasm. 'I wanted to buy somewhere in Oxfordshire where the scenery's a bit more gentle and the neighbours a bit less horsy but Stefano likes grand vistas. As usual he won.'

James frowned slightly in response to the little crease appearing between her fair eyebrows. 'Just be thankful he's not hooked on the views of North Scotland!'

She laughed, discontent vanishing like magic from her face. 'Oh, James, you're so good for me! I am pleased that you've come!' I had a good view of Stefano's expression as he appeared in the doorway. He didn't appear to share Cressida's pleasure. She patted the sofa next to her. 'Come over here and tell me all you've been doing since I last saw you properly. It must be at least two years since we had a really good talk.'

'All of that,' he said, sitting down beside her. 'It was when you told me you were going to marry Stefano.'

'So it was. You didn't come to the wedding, did you? Didn't you have an important sale or something you had to go to? What a shame – you'd have enjoyed it.' It wouldn't have occurred to me before now that seeing the love of his life get hitched to another might be James's idea of a good time, but you never know. 'It was a good wedding, wasn't it, darling?' she asked her husband.

'I thought so, certainly,' he agreed, pouring himself a cup of tea. 'But then I am prejudiced. It was my wedding after all.'

The conversation was becoming a little too loaded for

my taste so I cut in with, 'Have you been living here long, Stefano?'

'Only about two months.' He didn't move from his watchful position by the tea tray where he was able virtually to breathe down Cressida's and James's necks.

'You've moved to England from Italy in the middle of winter?' I said in genuine surprise.

'Cressida says we Italians don't understand central heating,' he said with a ghost of a smile that made me realise he could be very attractive if he chose. 'She claims we build our houses to combat the heat, not the cold. Since it is the opposite here, we will live in England in the winter and move to Italy during the summer.' His dark eyes flickered backwards to Cressida's fair head now bent towards James.

'Lucky you!' I breathed. 'And you're hosting the hunt ball already. How noble of you! And Cressida too. It must involve her in lots of organisation when she's barely unpacked. But is it usually held here? What's the history of the house? Do tell me about it.'

The look he gave me indicated he knew very well what I was up to but manners dictated he had to come and sit by me. He launched into an extremely terse history of the house: owned previously by only two families, the last plagued by expensive young men who sold off all the heirlooms and eventually forced the sale of the house. I did my best to indicate I found it all riveting. James leaned forward and interjected the odd remark, sensibly giving the impression that, unlikely as it was, he found local history just as interesting as the very pretty woman next to him. Gradually Stefano began to unbend as, bored by the problems of renovating a listed house, Cressida leaned back against the sofa cushions and daintily nibbled a corner of shortbread. Nonetheless it didn't make for the easiest of atmospheres and I was relieved when she stood up, saying, 'If you want to have a bath before getting changed, Laura, it'd be a good idea to have it before my sisters arrive and pinch all the hot water.' She sighed heavily. 'The heating and hot water systems were state of the art in about 1900 but it's such a big job we've got to wait until the summer when we're at the *castello* before we get them replaced.'

I'd have agreed to almost anything to get out of there to somewhere I could relax for a bit. A bath sounded just fine.

'I'll take you up and show you where everything is. Oh, hang on, could you wait a few minutes? I'd better go and make sure there isn't open warfare between the caterers and my staff in the kitchen.'

'It's all right, Cressy. I'll take Laura up, I know where everything is,' said James to my surprise. He'd looked remarkably comfortable stretched out in his chair, nursing the whisky Stefano had only just given him. 'It'll save you having to hurry.'

'I don't mind waiting, honestly,' I began as he rose to his feet.

He silenced me with a frown and took my elbow in a firm grip. 'Come on, sweetheart.' I almost tripped over the edge of the rug. Never before had I heard James express himself in that particular tone of sickening sweetness. Especially when accompanied by a weightlifter's grip. 'I'll be back for that whisky, Stefano, it's much too good to leave,' he said over his shoulder as he steered me out of the room.

'*Sweetheart?*' I echoed incredulously as soon as the door shut behind us. 'You might think the act needs a bit of beefing up to convince Stefano, but if you carry on like that he's going to think you've gone soft in the head! You'll be calling me Bunnykins next.'

'Shut up or I'll do just that!' he snarled. 'Look, there's something I've got to tell you—'

'Yes?'

'Oh, blast it!' he swore as a green baize door at the end of the corridor swung open and the plump woman walked towards us, carefully carrying a hanger which was supporting an elaborately flounced white dress that enveloped us in the crisp smell of freshly ironed fabric. She slowed down as she passed the pair of us standing motionless at the bottom of the staircase. 'Are you unsure of the way to your room? Can I help you?'

'No, thank you very much. I know where we're sleeping,' replied James. 'We were just admiring the carving on the balusters.'

'Yes, they look nice but they're the devil to dust,' she commented, doing a sort of agitated hover. I realised she was dying to get on but felt she couldn't leave us aimlessly hanging around. I pulled on James's arm and motioned him upwards. He sighed softly but began to walk up. We could hear her follow us, then come to a halt on the landing and watch to make sure James really was guiding me to the right room. After a couple more seconds she moved off, getting on with the important job of hanging up Cressida's dress.

James flicked on the light by the door and stood back for me to go into a large room wallpapered with an old-fashioned design of rosebuds contained within a criss-cross trellis made of twisted blue ribbons. The air was heavy with the sweet smell of hyacinths from a bowl placed on a bow-fronted chest of drawers between two windows hung with blue velvet curtains.

'Laura—'

I wasn't paying attention. Instead I was staring open-mouthed at an enormous four-poster that was to be my resting place for the night. The deep rose pink of the silk curtains, faded now from their original ruby red, was echoed in an exquisite patchwork quilt in a ring design that covered the bed itself. I walked over and stroked the fabric. To my relief it didn't feel nearly as brittle and fragile with age as its appearance suggested or I would have been afraid to turn it back lest I damage it. 'Gosh, isn't this fantastic?' I said. 'I've never slept in a four-poster before. It's *enormous*! There's room for about six of me.' I twirled around – 'What a super room' – and peered through a door cut in the panelling. Gosh, I had my own enormous bathroom too, with a claw-foot iron bath and what must have been one of the earliest showers in existence suspended over it. The head was about the size of a meat dish. A bowl in the middle of a marble-topped table was heaped with bars of soap from Floris and L'Artisan Parfumeur, and several exotically shaped bottles of bath oil were ranged neatly on a shelf above the bath. There was even a long, snowy white towelling bath robe hanging on the back of the door just in case I'd forgotten my M & S dressing gown.

'I can't believe this! It's amazing!' I burbled, skipping back into my room and nearly falling over one of my suitcases. I seemed to have a lot of luggage, I thought idly, and then slewed to a halt. Neatly aligned against my two tatty and battered suitcases, one with a rip in the canvas that allowed an embarrassing scrap of lace to peep out, was one of those strong and expensive black moulded models that people who travel a lot on aeroplanes use.

'This isn't mine. Isn't it yours? Why's it been put in here?' James was standing by the door looking distinctly hunted.

I must be very slow on the uptake because it took at least twenty seconds for the truth to sink in. 'Oh, no. No. *No way*,' I said firmly, my voice rising to a shrill note of outrage. 'I am not, definitely *not*, sharing a room with you. What the hell do you think you're doing, James? You *promised* that it was just a pretence . . .'

'It is, it is!' He shut the door behind him hastily. 'And keep your voice down, for God's sake! They'll be able to hear you all over the house.'

'So what?'

'From the noise you're making anyone would think you were some Victorian miss afraid of being ravished.'

Presumably it hadn't occurred to him that given he must have told Cressida we were sleeping together my fears were not unreasonable. So he'd said he wasn't asking me to commit adultery, had he? Granny Lovatt, right-eously indignant about James's carryings on with an older and unsuitable girlfriend (a so-called 'exotic' dancer), had once been unwise enough to accuse him of breaking the commandments. James had taken enormous pleasure in pointing out to her that since neither Cheryl nor he was married all they were doing was committing fornication, which hadn't actually been forbidden. Granny hadn't cared to tackle him on that issue again.

I shook my head. 'You are missing the point, James! Let me repeat, there is no way I'm spending the night in the same room as you. We'll have to tell Cressida she's made a mistake.'

'We can't! It'll ruin everything.' My face must have showed I did not consider this in any way a convincing reason why I shouldn't go straight to our hostess. He dropped his voice. 'It isn't just you and me who'd be embarrassed by that.' He didn't look particularly embarrassed, merely worried about the sort of scene I was going to kick up. 'It'd be mortifying for Cressy. The first time she's entertained in a big way in her new house and she goes and makes a bosh of it! Is it really fair to upset her like that just before everything gets going?'

I was halfway to agreeing with him when he went and spoiled it. 'Why create a drama for no reason?' Naturally steam started coming out of my ears again at this. He backtracked rapidly. 'I'd sleep on a sofa if there was one, but that little day bed is barely long enough for me to sit on, let alone lie down, and as you said yourself, the bed is plenty big enough for six. You won't even know I'm in there, I promise. I won't lay a finger on you. You have my word on that.'

He walked towards me, holding his hands wide apart in a faux-ingenuous gesture of total innocence. 'Don't come anywhere near me, James,' I hissed. 'If you get within arm's reach you're liable to go down to dinner with a black eye, and that'll sure as hell spoil your cover story.'

Prudently he backed away out of range. 'And I'm *not* creating a drama out of nothing,' I continued. 'Out of the goodness of my heart I agreed to pretend to be your girlfriend, but *you* neglected to tell me exactly what the role entailed.' I was working myself up into a fine rage. It was rather fun, since for once I was absolutely in the right. James glanced at the door in a worried way as if he feared that at any moment there might be a knock and a query as to whether everything was all right. 'Don't you *dare* give me that nonsense about the bed being big enough for both of us and that I'm making a fuss about nothing! You give your word that you won't try to lay a finger on me? Huh! I'd sooner trust the word of an octopus!'

'I won't, I swear,' he said earnestly. 'I wouldn't dream of going anywhere near you.'

'Thank you very much!' I snapped.

He stared at me blankly for a moment. 'Oh, God! I can't say anything right, can I?' he asked gloomily. 'You know I didn't mean it like that. Oh, hell! Look, Laura, I *swear* I didn't set this up.' He frowned and shook his head. 'I didn't say anything to Cressy that suggested we were sleeping together. Well, I mean I know I said we were an item, but why she presumed that meant . . .'

'What you actually mean is that, knowing you, Cressida instantly assumed that no girl going out with you could possibly resist the allure of your finely honed body for more than five minutes so we *had* to be sleeping together,' I said with withering sarcasm.

It rebounded immediately. 'Something like that.' If I'd

had something within reach I would have thrown it at him. James laughed. 'You asked for that! Look, I don't know why she's shoved us in together, perhaps she hasn't got enough rooms or something, but I promise it wasn't anything to do with me.' He gave me the wide-eyed and innocent look that proclaimed he was all that was fine and upstanding in British manhood and naturally would never dream of deliberately putting a girl in a situation like this. It was almost convincing. Except to those who have seen James playing cards. It is always he who ends up with the pile of matchsticks in front of him during marathon sessions of Cheat played on winter afternoons. He wins at Liar Dice too.

I perched on the side of the bed and looked at him steadily. 'Really?' I asked sarcastically.

He nodded vigorously. 'I promise. Look, if I'd had seduction on my mind when I asked you to come away, do you really think I'd be so crass as to ask Cressy to put us in the same bed and assume it would automatically lead to a leg-over situation?'

Actually that was the most convincing thing he'd said so far. James was adept at wriggling out of difficult situations but I couldn't imagine him deliberately engineering one where he could have predicted I'd kick up a stink. Besides I had the feeling that getting in a leg-over situation with me, as he so elegantly put it, was the last thing on his mind just now. He had too much unfinished business with Cressida. I just hoped that wouldn't land us in really hot water. Maybe it'd be safer if I was there to keep an eye on him at all times . . . He must have sensed I was weakening for he cocked his head on one side. 'We could put bolsters all down the middle of the bed if that will make you feel safer?'

'I don't *need* to be made to feel safer,' I informed him loftily. 'I'm a dab hand – and foot – at karate.' Completely untrue but never mind. I got up to open my case and as every inch of James's body language began to express relief that he wasn't going to have to cope with any further major displays of female displeasure, another thought occurred to me. 'You'd better have brought a pair of respectable pyjamas with you,' I said in a grim voice.

He looked at me guiltily. 'Well, actually . . .'

CHAPTER 6

A white-haired old man was standing sentry at the bottom of the staircase as James and I came down before dinner. I wondered if he was some kind of butler. He certainly had the requisite air of gravitas and his tail coat had been made in the days when he had less of a paunch, but surely butlers don't normally wear embroidered slippers? He looked up at both of us with slightly red-rimmed eyes. Butlers don't usually examine the quantity of flesh spilling out over a lady's bodice either. He proclaimed grandly, 'The party is assembling in the Blue Drawing Room. You may not be familiar with it. Would you care for me to show you the way?'

I quelled a giggle with difficulty. 'Thank you, yes.'

The old man inclined his head in a sort of regal bow. 'I have not had the pleasure of making your acquaintance before, I'm sure, for I'd never forget a pretty young thing like yourself.' The grand manner of his speech was only slightly spoiled by his second close inspection of my cleavage. 'May I introduce myself? Ambrose Twistleton-Bright, a very old friend of Cressida's family. I was asked by dear Cressy to wait for you.'

Thank goodness I hadn't done anything really gauche like try to tip him! His guidance wasn't really necessary as we could hear the buzz of conversation coming from an open door down the hallway, but seeing the deft way his hand shot out to claim a glass of champagne from a hovering waiter by the door, empty it and pick up another before James and I had even had time to touch ours I decided Cressida must have sent him out in an attempt to make sure he stayed on his feet until dinner.

About ten people were standing around taking up a very small part of a very large gilt and cream room. Cressida excused herself from the couple to whom she was talking and glided towards us so quickly across several acres of beautifully faded Indian rug that we might have been forgiven for thinking she had been on the look out. She looked exquisitely pretty in layers of ruffled lace and broderie anglaise, her hair tumbling around her face and shoulders in a carefully styled profusion of wayward curls held back by strings of pearls woven into it somehow. 'You look gorgeous!' I exclaimed. 'Just like a portrait by Winterhalter.'

Cressida's face went completely blank. 'She does, does she not?' agreed Stefano, from behind her. I was sure that seconds ago he had been at the other end of the room talking to a middle-aged couple. 'You are a student of art, Laura?'

'Not really,' I said, shrugging. James squeezed my elbow slightly. Too late, I remembered Stefano was quite a connoisseur himself. 'What I mean is, I've never actually studied art or the history of art, but I was brought up to believe that going to a gallery was as much of a treat as going to the zoo.'

Stefano's face assumed a mask of polite boredom. 'And so you were an expert on both at six years of age?'

I grimaced and shook my head. 'I'm afraid I preferred the zoo.'

He laughed, a rich deep sound that made me feel ridiculously pleased with myself for amusing him. 'Quite right too! You are honest, I like that.' I got the impression he didn't make that sort of statement lightly. 'I do not like those who pretend to be what they are not.' Was that a warning? I wondered uneasily.

'I love your dress, Laura,' Cressida broke in. 'I wish I could wear sophisticated styles like that.' She looked down at herself with a wry grimace. 'But I'm just not big enough. I look like a child dressing up in its mother's clothes.' From anyone else there would have been six-inch barbs attached to that remark, but she looked so transparently sincere it was difficult to believe she would say anything deliberately spiteful.

'And I've spent most of my life longing to wear ruffles like yours!' I said. 'The last time I wore frills was at my christening, and even then the photos show me looking like a bad-tempered loo roll cover.'

'In that case the two of you had better form a mutual admiration society,' said James. 'I'll be its founder member. You both look fantastic. Don't you agree, Stefano?'

His dark eyes had already examined me with considerable attention. 'May I say how charming you are looking tonight?' From his expression I gathered that tight, boned black silk was a lot more to his taste than the rust-coloured tunic and tweedy trousers I'd been wearing earlier that day.

'Thank you.' I smiled and leaned closer to James. 'I don't remember *you* describing me as looking "fantastic" earlier this evening,' I murmured. It had been more along the lines of 'are you really intending to appear in public wearing *that*?' when I tripped out of the bathroom after finally managing to do up my zip. (Given our sleeping arrangements and that the dress demanded I wear virtually no underwear, I thought I'd better dress on my own. James might have sworn he wouldn't lay a finger on me but I didn't come down with the last shower of rain. Give a man a good party, a lot of champagne, lust for an ex-girlfriend . . . and any reasonably soft female body in the bed next to him is going to seem pretty attractive, especially if he's had a visual appetiser earlier on.) I thought I looked pretty good, the dress had a decidedly slimming and curve-enhancing effect, though the curves on top seemed liable to burst free from their mooring at any moment. James had taken one look and snorted with laughter in a most ungallant manner. It nearly led to my calling off our whole arrangement. His hasty excuse that I hadn't seen him goggling with admiration just before his outburst didn't cut much ice. His next effort was better; that he'd had a vision of middle-aged and elderly men being laid low in rows from palpitations caused by the excitement of seeing my cleavage. At that I began to think about forgiving him. Only began, mind you.

'No, I said something along the lines of, I wasn't going to allow you out wearing that because I wanted to keep you all to myself,' he said, straight-faced and loud enough for Cressida and Stefano to hear. Then he dropped a quick kiss on my bare shoulder. It tickled. I jumped, spilling most of my glass of champagne. With poetic justice most of it went over his white dress shirt.

'What an original way you have of delivering a cold shower,' he said with a slightly forced smile and muttered out of the side of his mouth, 'Laura, are you incapable of remembering we're supposed to be *lovers*? Try acting the part a little.'

'Not if you're going to ham it up by mauling me in public!' I hissed back while making a great show of trying to mop him down with a handkerchief.

His eyes narrowed. 'If you think that was mauling, I can always give you a demonstration of the real thing. You won't make that mistake twice.' He took the hand-kerchief out of my hand. 'If you go on doing that you'll undo all your good work, sweetheart,' he said in his normal voice. I stepped back as if I'd been scalded, and heard Cressida give a little snort of amusement.

I could actually feel my cheeks growing hot. 'Oh, dear, so clumsy of me. I do hope it hasn't gone on your lovely carpet,' I said to Stefano, hardly knowing where to look.

He made as if to pat my hand in an avuncular manner (or maybe not so avuncular) and then, perhaps recollecting my tendency to chuck drink over men who touched me, withdrew it. 'No matter, champagne doesn't stain. If a carpet is too delicate to have something spilt on it, it should be hanging on a wall. I like to keep all my possessions around me.' Was I imagining the look he gave Cressida as he spoke? 'I don't believe in keeping things in a safe.'

'Unfortunately Stefano believes that about jewellery too. He won't let me have anything the insurers insist must be kept in the bank,' she said with a slight pout. 'It's so mean of him.' Considering she was wearing peardrop diamond earrings and a lovely filigree gold and diamond pendant at the base of her neck, I wondered if she was serious.

'But, *cara*, you do not need big heavy jewels,' Stefano protested, quite reasonably in my opinion.

'Maybe not, but whenever has not needing something stopped a woman from wanting it?' asked James.

Stefano smiled briefly in acknowledgement. 'Come, James, your glass is empty. We will go and fetch you another glass of champagne.' And firmly bore him off to the other end of the room. A minute later I saw James locked in conversation with the couple Stefano abandoned.

Cressida gave a little sigh, her eyes following them, then recollected her duties as hostess and began to introduce me to some of the other guests. Fortunately for my nerves more people were arriving all the time, the women in full ball regalia, the men in pink hunting coats, sometimes stretched rather tightly over the midriff, and she was kept too busy to cast any more languishing glances. Stefano, walking around checking that everyone had champagne, was relaxed and jovial now he had ensured there was a good forty feet and fifteen people between his wife and her ex-lover. I shared his feelings entirely.

Old Ambrose buttonholed me, saying he liked talking to 'pretty young fillies'. That would have been fine if he'd kept it to talking. I didn't mind the way his eyes kept straying to my cantilevered front, but I wasn't so keen on the hand that kept wandering to check out my silk-clad behind. I stepped backwards to avoid it. A minute later there it was again, and I had to retreat once more. I find it difficult to be rude to old men who are enjoying some of their last gropes so we sort of sidled backwards until I ended up plastered against the wall. It was a relief when dinner was finally announced by a magisterial butler and we trooped into the dining room to see that Cressida's idea of a 'decent-sized' dining-room table was one that seated twenty-four. With considerable confusion everyone found their places. If you got on the wrong side of the table you had to walk about half a mile before you got back to your place again. One man, severely hampered by poor eyesight and the misspelling of his name on his place card, went around twice. Various members of the local youth, dressed in short black skirts and Doc Marten's, got in each other's way, giggling, as they served the food, but luckily for Cressida's peace of mind at her first big party all went fairly smoothly even if a crown roast of lamb only narrowly avoided being planted in a substantial taffeta lap opposite me.

The first guests for the ball started arriving as our coffee was being served in tiny little gold and red Crown Derby cups. The hunt big wigs, Stefano and Cressida went to the marquee to say hello to anyone who wanted to speak to them and there was the normal rush from the rest of us for loos and mirrors to repair make up. Since, along with the general plumbing, the bathrooms had been installed in 1900, facilities were in very short supply. I headed for my own room and bathroom, and seeing James make a face indicating that he wanted to talk to me, meanly didn't offer to let any of the other women use it.

He appeared as I was refixing my precarious chignon. 'Here, let me,' he said, watching me trying to catch up a hank of hair and push it back into place with the aid of a diamante butterfly comb. I told myself that the shiver that ran all the way down my spine as his fingers brushed the back of my neck was a purely physiological reaction. It was normal, natural, it'd be like that if anyone touched me there, I told myself. I wasn't sure I believed it, though.

'Thank you,' I said into the mirror, outlining my lips with more care than was necessary. I hoped that the slight fogging of the elderly glass hid the touch of colour in my cheeks that hadn't been there before. James moved away, to my relief, and sat down on the chaise longue set at the foot of the bed. He cleared his throat ominously. 'I thought I'd better warn you – my partner at dinner was prattling away about her friend who's staying nearby and is joining them later on. It's Aunt Jane.'

Any vaguely naughty thoughts were doused abruptly in a cold rush of horror. 'Oh, lord!' I'm very fond of Aunt Jane, but to call her garrulous is like saying Harrison Ford is quite a successful actor. And it's Aunt Jane who is Imogen's bosom buddy and confidante. Within twenty-four hours of seeing us here, probably less for I wouldn't put it past Jane to ring Imogen in the early hours of the morning with important news, it would be all around the family – my seven step, full and half-brothers and sisters, two ex-stepfathers and God knows how many real and step-aunts, uncles and cousins – that James and I were an 'item', and if we were really unlucky, and the truth about our sharing a bedroom leaked out, that we were a very close item at that. My father's always been suspicious of

James and I quailed to think what his reaction would be when he discovered that his worst forebodings had been perfectly justified. There was no way he was ever going to believe James's intentions were honourable. Perhaps I should have a migraine so I'd have to go straight to bed and miss the party but then if Aunt Jane saw James she was bound to ask who his partner was ... so that wouldn't be any good. If we *both* had migraines ... Brilliant idea, Laura. Just think of all the nudge, nudge, wink, wink. Besides James might easily see it as an invitation. 'What are we going to *do*?' I wailed.

He shrugged with maddening insouciance. 'Nothing. We'll have to brazen it out.'

'It's all right for you,' I muttered. 'Have you any idea what my life is going to be like once this gets out?'

He smiled. 'Much like mine I should imagine.'

I paced agitatedly across the floor, thinking. On my third tour I said, 'We'll have to make it quite clear to Aunt Jane that I'm only here to help you out in the role of a partner because you don't have a special girl on the go right now.'

'Too many people here already know, or think they do, that we're lovers. If we change the story now it'll send the grapevine really haywire,' he pointed out with maddening calmness, 'and all they'll probably think is that we've had a lovers' tiff.' He was horribly right. 'And if we tell Aunt Jane the truth, what's Stefano going to think when we virtually admit in public that we've been pulling the wool over his eyes?'

That clinched it. I had my doubts about how convincing we were being, but that didn't make me any keener to discover what it'd be like to be the recipients of Stefano's anger if we openly admitted we'd been trying to hoodwink him. I took a deep breath and said aloud, 'OK, we're on for tonight, but I'm not draping myself all over you in front of Aunt Jane. Understood?'

'Yes,' said James so readily that I looked at him with deep suspicion.

I fixed him with a severe glance. 'And don't you even *think* about kissing me in front of her either!'

'Shame, I was looking forward to that.'

He was so blatantly not telling the truth that I ignored that remark entirely. 'And we break up on Monday. Sadly. But definitely. With no hope of a reconciliation. Agreed?'

If he was planning anything else it wouldn't do any good. I was turning out to be completely useless at this lark, my nerves wouldn't take it. My mind was made up even if we didn't run into Aunt Jane tonight, and that was a distinct possibility, I concluded hopefully. Surely amongst four hundred people spread around three different rooms and a marquee we could manage to avoid one middle-aged lady? Given her size and taste for flowing garments in bright colours it should be easy enough to spot and avoid her.

Feeling much more cheerful I walked down the stairs, past a couple of the dinner guests still waiting in some agitation for the loo on the landing. They gave me a reproachful look as I wandered past. I pretended I hadn't noticed.

Strains of Glenn Miller wafted down the hallway from the band (from the Hunt Secretary's regimental association) playing in the as yet empty ballroom and mixed with the distant thump of bass notes as the discotheque (Master's daughter's boyfriend) tried out the amplifiers. About a hundred people hung around in the marquee near the all-important bar, looking rather beginning of partyish and not entirely sure whether they wouldn't be having a better time elsewhere. The Doc Marten brigade hadn't got the serving behind the bar quite up to speed yet. As the number of hands holding glasses began to increase so did the noise level until after an hour or so I was hearing people say, 'Splendid party, what?' and 'Best ever this year, don't yer think?' I stopped looking around nervously for Aunt Jane and began to enjoy myself somewhere around my third glass of champagne. So what if the whole family began to buzz with gossip? It was only talk, I thought as I was whirled around the dance floor by Cressida's father. I discovered I could waltz rather well, especially when partnered by someone who had been forced to attend dancing lessons as a small boy. He was adept at catching me when I stumbled. Old Ambrose proved a dab hand at the fox-trot too (as well as the bottom pat) though that was early on in the evening. The last I saw of him he was peacefully stretched out on a Chesterfield in the drawing room, several empty glasses on the floor beside him.

I was having a marvellous time. The men had impeccable manners so they all felt obliged to ask every woman in their party to dance if she wanted to, and this one most certainly did. I was twirled round the ballroom and grooved around the discotheque to my heart's content. (The attempted grappling session by one of Cressida's brothers-in-law wasn't quite such a happy experience, but that was another matter.) Once everyone had performed their duty dances James drifted to my side, giving a masterly impression of having only a polite interest in his hostess and playing the devoted boyfriend to the hilt, making it clear I was saving the last waltz for him as well as a lot of those in between. I could only admire his technique, especially the way he glared at the brother-in-law when he demanded another clinch to music. The brother-in-law promptly retired to the other side of our table and didn't speak to me for the rest of the evening.

Cressida was fluttering around the tables, eyes sparkling and cheeks flushed with pleasure as she stopped to speak to people she knew. She was in her element as the centre of attention, being congratulated on putting on such a good show after barely having moved in, arranging all the spectacularly large displays of flowers in the marquee and house, and being told how lovely she looked. She bounced up to our table, bubbling over with pleasure. 'Stefano was absolutely right to say that we should buy a house near where I grew up. It's so nice knowing all these people and catching up with old friends. There are people here I haven't seen since I stopped going to children's parties,' she declared, then lowered her voice. 'One boy had lovely golden curls, do you know, he's going quite *bald*! He's only a year older than me too. I didn't recognise him, it was *so* embarrassing!'

She pulled out a chair to sit down and then as the discotheque started up with a particularly loud rendition of 'Good Golly, Miss Molly', exclaimed, 'Oh, I love this!' Tapping her foot, she turned to Stefano. 'Darling, I know you're much too stuffy for rock and roll, but you aren't, are you, James? Don't you remember when I got you to take me to those classes in Wandsworth? Weren't they in a church hall? They were really fun.' She beamed around the table. 'Though I say so myself, we were quite the best, weren't we, James? Come on, dance with me, please.'

He glanced quickly at Stefano, then stood up with a smile. 'How could I possibly refuse? You know I'd love to.'

I wondered if Stefano had decided James was no threat after all, for he didn't even bother to glance in their direction as they wove their way through pushed back chairs and people standing in gangways gossiping, their progress considerably impeded by the way Cressida kept stopping to talk to James over her shoulder. Stefano turned to me and began to talk idly, something about his plans to plant a rhododendron hedge at the bottom of the garden.

By the end of the second record his eyes were scanning the room restlessly. Halfway through the next, he stood up abruptly. 'I'm sure you want to dance, Laura.'

It was an order, not a request. I obeyed. He expertly manoeuvred me around the crowded strobe-lit disco-theque until he had a view of his quarry. My worst forebodings that we would find them locked together in a little oasis of stillness while everyone else jived around them weren't realised, though to my over-sensitive nerves it seemed as if they might well have been standing like that only thirty seconds before our arrival. Having got himself in guard dog position Stefano seemed prepared to devote his attention to me, or about ninety percent of it anyway. He was a good dancer, light on his feet and with an excellent sense of timing though I gathered from the occasional pained expression that pop music wasn't really to his taste. Then the music changed again, to something really slow. Cressida stepped towards James, arms held aloft. He glanced over her head, saw me, then Stefano, and his eyes widened in horror. I smothered a giggle. It wasn't normal for James to be so appalled by the idea of a pretty woman wrapping her arms around him. He bent his head and said something to her. Probably 'Shall we go and get another drink?' She made a moue of discontent, but despite her reluctance he put his hand in the small of her back and steered her firmly towards the exit.

It didn't surprise me that Stefano immediately lost interest in dancing. He cut purposefully across the floor and met them by the door. I made rather a poor fourth in the race. James turned to me. 'I didn't see you in there,' he said with a distinctly syrupy smile. 'What a pity. This is our song, isn't it?'

It was the Pointer Sisters with 'Slow Hand'. I could have killed him. 'It might be mine. I think "My *Little* Ding-A-Ling" is more appropriate for you,' I told him in a low voice.

He didn't bat an eyelid. 'What an unkind – and untrue – thing to say!' And just to show Cressida and Stefano that there were no hard feelings between us, he put his arm around my waist and dragged me towards him until I was glued so close to his side I felt as if I'd been transmogrified into a Siamese twin. He pressed a brief kiss to my forehead before smiling sheepishly at our audience.

I nestled my head against his shoulder and hissed, 'Loosen up! I can't breathe.'

'You shouldn't have eaten so much at dinner,' he retorted, but did relax the iron grip just a little. I took a deep gulp of air in relief.

With his arm still around my waist, James headed back towards our table. It was like doing the three-legged race. I'd been concentrating so hard on playing my role properly that I only dimly registered the well-upholstered woman who was looking our way. Then I realised there weren't many women of her age who would dare to dye their hair that particularly unlikely shade of bronze. I nudged James as hard as I could – difficult when your arm is pinioned against you.

He looked. 'Oh, hell!'

Aunt Jane advanced on us, beaming. 'James, how *lovely* to see you. I didn't know you were coming. I would have thought it would have been too difficult for you, dear boy, but you must have stopped carrying a torch for her at last. I'm so *pleased*.' I felt the dear boy go rigid as Aunt Jane's clarion tones reached most people within a ten-yard radius. I hoped Cressida and Stefano weren't following us too closely.

'And won't you introduce me to your—' Aunt Jane went on happily. I gave up trying to hide my face against James's shoulder and raised my head. 'Laura!' Her beady eyes went quickly from him to me and back again. She smiled roguishly. 'And how long has *this* been going on, you sneaky things? You've been keeping it *very* quiet, haven't you? I had no idea, James, I thought—'

Sure that she was about to proclaim to the whole room her regret that James and I had never previously looked at one another, I butted in with, 'We're staying here, aren't we lucky? Let me introduce you to our host and hostess. Aunt Jane, may I present Count Stefano Buonotti and his wife Contessa Cressida.' Aunt Jane's face was a picture. 'Stefano and Cressida – this is Mrs Cartwright. Oh, dear.' I looked at Stefano. 'I'm sure I got that wrong, didn't I?'

He smiled, 'A little, but does it matter? At least we all know who we are.' He picked up Aunt Jane's hand and kissed it, to her fluttering delight. 'I am delighted to meet you, Signora. Any relation of the enchanting Laura is doubly welcome in my house.'

Aunt Jane fluttered again. An impressive sight on someone of her bulk. 'But I'm not *Laura's* aunt, I'm *James's*,' she said in a doubtful tone as if she expected the welcome would instantly be withdrawn.

'James's?' echoed Stefano, looking puzzled, as well he might.

'But Laura's stepmother is my oldest friend,' added Aunt Jane helpfully.

Stefano looked even more confused. His gaze went from James to me. 'So you are childhood friends?' he asked suspiciously.

'Certainly not!' I said promptly, earning myself a dig in the ribs from my supposed beloved. 'I didn't even meet James until I was nearly fifteen.'

'But you were nutty on him even then, weren't you?' asked Aunt Jane in a soapy voice.

I longed for a nice deep hole to open up and swallow me. James leaned against me and whispered in my ear, 'Were you really?' with obvious relish.

'They're stepbrother and sister,' said Aunt Jane.

Stefano was looking like a man who feels he's been well

and truly taken for a sucker. 'But why have you not told us this interesting information before?'

James shrugged. 'Because people either react as if we're committing incest or instantly presume it's not possible and there must be something fishy going on.' He stared hard at Stefano for a loaded moment then down at me with an adoring expression that should have failed to convince anyone who knew him well. 'Besides Laura isn't my stepsister any longer. Hasn't been for several years,' he said with emphasis. And smiled at Stefano man to man. 'And if I tell you that Aunt Jane is still friends with Laura's mother, that my father sits on a committee with Laura's second stepfather, and that Imogen, Laura's current stepmother and Aunt Jane's best friend, looks on it as her duty in life to keep the whole of Laura's real and step families – and mine – up to date on all the family news, you'll understand why we weren't too keen to shout our business from the rooftops.'

I watched Stefano trying to digest all of this. At last he said, 'I think perhaps a drink would be a good idea.' I, for one, thought it an excellent one. He turned to Aunt Jane and proffered his arm. 'Signora, would you care to join us for a glass of champagne?'

Aunt Jane fluttered again and accepted. I was on tenterhooks lest, due to the way Stefano kept refilling her glass, she said something really indiscreet, such as, 'Is that *really* the girl who jilted you, James?' or 'What about that pretty blonde you were all over three weeks ago?' or 'But aren't you walking out with that writer, Laura?' Mercifully she couldn't think of anything but the delightful surprise that was James and I. At long last she remembered she had come with a party of her own friends and that she'd better go and find them. As we watched her substantial bulk casting off, tottering slightly to the alarm of those who feared she was about to land on their laps, Cressida said curiously, 'How many are there in your family, Laura?'

'Including steps and ex-steps? I lost count ages ago, but my sister and I worked out once that we have some sort of current or former relative in every county of England,' I said. 'The Christmas card list is murder.'

She sipped her champagne. 'And I thought Stefano's mother and sisters were bad enough! They all live near the *castello*. They like to drop in,' she added expressionlessly.

'At least you left them behind in Italy.'

'They telephone. And threaten to visit.' She spoke with a surprising amount of bitterness. 'Stefano insists that he's head of the family and it's my duty to welcome them whenever they want to come, and I would if they were halfway decent to me. But because I'm twenty years younger and a foreigner, they assume I know nothing about running the household. Or making Stefano comfortable. So they tell me how to do it. But even so, according to them, I'm not very good. I don't make my own pasta, you see.'

James leaned across me and asked, 'But do they make their own steak and kidney pie?'

The air of resentment vanished in an infectious giggle. 'No, nor apple crumble either! And Stefano loves that.' She put out her hand and covered James's for a moment. 'You've always been able to stop me getting worked up about things.' She glanced at me with a rueful expression. 'I try not to lose my temper but it's difficult sometimes!'

In my opinion her hand lingered a fraction too long before she took it away again and swiped a stray tendril of hair away from her face. I purposely didn't look at Stefano to see what he thought about it.

Slowly the ball was beginning to wind down. We all queued for our enormous breakfasts of bacon, eggs, sausages and tomato. James ate most of mine since a corset-like dress does wonders for taking the appetite (or the capacity to eat) away. Perhaps I should take to wearing one a little more often. By three o'clock the Doc Marten brigade were telling the last punters they were very sorry but all the drink had run out, though I knew for certain that one of them, a spotty youth with a cowlick, had been steadily stashing bottles behind the flap of the tent for a second party later on. I was just about danced out, flexing my toes in shoes that were no longer so comfortable as earlier in the evening, and I could feel my hair coming down at the back. James was slumped in his chair, bow tie dangling out of his pocket; Stefano looked much the same except that his tie was still in an immaculate bow. The lecherous brother-in-law was staring blankly into space, nearly comatose. One of Cressida's sisters had already given up and weaved her way to bed. Only Cressida still seemed to be alive with energy, darting about restlessly, telling people they couldn't go yet, it was still *early*, and demanding that someone come and dance with her. Stefano looked up indifferently while she pulled on one of James's hands. Maybe exposure to Aunt Jane had convinced him that James and I wouldn't dare fabricate gossip fodder or more likely he knew perfectly well that James was far too tired to get up to anything. James smiled lazily. 'You know I'd do almost anything for you, Cressy, but I couldn't dance another step.'

Her face creased in disappointment while I thought regretfully that I wouldn't have minded having one last dance with him myself. We fit well together, his shoulder is just the right height for my cheek, that's all.

Before she could plead a second time he smothered a yawn and said, 'I'm bushed. I think I'll go to bed. Coming, Laura?'

Oh, God! A minute ago I'd been wistfully thinking of resting my head on his shoulder on the dance floor, and now within minutes we were going to be in bed together. I wouldn't call myself a complete innocent, there'd be something wrong if I was at my age, but I didn't know the etiquette for this sort of situation. I mean, who gets the bathroom first? What happens if you roll over into the middle of the bed during the night and accidentally touch? Would he get ideas? Without the rose-tinted effect of sated lust would he survive the shock of seeing my face first thing in the morning? Swallowing a sudden attack of sheer funk I got up and said goodnight to the others. 'I think that went off quite well, don't you?' said James as we began to go up the stairs. 'Er, yes,' I replied inanely, looking at him sideways in an effort to gauge exactly what was on his mind. Only the slight glitter in his eyes and his grasp of the banister gave any clue at all that he'd been drinking, but that didn't mean his inhibitions were all firmly in place. 'Has Cressida really got a temper?' I asked by way of diversion. 'She looks far too sweet-natured.'

'Not always. She's been known to throw the odd plate or two.'

'Are you speaking from experience?'

He chuckled. 'I still have a scar. She doesn't do it often so I shouldn't think it'll be necessary to appear at breakfast wearing your tin helmet!'

That of course immediately set me back to thinking about what was going to happen in the hours *before* breakfast.

Needless to say I hadn't got around to unpacking properly before dinner so James, claiming that ladies always had first shot at the bathroom, lounged on the bed and watched while I rootled around in my case for my make up remover and night-dress – fortunately my most decorous, a voluminous floor-length affair of completely opaque navy sprigged cotton. I shot into the bathroom and locked the door. Two minutes later, red in the face with frustration and fury, I had to open it again.

James was in the middle of taking off his shirt. Luckily he'd started disrobing from the top. 'Can you help me? The zip's got caught on something and I daren't force it in case it tears.'

He flung the shirt in an untidy heap on the floor, giving me an admirable view of his torso, nicely honey-coloured and no flab, before I hastily turned around and presented my back with the half-undone zip. It seemed to take ages as he gently worked at the zip, teasing out the tiny scrap of fabric that had got caught. I stared rigidly ahead, clinging on to the front of the dress which was liable to fall down completely once the zip was undone and trying to ignore the way his fingers brushed against my bare skin as he worked. At long last he said, 'There you are. Done,' and the zip slid free. His voice sounded a bit unsteady.

I breathlessly said thank you and shot back into the bathroom again. I took as long as feasibly possible over the cleaning, toning, nourishing routine. I wasn't going to risk catching James undressing again. He was respectably covered up in a silk dressing gown when I came out, though as I'd suspected there was no sign of any pyjamas. I got into bed quickly and lay down facing the wall, my heart beating uncomfortably.

A couple of minutes later the covers were lifted back and a figure, smelling strongly of toothpaste, got in and turned off the light. 'Goodnight, Laura, sleep well.' He turned over. Within minutes his steady breathing proclaimed that he was asleep.

It was hours before I forgave him for not breaking his word. He might at least have *tried*.

CHAPTER 7

Stefano was positively effusive in his friendliness towards us when we appeared in the drawing room the next morning. It didn't take long for the sneaking suspicion to occur that this metaphorical falling on necks had a lot more to do with the other occupants of the room than with our personal charms. Cressida's elder sister and her husband talked nothing but horse, and the husband's sister talked endlessly about the self-improvement course she had just been on. 'All I can say is it didn't work,' muttered James sourly after several minutes.

'At least she's up,' I pointed out. He looked as if he thought this a doubtful blessing. Most of the house guests were still in bed. Cressida's other sister was reported to be suffering from tired eyes – the type of ailment which involves wearing dark glasses at breakfast – and the rest were suffering from migraines. The two men standing with me idly watching the caterers scurrying backwards and forwards with piles of plates and boxes of glasses were comparatively speaking pictures of health. Admittedly Stefano's eyes weren't quite as sparkling white against the darkness of his skin as they had been yesterday and James was displaying a slight tendency to wince at any loud noises, but that could have had as much to do with the subject matter as the actual volume of Arabella Featherington-Meade's voice.

'You have to decide how you yourself are going to interpret the events that happen in your own life. It is up to you to decide whether they are good or bad things,' she pontificated.

'Even if you're burgled?' ventured Cressida, with a tiny frown. She'd already been pityingly corrected several times for having no inner understanding.

'Of course. You can either mourn your lost possessions or look on the sudden freedom from being tied down to material goods as an enriching opportunity for spiritual development.'

'A welcome opportunity to claim on the insurance, more like,' muttered James. 'If I have to listen to any more of this twaddle I'll gain enough inner certainty to stuff one of those cushions in her mouth!' Stefano looked at him in a moment of complete empathy. 'I think I'll go for a walk outside,' James said in the voice of a man at the end of his tether, looking without enthusiasm out of one of the floor-length windows. The sky was suspiciously dark and the long grass on the bank halfway down the garden was being flattened by the wind.

'I have a better idea than walking in the wet,' said Stefano with a faint air of distaste, glancing at his highly polished loafers. 'Maybe you would like to look around the house? Nothing we bought with it is very good, of course.' He sniffed slightly. 'The best was sold years ago. From what was left behind I do not believe there was ever anything of much taste or quality, but some of the internal features are good.'

I hoped that James realised this was less likely to be an olive branch than an expression of complete boredom. He still accepted with alacrity. 'And Laura, would you like to come too or do you still prefer zoos?' Stefano asked with a faint smile.

'I'd love to.' I would have been interested anyway, but to get away from the details of the self-help course I'd have jumped at a chance to visit the local sewage farm.

We meanly left Cressida trapped listening to the ten easy steps towards spiritual cleansing and sneaked out like schoolboys ducking morning prayers. In the dining room the two men examined in exhaustive detail a reputed Adam fireplace and got very much in the way of the staff who were trying to prepare the room for lunch. The question of its provenance was finally left in amicable doubt when to the staff's relief Stefano took us to look at a pair of dubious Gainsboroughs in the morning room.

It was the first time I'd seen James in anything approaching work-mode and I have to admit I was surprised by how authoritative he was once he dropped the laid-back persona he usually wears like a cape. Stefano's slightly amused and patronising air faded and vanished as James, face alive with the energy of the true enthusiast, explained kindly but firmly why it was highly unlikely the master had ever laid brush to canvas in either of these portraits (primarily because he would have been about six when they were painted, and he wasn't *that* precocious), then moved on to the possibility of tracing furniture made by Simon Harker, a master cabinet maker who had worked locally and might even have been commissioned to make things for the house. The discussion became increasingly technical and though I have a reasonably good eye, nurtured by holiday jobs in the shop spent polishing and dusting, I am in no way an expert so I wandered on ahead taking a butterfly look at everything and daydreaming idly of what it would be like to live somewhere of this size. Horatio would love the space and the opportunity to go out and massacre the local rodents but he might pine if he was taken away from his supply of dustbins. So really it was a good thing I wasn't being given the choice.

We ended up in Stefano's office, one of the prettiest rooms in the house in my opinion. I suppose if you're going to spend most of the day working you ought to give yourself somewhere nice to do it in. (Management tends to believe in this for themselves but not, I fear, for their menials.) It was on a corner of the house, and had a lovely moulded ceiling in dire need of painting and floor-length shuttered windows on two sides. A huge desk with a well-weathered green leather top was positioned so that he could look out through either window to the garden. I'd have spent most of the day staring out of the window at what, even at this time of year, was a spectacular view, but I expected Stefano was made of sterner stuff than me. A computer terminal and five different telephones were arranged with scary precision on the desk while a printer, fax, copier and espresso machine stood lined up along one wall. Above them, incongruous against all this modern gadgetry, hung a small painting of the Grand Canal in Venice. I drifted over to look at it and my eyes nearly popped out of my head. I cleared my throat. 'Stefano,' I asked, afraid of making a fool of myself, 'is this a Canaletto by any chance?'

He broke off a fairly amicable discussion with James about whether the restoration of pictures should include repainting and looked up. 'Yes, but not one of my good ones.'

I had known he was rich; I hadn't appreciated quite *how* rich. 'How many have you got?' I asked timidly, afraid I was asking a very indelicate question. I gathered from James's expression that I was.

'Three.' I goggled again. 'My great-grandfather was a collector. He almost bankrupted the family by buying pictures – a lot of our estates had to be sold,' he said sombrely, then his face lightened. 'Luckily my father had a head for business so we have been able to keep hold of what Great-Grandfather left us.'

Even I could work out from James's anguished expression that I was *not* to ask what line of business Stefano's father had been in. Something extremely profitable to make so much so quickly, evidently. I found my thoughts drifting uneasily towards the rumours about Stefano's own business dealings. Surely just because you were Italian and had turned a quick buck it didn't mean you were automatically in the Mafia? I told myself sternly. I wished *my* grandfather had gone in for collecting – well, he had actually, betting slips and ladies of dubious morality, but neither passion had done anything like as much to improve the family coffers as a few old masters would have done. 'I think it's lovely,' I said, giving the little picture a wistful look, and added hopefully, 'I don't suppose you've got any Turners – good or otherwise – have you?'

Stefano laughed. 'I am afraid not. Much too modern for my great-grandfather, and he did not like the English school of painting. Said it was too solid and heavy, like your meals and your weather. I am afraid to say his visit to England was not a success.'

I wandered along, looking at a couple of pretty little drawings. 'Do you collect pictures yourself?'

'Not at today's prices and anyway I do not like modern art. Badly executed daubing and too many gimmicks,' Stefano said flatly. Thank heavens I hadn't said anything about enjoying the Saatchi Collection! 'But I amuse myself by collecting some little pieces here and there, nothing particularly important. I'll show you if you like?'

Inevitably we agreed. The 'little pieces' with which Stefano liked to amuse himself included several clocks – just a few of the English ones, mind you, since the French and Italian ones were in Italy. James said they were 'very nice' and 'very attractive'. I was getting used to his shorthand by now and translated this to mean that they were good but not in the top rank, except for an oak longcase clock with a beautifully painted face that he proclaimed 'super' and which even to my untutored eyes was in another league. Unbending under our obvious appreciation, Stefano brought out an enchanting set of silver doll's house furniture which he had started collecting for Cressida. There were tables, chairs, beds, a cot and a minute tea service. 'The *bambini* will enjoy playing with them when they come,' he said in an indulgent tone. I was turning the tiny spindle on a miniature spinning wheel with one finger while Stefano went to check a fax that had just come in, when the door opened and Cressida poked her head around it. 'There you are, I was wondering where you'd gone.'

'Are you much improved?' teased James with an unrepentant grin.

She came in and shut the door. 'Actually Arabella had some very interesting things to say,' she said earnestly. 'Oh, you may laugh, James, you never take anything like that seriously, but Arabella's quite right. If we took more responsibility for our own actions and found out what it was that we *really* wanted to do, we'd all be much happier.'

'And you need to go on a course and pay several hundred quid to work *that* out?' asked James. 'Money for old rope! All I can say, Cressy, is that if you're intending to go and throw your money away on one of those things, don't tell Stefano what you're doing. He strikes me as the sort of person who thinks of seminars as sheer self-indulgence for the terminally spoiled!'

'You are quite right, James,' said Stefano, the fax in his hand. 'I do not hold with all this looking at your belly button. Find out what you want and go and get it, *that* is the secret of happiness. For instance, I saw Cressida, I wanted her . . .' he reached over and picked up his wife's hand to kiss it '. . . and I got her.' He couldn't have given a more pointed reminder of who had won and who had lost in the romantic stakes if he'd got on top of his dunghill and crowed. I glanced at James; his face was completely, unnaturally, expressionless.

Stefano dropped Cressida's hand and looked at his watch. 'We've disturbed you long enough,' I said, taking the clear hint. 'Thank you, I enjoyed that.'

'Have you seen the china yet?' asked Cressida.

'It will have to be later, *cara*,' said Stefano, 'I have something that should be attended to.'

'It's all right, I'll show them,' she said blithely, and without waiting for an answer headed for a concealed door in the panelling, opening it on to a small room that could only be entered from the office, furnished with a leather sofa facing a miniature fireplace, two battered old armchairs and a table covered with newspapers and journals in English and Italian. It was a perfect masculine retreat from the outside world, an upmarket version of a garden shed. 'This is Stefano's own domain. Even the staff are only allowed in once a week under supervision to clean,' Cressida said with a conspiratorial grin. 'He's terrified one of them will flick a duster over those,' she gestured towards the figurines and china boxes arranged on shelves in two alcoves to either side of the fireplace, 'and knock about six of them off. They're nice, aren't they?'

'They are,' agreed James in heartfelt tones. Stefano had followed us in and was hovering in an agitated manner. I imagined he was worried lest we touch something and couldn't blame him. The little lady sitting at her tea table being waited on by a blackamoor page looked so fragile she might crack if we so much as breathed on her. James was standing back at a respectful distance making admiring noises as he looked at Chelsea ware bonbonnières and patch boxes, while I was eaten up with covetous desire for a tiny enamel box covered in paintings of exotic birds.

'Stefano gave me that one,' said Cressida, pointing to an inch-high Cupid nestling dangerously close to a tiger. 'He says men used to give presents like that to their lady love so it was fitting. The inscription says "Love conquers all" in Latin. Isn't that sweet? I think I'll take it up to my bedroom and have it on my dressing table.'

James looked completely horrified. 'You can't! You can't put anything like that where it might get knocked over, it's irreplaceable. And,' he added firmly as she looked as if she didn't find this a completely convincing argument, 'it's putting unfair temptation in the way of whoever cleans your bedroom. It's worth more than he or she will earn in half a lifetime.'

'I didn't realise it was so valuable,' said Cressida wonderingly. 'Oh, well, I'd better leave it here then. Could I have these in my room then or are they worth too much as well?' She looked questioningly at James while she pointed to a few of the boxes and a couple of figurines.

He shrugged. 'I should think so, but Stefano will know more than I do. It isn't really my field.'

She touched one of the figurines gently with the tip of her finger. 'Isn't it funny that while Stefano doesn't think I should have any decent jewellery because it has to be locked away, he's quite content to collect china that's too valuable to go on public display?'

James looked as if he agreed with Stefano that any spare dosh was better spent on antique china than jewels. 'Men can always justify spending money on their own pet obsessions,' I said quickly. 'Think how many of them swear blind it's absolutely *necessary* to have a Porsche as a town runabout.'

Cressida smiled faintly. 'Stefano has a Ferrari.' And added in a slightly obstinate tone, 'I still don't think it's very fair.'

'But, *cara*, I have promised you that after the first *bambino* I will take you shopping at Garrard's and you may choose whatever you like,' said Stefano indulgently. Then hastily added, 'Within reason!'

Cressida gave him a slightly strange look. 'So I'm not allowed Marie-Antoinette's diamonds?' She laughed, her good mood completely restored as she saw that for a minute Stefano had taken her seriously. Bits of her hair had come loose and were waving in tendrils around her face. With an impatient sigh she reached behind her head and reknotted the thick mass of hair into a casual bun. I observed with a certain amount of cynical interest that both men studied with keen attention the way her small breasts were pushed out as she performed this manoeuvre.

'I think you should return to the others, they will be ready for their pre-lunch drinks,' said Stefano, moving towards the door and holding it open.

Cressida nodded obediently, pulling her crossover top back into place. That manoeuvre didn't go unobserved either.

He waved the fax he still held in his hand. 'Go ahead, I have to reply to this. I'll join you in about five minutes.'

We headed for the door in a group. James suddenly stopped dead and I bumped into his back. I craned my head over his shoulder to see what he was looking at, but couldn't see much other than Stefano's cashmere-covered chest. James stepped around him, moving like a sleep-walker as if he couldn't believe his eyes. 'Look at *this*!' he breathed. 'It's one of the most perfect things I've ever seen.' I peered around his elbow to see a little statuette standing in a curved niche on the other side of the door, softly back-lit by two low-wattage lights. It was a dancing faun, about nine inches tall, seemingly ready to break into movement at any moment, one furry leg lifted in a minuet, a pipe held to his smiling lips, eyes slanted and mischievous under winged brows. 'What is it? Fifteenth century?'

'Sadly not,' said Stefano, who was standing very still, watching James intently. 'An eighteenth-century copy.'

'Really?' asked James incredulously. 'The copyist must have been incredibly skilled. I'd give my eye teeth to have something like this . . . it sends shivers down my spine.'

'You have taste. It is a special favourite of mine too. It was my father's, he found it in Milan after the war,' said Stefano, edging forwards.

James bent to look at it more closely, muttering something about was he *sure* it was a copy? Stefano rustled the paper in his hand and looked pointedly at his watch. James took no notice so I pulled on his sleeve and practically dragged him backwards out of the little room. He was still musing aloud on the statue's perfection when the three of us found ourselves on the other side of the office door.

'I'm sure I've seen a photograph of that somewhere,' he muttered.

'You probably have,' said Cressida. 'The original's quite famous. It was looted from the Orezia Palace near

Florence during the war with a whole lot of other stuff which then vanished without trace – just like the Amber Room. It's probably in a vault somewhere in Russia. Stefano told me all about it once – naturally he's curious about the story because of ours.'

'Interesting,' said James thoughtfully, and muttered almost as if to himself, 'I'd be prepared to bet the contents of the shop that's no ordinary copy,' as we went into the drawing room. It was fuller by now, though most of the occupants looked rather wan and the conversation was definitely on the muted side. Even Cressida's horsy sister had lowered her voice in deference to the prevailing headache level. There was a perceptible lightening of the atmosphere as Cressida asked who would like a drink. I almost expected a forest of raised hands. She began doling out Bloody Marys from a huge cut glass jug and James handed them round. Refills were requested before he had finished the first round.

I was talking desultorily with Arabella and her boy-friend, an ashen-faced banker who barely had the strength to string two words together and looked as if he would have loved the courage to wear dark glasses indoors, when Stefano materialised at our side. 'Oh, hello,' I said, 'I didn't see you come in.'

'You keep watch?' he demanded in a low voice. Both Arabella and her boyfriend's head jerked in surprise. So venomous was his tone that they melted away almost immediately like snowflakes on a windowpane.

'Why, no. What do you mean?' I didn't have a clue what he was talking about.

He pulled savagely at the collar of his shirt, as if despite its being open it was strangling him. 'There,' he hissed, 'behind you! You are on guard for them?'

I turned around slowly and scanned the room. Right at the end, on a sofa flanking one of the long windows, sat Cressida and James, deep in conversation. Her head was lifted to look into his face; he wasn't touching her, but his body was bowed protectively towards her as he listened with complete attention to what she had to say.

'Certainly not!' I snapped, my heart sinking.

My tone must have convinced him of something for he took a long shaky breath then said incredulously, 'You do not mind that James, *your* boyfriend, is making up to my wife in front of you?'

'They're just talking, in full view of several other people too. What harm can there be in that?' I said uneasily, for though they could easily be seen by everyone in the room they were locked in their own little bubble of privacy, oblivious to anyone or anything else. What the hell did James think he was up to? He'd behaved himself so well last night, you wouldn't have had a clue from the way he'd been acting that Cressida was anything more than an old friend, and now he was well on the way to blowing the whole thing. I couldn't think what had got into Stefano either. Earlier on he had been, if not positively benign, at least neutral in his attitude towards James. I'd begun to hope he was finally convinced that James had no intention of laying his wife. From his expression now you would have thought James was doing just that, and selling tickets to spectators. Even if something in that fax had put him on edge, it looked as if it was now up to me to get him back on an even keel.

I licked my lips. 'I expect they're just talking about your statuette. James was really interested to hear the story about the original.' As a consolatory measure it failed completely. If possible Stefano went even more rigid then said in a voice of the deepest contempt, 'Do you really believe that?'

'Well, no,' I admitted. I took a good swig of my Bloody Mary, concentrating on the welcome feeling of alcohol hitting my stomach. It gave me a badly needed illusion of courage. 'They're probably just going over old times, which is perfectly natural.' I lifted my eyes to look at him. 'Personally I'd rather they had never been involved, but neither of us can alter history. I don't think there's anything more to it. Cressida's in love with you,' a funny expression crossed Stefano's face at this, 'and though I'll admit that James *isn't* in love with me, I'm more than just any other girlfriend whom he can love and leave with impunity. He's not going to muck me around, not if he's got any sense. You've met Aunt Jane, and there are plenty more like her in the family.' Stefano looked horror-struck as he contemplated this awful prospect. To my relief his hunched shoulders were beginning to drop. I laid one hand on his arm. 'Look, Stefano, you don't seriously think I'd have come here if I didn't believe James utterly when he says that all he feels for Cressida is friendship? Believe me, I'm not into the sort of humiliation that involves seeing your boyfriend slavering over his ex in front of you.'

Stefano smiled mirthlessly. 'Aren't you? I wonder then if you have ever been really in love, Laura. If you love someone enough, you will go anywhere, watch them do anything, just for a chance to hold on to them.'

'Not me,' I said firmly, though I was uneasily aware that some of my behaviour towards Daniel wouldn't stand too close a scrutiny in that particular area. 'James and I don't have that sort of relationship.'

'I am surprised you and James have any sort of *relationship*.' Stefano pronounced the word with distaste. 'Even that wet fish there,' he flapped his hand vaguely in the direction of Arabella's boyfriend, 'has some cord of desire that binds him to a woman, though in his case it is not powerful, maybe because she is more of a man than him. With a couple like you and James, he should be wanting you with him at all times, he should be wanting to take you into corners, he should want you in his bed, he should be *thinking* about what he wants to do with you, to you, every hour, every minute of the day. That is what a man does with his woman. I do not see that in him.'

'We're British, we're very private in our emotions,' I protested feebly, rocked by the intensity of what he had been saying. I felt a tingle go down my spine at the very thought. Gosh, it would be exciting to have a lover like that, if perhaps a little tiring.

'That is not being *private*, that is being *frozen*,' Stefano informed me pityingly.

I was heartily glad that his attention was on me and not the little tableau down the other end of the room for James's body language was anything but frozen as he leaned forward to say something to Cressida. I wasn't the only person to have noticed for Cressida's sister, the one with tired eyes, touched her husband's arm and they both looked towards the window seat. The sister whispered something then advanced purposefully, ready to break up what she saw as a dangerous and indiscreet situation. Actually I was getting pretty annoyed myself. I didn't care if James and Cressida were making plans to elope or simply having an in-depth discussion of the weather, whatever it was they should do it in a way that wasn't calculated to bring out the jealous beast in her husband. A beast that it seemed to have fallen to me to tame, and receive little homilies into the bargain. I'd come here as James's girlfriend, albeit a pretend one, not as a large gooseberry, and he should be damn well playing his part with a bit more verve and conviction.

Stefano raised his eyebrows. 'Perhaps you do not have so much of that English cool after all. You look positively Latin at this moment.' He was still smiling to himself as he turned away to talk to another of his guests.

The magisterial butler appeared to announce lunch and we all filed into the dining room where the table, denuded of several of its leaves and laid for a mere ten, stood looking rather small in the middle of the huge room.

Since I was put on the opposite side of the table, I didn't get a chance to speak to James until after lunch when Cressida, proving that under her fragile loveliness there beat the heart of a true Englishwoman, declared that even if it was drizzling slightly we must all go out for a walk. Even so it wasn't for a good twenty minutes that I got him to myself. Cressida had quite reasonably balked at the mire in the fields so we were parading decorously around the gravel paths in the grounds, which heaven knows took us far enough for all but the most dedicated of walking enthusiasts. We were in a tight group, no stragglers had lagged behind or braver spirits gone on ahead, though Stefano hadn't even made it as far as the starting gate. He declared firmly that walking in the damp and cold was a peculiar English aberration he didn't intend to share and that he would get far more pleasure from observing our peregrinations from his office windows. Maybe it was this not so subtle hint that he was watching that made Cressida's sisters and brothers-in-law determinedly hang on in there, despite at least two debilitating hangovers. I could have told them that their sacrifice was for nothing since I myself was going to make sure that James didn't have a chance to have another tête-à-tête with his hostess. I stuck to his side like glue, even when he started discussing the finances of arable farming with Portia, the eldest sister. At last she must have decided she could safely leave him with me, even though I was half comatose with boredom by now, and walked on ahead, saying that she needed to talk to Viola and Cressida about their brother's birthday present. I smothered a yawn and said, 'All she's got to do is choose something from one of those catalogues that come in plain brown wrappers.'

James smiled. 'Oh, it's not for Orlando. It's for Viola's twin, Sebastian.'

'You're kidding!' I exclaimed. 'Are there any more? Tybalt perhaps?'

He shook his head. 'Cressy's mother trod the boards until she decided that a wealthy husband with five hundred acres was preferable to being a walk on at the RSC. But she's never forgotten her calling; the girls are all named after roles she understudied.'

'And the boys?'

'Reputedly boyfriends.'

'Lucky she never went out with someone playing Pyramus or Malvolio!' I said with a giggle, then exclaimed in a tone of artificial surprise, 'Oh, look! Aren't those pretty?' I stopped to peer at a rustic bank where two semi-circular seats were artfully placed so that visitors could enjoy the view at leisure – on a day when the clouds were slightly higher above the horizon.

James obediently stopped and looked without discernible astonishment at snowdrops in February. There were quite a lot of them. 'So what's all this about then?' he asked, raising his brows. 'What's with the sudden interest in horticulture?'

I made a face and looked on ahead. The party had separated out, Cressida and Arabella in front, no doubt discussing personal fulfilment, the boyfriend close behind, every dragging step proclaiming that lunch, something to drink and a walk hadn't made much of an improvement in his condition, Viola, Portia and husbands forming a protective cordon behind. It was too cold to stay still, so digging my hands in my pockets, I walked on as slowly as I could, giving the others a chance to vanish into the shrubbery. Then I told James what the matter was. I tried to be reasonable and measured about it, but simmering resentment over his lack of discretion and how he'd left me open to that disturbing speech from Stefano suddenly boiled over. I may not have red hair like my sister but I've got the temper that goes with it, in spades. James's isn't too even either.

'For God's sake, Laura, be reasonable!' he said after a couple of minutes during which we'd exchanged free and frank opinions on each other's character. 'All I was doing was talking to her in a room full of people! What harm was there in that?' From the slightly shifty look in his eyes he knew very well. 'She wanted to talk to me, she's not very happy at the moment.'

'And she was testing the water to see if she could go back to where she was two years ago?'

'Of course not!' he said stiffly.

I made an unconvinced noise.

He wheeled around and grabbed my shoulders as if he was about to shake me. 'She's got a few problems and needs a sympathetic ear.'

'So she chose the man she dumped to act as marriage counsellor? And in front of her husband too? You've got to be out of your mind, James! You were supposed to be convincing Stefano you were far too content in your personal life even to give Cressida a second glance, not imply you'd run off with her given half a chance! I might as well be your real sister for all the attention you've paid me.'

James drew in a deep breath and his look sharpened. 'Is that the problem?' he asked softly. 'You're feeling ignored?'

He was standing close before me, too close for me to glare at him comfortably. I backed up a step and met a high ornamental box hedge. He had hit the nail uncomfortably close to the head, but I'd see him in Hades before I'd admit that. I licked my lips and said, 'No, I'm just fed up of doing my best to convince Stefano we're having a rip roaring affair when you aren't bothering to pretend that you fancy me rotten – or even fancy me at *all*. It makes me look a complete dork, like one of those frustrated spinsters who have to enliven a non-existent sex life by fantasising!'

'How do you suggest I indicate to all and sundry that we have the sort of sex life that brings down the ceiling?' he asked a touch sulkily. I had a feeling I'd struck a nerve there. Maybe he'd thought everyone would automatically assume it. 'Pant enthusiastically every so often while I dive my hand down your bodice?'

'Don't be stupid!' But even looking at my bodice occasionally with some show of appreciation would be an improvement. 'Stefano says you lack passion,' I informed him, perhaps a tad unwisely.

'The Devil he does!' exclaimed James. 'And what other nuggets of wisdom did he pass on to you to get you so worked up?'

Even more unwisely, for I was still suffering from vestiges of bad temper, I told him.

James laughed.

I could have hit him.

Then he said in a tight voice that showed he didn't think Stefano's comments on his lacklustre performance nearly so funny as he pretended, 'So I should be taking you into corners? I should be fondling you, tumbling you, generally making a spectacle of myself and frightening the horses into the bargain! Well, we can certainly do that if that's what you want.'

'It isn't!' I said quickly.

James smiled, in a more friendly fashion this time. He

put his hands on my shoulders and looked down into my face. 'But, Laura, this is a golden opportunity. You said yourself we've been falling down in the acting department.' We? 'And here we are, right under the house. If Stefano lifts his head from his desk he can't fail to see us. You're so right, we need to give him an Oscar-winning display.'

My first reaction was to tell him, no way, buster, on your bike, etc, etc. Actually it was panic, putting it into words came later. My *second* reaction was that I'd wanted a tussle with James since I was fifteen and this was the first time I'd even got near it. So who cared what motivated him to pounce? I'd still have the chance to see to what degree my fifteen-year-old fantasies had been wildly overinflated. 'OK.' I lifted my head and pursed my lips. 'Earn your Oscar.'

James looked startled, then to my relief a look of enthusiasm lit his face. About three minutes later I had to come up for air. My heart rate wasn't making it any easier to breathe. I was pressed up against the hedge, only James's arm around my back preventing me from collapsing into it altogether. 'Well?' he asked a bit raggedly, brushing a bit of hedge out of my hair. 'Did the Academy give me the vote?'

I couldn't think what he was talking about. 'I don't know,' I said vaguely. I was too busy thinking that my fifteen-year-old fantasies had been quite wrong. They were far too innocent.

'You don't know?' he echoed indignantly. I tried, not very hard, to stop him from helping me make up my mind. It was just as good the second time round. This man was a seriously good kisser, I thought, as at long last it had to end. I had my arms wrapped around his neck, and was pressed as close to him as was possible without actually melding into him. It left me in no doubt either that, right now at any rate, he was harbouring some very unbrotherly feelings towards me.

'You get the vote,' I said, smiling up at him.

'Thank you. I rather thought I should have got it first time round,' he said complacently, linking his hands around the small of my back and pulling my hips towards him. I stood enjoying the feeling for a moment then pulled away. James held on for a second then let me go and stood looking down with a pleasingly disappointed air.

'Well, we certainly gave Stefano something to think about there,' I said cheerily, swiping a leaf off my coat, 'though perhaps any more would be rubbing his nose in it somewhat.' Actually any more would be downright pornographic. As they say in soppy romantic novels, there were bits of me quivering that I had never known could quiver, that I'd never realised could feel anything at all, especially as the result of a mere kiss. But I knew James too well to want – no, amend 'want' to 'be prepared for' – more. His expertise at pressing the right buttons came from long practice, and I had no wish to join the line of willing victims. Also, though embarrassingly I seemed to have forgotten about it until now, I had a boyfriend of my own, a current one who was a fairly dab hand at pressing buttons too – when he got around to thinking about it. At the risk of sounding sanctimonious I don't muck around with more than one man at a time – not that I've often been given the chance.

To my chagrin James didn't try to make me change my mind. He said, 'Well, if you're sure,' in a tone that suggested I was going to be the loser. Is it surprising I've frequently harboured fantasies of violence towards him?

CHAPTER 8

Needless to say James managed to wheedle me into agreeing I wouldn't announce straight away to the whole world that I had metaphorically cast his dust off my shoes. As he said, quite reasonably, Stefano hadn't absolutely refused to do business with him, though he had to admit the chances weren't high, and if I cared at all about my poor old mother continuing to receive her maintenance it would be a good idea if we didn't let Stefano know that our affair had fizzled out suspiciously quickly. The last was the most convincing argument. Not that I don't care for my poor old mother (who would personally disembowel anyone who used those adjectives about her), but I'd already learned quite enough about Stefano to be wary of doing anything that might get me on his bad side. And so I agreed that we should maintain our fiction of being 'good friends' for a bit longer. Actually I rather enjoyed the refreshing change of spending the odd evening in the company of someone who concentrated on me rather than his art. It had absolutely nothing to do with the possibility that sometime it might be necessary to put on another display of unbridled lust. When it's acting and in a good cause it doesn't count as being unfaithful.

I can't say that as we left Stefano was particularly assiduous in echoing Cressida's entreaties for us to come and stay again, but he certainly didn't look disapproving when she asked for my telephone numbers at work and at home. She thought she would be coming up to London soon and said we must meet for lunch.

I didn't expect to hear from her. I reckoned Cressida was the sort of person who extends an impartial friendliness to nearly everyone but unless she's reminded by someone won't do anything to fulfil half-meant promises. In any case I was too busy trying to field the curiosity of my family over exactly what I'd been doing 'wrapped around James' as Aunt Jane had so succinctly described it. I tried putting out the 'good friends' line, but that didn't wash very well. 'Come on, love, you know quite well you've never been good friends with James,' pointed out his brother Harry, who thought there was more chance of getting all the hot goss out of me rather than his close-mouthed sibling. (For once he was wrong.) 'Pull the other one!' advised my sister Katie. 'You've been waiting to get your hands on that man for years! Good on you!'

It was embarrassing how many people seemed to know of the teenage crush I thought I'd hidden so well, and positively mortifying that no one, but no one, thought fit to say that James had been nurturing a secret passion for me over the years. I favoured Katie with the whole story (well, I left out the clinch), much to her amusement; she found our sharing a room highly funny, much more than I had. 'You must have thought all your Sundays had come at once!'

'No, I didn't,' I said primly. 'I'm going out with Daniel, remember?'

'So you are,' she said in a disparaging tone. She'd said once that Daniel's book was 'trite, full of clever tricks designed to impress'. I suppose she's entitled to give an opinion; she's the only person I know who's actually read the whole of *Ulysses*. Has done twice in fact. 'No reason why that should stop you road testing another model, though,' she offered thoughtfully.

Luckily the heat was taken off me after a week by the far more interesting news that one of my cousins was pregnant by a Spanish waiter she'd met in Ibiza last summer who'd come over to visit her. There was much hand wringing and pleasurable disapproval until it was discovered that the future father had actually been waiting in his own father's hotel so he could learn the trade from the ground up and that he was quite prepared to Do The Right Thing by Amelia. Arrangements for an immediate white wedding were hastily put into place and the topics of conversation moved to 'Can we have asparagus rolls and smoked salmon wheels or must we be fashionable and have coriander filo parcels?' and 'Do you think it'll *show* on the day?'

I accepted an invitation to Amelia's baby shower, buying her an extremely glamorous nightie to wear in hospital as a means of expressing my gratitude for her news worthiness.

Then I settled down to putting the final dots and crosses on the arrangements for the sales conference in France. I was planning to leave a couple of days early and go via Paris to visit my mother who was being kept in

happy immorality by two different men. They both con-
tributed towards the costs of her apartment in the 7th
arrondissement; one, a banker, visited her during the week
and the other, a commissioner for the EC in Brussels, sped
over at the weekends. They both knew about their rival,
but somehow she had managed to convince each that her
relationship with the other was entirely platonic. All the
juggling was a bit time-consuming, she said, but worth it
since her boredom threshold with men is very low.

I was looking forward to seeing her, if I ever got away.
Darian had only given me permission to take days off if I
got my work right up to date, which would have been fair
enough if I hadn't spent most of the last week assisting on
a huge pitch the agency was doing for a new line of
organic soft drinks. Not that I minded, I love doing
pitches. Most of the agency gets involved in brain storming sessions, tossing ideas around over lunches of Marks
and Spencer's sandwiches. Even the most humble member
of staff like yours truly gets to contribute. The whole
place buzzes as we rush around frantically doing story
boards, making up reports, finding exactly the right colour for the cover of the binders, getting mock ups made,
checking the proposal for glitches. Rumour has it that the
agency once pitched for a firm that made paints in
heritage colours and that after days of work the twentieth
and final version of the presentation document rolled off
the computer long past midnight on the morning before
the big meeting. It wasn't until everyone was in the
boardroom and David had already started his introduc-
tory spiel that someone noticed that the title page read
'Proposal for Torrington Bros, makers of fine old *pants*'.

Now the adrenaline surge was over. David and two executives were upstairs in the boardroom presenting our efforts to the drinks company's hardened marketing people while the rest of us were rubbing our eyes and swapping stories about how late we'd got home last night. Morning gossip finished, I was wondering idly if a colouring competition sponsored by makers of children's toothpaste would be the ticket – it might get some coverage in those parts of the provincial press really desperate for something to fill their pages – and deciding if it was still too early to ring Liv who had made me swear that I'd call her for a really extensive chat once the immediate heat was off. I'd hardly said a word to her for two weeks, I thought, yawning slightly. Then the door crashed open, slamming against the wall and making the coffee machine rattle. Stefano stood framed in the doorway, dressed in a dark suit with a camelhair overcoat on top, gloved hands flexing and unflexing. His eyes were sunk deep in a set white face, jaw rigid under the shadow of a beard already coming through. Only an idiot would have failed to realise he was pretty upset about something and in a blinding rage too. And it didn't take two guesses to work out who he was looking for either. Unfortunately my desk is plumb in front of the door so I couldn't dive for cover under it. I didn't even have time to duck my head behind my computer screen before he pointed a shaking finger at me and snarled, 'You! Yes, you, Laura! You will tell me – do not think you can refuse. Where is my wife?'

'Cressida?' I said stupidly. 'I don't know. Did you think she was meeting me for lunch?'

He strode across to my desk. 'No, I did not! But she has gone – and I know where!' I gaped at him open-mouthed. He hit the desk with one gloved fist, making my jar of chewed Biros jump and the figures on the screen wobble. 'She has gone running into the arms of that so-called lover of yours. Lover?' he shouted. 'Ha!' And hit the desk again.

The others in the office were listening with shocked expressions – and keen interest. Unfortunately none of them had the nous to *do* anything except sit and stare while Stefano leaned over me threateningly and I cowered. 'I'm sure that's not true,' I said, trying desperately to aim for a soothing tone to calm him down. It didn't work. Even I could hear the tremor in my voice. He bent his head so he could eyeball me even more menacingly. I cowered so far I almost went through the back of the chair.

'I know all about you and your little tricks!' he spat out contemptuously.

'What tricks?' I asked, bewildered.

'Your lie that you are lovers with *him*!' I thought it would be wiser not to point out that I had never actually said that. 'You have your own lover – a pasty-faced writer with a tail like a horse!'

My heart hit my boots. How the hell had he found out?

It was damage limitation time. I licked my lips nervously. 'Whoever told you that is wrong,' I said as coolly as I could. 'He might have *been* my lover, he isn't any longer.'

'You lie!' said Stefano flatly. 'You have been with him since sleeping in our house with *him*.'

I realised gloomily from the riveted expressions of all those listening that they'd had no trouble at all in interpreting that slightly elliptical statement. 'Um, well, Daniel's my smokescreen to cover up what's been going on with James,' I said, reckoning it was worth condemning my reputation to perdition if it would calm Stefano down.

Unfortunately my noble gesture was completely wasted. 'Ha!' he shouted again, thunderous expression darkening further. 'What you mean is that *you* were his smokescreen while he was planning how to take my wife from me! Did you plan it with him?' he asked, flexing his hands in a meaningful way.

Too petrified to speak, I shook my head.

To my intense relief he straightened up and stepped back a pace, though he was still a lot too close for comfort. 'I wish I could believe you,' he said in a voice of deep contempt. 'But how can I trust a word you say?' For a hopeful moment I thought he'd decided that due to my general untrustworthiness I wasn't worth cross questioning any further and was about to storm out in much the same fashion he'd come in. Unfortunately he took a deep breath and shouted, '*Where is she?* Answer me! I must know! I have been to his house and to his shop, and the staff say he is not there. Maybe he is in hiding somewhere. That is a good thing for him. When I find him I will make him wish he had never been born, that he never dared to call himself a man, *il . . .*' Here he described James in a few choice Italian phrases which I had no trouble at all in understanding though I'd never heard them before.

'What is the meaning of all this racket?' Darian

demanded in her usual crushing-the-underlings tones, standing in her office doorway with her hands on her hips. I would never have believed until that minute that I could be pleased to see her, but I was. I was delighted. I could almost have fallen on her neck and kissed her. She looked down her nose at Stefano. 'And just who are you?' she asked frigidly.

He turned around and stared at her with a faint air of disbelief. I don't expect he's used to women speaking to him in that tone of voice, especially ones like Darian. She's too bony and angular to be conventionally pretty, but a certain natural style and eyes that can skewer you at a hundred paces easily make up for that. He drew himself up and said, 'I am Count Stefano Buonotti, Signora.'

If he'd been hoping that Darian would be impressed by his title he was doomed to disappointment. She's resolutely unmoved by titles, a dedicated republican through and through. 'What do you think you're doing disturbing my staff while they are supposed to be working, Signor Buonotti?'

Even in my somewhat befuddled state I was interested to see that her snotty tone got Stefano as much on the raw as it does all of us. He cast her a murderous look and said in a clipped voice, 'I need to speak to Laura.'

'So I heard, as did the rest of the building,' Darian said acidly. 'But, Signore, firstly my staff are not allowed to receive visitors on personal business in working hours and secondly we have a very important meeting going on upstairs. If you persist in creating a scene I shall be forced to call the police.'

Emma met my eyes from across the room and we both

raised our eyebrows in reluctant admiration. We'd heard Darian on her high horse before but never like this.

Stefano's whole stance shouted, 'Just try it!' Now that the threat of imminent strangulation had been removed my wits were slowly coming back. Stefano didn't look in the least likely to leave peacefully if I didn't tell him what he wanted to know and it was going to take quite a bit of persuasion to convince him that I really didn't have a clue where Cressida was. Surely James wouldn't have been crazy enough to elope with her, would he? Yes, he might easily have been, I decided, but couldn't believe that he would have done it without warning me. Rushing off to do things without any thought for the consequences for others wasn't one of James's faults; he would have known that Stefano would eventually come after me. Better that he should talk to me rather than James. I was fairly, not absolutely, confident Stefano wouldn't physically hurt a woman, no matter what threats he made. I was equally confident that right now, given the chance, he wouldn't have any hesitation in taking a swing at James. So, feeling rather like Wonderwoman, the upholder of justice and the sorter outer of all problems, I bravely put my head above the parapet and said, 'I'll tell you whatever I can, Stefano, which isn't much. But we can't do it here. The place is crawling with prospective clients. Shall we go to the coffee bar around the corner and talk there? If that's all right with you, Darian?' I added.

'I don't know,' she said, obviously torn between a desire to see the back of this still enraged male and a deep reluctance to allow me to indulge in what she would see as a form of skiving off.

Stefano gave a formal little bow. 'Madam, I can assure you that you need have no fear for Laura's safety,' he said coldly, entirely misreading the reason behind her hesitation.

'Well . . .' She glanced doubtfully towards me. 'Are you quite sure, Laura?'

'I am,' I said, lying through my teeth. I wasn't at all. Wonderwoman had just caught sight of a whole load of kryptonite and was in a complete funk. I reminded myself that Costas, the owner of the coffee bar, was bigger than Stefano which was why I'd decided to go there in the first place, and Stefano was hardly likely to do anything to me in the fifty yards between there and the office. As a backbone stiffener it was moderately successful; my legs weren't actively shaking with nerves as I got up.

I chose a table that was far enough away from Costas as he made the lunchtime baps for us to talk in privacy but still within his eyeline and close enough for him to nip around the counter and collar Stefano if necessary. From the slight curl to his lip as he brought a cappuccino and an espresso to the table, Stefano knew exactly why I'd chosen it too.

I scooped a bit of the froth off my coffee, the bit with the chocolate granules on it, and sucked it off the spoon. 'Tell me what's happened, as if you believed I knew nothing about it,' I said after we'd sat in silence for a bit.

Stefano gave me a long measuring look indicating he no longer believed anything I said, but at least his rage seemed to have evaporated during the short walk here. Now he looked deeply miserable and lost. His hand tightened around his cup convulsively as he began to speak, in slow broken sentences with none of the aggression he had shown in the office. There didn't appear to be much to tell, or at least not the way he told it. Cressida had been in a very strange mood ever since the ball, and he had no doubt about the reason why, particularly as she had on more than one occasion compared him unfavourably to James. I closed my eyes briefly, praying heartily that she hadn't been mad enough to make certain specific comparisons. They'd had a row last week, he declined to say about what, except that surprisingly enough it wasn't over James, but it had all been sorted out and Cressida had come around to his point of view. (Really? Sounded like wishful thinking to me.) He'd had to go to Milan on business for a few days, leaving what he thought was a loving, faithful wife, and when he'd got back last night he'd found she'd flown the coop several days before. She had left the proverbial note on the mantelpiece (not strong on originality, Cressida) but what parts of her scrawl he could read didn't say anything useful like where she was going or why, just that she would be in contact later. According to the staff she had told them she was going away for a few days with her sister which naturally enough they didn't question, and as by chance his telephone had been out of order all weekend Stefano hadn't been able to make his normal daily call to check on the well-being of his wife, so she'd had four clear days in which to cover her tracks before he finally returned.

'That doesn't give you any reason to think James is involved in this!' I protested.

'Cressida would not leave except for another man,' he said with utter certainty. He thumped the area of his heart dramatically with one fist. 'I feel it *here*. She is not one of your liberated women who imagine they have no room for a man in their life. She needs a man like a vine needs a wall.' I had to agree with him there. 'Who else would she go to except Lovatt?' he demanded with a murderous expression. 'There is no other possibility, Cressida is not on close enough terms with any other man.'

I thought it wiser not to say that if she was he'd be the last person to know.

'Also,' he said, looking at me pityingly, 'I have other proof. He has been ringing her at the house while I am away, his number is recorded in the telephone's memory. There is no reason for him to be ringing another man's wife unless he has black deeds in his heart.' Actually it was quite possible the calls were entirely innocent, but Stefano wasn't in a mood to hear that. 'This I already knew, I was sure, then last night I had a call from someone who has seen them together.' He shuddered convulsively and looked as if he was having difficulty getting his words out. 'Kissing.'

'What!' I exclaimed. 'Who? Where?'

His lip curled in distaste. 'A journalist from one of the tabloid gossip columns. She wanted my comments on my wife leaving me for *him*. When I denied it she told me that all of London knew of it, they were not bothering to hide their affair. They had been seen in La Cucina on Friday – embracing.' He shuddered. 'It is Cressida's favourite restaurant,' he added slowly, 'I have taken her there several times.'

I couldn't think for shock. All I could say was, 'You know journalists never tell the truth. They feed you a line hoping you'll say something else to give them a story.'

Stefano looked at me as if I was trying to snatch straws out of thin air, which of course I was. 'I don't believe it,' I said distractedly. 'Even if James were still head over heels in love with Cressida – which he swears he isn't – he'd never do anything so *stupidly* indiscreet as to have dinner with her in a public place, let alone be seen in a clinch. He's got far too strong a sense of self-preservation.' Stefano looked even more savage so perhaps that wasn't the best thing to say. 'Hang on, though,' I added sharply, my brain beginning to work a little at last, 'James can't have been canoodling with Cressida in a darkened restaurant on Friday night. It was his father's birthday and he was having dinner in the country,' I said authoritatively. Actually I just presumed he had been there, but I didn't think James would have let his father down at the last moment. If so I'd certainly have heard, via Aunt Jane and Imogen, how cruelly he had upset his aged parent (and by virtue of my supposed romance been accused of having a hand in it too). 'Don't you see, it *proves* that journalist was just making everything up!' I went on, encouraged.

Stefano shook his head slowly. 'All it proves is that they may have got a fact or two wrong,' he said flatly.

And that you're completely bull-headed! I thought crossly. 'Has got *everything* wrong,' I corrected firmly, and decided to try a change of tack. 'One thing about James is he's got his feet firmly on the ground. He was hoping to do business with you, Stefano. He would hardly have been planning to pinch your wife while trying to sell you a few hundred grand's worth of chairs and cupboards for your hotel, would he?'

Stefano looked at me as if I were totally stupid and then said darkly, 'He will not need to worry about his business now, will he?'

'What do you mean?' I said with foreboding.

His fingers gripped the edge of the table. 'Cressida did not only take herself. When I returned home I found the shelves of my study literally bare. She had helped herself to most of the china collection, one which your so-called lover had valued for her only a few days before!'

'Oh, no!' I said in horror.

'So, you see, your James will not have to worry about not doing business with me. My wife will be coming to him with a very valuable dowry – all collected by me! Or so he thinks. He will not enjoy it for very long.' The savagery of his voice made me feel sick with fear. His mouth stretched into a ghastly parody of a smile as he saw my expression. 'Oh, do not worry, Laura, I am not like our Sicilian cousins. He will not suffer any physical harm but I will still destroy him – completely. I am a better and more ruthless player at this kind of game, he will be no match for me. By the time I am finished with him he will have nothing – no business, no home, no reputation.' He paused reflectively. 'Maybe not his liberty either. It is very easy to make it look as if a man has committed a crime. In fact he has. My Cressida would not have dreamed of taking my china if not at his urging. And he need not imagine that my wife will stick with him through his troubles, she will not,' he added with calm certainty. 'She will come back to me.'

I couldn't speak. It seemed as if my tongue had grown too big for my mouth. I had never heard threats being made against someone else before, except the 'I'll make him sorry he ditched me' sort. I couldn't think what to say. It didn't seem there was much point in saying anything, Stefano had made up his mind with a blind, unstoppable obstinacy and I couldn't see that any words of mine were going to make any difference. I half lifted my coffee cup and saw to my surprise that somehow I'd drunk it without noticing. I swallowed hard, pushing against the lump that was blocking my throat, and shook my head to clear it.

Stefano's dark eyes were boring into me. 'You do not appear to be shocked,' he said finally when it became obvious that I was still struck dumb. His tone sharpened in suspicion. 'So you *were* planning this along with them? Your visit to us was all part of an elaborate trick!' I flinched at how uncomfortably close to the truth at least part of his accusation was. His expression changed and he half rose, saying furiously, '*Putana!* You did know!'

I shrank back in my seat. Costas dropped the towel he was using to polish water glasses and moved pointedly around the counter to our table where all six foot four of him loomed comfortingly over the pair of us. 'Anything you need, Laura?' he asked meaningfully.

Stefano subsided, looking shocked with himself, the flash of rage dissipating. 'A glass of water, please,' I whispered, and gathering all my reserves of acting ability looked at Stefano. 'If I'm calm it's because your accusations are so outrageous that they're laughable!' I said coldly. 'I don't believe it. I especially don't believe James would encourage Cressida to nick your china. He isn't dishonest.'

Stefano laughed hollowly. 'If you believe that you are either really in love with him or very foolish!'

The patronising, pat the little girl on the head edge to his voice really got me annoyed, especially as apparently he himself was a fine one to talk about dishonesty. And he was following a fine parental example too. 'Why are you so blindly determined to believe that your wife is adulterous? I think you'd rather she has a lover than that she left you for some other reason – such as being unhappy over something!' I snapped.

He stared at me in surprise and outrage, a red flush spreading over his cheekbones. I wondered if I'd inadvertently hit a sore spot and leaned closer to him over the table. 'If you go around telling people she's left you for a man when it was for something else entirely then she'll never forgive you and you'll have lost her forever.' His eyes under their hooded lids widened in attention. 'I'll go and see James to find out if he knows or not what Cressida is up to.' I held up my hand as Stefano began to speak. 'No, listen,' I said with amazing firmness. 'He'll tell *me* the truth, even if it's something he knows I don't want to hear.' Despite the fact I was sitting down my legs were still shaking like jelly. 'But you aren't to go near him.' Stefano looked as if he was about to start objecting loudly so I added quickly, 'Be sensible. If you go near James in your present mood you'll end up hitting him. I don't want to see either of you hurt – and, yes, he's very strong – and you'd end up charged with assault too.'

He shrugged. 'It would be worth it.'

God save me from macho males! 'Worth looking stupid if it turns out you've beaten him up for nothing?' I enquired. 'And I doubt you'd be allowed bail. If you so much as lay a finger on James – or do anything else to harm him – I wouldn't have any hesitation in telling the police of the threats you made against him.'

For the first time since he had burst into the office I saw Stefano relax a little. He smiled slightly. 'Dear Laura,' he said patronisingly, 'one of the advantages of being very rich is that you have access to justice which the poor don't have – the most expensive and influential counsels in the country. People like me do not go to prison.'

I had a horrid feeling he was probably right. 'Well, anyway,' I said weakly, 'it wouldn't endear you to Cressida, would it?'

He stared down at the table top for a few moments, then raised his head. 'No, you are right,' he said slowly in a voice suddenly devoid of all its underlying aggression. 'She does not like violence.'

I hadn't realised I had been holding my breath. I let it out in an enormous rush, feeling almost light-headed with relief that for the time being Stefano wouldn't be rushing around to the shop with intent to cause bodily harm. 'So I'm the one to go and see James. Agreed?' As he hesitated I added wryly, 'Don't you think I have an interest in this too? I'm just as keen as you are to discover the truth. I promise that if she is with James I won't hide it from you – though I might give them time to hide!'

He sighed, all the pent-up rage seeming to slip away, leaving him curiously deflated. For the first time he looked every day of his age, older in fact, with tight lines of despair drawing down the corners of his mouth. He really did care about her, I thought, this wasn't just bombast or infuriated pride at a trophy wife slipping out of his grasp. Maybe he had needed to whip up his anger against James to stop himself from collapsing entirely. I felt the beginnings of pity towards him and reminded myself you might feel sorry for a wounded tiger but that still didn't mean you put your head in its mouth. He groped in his coat pocket and brought out a wallet, extracting a card which he flipped across the table to me. It had his name on it and several telephone numbers including a couple with international prefixes.

'You can always find me on one of those, the last is a twenty-four-hour answering service. I will give you until tomorrow. After that I will feel free to do as I think fit.' He looked at me with chilly dark eyes. 'This does not mean I trust you, Laura. The only reason I am allowing you to do this at all is that I think you too do not want James Lovatt to run off with my wife.' He pushed back his chair with a screech that set my already tattered nerves even more on edge, and threw a five-pound note on the counter with an instruction to Costas to keep the change. He turned his head and fixed me with an uncomfortably piercing look. 'I will not tolerate you trying to deceive me again, Laura. Remember that.'

CHAPTER 9

It was some time and a coffee on the house before I could get my shaking legs in order and walk back to the office where our secretary, Lucy, slid out on to the landing and caught my wrist before I could go in. 'Oh, Laura. I'm so sorry, it was all *my* fault!' she said tearfully.

I looked at her in surprise; the whole agency knows that Lucy has the brains of a gnat and owes her job to Daddy being one of our largest clients, but surely even she couldn't really think she was the cause of Stefano's jealous outpourings?

Her eyes filled with tears. 'He came around last night after you'd gone. He said it was urgent so I told him you'd said you were meeting Daniel in Bruce's.'

'So he asked who Daniel was and you told him?' I said. She nodded, lower lip trembling. And luckily for my social credibility Stefano must have decided against creating a scene in a crowded wine bar. That was one question answered, at least he didn't have superhuman deductive powers. I hoped the local axe murderer never rang Lucy asking for details of my itinerary, that was all.

I assured her no real harm had been done, with my sort

of luck Stefano would probably have found out some other way, and went inside to be bombarded with excited questions. As Emma pointed out over coffee, biscuits and second-hand cigarette smoke over the photocopier, what with Hugo and now Stefano I was rapidly becoming a one-woman source of vicarious thrills and gossip for the whole agency. She didn't think it quite so funny when I told her of Stefano's threats. 'Would you like to come and stay at my flat for a bit? Then at least he won't know where you're living,' she asked in a worried voice.

'Bless you,' I said and meant it. Emma's hot date had gradually metamorphosed into a hot prospect and she was reeling him in with all the skill Helen had used on Paris. The last thing she needed was an onlooker while she was trying to entice him with her superb cooking (local catering firm), skill at home-making (local cleaning agency), brilliant personality and superb figure in bank-balance-busting new dress (both Emma). 'I'm not afraid of Stefano – not for myself. I don't suppose you'd like to have James to stay, would you?' I asked teasingly.

She pretended to consider for a moment. She'd been rather taken with James's looks when she was doing her spying in the wine bar. 'Nah. I wouldn't want to spoil a beautiful friendship when you got antsy wondering what we were up to.'

'I'd do no such thing!'

She gave me a long and disbelieving look. 'Since when have you been prepared to hand over one of your lovers to a friend, Laura Moreton?' she asked loftily.

I could feel myself blushing to the roots of my hair. 'I've already explained that he's not my lover,' I said in a stiff voice. 'So we shared a room – OK, a bed too – but that doesn't mean anything happened!'

'Talk about wasted opportunities,' muttered Emma. 'If it's really true, which I doubt!'

'Well, it is!' I snapped grumpily. 'James and I are just friends – and we aren't even that a lot of the time,' I amended, remembering what he could be like.

She gave me a superior look. 'Oh, yeah? Then why are you tangling yourself up with a nasty piece of work like that Stefano for a part-time friend, eh?' She walked casually around to the other side of the photocopier so she was out of reach and rested her elbows on the top. 'Bet you wouldn't stand up to this Stefano for Daniel. Think about that.' She retreated into the safety of the main office before I could get at her.

It was complete nonsense, I thought indignantly, which was why, during the course of what turned out to be a very long telephone conversation indeed with Liv, I just didn't happen to mention Emma's outrageous suggestion. I mean, there's no point repeating rubbish, is there? It just wastes good gossiping time and even I can't spend *all* day chatting. Liv took a far more phlegmatic view of Stefano's threat than Emma did, saying she doubted he represented much of a danger to me apart from acute nuisance value. 'It's not as if Cressida's run off with *you*, is it?' she asked practically. 'Then you'd really need your tin helmet! Men like him don't persecute women. Instead he's going to be feeling sorry for you – which'll *really* get up your nose – because you've been hoodwinked into helping your lover while he was planning all the time to go off with someone else—'

'He's *not* my lover!' I interrupted crossly. That little story was running a lot too far in my opinion. And I still hadn't made up my mind if what infuriated me most of all was that there was no truth in it. 'Nothing, absolutely *nothing*, happened! I'm going out with Daniel, not James.'

'Fidelity can be a real bind at times, can't it?' said Liv with suspicious sympathy. 'Still I suppose it's worth it to be able to look Daniel in the eye and swear James never laid so much as a finger on you.'

I had a sudden vision of Stefano pointing out, with a completely straight face, that I had a piece of box hedge in my hair. Thank God we aren't in the age of video phones! Liv would never have let my scarlet face go by without commenting. 'Daniel trusts me,' I said loftily.

She laughed. 'Enough for you to tell him that you shared a room with James?'

'Well, no,' I admitted.

'Thought not!' she said triumphantly. 'What does he think about all this?'

'I haven't told him,' I said uncomfortably. 'You know what Daniel's like. It would only upset him and he's on a really good roll with his writing at the moment. I don't want to do anything that might disrupt it. And of course he'd feel bound to try and help me.' Liv snorted in a way that threatened to put a severe strain on our friendship, so I continued hastily, 'Besides it'll only make Stefano even more suspicious if I involve Daniel now. You see, I told him Daniel and I weren't going out any more.'

To my relief she accepted this excuse, and we moved on to a series of highly pleasurable speculations about what

Cressida could be up to if she hadn't done a runner with James, until the tap of heels coming up the stairs reminded me that Darian was unlikely to regard emotional upset and the need to get it off my chest as a valid excuse for not starting her press release. I can work speedily if necessary. I had half a paragraph done by the time she strode over to my desk to check on my progress. She said it was complete rubbish, but then she always says that on principle about first drafts.

Later on that evening I was sitting in Lovatt and Barnes, Fine Antiques (Barnes sold out his share long ago), literally swinging my legs and looking impatiently at my watch, wondering if James would come back before locking up time. Neither of his current staff had met me before so I could hardly ask them to let me wait in his office and he hadn't replied to any of my increasingly urgent calls to his message service to meet me here. A niggling little voice was suggesting that his silence might mean something after all. But at least there weren't any Battersea ware or Chelsea boxes on sale in the crowded display cabinets. I'd looked. I got up from my chair and wandered around, breathing in pleasurably. The smell, a mixture of antique wax polish, dust and an undefinable hint of pure age, reminded me of that wonderful feeling when after a summer spent working here I realised I had enough money for the first time in my life to buy the clothes I wanted, rather than the ones my mother or Imogen thought suited me. Sabrina, fresh from a stint behind the front desk at Sotheby's, winced slightly as I ran my fingers down the outside of a large Wedgwood vase, and I smiled at her to indicate I wasn't a Goth and knew what I was doing.

I had flaked off all my nail varnish and was contemplating taking up nail biting again when James finally arrived just before the security grille went down. He walked in, shaking raindrops off his hair, and said cheerily, 'Hello, Laura. What's all the panic about? Sorry I didn't ring back, but I've been in Cheshire at a sale and good boys don't use their mobiles while driving down the M6. You two go home, I'll do the locking up. Come into the office, it's more comfortable and we can have a drink while you tell me what's up.'

If James really did have Cressida hidden away somewhere, was even he capable of such a masterly assumption of ignorance as to why I might want to see him? My hopes began to rise a little. 'I got a couple of really good pieces,' he said over his shoulder. 'Including a French Empire credenza covered in verdigris for Mr Carter. He was saying only the other day that he needed sommat to get his dentures into.'

'It sounds just his cup of tea.' Mr Carter was a retired master restorer and generally cantankerous old boy who liked to keep his hand in with the occasional piece. (And it keeps the big bugger out of my kitchen, as his wife said.) Since he grandly and noisily refused to work on anything that was not of the highest quality it had become a game with James and his father to see what they could find that was both neglected and good enough for Mr Carter's meticulous if slow restoration.

'Sit down,' said James, waving a hand as we entered his office. He was not a believer in the maxim that a tidy desk means a tidy mind. Files and pieces of paper lay heaped all over it; Post-it notes were stuck to the screen of his computer, presumably the only place you could be sure they wouldn't get buried; a stack of empty picture frames in various states of disrepair leant against one wall and a pile of Sotheby's *Reviews of the Year* dating back to the mid-seventies was tilting precariously towards another. He lobbed his jacket in the approximate direction of a chair and, without bothering to wait and see if it hit anything, went into the little kitchen behind the office and came back with a ready opened bottle of wine and a couple of glasses.

He handed me one and settled himself comfortably in a battered leather director's chair that had seen better days. 'What's up?' he asked casually.

I eyed him, wondering what the best approach was for what might be a somewhat delicate subject. In the end I decided directness was the answer. 'Where's Cressida?'

James nearly choked on his drink. 'Cressida?' he said with what looked like genuine surprise. 'I haven't the faintest idea. Why should I?'

I felt something tight inside me relax in relief. 'Because she's left Stefano, and he's convinced it's because of you.'

James jerked upright in his chair so that the wine in his glass slopped around dangerously. 'It certainly isn't!' He took a deep swig and gazed unseeingly towards me. 'She told me she was thinking of leaving him but I didn't believe her.'

'She what?' I stared at him incredulously, wondering how on earth he had managed to keep such a riveting piece of information to himself. OK, so James was very close-mouthed when it suited him, but as his partner in crime, so to speak, I reckoned he'd owed it to me to share the news. He might have known it would reverberate on us eventually.

He shrugged, looking embarrassed. 'When we were staying at Hurstwood she was telling me she wasn't happy – said that Stefano doesn't respect her, she hates living in Italy and loathes his family who make her feel she's nothing like as good as his first wife and certainly not good enough for Stefano. You know the sort of thing.' I could just imagine. And naturally he hadn't had the common sense to tell Cressida she had a simply splendid husband, to hold on to him with both hands, and that everything would work out in time. 'Cressy's always lived life in high alt so I didn't know whether to take it seriously or not. She rang last week, left a message on the answerphone saying that Stefano was making unreasonable demands—'

'What sort of demands?' I interrupted in fascination.

'Haven't the faintest idea, she didn't say,' he said, looking at his feet in a slightly self-conscious fashion, as if his mind too had been running amok with wild speculation. 'She said she couldn't live with him any longer and wanted to come and see me.'

'What about?'

'Oh, to discuss what she should do with her future, I imagine.'

'She did?' I murmured. I couldn't conceive of approaching any of my former boyfriends to ask for advice as to what I should do next. With at least one of them the advice would run along the lines of 'find the nearest lake and . . .'

'Of course I rang back as soon as I got the message but

her housekeeper said she'd just left to spend the weekend with her sister and would be back on Monday. I reckoned that whatever Cressy had been rowing with Stefano about hadn't proved to be so marriage-shattering after all and everything was back to normal. I haven't spoken to her since.' He made a face. 'Frankly, whatever my feelings about the man, I didn't particularly want to be directly involved in the breakup of Cressy's marriage.' But that didn't necessarily mean he wasn't pleased about the outcome. 'So whatever Stefano may think, I'm not the one responsible!' James went on. His eyes glinted. 'You needn't worry, dear heart, I haven't been unfaithful to you!'

'I wasn't worrying,' I said tartly. He made a grimace of mock distress and reached over to refill my glass. 'It's worse than that, James,' I said, and told him the full story of my meeting with Stefano – was it really only that morning? It seemed I had been sick with fear for aeons longer than that.

Typically enough James immediately seized on what to me seemed the item of least importance. He was incandescent about Stefano's approaching me at all, and even though I'd read enough of his reaction to leave out the bit about Stefano's warning me not to deceive him again, he went on blowing the protective male trumpet at full blast and informing me I mustn't speak to Stefano again. I had to point out firmly that I'd had enough male posturing for one day, and like it or not he had involved me from the moment he'd pressurised me into going to Hurstwood House for the weekend, so he could just shut up about it. Surprisingly enough he did. It was the first time I've ever been able to do that. Then instead of concentrating on Stefano's threats of revenge, he started worrying about the possible damage to Stefano's china collection if Cressida hadn't packed it properly. I gritted my teeth, refrained from saying that the silly girl deserved all that was coming to her if she had broken anything, and told him there were some things of more immediate importance, such as the false story from the journalist who was doing such a good job of fuelling Stefano's rage. We needed to get that repudiated immediately.

James put his hands behind his head and looked at me with studied nonchalance. 'What's the point? The damage's been done. The whole of Cressy's crowd gossip like mad. One of them said something which was passed on to the next in an improved and more dramatic version like Chinese whispers until it reached a stringer for the paper. We'd never manage to unravel it. Stefano'll find out soon enough from someone else that I wasn't there.'

He didn't appear to take the threats of revenge against him seriously either. 'Bluster,' he said, shrugging.

'I don't think so,' I replied seriously, trying to repress a shiver when I thought of Stefano's expression as he told me that effectively he was above the law and could do what he liked. James, who should have been much more wary of Stefano than me, seemed to look on him as a comic opera character, full of noise and bravado. But I couldn't help remembering just how ruthless a lot of those operatic tenors were. I had to settle for getting James to agree not to go into any dark alleys with Stefano and to be very careful if he was offered anything stunning at a rock bottom price, since it would certainly soon be followed by the fine art squad who would finger his collar for the receipt of stolen property.

That last did get his attention at least. James takes his business and reputation seriously. He stared into space, twirling his glass abstractedly. 'Bloody hell,' he finally said gloomily, 'I suppose the only thing to do is to get hold of Cressy and make her tell Stefano that firstly I haven't anything to do with her leaving him—'

'Do you think he'll believe that?' I interrupted. 'Especially as she'll be doing it at your prompting.'

He raised his brows. 'It's the truth,' he said loftily, 'and it's worth trying. She could always tell him why she really left him. I expect he'd like to know. Secondly, she can inform him I didn't commission her to pinch his bloody collection.'

I supposed it might work. 'But you said you didn't know where she was,' I pointed out, doubt raising its ugly head again.

'I don't,' he said flatly, and caught my sceptical expression. 'In that I really don't know whether she's in London or Aberystwyth, *not* in that I don't know if she's in the bath or going downstairs in the lift. But we could try some of her friends, I still know them. Though,' he grinned at me wickedly, 'I don't expect Serena'll feel much like helping us.'

'*She's* Cressida's friend?' I gasped.

'Not exactly, but they've known each other forever, their mothers were at school together or something.' He drummed his fingers in a rare clear space on the desk top. 'Abby? Perhaps. Didn't Cressy say she was travelling in Europe, though? Georgina? Don't know her number,' he muttered. 'Fiona? Don't have a clue where *she* is now.' His head jerked upwards, eyes alight. 'I know! Arabella!'

'Self-improvement Arabella?' As he nodded, I said, 'You could be on to something. They did spend a lot of time talking.'

'Arabella did, Cressy just listened,' James said dryly. 'But that sort of improve your own psyche lark is just Cressy's cup of tea. Let's see if Arabella knows anything about her whereabouts.'

Unfortunately there weren't any Featherington-Meades listed in the telephone directory and a call to Viola and Richard Featherington-Meade's home in Northumberland only produced a Spanish au-pair who hadn't got very far with learning English and nowhere with looking up numbers in the book. We'd have to get it from Arabella's boyfriend at his bank in the City, but that was going to have to wait until the morning. Banks worked jolly short hours, I thought with disapproval, not like us in PR. Slightly against James's judgement I decided I would ring Stefano later and for what it was worth assure him James had no clearer idea than he did where the errant wife was – though perhaps not in quite those terms. I hoped he'd believe me. Somehow, without mentioning it, we both assumed I wouldn't be telling Stefano that we had a possible lead on her. There was enough female solidarity in me to support her decision to leave him and keep her secrets if necessary – unless, of course, it became a choice between her and James. Then I'd let her sink. Stefano would certainly throw her a lifebelt.

James stretched, yawning slightly. 'That's about it. I'm starving, I didn't have time to do more than snatch a sandwich for lunch. Fancy coming back to my place? I'll show you,' he leered exaggeratedly, 'the contents of my freezer. Or even better, the outside of a takeaway pizza.'

It sounded like a nice idea. I was surprised to realise how much I enjoyed his company these days. I might even get a chance to break down his reserve and find out what he really thought about Cressida's leaving Stefano. He wouldn't be human if he didn't feel at least a smidgen of satisfaction, but the question was, was he planning to charge in and sweep her off her feet for himself? (I wasn't being nosy – well, I was – but feeling quite justified concern for James's well-being and needed information to quell, or fuel, my fears.) Then I realised with a pang of dismay that I was supposed to be looking at the contents of Daniel's freezer this evening, or rather inspecting his fridge to see if I could salvage something that wasn't growing hairs or actively moving. I was already late, though why I ever feel guilty about that I don't know since Daniel always is. But, of course, true artists aren't expected to have a sense of time. 'So you're still carrying on with the etiolated boyfriend?' James asked with a malicious smile.

'He's not etiolated!' I protested.

James's grin widened. 'Dear Laura, he looks as if he doesn't cast a reflection in the mirror!'

I got up angrily, making several piles of paper wobble ominously. 'You haven't changed much from when I was fifteen, have you? Always ready with a cheap unfunny crack!'

'I thought it was very funny,' protested James innocently. 'And speaking of when you were fifteen – do you still fancy me as much as you did then?' he asked with a straight face.

'I didn't!' I said with what dignity I could muster. 'That was just Aunt Jane romanticising.'

'Liar,' he said. 'I have it on good authority – your sister. We had a very interesting chat. According to her you were being disappointingly reticent about the weekend at Cressy's, which she said must mean something. She then went on to tell me exactly what she thought it was too,' he added gleefully.

'Did she?' I muttered, making a vow to do something unpleasant to her as soon as I got the opportunity. In fact I might take the day off work tomorrow and drive down to Oxford to do just that. 'My taste has improved a lot since then,' I informed James coldly.

He leaned back in his chair and put his feet up on the desk, regarding me under half-closed lids. 'That's the most insulting thing you've ever said to me,' he murmured. 'At least I come out in the day time.'

I was a bit slow on the uptake because it was at least twenty seconds before I threw something at him. He just laughed.

CHAPTER 10

Arabella sounded curiously reluctant to meet me for lunch when I rang and suggested it the next morning. Since, so far as I'm aware, I don't smell that bad and I hadn't done anything dreadful like make rude remarks about the self-awareness course (that had been James, which was why I'd been elected to speak to her), I was fairly sure it meant she had something to hide. Detective Laura was determined to find out and gently but firmly insisted, saying she was about to go off to France (quite true) and really must speak to Arabella before she went. Grudgingly she agreed to meet me at a wine bar near her office at one o'clock, saying she'd have to make it brief because she was very tied up. I made a point of getting there at a quarter to, just in case she came in early and then left saying she'd waited and I hadn't turned up.

She was already seated when I pushed my way through the door and looked thoroughly put out when I plumped down on the chair opposite her. I ordered myself a white wine and soda but refused anything to eat; it's not easy to interrogate a reluctant witness with your mouth full. We skirted around the main subject for a few minutes while she eyed me uneasily. Despite the famous self-assertiveness course she still didn't ask me why I wanted to talk to her.

Eventually I thought I'd better put her out of her misery. 'Do you know where Cressida is?' I asked.

She flinched and went bright red. 'Cressida? Why should I?' she mumbled, digging intently in her lentil and rocket salad with her fork. 'I mean she's at home of course.' Her hand shook and lentils showered off her fork back on to the plate. 'I haven't heard from her for ages, so how would I know?' A ham acting school couldn't have given a better demonstration of how to express guilt.

'I just thought you might,' I said. 'You two seemed so close the other weekend.' Her fork clanged noisily as it hit the floor. 'Stefano's been to see me,' I said once she'd managed to pick it up. 'He's convinced she's gone off with James, which I know isn't true, but unless I can get *her* to tell Stefano that James has nothing to do with this, I'm really worried that Stefano might do something to him.'

Arabella didn't look as if this was a serious consideration for her. I tried telling her about Stefano's threats but she was quite unmoved about potential danger to her fellow man (James's mockery of her course must have got her more on the raw than we realised) and continued to insist, completely unconvincingly, that she didn't have a clue where Cressida could be. She hadn't heard a word about Cressida's leaving Stefano, but if she *had* left him Arabella thought that Cressida needed all the support she could get while she tried to take control of her own life and learn to live with the wreckage of a marriage that was in ruins entirely because of the insupportable behaviour of her husband. The last thing she needed was to be bullied back to someone she didn't love any longer.

I broke in on this breathless twaddle with some irritation. 'I haven't said a word about forcing Cressida back to Stefano!' I said crossly. 'Frankly I'm tired of the pair of them and really don't care if they never see each other again. But if she wants control of her own destiny she'd better learn how to do it without trampling all over others! And the first thing she must do is sort out this mess for which she's responsible.'

'You can't blame Cressida for Stefano's jealous fantasies,' bleated Arabella.

'Oh, can't I?' I retorted grimly. 'If she'd had the sense to stop throwing her arms around James at every opportunity, Stefano wouldn't have got the idea in the first place.' I knew this wasn't strictly true but there's no point in spoiling a good remark for pedantic reasons.

'Well, I've already told him I don't have a clue about it,' said Arabella triumphantly, realising a fraction too late she'd just given the lie to what she'd said before.

I leaned forward and fixed her with a basilisk glare. 'Just get this, Arabella, I'm not letting you or Cressida push me around. Either you tell me what you know about Cressida, or the moment I leave here I'm off to the nearest phone box to ring Stefano. I'll tell him that whatever you said to him before about being completely ignorant isn't true. Then you can have a nice little chat with *him*.' I smiled slightly, and I hoped nastily. 'He really does know how to bully people, and from what he's told me he makes a bad enemy. I wouldn't envy you if you got on his wrong side.'

I could almost see this notion taking root in Arabella's brain. Her eyes grew wide and her expression slightly sick. She looked as if she was see-sawing between the desire to stay devotedly at the barricades, risking all in her loyalty to her friend, and a cowardly wish to dump the whole problem in my lap and get the hell out of there. Luckily cowardice won the day. She licked her lips nervously. 'You promise you won't tell Stefano?' she asked to salve her conscience.

'Of course I won't,' I assured her. 'All we want is for Cressida to tell him that she isn't having an affair or anything else with James.'

'OK,' said Arabella miserably. She pushed her unappetising lentils around her plate and blurted out, 'She's in Folkestone.'

'Folkestone?' I echoed in blank astonishment. 'What on earth is she doing in *Folkestone*?' I mean, if you really want to go to the seaside in the depths of winter, almost anywhere along the South Coast is more glamorous and lively than Folkestone.

Lifesigns, the company that ran the self-awareness courses, had their headquarters in Folkestone for the good reason that their founder and head guru had a house there. Arabella had been to a couple of follow on seminars down there. Her rather equine face lit up. 'They were really enriching. I got so much from them. You wouldn't believe it! I was so empowered.' I firmly nudged her away from describing her own spiritual experiences and got her back to the point. Something about Arabella's undiscriminating enthusiasm for her course had got through to Cressida, or maybe it was akin to subliminal advertising. She heard

Arabella going on about it so much over the weekend that she must have begun to imagine she herself actually thought some of what was being told to her. With the zeal of the born again convert Arabella had sensed that interest and continued to bombard Cressida with telephone calls telling her all about Lifesigns' next seminar and trying to persuade her to attend. Cressida had demurred, afraid of Stefano's no doubt scornful reaction. (So much for taking control of her life.) Last week Arabella had rung again and caught Cressida just after she'd come back from seeing Stefano off at the airport and, contrary to his fond imaginings, in no way feeling that their row had been made up. Disappointingly Arabella didn't know the full details, except that Stefano was quite unreasonable and made Demands That He Shouldn't. Cressida had declared tearfully to her that Stefano was impossible and would never change (probably a fair character assessment) and that if she wasn't to be ground into the dust like a chattel of the last century she had to leave, because he was forcing her into an Intolerable Position. Cunningly Arabella had slipped in a suggestion that if Cressida were to gain some inner knowledge and insight on how to manage her own life she might be able to stand up to Stefano in the future. Cressida had been tempted but still havered.

On Friday Arabella struck pay dirt. She'd rung with the exciting news that there was a seminar starting the next day and though they were always fully booked she had managed to persuade Sam to squeeze in Cressida as a special favour. Cressida fell for it hook, line and sinker and within half an hour she had arranged a mythical visit to her sister and was heading off up to London with her bags and Stefano's china collection. (Presumably she had decided in the meantime she couldn't be bothered about learning to stand up to him. After nicking his precious collection it was going to take much more than a course to enable her to do that.) She had a wild night out with Arabella and a couple of other friends, paying for a really good dinner for all of them at, interestingly enough, La Cucina, and slightly hung over had staggered off the next morning to do the seminar. (At £500 for a weekend I wasn't surprised Sam had been able to squeeze in an extra person.)

Cressida had been really bowled over by it, reported Arabella. She felt enriched, empowered, a new woman. She expressed this by going shopping with Arabella and buying a whole lot of clothes that Stefano would hate. But it seems being empowered and enriched isn't enough and that if you're really interested in personal self-advancement there are inevitable follow up sessions. (At a price, of course.) Sam had suggested that as a successful graduate of his seminar Cressida might be interested in helping out at a couple more he was running in Folkestone that week. She had shot off down there, full of enthusiasm, like a bullet from a gun.

'Is she staying with this Sam?' I asked doubtfully, seeing more problems ahead. Much to my relief Arabella said that he and his wife had a rigid policy never to allow their graduates to stay with them and had arranged very preferential rates with a local hotel for those who wanted it. 'So what's the name of the hotel?' I demanded, half expecting Arabella, who was visibly beginning to regret spilling the beans, to claim defiantly that she wouldn't tell me.

Rather sulkily she muttered it then added with a flash of spirit, 'But don't ask me for the telephone number, because I don't know it!'

'It doesn't matter,' I said mildly, 'I can get it from Directory Enquiries.'

'It won't do you any good,' she said triumphantly. 'She's not taking any calls. In fact the staff have been told not even to admit that she's staying there.' She lowered her voice importantly. 'It might be Stefano.'

If he got wind that his straying wife was anywhere near Folkestone he was unlikely to be content with making an exploratory telephone call. He'd have the heavy mob down there turning over every stone until they found her. 'I'll send her a letter then,' I said, shrugging. 'Not even Cressida could believe Stefano would *write* to her.'

I got the distinct feeling Arabella felt I wasn't taking all this seriously enough. I received a very old-fashioned look and a heavy sigh. More annoyingly she claimed not to know when Cressida was planning to return to London though she did go so far as to admit that presumably she was going to sometime since half of Arabella's bedroom floor was occupied by suitcases Cressida hadn't deemed necessary to take with her to Folkestone. Still I felt that Detective Laura hadn't actually done too bad a job. We now knew where Cressida was and James could drive down to Folkestone later that afternoon to talk to her.

It turned out he couldn't. When I rang him, full of my news, he congratulated me and said, 'There's just one problem. There's a bloke parked outside in a Ford Escort. He's been there a couple of hours now, apparently having a kip in the front seat of his car, just like the guy in the

Peugeot 205 who was in that space before him – except that he woke up in time to decide to come and have a pint and a sandwich in the same pub as I did. Either Stefano's put the rozzers on me and they're keeping watch to see where I've stashed the loot, or more likely he's got private detectives following me to see if I can lead them to Cressida.'

'Oh, dammit to hell!' I said loudly, causing Darian to give me a dirty look as she swept through the office. 'Bloody Stefano! Why can't he keep his sodding word?' At Darian's second glare I lowered my voice. 'He swore he'd leave you alone and now look what he's doing. I thought I'd convinced him you had nothing to do with this.'

'Obviously changed his mind overnight,' James replied dryly. 'If Cressy won't come to the phone someone will have to go down to Folkestone to speak to her. It can't be me.'

'Let it be Stefano then,' I said in irritation. 'If her seminar was that successful she'll easily be able to stand up to him.'

There was a long meaningful silence. I could almost feel the waves of reproach washing down the telephone wires and out through the receiver. 'You know you don't mean that,' said James reprovingly. 'Whatever happened to female solidarity? Besides you made a promise to Arabella.'

There was another silence. I broke it first. 'James, I *can't* go to Folkestone!' I wailed. 'I'm going to France tomorrow morning and I've got loads to finish here before I go. I haven't even packed! I simply haven't the time to get to Folkestone and back after work.'

I might have known I wouldn't be allowed to get away with that. There was a pause then he said brightly, 'You're going on Eurostar, aren't you? You could go to Folkestone first thing in the morning, see Cressy, and then catch the train from Ashford. You'll still be in Paris by lunchtime if you get cracking early enough.'

He made it all sound so easy. Apart from the matter of having to get up at five in the morning and driving for about three hours in my elderly Renault 5 with its dicky heater and broken radio, without any guarantee that Cressida hadn't left instructions to turn away personal visitors as well as telephone calls, and then finding the station in Ashford, changing my ticket and no doubt paying for it as well, there weren't too many objections I could make, though I tried. Believe me, I tried. I asked why Harry couldn't go. Surely this was a fraternal duty? Harry and Cressida didn't get on, according to James. We couldn't involve any of her family as I'd made a promise and I didn't break my word, did I? I was beginning to think I could, quite easily. I even offered to come along to the shop with a wig, a large raincoat and some size 10 stilettos so that he could sneak out in disguise and go to Folkestone himself. James was quite taken with this idea but decided he would never live it down if he were stopped by the police in rather amateur drag. Eventually, as he knew I would, I heard myself weakly agreeing that, yes, I would get up at the crack of dawn, or before dawn to be accurate, and go and try to persuade Cressida to do the right thing. I had a feeling, even then, that I was going to regret it.

The only good thing I can say for my car's heater, or

lack of it, is that the frigid cold did at least help to keep me awake after about three hours' sleep, and the pain from the chilblains developing on my fingers and toes effectively took my mind off the slight hangover that was niggling away behind my eyes. James had employed himself usefully by ringing the hotel and asking for directions as to how to get there and had said he'd drop by the flat with the details. And it wouldn't do any harm if his tail reported he'd gone around to visit me either. He turned up laden down with wine and a takeaway for which I was most grateful at the time (I think it's the first occasion any member of the male species has arrived with food that I wasn't expected to 'do something' with), but for which I found myself cursing him now. Actually I was cursing him for getting me involved in this at all, and myself too. If I'd been a bit stronger minded I'd never have given in to him – on several occasions – and right now I'd be at Waterloo buying a magazine to read on the train instead of sitting in the car trying to make head or tail of his map. It had seemed so simple last night when he explained it to me, but map reading has never been one of my strengths. I can't even use the *A to Z.*

At least I could identify one thing on the map – the squiggly line with 'sea' written on it. The real thing lay to my right, reflecting the grey and sullen sky, with the odd ship dotted around on it, looking thoroughly unprepossessing. There was a grassy expanse which stretched along the cliff top almost as far as the eye could see and which was bordered by large Victorian and Edwardian hotels with fine sea views to one side, which must be the oblong marked 'The Leas' on the map. In better weather you would have expected dog walkers, strollers heading for the pretty bandstand further along, the odd attendant pushing a wheelchair, but right now with a chill wind blowing the sparse winter grass almost flat it was completely deserted. Even those of the hotels which had escaped being converted into apartments looked as if they had been closed for the off season. But none of the spider tracks on the piece of paper in my hand bore any resemblance to the roads I could see around me. At last I found the hotel. I had been, justifiably I think, misled by the name, 'Bosun's View'. It hadn't occurred to me that having spent most of his life afloat the bosun would make sure he never had to look out of his window and see bloody water again. I imagine whoever had been giving the instructions to James hadn't been keen to stress this point either. It depends if you think that 'a short walk' from the sea is about a mile.

I was prepared for enormous difficulties in getting to Cressida, having to stand my ground and insist on seeing her in the face of denials that she was there at all, threatening to chain myself to the railings, etc, but to my surprise the angular woman who answered the bell at the desk in the dark little reception area simply sniffed and said she dare say Mrs Buonotti would be coming down soon. She'd have to or she'd miss breakfast because the dining room was closing in five minutes, she added, thin lips snapping with satisfaction. I could wait over there, she indicated, waving at a cretonne-covered sofa in one corner, and if I'd excuse her she'd have to get on, she had a lot of work to do, low season or no low season.

I sat down and occupied myself with reading last

summer's timetable for the Hythe-Dymchurch miniature railway. It looked quite fun, the sort of thing Imogen's two boys who are still at prep school would like. There was a slightly more up-to-date programme for the local theatre group. I'd just finished reading the cast list for the Christmas pantomime when I heard footsteps on the steps and Cressida appeared. She was dressed in a fine wool polo neck in the pale grey she seemed to like so much, tucked into the enviably narrow waistband of a pair of designer jeans. She was looking tired and strained, her eyes even huger than usual in her pale face, shadows like camouflage stripes underneath them. I stood up. 'Hello, Cressida,' I said.

She wheeled around with a squeak of alarm, hand pressed to her mouth. She was so white I thought she was about to faint and leaped forward to take her arm to support her. 'I'm sorry, I didn't mean to startle you like that,' I said quickly. 'It's all right, Stefano isn't here.'

To my relief the colour began to return to her face. 'It was just the surprise,' she whispered, and smiled at me tremulously. 'It's nice to see you, Laura. Come and sit with me while I have my breakfast. I'm sure we can persuade Mrs Jessop to make you some coffee. Even if she is a miserable old witch,' she said, dropping her voice.

The dining room had last been decorated circa 1967 with an embossed design of gold, silver and yellow circles and squiggles against a dirty white background. Framed prints of sea views, to make up for what you couldn't see from here, hung with military precision in the middle of each wall. There was a pervading smell of damp. It wasn't surprising that in these dismal surroundings Cressida had no appetite for anything more than toast and marmalade, though if the cooked breakfast was anything like the coffee that was grudgingly brought to me ('It'll have to go on your bill, Mrs Buonotti, we didn't agree anything about entertaining guests') it was probably better for her digestion that she refrained. I wondered idly if she had ever stayed anywhere before where she wasn't valued as an honoured guest but instead treated as just another blooming tripper, unlikely (with good reason) to return. Her downcast expression didn't give the impression she was finding this a jolly adventure.

I wittered on brightly about going to Paris, giving her time to have two triangles of soggy toast and a cup of tea so brown you could have used it for dyeing your clothes, before I launched into the reason why I was there. Perhaps I should have left it longer but I had a train to catch. As it was, despite James's airy promises, I was going to miss *moules marinière* at my mother's local brasserie. I'd been looking forward to them all week too. Maybe I could persuade Mum to go there for lunch tomorrow. I cut ruthlessly into Cressida's colourless description of the seminar and began to tell her about Stefano's visit to me. She wasn't surprised – not even Cressida could imagine I just happened on her hotel by chance. But she was horrified about his invading the office. 'You see why I simply can't live with him any longer,' she murmured. 'That temper! Please don't even suggest I should go back to him.'

'I wasn't going to,' I said promptly. It occurred to me that she looked not so much angry with him as frightened, and naturally I made the gigantic leap to a damning conclusion. 'Has he been beating you up?'

Her eyes widened. 'Of course not!' she said indignantly. 'Stefano would never do *that*!'

'Thank God!' I said with a sigh of relief. 'But I swear to you I don't want you to go back to him if you don't want to, nor am I going to tell him where you are. All I care about is that he stops getting the wrong end of the stick about James.'

'But I can't help that!' she protested.

I could have given her chapter and verse on how she could, starting with comparing her husband unfavourably to her former boyfriend. To his face. With rare tact I didn't. I did say though, 'Stefano thinks it was James who persuaded you to take his things.'

She went rigid. 'What do you mean?' she asked.

'Why, the china of course! Because James told you how much it was worth. He thinks you're planning to sell it and set yourself up with the proceeds.'

Cressida laughed shortly. 'I hadn't thought of *selling* it. I suppose it's not a bad idea. I need some money.'

'Would that be wise?' I ventured. What could she need that amount of money for? The diamond necklace that Stefano wouldn't give her? 'I mean, he really is very upset about it – you don't want him publicly accusing you of theft.'

Her face set like stone. 'He won't. I had a perfect right to them,' she said flatly in a way that indicated she didn't want to talk about it again.

Afraid of really putting her back up I decided not to pursue the rights and wrongs of pinching your husband's favourite things and said instead, 'That doesn't really matter. What does is that he thinks you're having an affair with James. I've tried to tell him he's wrong, and I've failed. You have to convince him.'

'But I can't do that!' she protested immediately.

I leaned over the table. 'Oh, you don't have to worry, Cressida,' I said eagerly, 'he'll listen to you. He doesn't really want to believe you've gone off with another man. He'd much rather hear you were having dinner with girlfriends and not James at La Cucina on Friday and that—'

'No! You don't understand,' she said. 'I don't want to talk to him – I can't! He'll find out where I am and make me come back!' Her eyes filled with tears and she sniffed. I saw with interest that her nose didn't go red nor her eyes pink like mine do when I'm on the verge of crying. What a very useful talent to have. It must make men go weak at the knees. It left me completely unmoved.

'Nonsense!' I said bracingly. 'That's one of the reasons you've done this seminar, so you can stand up to Stefano.' Right now, judging from her expression, it looked as if she was going to have to be ranked as one of the failures. 'Please, Cressida,' I begged, beginning to feel almost as tearful as she looked, but nowhere near as pretty, 'do it for James's sake. Stefano said something about how easy it would be to put James in prison – you can't let that happen to him.'

'I don't think he'd really do anything like that,' she said doubtfully, in a way that suggested she was fairly sure that he would. 'No, I can't let him,' she went on in a stronger voice, beginning to look encouragingly annoyed at the idea. 'How dare he think he can go throwing his weight around and threatening people?' she demanded angrily. 'He thinks he can do whatever he wants, walk over anyone to get what he desires—'

'Men in his position – whose wives have left them – don't always behave in the most rational and reasonable fashion,' I felt obliged to point out, not quite sure why I was defending Stefano in any way.

'He deserves to have someone do something like that to him – to see how he likes being treated that way!' she stated hotly. I felt we were getting off the point here – that she needed to talk to him herself – and said so. She nodded reluctantly. 'But if I ring him from here he can trace the number on that machine of his. He'd be down in a couple of hours.'

'I could drive you to a telephone box in another town,' I offered, wondering if I'd make Paris that day at all.

Cressida looked doubtful. 'I suppose so.' Then she brightened and sat up straight. 'I know!' she said excitedly. 'I'll come with you to Paris and ring Stefano from there!'

CHAPTER 11

She bounced up, looking in an instant much more like the lively, vibrant person I'd first met than the careworn, worried individual I'd just had breakfast with. 'It's a brilliant idea! He'll never be able to find me there!' I didn't know what to say as she gabbled on. 'I've got my passport with me, I always travel with it, and I can buy any clothes I need while I'm there. I want a few new things.'

'I thought you'd been shopping with Arabella,' I said, seeing my weekend with my mother vanishing like smoke.

'But I don't like them, I only bought them because they'd annoy Stefano,' Cressida said simply. 'Besides nobody understands underwear like the French do,' she stated authoritatively, 'and I could do with a bit of a holiday.'

I was sure deep in my bones that this was going to turn out to be a very bad idea. 'If Stefano ever finds out you came to Paris with me he'll believe that I – and by inference James – have been helping you to leave him all along. He'll be right back on the warpath again,' I pointed out.

Cressida's lower lip protruded in a manner recognisable to all owners of sulky four year olds. 'I can't risk his tracing me,' she said obstinately.

I was tempted to point out that even if Stefano possessed the technology to trace a telephone call to a certain place immediately he wouldn't be able to get from London to south Kent in the matter of minutes it would take for her to get in a car and drive away but I had a strong feeling it wouldn't be any use. That pretty face was looking uncommonly stubborn. She must either adore Paris or be extremely bored here. I suspected the latter. Well, I was also staying with Mum next weekend as I returned from the Freddie French do, so I would get a chance to see her properly then at least. 'What about the seminar?' I asked in a last ditch attempt to dissuade Cressida. 'Aren't you supposed to be helping at one of the weekend affairs?'

She grinned at me. 'What's the point of doing a seminar on self-assertion if you don't feel you can pull out if you want to?'

Which was how, three hours later, Cressida was sitting next to me as we passed under the Channel only a couple of miles away from where she had been having breakfast. I will say one thing for her: once she's made up her mind she's a fast mover. She had herself packed, bill paid (overriding Mrs Jessop's protest that she didn't like taking cheques, especially off people with foreign names) and ready to go around to Sam to tell him that she wasn't going to be present that evening in under twenty minutes. He certainly did well out of Lifesigns if he could afford to buy a seriously large Victorian villa set in what looked like acres of garden on the edge of town. Cressida shot up the path carrying two bulging carrier bags and came back less than five minutes later, saying breathlessly, 'Just returning some things he lent me and giving him a couple of things I don't want to lug all the way to Paris, to console him for my dropping out. He wasn't very pleased,' she added morosely. 'Said I had been so receptive to the messages of Lifesigns that he'd been thinking of giving me a job, but of course if I was going to be unreliable . . .'

My little car chugged out into the traffic. I glanced over at Cressida as she carefully buffed already perfect nails. 'I think it's brilliant to have someone even considering giving you a job this soon.'

'What do you mean?' she asked in surprise.

'Well, if you're really determined not to go back to Stefano you'll have to get a job of some kind, won't you?' I asked.

'Will I?' she queried as if the notion had never occurred to her before. It probably hadn't. She looked distinctly put out. She put a perfect fingernail in her mouth and nibbled on it absently, forehead creased in thought. 'I don't know what I'll be able to do,' she said doubtfully. 'I'm not very good at working.'

I let her ponder on that while I searched for the roadsigns to Ashford. I had an idea that it wouldn't do Cressida any harm to think about what life in the real world was going to be like.

I'd rung my mother from the train to tell her which one I'd finally managed to catch and she was standing at the top of the platform at the Gare du Nord waiting for me, looking ridiculously young for someone with two children in their twenties. Her hair had been restyled into an enviably smart layered bob and had gone from its former dark blonde to a fetching tortoiseshell effect of several different colours. It must have taken the hairdresser ages but my mother is never happier than when she can devote a good few hours to her appearance. She looked a bit surprised when she saw I had a companion; even more so when she heard who that companion was. 'James's Cressida?' she hissed in a whisper.

'I'll tell you about it later,' I hissed back. 'It's very complicated.' I gave her a hug and said, 'You look great, Mum.'

'Thank you, darling.' She looked at me with a faint air of disapproval, obviously wishing she could say the same. To her lasting regret neither of her daughters has her air of chic. We just haven't inherited her way with a belt, a lipstick, the perfect height of a heel. Or her come-hither look either.

'I had to get up at five,' I pointed out defensively.

My mother looked appalled; in her book if you saw five in the morning at all it was because you were on your way to bed after a really good party. Though even if she had got up at five her hair would still be immaculate, all her make up in place and she'd have remembered to polish her shoes. I hadn't. 'And where are you staying, Cressida?' she asked brightly.

'I don't know,' floundered Cressida. 'I only decided at breakfast that I was coming. I mean, Stefano and I usually stay at the Bristol but I don't want to stay somewhere I'm known – or where I might meet one of his friends.' She looked helplessly at me. 'What do you suggest?'

I in turn looked at my mother. 'I wish I could have you to stay in the apartment, but really my spare room's not big enough,' she said to my uncharitable relief. I don't see my mother that often and I didn't want to have to share that time with Cressida. 'But there is a nice little hotel around the corner that looks comfortable and clean and not too expensive. I often meet Madame Blanc who runs it at the charcuterie, I know she'll look after you properly. We can take you on our way.'

Well, it certainly wasn't the Bristol. The bathroom was so small that the bidet was attached to the wall by a stretch hose and was wheeled away under the sink when not in use, and the panels of blue silk that covered the walls were hiding plaster that was steadily crumbling away. But, as my mother said, it was clean and the elderly *bateau lit* bed was very comfortable though it was a good thing that Cressida isn't very tall; I couldn't have lain straight in it. But she seemed quite satisfied (compared to 'Bosun's View' it was the height of luxury and chic), smiled and said it was lovely in slow but intelligible French which pleased Madame Blanc no end; she approved of *les Anglais* who made an effort with her language.

Any hopes I had of being able to leave Cressida to get on with telephoning Stefano and shopping for her all important underwear were dashed at her miserably uncertain expression as she listened to my mother's explanation on how to find the nearest bank to change some money. My mother's ability to give lucid directions (on a par with my ability to read a map) had a lot to do with Cressida's woebegone confusion. Even so, only the sort of person who is mean to puppies could have walked away and left her to cope on her own. I heard myself say with gloomy resignation that I'd come back for her after I'd unpacked and had a chance for a chat with my mother, and then we could find the bank and a telephone together. From Cressida's incandescently grateful expression you would have thought I'd just saved her life.

We had already dropped my suitcases off on the way so Mum and I walked back slowly from the hotel while I tried to explain why I'd ended up with James's ex (and I hoped it was staying that way) love in tow. I was a bit curious about that myself. Since the hotel really was only just around the corner I'd nowhere near finished before we arrived outside the high wooden gates which open on to the courtyard of Mum's building. Traditionally these are guarded by a concierge, who sits at her post and beadily inspects each caller. Mum's concierge lives in a ground-floor apartment and the lace curtains twitch each time a door opens. You can feel a glare of concentrated malevolence checking that you aren't performing some major sin such as putting rubbish in the bin on the wrong day or not using the designated bags. We climbed up the three flights of stone steps to the apartment – one of the reasons that Mum's got a smaller waist than I have. She took me straight into a little kitchen decked out in Provençal prints and all the most modern equipment, for Mum's become quite French enough to know that the first thing you do with a visitor, any visitor, is to offer food and drink.

I was delighted to have a nice messy French bread sandwich. It seemed ages since I'd snatched a piece of toast while Horatio wound himself around my legs, puzzled but pleased at the notion of an early breakfast. Cressida had been too busy on the train telling me about the iniquities of Stefano's mother and sisters for me to be able to get to the buffet. They sounded so appalling that I stayed glued to my seat in reluctant fascination. In front of Stefano they were absolutely charming, praising Cressida's exquisite English looks and saying what a credit she was to him. When he wasn't there it was another matter. There were constant references to the sainted Angelica, Stefano's first wife, who, according to the old Contessa, was the pinnacle of every womanly achievement except that of producing babies. Cressida, naturally, hadn't even got on the foothills, and boy did they let her know it.

'Poor child, what a load of harpies!' said my mother sympathetically as I finished telling her all of this. 'But surely she wouldn't really have left this Stefano just because of them?'

Actually by the time we were passing through Lille I'd come to the conclusion myself that there was a heavy degree of gold-threaded embroidery going on here. The family sounded extremely tiresome but not marital break up material. Besides when the chips were down most men supported their wife rather than their mother and Stefano certainly didn't strike me as a man securely tied to Mama's apron strings.

My mouth was too full of bread and *saucisson* for me to answer Mum so I shook my head vigorously and swallowed hard. 'I was wondering if you could talk to her and try and find out why she's done a bunk.'

My mother stared at me hard for a moment and I worried that she might have taken one of her sudden offences, then she laughed. 'On the grounds that I've had loads of practice at doing bunks?'

'Something like that,' I admitted, though actually I had been thinking of her more in the light of an older, more motherly figure in whom Cressida might like to confide; luckily I realised in time that my mother would find being thought of as 'older' and 'motherly' really offensive.

'Well, if she wants to talk to me she's welcome to,' said my mother lightly. It occurred to me that Cressida probably wouldn't see herself as being in the same boat as Mum. Whatever it was that had driven her to leave in such a hurry, and it had to be more than not liking Stefano's family and a sudden urge for an in-depth study of self-assertion, I didn't think she suffered from the same eternally itchy feet as my mother. Mum glanced over to see if I'd finished and then delved in her handbag for her cigarettes. My paternal grandmother once said that you could fault her daughter-in-law Virginia on many counts (particularly her fidelity), but never on her manners.

We caught up on the most important bits of each other's gossip over our coffee – to my relief two partners seemed to be satisfying my mother's need for variety perfectly. I filled her in on my news – most importantly that no matter what she might have heard I was *not* having a hot romance with my ex-stepbrother.

'What a shame for you,' she said, leaning back in her chair and blowing a smoke ring into the air.

'Don't you start as well,' I said grumpily. 'I've already

had Katie telling James that I've been panting over him since I was fifteen.'

'Katie has never known when a discreet white lie is just the ticket,' said my mother with a reminiscent look in her eyes. (Obviously Katie still wasn't completely forgiven for a certain indiscretion committed when she was six.) Mum got up, brushing a stray crumb or two off her skirt. 'Come on, get yourself unpacked a bit and then we'll go and find Cressida.'

Mission Contact Stefano was a bit of a non-starter, a resounding failure in fact. Madame Blanc did not allow her guests to telephone abroad from the hotel so we spent ages buying a single packet of mints or one three-franc stamp and paying with a hundred-franc note so we'd have loads of small coins for the telephone only to discover that all the telephones we could find took telephone cards. We found a *tabac*, bought a card, went back to the telephone boxes, which having been empty were naturally now full, with queues. When Cressida finally got to the head of one, she couldn't reach Stefano on any of the numbers she tried. His mobile was switched off and she didn't want to leave a message with the bland-voiced woman at the answering service to tell him that in fact she hadn't run off with her former boyfriend but had gone for other reasons. She felt much the same about the answering machines in Derbyshire and the flat in London.

After the fourth try she began to look moist-eyed and trembly-lipped so my mother hastily asked if she would mind if we went along to Mum's favourite shoe shop where they were keeping a couple of pairs for her while she made up her mind which she wanted. Cressida was indeed most happy to have her mind taken off her troubles by a visit to a shoe shop. We staggered out an hour later leaving half the stock of the shop, tried and rejected, on the ground behind us. The other half was seemingly in boxes hanging from Cressida's arms. We dumped the parcels at the apartment and then to show that we weren't complete Philistines went to see the Impressionists at the Musée d'Orsay. Cressida even managed to forget her nail-biting preoccupation for a while as we each tried to decide which of the pictures we'd take home if we were allowed to take one off the wall and became positively heated in favour of our own choices.

Cressida got the same stalemate when she tried to telephone again after we left the museum. While I was choosing a postcard of Les Deux Magots to send to Daniel I flippantly suggested that perhaps she should send Stefano a postcard too. Maybe a Renoir or, if that was too exciting, a nice calming Monet instead. 'Do you think I should?' Cressida asked seriously, looking as if not having to speak directly to him was decidedly appealing. 'He might find it a little insulting, mightn't he?'

'Very, I should think,' said Mum, giving me a quelling glare. 'Never mind, Cressida, you'll find him at home soon.'

Unfortunately she didn't. She had declared herself starving so we removed to a café and ordered coffee and patisserie, sitting at a table on the pavement, not for the pleasure of being outside under a lowering grey sky but so that Cressida and I could feel ourselves being thoroughly French. My mother, not needing to make these gestures, sat with a resigned expression on her face and the collar of her coat pulled up around her ears. After nibbling a quarter of a *chocolatine* Cressida declared that she was full up and, assuring the waiter who was hovering in the most solicitous way that it had been perfectly delicious but she couldn't manage another bite, she headed off for the telephone box on the corner of the square, brandishing her phone card as if it was a talisman. No wonder she keeps so slim, I thought enviously as I licked the last crumbs of my *tresse à vanille* off my fingers. 'Oh, good, she's got through,' I said to Mum as I saw Cressida's head begin to start moving in the way it does when someone is speaking. But seconds later she had replaced the receiver and was coming back towards us with a white, shocked face.

Mum got up and put an arm around her, guiding her to a chair. 'What did he say to you?' she asked.

Cressida shook her head. 'There wasn't any answer again, so I rang Viola. I thought she could give him a message.' Her eyes began to fill with tears and she sniffed delicately. 'Stefano's already spoken to her. He says that I've damaged what is most precious in the world to him and he'll never forgive me for what I've done!' A single tear traced its path down her cheek. The waiter, who had hovered straight back the moment Cressida retook her chair, dashed forward holding out a handful of paper napkins. It was only a stern look from my mother that prevented him from gently dabbing at the tear himself. Cressida took some and wiped her eyes, smiling a watery thank you. The waiter looked as if he had just won the Loto. 'I don't know what to do! I can't talk to him if he's going to be like that, can I?' she asked, eyes swimming again.

My eyes met Mum's. I began to wonder how serious Cressida's precipitate departure from Hurstwood House had been. Rather than a final *coup de grâce* for her marriage, had it been more along the lines of a cry for help? She did seem prone to dramatic gestures. So did Stefano, come to that. They were well suited. Mum patted her on the shoulder. 'It's not uncommon for men to behave like that when they believe their wife has run off with someone else,' she said gently. 'So far as he's concerned you've just thrown away your marriage and so he's lashing out.'

Cressida sat up a bit, looking encouraged. 'Do you think that's what he meant by the thing he holds most precious in the world?' she asked.

'Of course,' I said firmly. 'You just have to look at him to see how much he adores you. He'd forgive you anything – except having an affair with James.'

Cressida looked as if the sun had just come out from behind her own particular cloud. 'Anything?' she echoed, eyes shining. 'You really believe that?' She sucked on her nail, her exhilaration dying a little. 'I wish I could be sure of that, but maybe I've left it too long,' she said soberly with another of her lightning changes of mood. She smiled bravely as if about to step into the dentist's chair. 'We'll see after I've spoken to him, won't we? But I expect I shan't be able to get him until after the weekend now, he seems to have switched off his mobile and he's not at home. I'll have to ring him on the office phone on Monday.'

There didn't seem to be anything else to do. I hoped that in the meantime Stefano wouldn't get too impatient at the lack of news and kept his hands off his wife's supposed lover. James sounded as if he was fervently hoping much the same when I rang him later on from Mum's flat before we went out for supper. I tried my hardest to be charitable – well, fairly hard – and to attribute his grumpy reaction after hearing my news to tension at being followed everywhere by the detectives, who were apparently still sticking to him like a pair of well-trained gun dogs. At least, as I pointed out, once Stefano realised that Cressida was in Paris and his detectives could confirm that James was in London all the time, he'd know that James wasn't having it off with his wife. Not necessarily, James informed me coldly. There was no reason to think that Stefano was going to be any more logical and reasonable than he'd shown himself already. I told him not to look on the dark side. He said that it was all right for me, swanning around Paris enjoying myself, to make silly and puerile remarks, but he was up against it and couldn't afford to indulge in such rank stupidity. The conversation went sharply downhill from there on.

'You two haven't changed much,' said Mum as I put the phone down with unnecessary force, 'though a couple of years ago you'd have been calling him names, so maybe Jane was right and you are mellowing towards each other!' She smartly left the room to change before I could commit matricide.

Mum sensibly chose a little neighbourhood restaurant with a largely female staff, so Cressida's rather lachrymose behaviour during dinner didn't have too drastic an effect on the service of meals to the other diners. She picked at her food and talked of Stefano to such an extent that I thought I'd scream if I heard his name mentioned once more. Fortunately Mum adroitly diverted her by planning a massive shopping expedition for tomorrow and Cressida was able to forget her woes temporarily in the pleasurable anticipation of doing serious damage to her credit card. I stayed out of the discussion about exactly which shops were to be hit, I was too broke to do anything more than window-shopping. Besides I was doing some serious thinking.

Halfway through dinner, luckily after I'd finished my *magret de canard* so my appetite wasn't spoiled, one of those stray film-like memories, exact in every detail, popped up for some reason. It was of Cressida in the telephone booth as she tried Stefano and then rang Viola. She had been standing side on to me so I'd seen her hands flashing around as she tapped out the numbers and I'd thought vaguely that perhaps it wasn't very wise to walk around even in respectable areas of Paris wearing two such large diamond rings. I was sure she had only dialled once. Well, nearly sure. I became less certain each time I thought about it, but had she in fact even tried to contact Stefano? It was pretty odd that a man like him should make himself incommunicado. No, not odd, downright unbelievable. Apart from anxiously awaiting news about Cressida, and presumably reports on what James was doing, businessmen like him, with fingers in loads of rather dubious pies, need to be able to be contacted at all times. Surely he wouldn't just rely on his message service? So why was she lying about trying to contact him? Probably to get me off her back. Maybe she was frightened to speak to him. But why? All she'd done was go to a seminar Stefano would dismiss as a waste of time, hardly a capital crime, and spend a lot of money, which I shouldn't think was anything unusual. I reckoned he'd happily forgive her both once he knew that she wasn't shacked up with James.

So *why* did she prefer him to believe that she was committing adultery rather than speak to him?

CHAPTER 12

'Gosh, you don't get much room in these trains, do you?' asked Cressida as we eased ourselves into our seats on the TGV to Bordeaux.

'There's more space than on the average aeroplane,' I said, doing an automatic check through my handbag for the umpteenth time to see if I had all the necessaries: ticket, voucher for the car hire, driving licence, passport in its pocket and not in my bedside drawer at Mum's, etc.

'Is there? I never fly economy,' said Cressida. There was no answer to that. Possessors of Gold Cards just don't understand how users of the ordinary variety can find the difference between fares of vital importance, even when the said Gold Card has stopped working in French credit card machines. 'Eet ees zee swipe,' the assistant had explained with a dazzling smile, which didn't leave us any the wiser. But it was now *my* credit card that was paying for the pair of us since Cressida had run her other card up to the limit buying a very eye-catching lined raincoat. Well, she was cold, she'd said.

'How far away from Bordeaux are we going to be?' she asked as I sat down.

'About forty kilometres, in the depths of the country. I'm afraid you're going to be dreadfully bored.'

'Oh, that doesn't matter,' she replied airily. 'I've got my driving licence with me so I can take the hire car while you're working and explore, but do you think the people at Freddie French will mind my coming along?' she asked doubtfully.

Fifty percent delighted and fifty percent ranging from not very to highly displeased, according to their sex, I should think. The last thing I'd intended was to take Cressida with me to the conference. Even if she'd agreed to it I didn't want her to return to England without making sure that she told Stefano the truth about James so I'd been thinking hopefully along the lines of leaving her safely in Paris under Mum's wing; she could have moved into the tiny spare room, and Mum could have gently bullied her into doing the right thing. I thought it a brilliant idea as Mum and Cressida had loads in common, primarily a passion for shopping. I like shopping too, but my enjoyment is frequently tempered by excess of spare tyre. The essential factor for a good time in the changing room is to feel thin; slimness is a state of mind and has little to do with your actual measurements. Cressida's got the sort of figure that looks good in a sack and my mother is blissfully convinced that she has too, so they made a good pair. But it would have been more sensible to suggest to Mum that she have Cressida to stay before we had a drink with Hervé, the weekend half of Mum's liaisons. She looked at me with raised eyebrows and said, 'Darling, you know I would do nearly anything for you, but no. Not this. Definitely no.'

I have to admit that it was the first time I'd ever heard a man say '*Enchanté*' and sound as if he meant it with all his heart. 'I can control Hervé,' Mum went on with a touch of grimness, 'but Christophe is very susceptible. Frankly, darling, I don't need that sort of competition. And from someone twenty years younger than me.' (Nearer twenty-five I would have said, but who am I to challenge my mother's mathematics?) So Cressida, with that sweetness and pliability of temperament that she seemed to show about everything other than contacting her husband, readily agreed that a few days in the south-west might be fun. My initial plan had been to park her somewhere in Bordeaux and leave her to sight-see, but that was scuppered by the Gold Card débâcle. Even my mother, who had been watching Cressida's shopping progress with an envy tantamount to awe, agreed it was quite impossible to leave someone of that profligate tendency alone if one was going to have to pick up the bill at the end of the week. So lucky Cressida was coming with me to the Moulin des Deux Ponts and I hoped, much more fervently than her, that the Freddie French contingent weren't going to be too displeased. I was hoping even more fervently, but I feared hopelessly, that this wouldn't get back to Darian either. I'd worry about that later.

As the train trundled slowly over the bridge and into the station in Bordeaux the sun came out from behind lowering clouds, bathing all the buildings along the curve of the river front in a yellowish light. Church spires pierced the sky line, towering over elegant eighteenth-century houses that had changed little in two hundred years. If you half closed your eyes to block out the stream of traffic going both ways it was possible to imagine that you were looking at a scene from ages ago. Cressida craned forward, staring with round eyes. 'It's like Stefano's picture, isn't it?' she asked in a voice that had a distinct wobble to it. 'I don't think he's ever been here, he'd love this.'

I reached out and patted her hand comfortingly. 'You're obviously terribly unhappy without him. Don't you think that perhaps . . .'

My voice died away as she shook her head, but I thought with perhaps less vigour than she'd used previously. Mum had said bluntly after dinner that first evening that the sooner Cressida was persuaded to go back to her husband the better. Anyone who talked so endlessly about someone was obviously completely potty about them. I hadn't agreed with her then. Twenty-four hours later I was coming around to the idea. At least it would mean I'd stop hearing his name every second word. But before I could even start persuading her to go back to him I needed to find out why she seemed to be so alarmed about contacting him. I'd tried to call her bluff when she declared she was sure he'd refuse to speak to her by saying that I'd ring him myself and then hand the phone over to her. But she just said it would make him even more angry with her if he discovered he had been tricked. It sounded completely reasonable; so reasonable, in fact, that I was still not absolutely sure if she was pulling a fast one or not.

'Maybe tomorrow when you've tried him at his office?' I said.

She nodded dismally. 'But it's no good, I can't go back. You don't understand. Things are too bad. And he wants... Oh, I can't tell you this now,' she said with a sigh. 'We're arriving.'

Blast it! I'd been impatient for this journey to end for the last two hours and now it had done five minutes too early, I thought in irritation as I started getting our bags down from the overhead rack. Who knew when Cressida was going to be in a confiding mood again?

Certainly I wasn't in the mood for an exchange of confidences once we got into our hired Renault Twingo. Cressida, who was supposed to be map reading, was rubber necking in every direction, saying, 'Look at that! Isn't that pretty?' then taking a quick look at the map and saying in a vague voice, 'Oh, I think we go down that road on the left. Oh, sorry, I didn't see it was a No Entry. What do you think that building with the roof like an onion is?'

My head was jerking backwards and forwards like a petrified turkey while I practised driving on the wrong side of the road in four lanes of traffic where even elderly women in rusty 2CVs were switching lanes at high speed and cutting me up. I surrendered any idea of taking even part of our journey on the autoroute and instructed Cressida, in a voice clipped by terror, to find a way cross country. Just before I got to the point of threatening to strangle her, she concentrated for long enough to direct me on to the right bridge over the river and roughly towards where we were supposed to be going. We came up behind a huge agricultural vehicle that looked as if it had just left a sci-fi movie and was going at about twenty miles an hour. It was too wide to pass safely so I had a reasonable excuse to slow down and let the sweat dry off my hands.

The sun had disappeared as soon as we got out of the train and fat little raindrops were beginning to leak out of the sodden grey sky. I hoped this wasn't a portent for the next four days but had a nasty feeling that the weather forecast I'd glimpsed in someone's paper on the train had large black clouds with lines coming out of them plastered all over this part of France. 'It's a good thing I bought myself that raincoat in Paris,' said Cressida, echoing my thoughts. 'I'm probably going to need it.' She glanced down at the brochure on her lap. 'I wonder if there are any decent walks near the hotel. It looks really pretty.'

It was. It was a converted watermill right on the edge of quite a fair-sized river, built of newly restored and cleaned honey-coloured stone, with red wooden shutters at all the windows. It was going to be lovely to sit in the shade of a large tree at one of the wooden tables dotted around the lawns, sipping a glass of the local wine and watching the gentle river, while fishermen sat in one of the huts on the opposite bank, gossiping and enjoying the occasional Pastis. In the summer. Right now the rain dripping off the leaves meant you'd need a full scuba diving outfit to sit anywhere and any self-respecting fisherman was going to be ensconced in the nearest bar talking about the one that got away.

But even in winter it was still pretty, if a little damp. We parked the car and made a dash for the door, dodging the puddles spreading over the tarmac. Luckily, despite

Cressida's map reading, we were the first to arrive. Darian had been very insistent that I help everyone settle in. I didn't believe that twenty-three of the country's finest sales reps really needed me to babysit them but I wasn't going to dispute orders, not openly anyway. Perhaps the others had had as much difficulty as we did in finding the two-kilometre *chemin rural* to the hotel which led off a minor road that led off another minor road. The hotel had included a helpful map. Unfortunately that had neglected to include one of the minor roads.

The assistant manager who spoke English to whom I'd talked before had departed on Friday on maternity leave. The manager had been so overcome at the idea of the money he could make from the thirty or so English eccentrics who were mad enough to come and stay when the hotel would normally be closed for the off, off season that he'd persuaded himself he would do as a stand in English speaker. He was wrong. His English bore little resemblance to any language I'd ever heard before. Knowing that the responsibility for this would somehow be laid at my door, I thanked whatever deity it was up there who had influenced my mother into refusing to give Cressida a billet for the week. I might even be able to get away with bringing her here after all, I thought hopefully, as I enrolled her as chief interpreter. She seemed rather pleased about it, saying that having something to do would take her mind off things. Putting her to work almost made up for having to share a room with her, not that I disliked her or suspected her of any dubious personal habits, just that with someone else there I wouldn't be able to be my usual incredibly untidy self.

Cressida was right about having something to do. Within half an hour she was embroiled in discussions – well, disputes actually – with the manager over those who claimed that they had booked a single room and were being made to share (too bad, there were no more rooms as we'd already discovered), those who insisted that a sit up hip bath didn't count as a proper bath, the grousing about the lack of blankets, the bolster pillows, and the slight smell of damp which hung over everything despite the brow-mopping level of the heating. Those grumbles were nothing compared to the howling level of complaint that arose when one of the wives (who had come along for a nice holiday in France and was furious to discover that it was raining) glanced at the menu for dinner on the wall and saw there were no vegetarian options. These were demanded but the chef considered himself an artiste of *la cuisine du terroir* and since vegetarian options don't feature in the cooking of the *Grande Sud-Ouest* he had absolutely no intention of providing them. Neither was he prepared to do low-cal meals for the two dieters who insisted these were now quite normal in any conference hotel in England. This provoked some impressive Gallic shrugging and muttering about *Sacrés rosbifs* and other comments on the state of British cooking which Cressida declined to translate. He was in such a state of offended culinary sensibility that it took her quite a quarter of an hour of eyelash fluttering and assuring him that his *pâté maison* proved he was indeed a master of his craft before he calmed down and graciously agreed to provide omelettes and undressed salads for those who were mad enough to want them.

'You're worth your weight in gold,' I said to her gratefully once we'd managed to make our escape and were slithering up the stairs towards our bedroom before we could be embroiled in another dispute. 'I don't know what I'd have done on my own.'

'Oh, thank you,' she said, going pink with pleasure. 'I was so afraid that I was being a real pain in the neck hanging around like this. I'm just glad I can do something useful.'

Of course I immediately started feeling guilty. I knew I hadn't been particularly gracious about having her with me all the time, and she was making me feel even worse by being so nice about it. I was going to have to make a bit more of an effort, and not let it show when I got irritated with her indecisiveness over whether she could ring Stefano just now (there was always some good reason why she shouldn't) or perhaps it would be better if she were to talk to her mother or one of her sisters and get them to ring him instead? (There was always a good reason why she shouldn't do that either.) It was now nearly six days since Stefano had burst into my office vowing vengeance on James and so far all he had to go on was my assurance that James had had no part in it. I couldn't see my word satisfying the patience of a volatile Italian for long. Well, it hadn't, had it? Look at the detectives. But if Cressida continued making excuses to avoid speaking to her husband I wondered how long it would be before he cracked completely, especially if that journalist went on trying to embroider a completely ficti-tious story. I looked at Cressida as she flung herself on her bed and lay down with a sigh of relief, and wondered exactly what had gone on. There had to be more than just a desire to find herself and be her own person. From what I could see Cressida didn't particularly mind not being her own person, she was essentially a pliant personality and quite happy most of the time if someone else led the way. So what were these annoyingly close-mouthed references to Stefano's 'demands' about? My irrepressible imagination had already created several unlikely scenarios, but I couldn't believe that the 'unreasonable demands' were of the type my great-grandmother would have referred to in a hushed voice when she was safely alone among her married female friends. Maybe our sharing a room would be a bonus after all, there's nothing like an after lights out chat for extracting confidences. I began to unpack and nobly, out of contrition for my former snappishness, allowed her to have three of the five coat hangers.

'Do you think I should change into this for dinner?' asked Cressida, holding up a lilac dress made of jersey so fluid and fine it seemed to drip through her fingers like water.

I thought of how she'd looked in it when she'd bought it yesterday, the material clinging to and flattering every curve, and shook my head decisively. 'No.'

Her face fell. 'Yes, I suppose I have put on a bit of weight recently. I can't think why, I haven't been eating much.'

'I didn't mean that!' I said quickly. 'It's just that half the wives are in a bad enough mood already due to being miles from any decent shops, not to mention vegetarian Mrs Bayliss and her gripes. The last thing they need is you walking in and knocking the spots off the lot of them! I know it's not possible for you to look plain but can't you choose something that makes you a bit less stunning?'

She giggled. 'Well, you don't exactly belong with your head in a paper bag yourself, and I can't see you bringing out the sackcloth and ashes.'

I sighed. 'I might not be in the mirror-cracking league, but whatever I'm in no one's tongue hangs out when I go past! And if you wear that several will, I can promise you. That dress is strictly X-certificate.' I made a pretence of arranging the contents of my make up bag – for the first time in its existence – and said casually, 'It's the sort of thing you'd put on if you wanted to get back with someone. No man could resist it.'

There was silence and I began to wonder if I'd really put my extra large foot in it. Then she said softly, with a catch in her voice, 'Yes, Stefano would love it,' and laid it down gently on the bed. I felt like a real heel when I saw the brightness of her eyes but perhaps it was no bad thing if she was reminded from time to time just how much she was missing him. She was very quiet as she put her hair in a single thick pigtail and got out a suede skirt and a russet-coloured jumper that did nothing to disguise the fact that she was a thousand times prettier than it was fair for anyone to be, but at least she wasn't going to look as if she was actively on the prowl.

I could feel the atmosphere simmering with discontent as soon as we set foot downstairs. Everybody was tired after a long journey (I thought regretfully of Le Touquet), and wanted respectively a drink and then dinner. The beer drinkers were put out because the lager was thin European pigswill (actually the term they used was considerably ruder), and the local dry white wine didn't go down at all well with those who fancied a glass of German Riesling. And the chef, who was still sulking over being asked by culinary barbarians to be a traitor to his art, had tossed his blow dried locks and declared that the work involved in taking the crispy bacon lardons out of his *salade composée* for the vegetarians meant that he was going to have to put back the serving of dinner by at least an hour if not more. The bar didn't sell crisps or peanuts. The shopping contingent had discovered that most of the shops in the local town were closed on a Monday and if they wanted to do any serious spending of money tomorrow they'd have to go to Bordeaux. 'As if I'd dare go on any road where there are French!' sniffed one. 'You can't tell what side they're going to be on.' Only the sales director was full of vim, vigour and in a generally good mood as he had every reason to be. He'd only travelled for about an hour, he'd watched a splendid rugby match yesterday and his team had won. He'd detoured via a local château on the way and was already halfway down a bottle of their perky little red while he made up his mind whether it would be worth buying a case or two to take back to England. I despatched Cressida to the kitchen to go and flirt with the chef and see if she could persuade him to hurry up a bit, and after arming myself with a satisfactorily large glass of wine did my duty and went and joined several stroppy-looking men and women who were huddled ostentatiously around the large stone fireplace, holding out their hands to the blaze.

'Whose flaming idea was it to come to bloody France?' asked one of the disappointed beer drinkers. I kept discreetly quiet, fearing lynching. 'Blooming stupid if you ask me. We'd have been better off in Torquay like we planned originally. At least you'd have been able to get something decent to drink,' he added bitterly.

'And it's not what I'd call cosy either,' said a sharp-nosed woman. 'All these stone floors. You'd think they could afford a decent bit of carpet at least.'

'I think they have the stone floors to keep the place cool in the summer,' I explained.

'But it isn't the bleeding summer, is it? Unless we've gone to the South Pole by accident,' said another, chortling loudly at his own wit. Someone had to, no one else was.

Cressida returned with the welcome news that Alexandre had graciously conceded that perhaps he could have dinner ready in about half an hour, providing that no one else made any completely unreasonable requests that disturbed the flow of his creativity.

'Alexandre?' I queried with raised eyebrows. 'Quick worker, aren't you? He'll be naming a dessert in your honour soon.'

Cressida grinned. 'We're having it for lunch tomorrow!'

The sales director had at last turned his attention from sampling Château Gonzan for long enough to realise that his troops were becoming seriously discontented and began to devote himself to jollying everyone up. Since he hadn't risen to be head of sales without a talent for getting on people's right side he did it pretty well. He radiated bonhomie and insisted that everyone had another drink. After all, this was the first evening, we were all entitled to treat it like a holiday, we could work tomorrow (even if we had to do it through crippling hangovers). As a final mood sweetener he announced the company would pick up the whole of the bar tab tonight. Twenty-three sales reps set about getting drunk with a vengeance.

All things considered the next two days went off fairly well, even if I was nearly at the point of committing the heinous crime of clonking one or other of the Freddie French team or their partners on several occasions. No one had thought to get continental adapters for the audio visual equipment that had been laboriously imported from England. Naturally it was I who had to dash to the nearest town to try and find a job lot of plugs. And then go back for a set of screwdrivers. There was a running stream of petty complaints: they didn't understand tea here and served it with hot milk, there was no de-caf, no Diet Coke, the electricity had a habit of fusing at regular intervals. Though there had been general unspoken agreement to stop complaining about the food after one quibble was followed by a highly audible plate-throwing session in the kitchen, each crash accompanied by an equally audible '*Merde!*'

And there was the rain which never let up. It either dribbled or it came down in torrents so heavy that it was difficult to see as far as the opposite bank of the river. Standing pools of water gathered all over the parking area at the front of the hotel as the river rose to lap the edges of the tarmac. The manager advised us to move our cars to the higher ground behind the hotel where we were assured the water never reached. Strangely even his limited command of English deserted him when he was asked if the water ever got into the hotel itself, and he broke into voluble French insisting that the Moulin was never *inondable*. 'In that case I wonder what that is,' whispered Cressida pointing to a tide mark six inches from ground level around the walls in the lobby.

'Did you manage to get hold of Stefano?' I asked casually as we were both getting ready for bed on Tuesday evening. I had a feeling I already knew the answer. Cressida looked up from where she lay sprawled on the bed stroking the hotel cat, a beautiful velvety grey Chartreuse with round yellow eyes, who was much enjoying the procedure judging by the rumblings that were filling the room. She shook her head. 'He wasn't there.'

I glared at her suspiciously and bit my tongue just in time to stop myself from demanding what the hell she was up to. Direct confrontation only made her cry. I'd discovered that already. 'Well, do you think you had better write to him then?' I suggested. 'Explain that James had nothing to do with your leaving. Tell him—'

'Tell him what?' she demanded, sitting up straight and disturbing the cat who gave an indignant yowl as it was shifted sideways. 'You don't understand, Laura, it's too late. He's not going to believe I only went off to do one of Arabella's courses now, is he? He's going to think I'm hiding something and if it's not James it must be something else!'

'Are you?' I asked directly.

She bent her head and to its displeasure fiddled with the cat's ears. 'No,' she said quietly. I didn't believe her. She raised her head and looked at me with wide grey eyes, limpid and guileless. 'The only things I'm hiding are personal, married things. You know, the sort of rubbish that accumulates between couples. Things that aren't very important and don't have any bearing on this.'

I believed her even less. James, imparting a rare piece of brotherly advice, once told me never to trust someone who looks you directly in the eye. They are aiming to deceive. And a master of the art like him should know. What was Cressida hiding?

CHAPTER 13

I awoke to the familiar sound of the rain striking the stonework outside our window. There was only the dimmest of grey light creeping around the edges of the shutters so I rolled over to readjust my pillow, knowing I could count on at least another half-hour in bed. I wriggled deeper into the warm heap of bedclothes, half listening to the wet slooshy sounds that seemed to be coming from just under the window, and conjured up a daydream about Daniel. It was a familiar one where we go through lots of exciting adventures and vicissitudes before he realises where his heart truly lies, though strangely enough this didn't enthral me as much as it used to and I found myself rushing through a lot of the bits I used to linger over – turning his profile, tossing his head meaningfully and so on – and getting on to the more interesting action bits (by which I don't mean action as in the women's novels on the top shelf of the newsagent, but action in the best tradition of female world savers. My daydreams always have a very large canvas). My mind was wandering slightly from a significant meeting with Daniel in the shadow of the Kremlin (I'm a great mental traveller too), when it occurred to me that the wet slooshy sounds really did sound as if they were under our window. I abandoned Daniel to the Red Guards, he could always be rescued later, and kneeling on the end of the bed pushed open the shutters and peered outside.

I squinted slightly into the grey light and saw that the river seemed wider than yesterday. I blinked to clear my head. It *was* wider, a lot wider. The trees on the bank opposite now had their trunks in the water and as I craned my head to take a closer look I saw that a dark grey sheet of water, glinting like unpolished metal under the lightening sky, had crept right up to where the hill rose sharply on the other side. In contrast to the tranquillity of the flood water the middle of the river was a fast-moving torrent, carrying a fallen tree faster than I'd have been able to run. It wouldn't be very nice to fall into that, I thought with a shiver, as I leaned out of the window then prudently withdrew a little so that there was no chance of tumbling out into the water lapping against the walls of the hotel. Against the *walls*?

A quick experiment with my bedside light proved that yet again we had no electricity. Ignoring Cressida's sleepy queries I pulled on my tatty old dressing gown and slippers and padded along the corridor to the top of the stairs to peer down to the lobby and reception. The stone floor was shining – with water that was already lapping around the ankles of Alexandre and the manager as they frantically splashed around trying to plug the gaps around the door where the flood was trickling in.

'Oh, hell!' I said out loud. 'There's going to be the devil to pay for this.'

There was. From the fuss made by some of the party you'd have thought we'd been booked on to a cheap weekend excursion on the *Titanic*. Panic was in and stiff upper lips were out. It was in vain that the manager repeated time and time again that we could wait on the first floor in perfect safety for rescue by the *pompiers*, the general emergency service, who kept boats for just this sort of thing. He had to point out rather sharply that so far the mill had withstood two hundred years of being flooded and had not ended up down river in Bordeaux yet, so was unlikely to do so this time. A couple of gung ho types said that as the water was as yet barely a foot deep we could wade to safety. With a lot of expressive gestures the manager demonstrated what would happen to anyone who lost their footing in the floodwater. Bordeaux here we come. We meekly agreed to wait upstairs while the sales director, obviously afraid that the mutterings of 'Who's the bloody idiot who suggested this flaming place?' were going to rise to fully audible, organised the fittest men into salvaging as much of the wine cellar as they could carry. As Alexandre's first priority had been to save the contents of his kitchen we were going to be able to have a splendid picnic while we waited, though the manager looked distinctly askance at the only half joking suggestion from the rep for the North West that we break up a couple of the beds to make a fire.

Every time we went to the top of the stairs and looked down the water had risen a bit more. Within an hour it was lapping against the sixth step. The manager confessed that the building had been flooded many times before, its position near the mouth of a much larger river which made water back up into this valley made it particularly vulnerable, but this was unusual. It was all to do with the exceptionally heavy rainfall, the several smaller rivers which were bringing all their flood water here, and something called the co-efficients which mystified all of us, even the red-bearded sales rep for Cornwall who could usually be guaranteed to know about things that the rest of us didn't. We all nodded wisely and had another glass of red wine to keep the chill out.

It was several hours later and the novelty of being marooned was wearing off before we finally heard the welcome sounds of our rescuers. We rushed to the windows to watch two brawny young men, looking as if they were having the time of their lives, motoring up underneath one of the windows while a third instructed the manager to let down the rope fire escape ladder. He swarmed up it in a very macho way and scrambled inside. He informed us in a strong accent that his name was Jean-Baptiste and that he'd been chosen to guide us because his English was so good. I suspected it was actually because he had the best line in flirting (and out of a party of fit young Frenchmen that was quite something, believe me). Certainly even the most frightened woman tended to forget, as she gazed into his smouldering blue eyes, that she was entrusting herself to a wobbly rope ladder suspended over a lot of rushing water. It took quite a long time, what with the ditherers who froze half in and half out with one flailing foot kicking at the ladder while Jean-Baptiste muttered sweet nothings or barely concealed curses depending on what sex they were. The general idea was that the women would go first (I'm not sure all the men agreed with that, especially the ones who claimed they suffered from asthma and such like and shouldn't be kept in a damp, cold atmosphere, but Jean-Baptiste was calling the shots). In fact Cressida and I ended up being amongst the last as she declared we had to find the cat and take it with us since it was having kittens and needed looking after. I wondered who was going to have the enviable task of going down that ladder holding a no doubt highly displeased cat but obediently followed her as we searched each room. In a typically cat-like way she had concealed herself at the back of an unmade bed, almost invisible behind the tumbled covers, and didn't deign to let us know she was there. We only found her the second time around.

At first Jean-Baptiste refused flatly to have anything to do with lowering a cat in a shopping basket (the best carrier we could come up with) out of the window but when Cressida declared tearfully that in that case she wasn't going either, he pulled out a large white handkerchief from his pocket and said that of course he would be only too happy to oblige mademoiselle in anything she wanted. I just hope he found the dazzling smile Cressida bestowed on him sufficient reward for the deep gouges in his hands administered by the expectant mother.

We were offloaded on a grassy bank to join the others as the *pompiers* went back to get the last load. Most of the group were milling around uncertainly, those who'd been unwise enough to ignore the advice last night to move their cars were gazing appalled at the sight of roof top luggage racks just visible above the water level, young Patrick from marketing was worrying aloud how he was going to explain to the accounts department that he'd lost *all* the audio visual equipment, and someone else was speculating on the possibility of looters taking our luggage. Looters in wetsuits perhaps. Cressida stood alone, cuddling the cat, who with unusual gratitude for a feline was purring, while I watched a photographer from the local paper focusing his tele-photo lens on a spider-like figure climbing down the ladder (since it was one of the chip-butty-favouring reps it was rather a large spider) and getting a real live action photo of a rescue. It was going to look almost too good to be true. The rain had stopped about an hour ago, and the sky was filled with heavy, broken dark clouds which glimmered around the edges from the weak sun behind. It formed an almost Hollywood backdrop to the square bulk of the converted mill rising straight out of a deceptively placid-looking lake. Naturally enough the photographer was quick to seize on the photo opportunities of Cressida and the cat and insisted on taking several of the two of them, then more of them with Jean-Baptiste, who made sure he kept a safe distance, then even more of everyone. He seemed to think that the story of a whole lot of English who were crazy enough to book a conference by a river in February and then had to be rescued would be the sort of light item that would greatly amuse his readers. When I told him what the name of the company was he laughed so much that all three of his chins began to wobble. '*L'équipe française*,' he roared, digging the manager in the ribs and making further, very weak puns on the lines of the French team, the French contingent, watch out the English are coming even though they call themselves French, and other such jests which he seemed to find much funnier than anyone else did.

We were hustled off to the local village hall to join other refugees from the flood, where instead of a reviving cup of tea and a biscuit we were offered a fortifying plastic glass of wine and bread and *pâté*. The noise level was tremendous; tomorrow or the next day there was going to be the depressing business of cleaning reeking river mud out of houses, outbuildings and gardens. For now everyone was enjoying the excitement, competing to see who had the most dramatic story to tell and, as we could see, several were making short work of the copious quantities of food and drink laid out on trestle tables. The manager had taken charge of the cat to my relief, assuring Cressida that his mother would take good care of it and the kittens. Apparently even crossbred Chartreuse were very sought after so there would be no question of their meeting a nasty fate. I could see from Cressida's set jaw that if there'd been even a hint of anything untoward in store for them, she'd have insisted on smuggling cat and contents back to a kind home in England. And the first thing I would have known about it was when we were arrested at Customs.

It was generally agreed amongst the Freddie French lot that this year's sales conference was now officially over; the lone voice who suggested it might be possible to find somewhere else for the last day was firmly shouted down. The moment our luggage, only slightly damp around the edges, arrived Cressida and I sloped off, meanly deserting those who still had to deal with waterlogged cars, or were speculating and not doing anything about finding another place to stay.

We drove halfway to Bordeaux and then stopped at a

little hotel in the middle of a small market town where the only water in sight was running decorously along the gutters by the pavement. My ticket back to Paris wasn't for another two days and I didn't feel like paying to have it changed so we agreed that we'd take a holiday and just do some sightseeing the next day. It was also tacitly agreed that I wouldn't hassle Cressida about Stefano either, though I wasn't particularly happy about that. We had a really nice time; being able to poodle around on minor roads at my own speed meant that I finally got confident about driving on the right, though there was nearly a nasty incident with a removal van. I'm still sure I was in the right. Most of the towns and villages were still charmingly undeveloped and even if they had nothing of particular architectural importance in them, wandering around the narrow streets still felt as if you were entering some earlier age. We lunched off superb *cassoulet* and hearty red wine in a small café with a splendid view of a church, or rather I did. Cressida merely pushed her food around her plate saying that she wasn't very hungry. She looked desperately tired, with dark circles under her eyes and pale cheeks, though I have to say that all it did was make her look interestingly fragile whereas I, in that state, look as if I've recently been dug up. I didn't think she was sleeping well, she'd woken me up several times tossing and turning, but there was no point in asking her what the matter was. It was painfully obvious that she didn't want to discuss it.

I decided regretfully that I'd have to junk my plans for seeing Mum again and get Cressida back to the UK as quickly as possible. Once we returned to real life she wouldn't be able to go on procrastinating forever. If necessary I could even frog-march her around to James, detectives or no detectives, and get him to force her to pick up the telephone. I knew from experience how compelling he could be when he wanted you to do something. The only problem was that I had a gloomy feeling that Cressida's large tear-filled grey eyes would have exactly the same effect on him as they had on half the waiters in Paris. But we were going to have to do something. In my last brief call to James, the night before the flood, he'd sounded stressed and had muttered something about Stefano 'putting the pressure on', though he then went on in an infuriatingly masculine way to tell me not to worry about it. ('Your pretty little head' was left unsaid, but reverberated distinctly down the line.) In my nastier moments I thought that if Cressida went on putting off speaking to Stefano I'd tell him where she was so he could come and get her for himself. At least then we'd get something resolved. I never seriously thought of doing it, but it was comforting to consider it when my patience was being tried.

Cressida wasn't thinking very happy thoughts either. She stared morosely out of the window at the water-logged landscape, chin resting on her hand as we sped towards Paris in the TGV, eyes shadowed and heavy, though that was probably more to do with our early start than worry. Someone getting out at Poitiers had heard me speak English and offered me his copy of yesterday's *Daily Mail*. I glanced blearily at the headlines but couldn't concentrate, even on tabloidese, so I stuffed it in my tote bag to look at later.

At Tours a woman slid into the seat opposite us with her baby. I'm not usually that wild about babies in general, even those that are related to me in some way. Having a baby must trigger some strange gene in you that wasn't there before. I mean, you aren't born finding mashed peas in the hair funny and not disgusting. But this baby was something else. She was wearing the most splendid bow affair around her head, presumably to disguise the fact that there wasn't much hair underneath. The ends kept dropping over big, button black eyes so she would raise one chubby fist and push them out of the way, then give us an enormous toothy grin. Even Cressida came out of her mood of abstraction and began to smile back, and then play peepo which made the baby almost fall over backwards with delight. She slapped the table with her rattle and gave an enchanting giggle. Cressida did it again.

I got tired of playing games long before the baby did so I was secretly pleased when she and her mother got off at the next stop, though Cressida cast a wistful look after the departing pair. 'Wasn't she *gorgeous*? None of Viola or Portia's was as nice as that.'

'So that's where you get your skill at playing pat-a-cake,' I said.

She smiled. 'Yes. Isn't it funny how much prettier the babies seem to be over here?'

I can't say that I'd noticed, but the heavy sigh that accompanied her statement set bells ringing even in my befogged brain. Was this the problem? But surely Stefano had been talking about when the children came, I thought, confused, so he couldn't be refusing to let

Cressida have any. Oh, lord! Another possibility raised its head. You read about it all the time, don't you? Even people like me. As Cressida continued to look longingly out of the window in the direction of the now vanished baby I cleared my throat nervously and, desperately afraid I was about to put my foot in it, said carefully, 'Do you want to have a baby, Cressida?'

She turned her face towards me with a slightly surprised expression. 'Well, yes, I do. But it's all so difficult.'

'Can't the doctors help with problems these days?' I asked.

She stared at me in astonishment. 'What for?' she said indignantly. 'So far as I know I don't have anything wrong with me. Neither does Stefano for that matter!' she added furiously as if I'd just accused him of impotence.

I felt like going and hiding my burning face in the loo for a quarter of an hour. Talk about offending people. 'Look, I'm sorry, I just thought that when you said it was difficult . . .'

'That I was in need of IVF?' she finished for me. 'Well, I'm not.' She sighed again. 'It's all so *complicated*,' she said plaintively and began gazing out of the window again. I waited hopefully, praying that my silence would make her feel the need to rush in and fill it. To my faint surprise it worked. She turned tragic eyes towards me and said, 'You see, Stefano said before we even got engaged that he'd want me to start trying for a baby soon after we got married. He doesn't have any children from his first marriage, his wife kept miscarrying, and he's desperate for a family before he gets, as he puts it, too old to enjoy his own children. And I agreed that after six months I'd go off the pill and we'd see what happened.'

She began tracing invisible circles on the table top in front of her with the tip of her finger. 'I really meant it at the time, I was going to, but I didn't know what it would be like! I mean, he virtually forced me into saying I'd have a baby. Said he wouldn't marry me unless I agreed.' Her voice was indignant. 'I understand his wanting a baby, and I want one too – eventually – but I'm still young. There's lots of time. I think a promise that's been forced out of you like that doesn't really count. Don't you agree?'

I didn't know what to say. Actually I didn't think I did agree but I knew it wouldn't be sensible to say so. I kept my eyes down as I said, 'So what did you do?'

'I went off the pill,' she said promptly.

I raised my head and stared and her in astonishment. 'But you said . . .'

She tapped the side of her nose. 'I'm not always as stupid as I look! I knew I couldn't risk Stefano's ever finding them and the chances were, since I'm always leaving things about, he would, no matter how carefully I hid them, so I went off and had a coil put in. He had no idea!' She smiled at her own cleverness and then seeing my expression said defensively, 'I *had* to do it that way! I couldn't have told him. He'd have worn me down until I agreed to do exactly what he wanted. You see, I'm not strong like you.'

'Me?'

'You don't let people walk all over you. Look how you stood up to Stefano when he came into your office, I could never have done that. I can shout at people, lose my temper, but I'm no good at standing up to people.' So instead of standing up to Stefano, I thought, she provoked him instead. 'I only got interested in Arabella's course because I thought it might show me how to be firm with him. It was no bloody use at all! But it was too late by then.' She looked down at her lap and said in a low voice, 'He opened a letter from my gynaecologist by mistake. It asked me to contact him because there had been problems with my type of coil.'

'Oh,' I said inadequately.

'Quite,' said Cressida grimly.

'So that's what the big row you had before he went to Milan was all about?'

Cressida looked funny as if just the memory of that cataclysmic argument was enough to make her feel queasy. 'He's never, ever spoken to me like that before. He said that he'd never be able to trust me again. He even said,' she laughed harshly, 'that his mother was quite right when she said that I was completely unreliable and not fit to have care of so much as a hamster!'

'People say dreadful things when they're angry, and often don't really mean them.'

'He meant it!' she said indignantly. 'He said he was cutting off my allowance until I was pregnant, and he was going to send me back to Italy where I could have a peaceful time with his mother, contemplating my familial obligations! As if I was just some form of baby-producing machine!' she added loudly enough for a couple of people to turn around and look at her curiously. 'And that he would visit every week or so for a service until we had the desired result!'

I didn't dare ask her to speak in a lower tone in case she shut up completely. I sank down in my seat and hoped with all my might that no one in this carriage spoke English. 'Um, maybe he was just hurt and upset,' I said, afraid to say too much.

'Furious more like! He'd even taken himself off to a fertility clinic to get himself tested on the QT, see if it was his fault that I wasn't pregnant. That hit his pride where it hurt most and he blames it all on me,' Cressida said gloomily.

This was one of the rare occasions when I found myself fully in sympathy with Stefano. 'But what I can't understand, Cressida, is why you've decided you don't want a baby. I saw you with that one just now and you adored her. You looked like a natural!'

She smiled at me, pleased. 'Oh, do you think so?' Then her face fell. 'You see, I'm so frightened—'

'You don't want to believe those old wives' tales about being in agony for days on end,' I cut in reassuringly.

'You should hear what the old Contessa has to say about biting through the bedpost having Stefano!' Cressida said dryly. 'I'm not afraid of pain but—' She cleared her throat. 'I know perfectly well that Stefano didn't choose me for my scintillating conversation, my keen mind or because I can take an active interest in his business interests like his first wife did. Or for my child-bearing hips for that matter,' she added with a flash of spirit. 'He wanted me for my looks, and because I can talk to people and I'm a good hostess who can make people feel comfortable. I can even run a house pretty well and knock up some classy flower arrangements. But it's my looks that are the most important thing. Once I'm pregnant I won't be attractive any longer.' I stared at her in amazement. 'Everyone knows that men go off their wives when they're pregnant. Once their wife has lost her figure and is being sick each morning and demanding coal to eat they're haring off in search of the next bimbo with a twenty-two inch waist and large breasts that are for them alone, and not about to be devoted to the next generation!'

'That's complete rubbish!' I said. Surely Cressida couldn't really have so little confidence in herself that she believed she could lose Stefano's affection like that? Or have such a cockeyed way of thinking that she'd been prepared to risk losing his love by her deception? But a quick glance at her pretty, frowning face showed she was being absolutely sincere. 'Lots of men find their wives even more attractive when they're pregnant. My cousin Helena complained that her husband would never leave her alone and she found it quite exhausting.' Quite untrue since Helena was a vinegary spinster in her fifties but what does a little lie matter when it's in aid of curing a heavy bout of self-pity? 'And so what if the first thing that attracted Stefano to you was your looks? There's got to be something that draws people together in the first place.' She was still looking unconvinced so I began to elaborate on my theme, as usual rushing in where angels fear to tread and not thinking about what I was saying.

'Look at me, for instance. James didn't go straight to the top of my personal hunk parade the moment I saw him for his nifty way of valuing tables and his good results from university. It was what he looked like in a pair of over-tight Levi's that set me going. I couldn't have given a damn what his views on anything were or what he spoke about – in fact, since he spent a fair amount of time putting me in my place, I'd have been glad if he was conveniently dumb – all I wanted was to get my hands on his body. Though I was a bit vague about what I'd actually *do* with it once I had,' I admitted.

'And now you've found out,' said Cressida demurely. 'Worth waiting for, isn't it?'

I went bright red and turned quickly to stare out of the window until the heat left my face. I can't cope with this! I thought in panic. Being me, I was bound to say something in a minute that would show I'd never had anything more exciting than a grapple in a box hedge with James (yes, OK, that encounter stood pretty, actually very, high on my list of things to be remembered with a smile and a raised pulse rate). Perhaps I should talk about Daniel and just substitute James's name. I realised with a pang of dismay that for some reason I couldn't think of a single thing about Daniel that made me want to do a pleasurable squirm. Usually when I tried this I was wriggling around as if there were ants in my clothes. I must be very tired.

When in doubt change the subject, or at least get back to the subject before last. 'But, Cressida, if you get pregnant Stefano's going to love you even more, not less, because you'll be beautiful *and* the mother of what he wants most in the world after you.'

Her expression gave me hope that I'd struck a chord. Encouraged, I ploughed on. 'Can't you see how much Stefano must love you if despite your – um – not being frank on the birth control front *and* his being assured you were seen virtually having it off on the table in a public place, he still wants you back? I can't believe he – frankly he isn't exactly in the forefront of liberal thinking – would be prepared to have an adulterous wife back unless he adored her.' I held up my hand at her indignant exclamation. 'I know you didn't rush straight off to bed with James, but he doesn't. I bet he's already forgotten all that stuff about no credit cards and putting you in seclusion until you're in a fecund state!'

'Do you really think so?' she breathed, eyes wide and hopeful. 'I suppose he did have reason to be quite angry with me over the coil. I had broken a promise. But some of the things he said, and the threats he made . . .'

'I never said he was perfect.'

She giggled. 'He certainly isn't. I love him, really I do.' Her eyes were very wide. 'I know you won't be able to understand why I preferred him to James.' She was certainly right there. She coloured slightly and continued, 'Some of my so-called friends said it was because he's so rich, but that isn't true at all.' She frowned. 'Only of course it's a bit hard to imagine Stefano being Stefano if he was *poor*,' she added seriously. 'But he's not always easy to live with and then I get angry and do stupid things. Like flirting with James to provoke him.'

'Yes, probably best to leave that out in future,' I agreed. 'It seems to be the one way to make Stefano go completely ballistic.' To say nothing of exposing James to more temptation than was good for him.

She sighed heavily. 'Oh, I do so want to see him again.'

I felt lightheaded with relief. 'That's easy. All you have to do is ring him as soon as we get back to London.'

My relief had come too soon. Her face fell. 'I don't know if I can,' she whispered. 'There's something else, something I did that was *really* stupid . . .'

What now? I thought in exasperation. One thing this little expedition had shown me was that Relate would have to do without my services. I just wasn't cut out for this counselling lark. The temptation to grab the subject by the scruff of the neck and threaten to throttle her if she didn't spill the beans, all of them, right now, was just too strong. I unclenched my jaw, loosened my fists, arranged my mouth into a nice smiley position and said in what I hoped was a calm understanding tone, 'What's that? I'm sure it can all be sorted out.'

The speakers crackled into life with an announcement as Cressida said doubtfully, 'Maybe.'

I waited for her to amplify this unilluminating statement, then a woman poked her permed head around the back of the seat in front of us. 'Hey, honey, did you understand a word of what that said?' she asked in a strong American accent. 'I just can't get my little ol' head around this French they speak here. It doesn't sound at all like the tapes I had back home. Did they say that we were going to be late getting into Paris? I've got a train to catch, your Eurostar to London, and I just know it'll take at least an hour to cross Paris in a taxi, my travel agent told me so . . .'

She had to pause to draw breath so I cut in quickly with, 'It'll be faster on the Metro if you're worried about the time.'

The woman pulled a face. 'Honey, I went on the Metro before we left Paris and I couldn't get anyone to understand me when I asked if I was going in the right direction. They pretend they don't get my accent, but I think they're downright rude!'

Cressida pulled a face. 'The Parisians do have a reputation for that. Why don't you come with us? We're going to the Gare du Nord too.'

'Oh, honey, I would be so grateful, you can't imagine,' said the woman, getting up and coming to join us in the empty seat opposite. 'I've gotten so tired of being by myself all this time. Not that I don't appreciate the trip but I miss having someone to talk to . . .'

Oh, well, I might get Cressida to produce what I devoutly hoped would be the last piece of this puzzle on the train to London. That is if we didn't have Mrs Darleen Litsky from Idaho in the same carriage. Mrs Litsky was a widow and a thoroughly nice discreet woman. Not by so much as the flicker of an eyelid, did she betray that she must have been able to hear all the most embarrassing parts of Cressida's and my conversation. She had won a return ticket for two to London in a lottery at her workplace, plus train vouchers for travel all over Europe, journeys to be taken in the off season, hence her travelling around in the rain. She'd taken another widowed workmate with her, but on their first night in London they had decided to sample the delights of the genuine English pub opposite their hotel and the workmate suffered a *coup de foudre* in the unlikely shape of the portly barman of the Golden Apple. Being a sporting character Mrs Litsky had wished her friend well and set off for two weeks around Europe on her own. She was going to discover tonight whether passion had continued to blossom over the beer glasses and if her friend was going to stay to learn how to say, 'And what's yours, lover boy?'

We had been placed at opposite ends of the London train so parted with best wishes and an exchange of addresses and promises that Mrs Litsky would let us know what had happened with the great romance. 'I hope she does,' I said to Cressida. 'I'm tempted to go to the Golden Apple to take a look at Fred the great Romeo, aren't you?'

'Mmm,' agreed Cressida, leaning her head back against the seat and closing her eyes. I can take a hint so I got out my book, a Mary Higgins Clark, and the sandwich I'd bought at the station and settled down to read as we began to speed through northern France.

Cressida woke up as we were coming into a grey and grizzly English afternoon, no different from Bordeaux actually except the fields had hops in them instead of vines. 'I don't know why I'm always so tired these days,' she said, yawning.

'Stress, I expect,' I said, nose deep in my book. I'd just got to the part about twenty pages from the end where it gets so tense that your heart starts to race and your mouth dries as you turn the page in anticipation of what's coming next. If Cressida wanted to tell me what was on her mind, too bad. I'd got to finish this first.

'Can I read that paper of yours?' she asked.

'Help yourself,' I said, pushing it over without raising my eyes, 'but it's only yesterday's.'

'Doesn't matter. It's got to be more amusing than my book, and I enjoy the gossip page.'

I grunted and there was silence for a minute, broken

only by the rustling of newspaper and the turning of pages until I heard her say, 'Oh, no! Laura, look at this!'

'At what?' I said a tad grumpily. The heroine had been buried alive in a coffin, for heaven's sake, and Cressida probably only wanted to point out something about one of her friends in the gossip columns.

'This,' she said, pointing.

I looked.

'Blimey, that's not going to go down well, is it?' It was the understatement of the year. There, under a heading of 'The French Contingent get rained out' was a winsome picture of Cressida, holding the hotel cat, against a splendidly theatrical background of cloud-tossed sky and flooded hotel. I was, unfortunately, clearly recognisable, standing a few paces behind her. The picture caption was surprisingly accurate for this sort of thing, saying that the Freddie French sales conference had had to be rescued from the floods that were causing havoc in south-west France and plucky Cressida Buonotti had refused to leave until, in the best British tradition, she had found the hotel cat, which, added heartstring pulling here, was about to have kittens.

'I suppose that photographer must be a stringer, or whatever you call it, for some of the English papers,' I said. 'You can't accuse him of not being able to recognise a good story when he sees it, and for it to have been you to have rescued the cat—'

'Why?' she asked blankly.

She was a bit thick sometimes. 'Do you think the *Mail* would have been as happy to print a large picture of Mrs Harris, the dieter with the salt problem and the dripping nose?' I demanded. 'It's because you're so pretty, you dollop!' She smiled faintly and I sighed, determinedly trying to look on the bright side. 'At least Darian will be pleased.' It was nice to know someone would be.

'Why?' asked Cressida with a palpable lack of interest.

I enlightened her anyway. It took my mind off the main problem for a little longer. 'It's the real tops if we manage to get a mention for one of our clients in the dailies, especially a company like Freddie French.'

'But that story isn't going to do anything to help the sales of baby products,' protested Cressida.

She was never going to make it in PR. 'Most of the mentions we get for our clients are of no practical use whatsoever, but the next time the Marketing Director is empire building, he'll say he needs a much larger budget than all the other departments so he can pay this red hot agency that gets him mentions in the daily press. And by that time everyone will have forgotten that the story was really about a pretty woman and a cat.'

'Except Stefano,' Cressida said gloomily, bringing the subject smartly back to her own problems.

'What can he say?' I asked with a leaden-footed attempt at lightness. 'Not even Stefano in his darkest imaginings could believe you ran away from him to go and do naughty things with the entire Freddie French sales conference!'

She laughed dutifully. 'But this has all got so complicated! It started off being so simple. We had a row and . . . I never *meant* to leave him for good,' she wailed. 'But I'm going to have to now, I'm never going to be able to explain all of this!'

My heart hit my boots. Damn it! Half an hour ago I almost had her sitting in Stefano's lap, kissing and making up. I took a deep breath and tried to look as if it was nothing. 'Don't then. What have you got to explain – that you went to France with a female friend? Where's the harm in that?' I embroidered on this theme for quite a bit, she was so worried and tense that for once I nobly didn't mention my own pressing concern; viz, that I had assured Stefano I didn't know where Cressida was. I was quite sure he was going to consider it entirely beside the point that when I spoke to him I *hadn't* known; that all too clear photograph of me with Cressida was completely damning. He was going to go ape. I could only hope he didn't lose his rag entirely. I looked at my watch surreptitiously, willing the train to speed its crawling progress through the gardens of Kent so that we could get to Ashford and I could find a phone to ring James.

When I finally got hold of him I rather wished I hadn't bothered. 'Where the bloody hell are you?' he roared down the phone. I held the receiver a prudent inch away from my ear. When the noise level slackened a little I put it back and said, 'Has there been any trouble?'

'Of course there has, you blithering idiot!' he snarled. 'Just imagine Stefano's reaction when, after telling everyone that his wife was at a health farm, there she was appearing on television rescuing a *cat* in France. Why the hell didn't you warn me that the pair of you were about to become media stars?'

'Television?' I repeated blankly. 'How can we have been on *television*? We didn't even get rescued till mid-afternoon.'

'Modern communications, sweetie,' James said in an annoyingly sarcastic tone. 'And bad luck that there weren't any earthquakes or hooligans to take the place of a nice little human-interest story. It was just a small filler at the end of the news using still photos but quite enough to do the damage.'

I wondered if I should commit hari kari now before Stefano or James did the deed for me. 'I'm so sorry, James, we didn't know anything about it.' For the next two or three minutes I metaphorically licked his boots as I apologised in a humble voice that I'd never normally use to any member of my family, especially not him.

My self-abasement worked. Eventually he said in a more mellow tone, 'Stefano's beside himself with rage, and apparently now convinced you're right up to your pretty little neck in it. One of the gossip columns picked up on Cressida's being abroad without him and led with an article this morning asking if there was trouble in the Buonotti marriage – and saying that Cressida and I continued to be very good friends. The inference was obvious.'

I closed my eyes in dismay and leaned my head against the side of the hood over the phone. 'Has Stefano contacted you?'

'He wouldn't lower himself. But he moves quickly. The police were around yesterday morning to ask questions about the theft of Count Buonotti's china collection and other "artefacts of value" from his country establishment.'

'Oh, no,' I breathed. 'But why would they take Stefano's word that you're connected with it?'

'To start with being stinking rich means you get listened to a bit more closely than your poorer cousins.

Also a witness claims he saw a car with the same number plate as mine parked in the woods by the house the night the china is supposed to have gone missing.' I made a sort of squeaking noise and James laughed. 'Unfortunately for Stefano some kind warden had my car taken to the pound that night so even the least intelligent copper can work out I wasn't using it as a getaway vehicle, but I daresay it won't take Stefano too long to come up with some other way to pin it on me.' There was a pause and he added in a weary voice, 'Could you ask Cressy if she wouldn't mind ringing the police and telling them what she's done with the wretched stuff?'

'I hope she didn't take it to France in her suitcase,' I said distractedly. 'They were dropping the suitcases out of the window into the boats with terrific crashes. Her new one has a dent in it already. It won't have done the china any good.'

'Then she can present Stefano with the pieces, I don't care,' said James. 'It'll get him off my back at least.'

I was beset by a new worry. Was *that* the really stupid thing she'd done? Smashed some of Stefano's china? Still, best cross that bridge when and if. 'We'll set off straight away. Where will you be? The shop or your house?'

'At home, I think. The bloodhounds are still at my heels, so it'd be best if you don't bring Cressy here.'

'Something the matter?' asked Cressida as I got into the car.

'You could say so,' I retorted grimly, gunning my poor little car into reverse and shooting out of the car park at a faster speed than it was used to. I filled her in on the latest developments. To my annoyance she seemed far more concerned about the gossip column piece than the suspicions the police had about James.

'Once the police find they have no evidence he's behind the thefts they'll have to drop it. I do wish Stefano would stop thinking that James is behind everything, but then he must be beside himself,' she added indulgently. 'He adored that collection.'

My head swivelled in her direction and I nearly drove into a parked car. How could she possibly sound so innocent? Was she a schizophrenic or something, someone with no recollection of what she'd done? 'Cressida,' I said carefully, 'of course he's beside himself. Particularly because he knows quite well it was actually his wife who took it!'

'Me?' she said. 'Me? *I* didn't take his china. I wouldn't be so stupid.'

CHAPTER 14

Luckily there was a long patch of empty curb for me to draw into otherwise there might have been a serious accident. I took a deep breath. 'But, Cressida, you said you had! In that horrible dining room in Folkestone, remember? You said you had a right to it.'

'I do,' she repeated stubbornly. 'To what's mine. I took the two bonbonnières Stefano gave me. Even if he didn't really mean me ever to take them from his collection, they're still mine to do with as I please. And I couldn't have left "Love conquers all" behind.' Her voice was redolent of misted eyes and fond memories. Then she sat up and said crossly, 'And I'm not a thief either!'

Given the merry dance she'd been leading me her righteous indignation was a bit excessive, but it still didn't stop me from feeling both pretty stupid and more than a little embarrassed. 'Then what is it that you're selling?' I asked, confused. 'I thought you'd decided to sell the china.'

'Just how thick do you think I am?' she demanded. 'Stefano would tear me into tiny little pieces if I even thought of selling one of his things!' She looked down into her lap as if some very nasty thoughts had just occurred to her and said in a low voice, 'It's some of my jewellery, so I can pay for something urgent – something I don't want Stefano to know about.' Or me, judging by her uninformative expression. 'And they're pieces my grandmother left me so it's not even as if I'm selling Stefano's presents,' she added in an offended tone.

She was gripping the door handle convulsively as if about to jump out of the car in high dudgeon and make her own way back to London. 'Cressida, I'm sorry.' This was the second time in five minutes that I found myself grovelling. It was becoming tiresomely familiar. 'But Stefano told me himself you'd taken the whole collection. I presumed he knew! It seemed unlike you,' I said quickly, seeing her face still set in lines of offence, 'but I thought maybe you were getting back at him. I wasn't to know that when you said you had a right to it you were talking about two pieces, not thirty!'

'Forty-three,' she corrected absently. 'I suppose it was a natural enough mistake,' she said with just a hint of offence left in her voice, as if her probity should automatically have been above suspicion. She put her hand to her mouth in dismay. 'Gosh! No wonder Stefano's so ragingly furious if he really believes James nicked the whole china collection.'

'And took his wife too, which is worse.' At long last she appeared to be appreciating the gravity of the situation. 'You may not believe it, but I reckon you're slightly more important to Stefano than the china.'

'I don't think I'll put it to the test. I might not get the answer I want!' she said with a gurgle of laughter, more light-hearted than I had heard her all week. Then her face sobered. 'I wonder if the thieves took anything else? Oh, dear, poor Stefano. I hope they didn't get his Canaletto as well. But that's got a special alarm system attached to the back of it. It'd be very difficult to take it off the wall without setting off all the alarms in the house. I don't suppose we'll ever get the china back, it'll be on the continent by now. It's too recognisable to try and sell over here.

'And that's why if Stefano would calm down for a moment he'd realise James certainly wouldn't have taken it,' she added, rapping her fingers thoughtfully on the dashboard. 'He knows perfectly well that James is far too streetwise to take the china equivalents of a Gainsborough or a Turner. They're much too hard to get rid of!' She sat up and said briskly, 'We'd better get back to London as soon as possible. At least the two pieces I took have been saved, I hope poor Stefano finds that some consolation. Don't worry, I'm sure I can convince him that James wouldn't have been crazy enough to do this.'

I meekly obeyed and started the car, swinging out into the traffic.

She grinned wickedly. 'It's a good thing I've been pretty comprehensively chaperoned for the time I've been away, isn't it? Even darling Stefi can't really believe I'd get up to anything under the eye of your mother.'

'He would if he'd met her!' I retorted. Cressida seemed curiously unperturbed by the news of a burglary in her house; no skin-crawling revulsion that strangers had been in to invade her space, maybe paw through her belongings, even take some of her own things. Instead she was staring out of the window with what looked uncommonly like a smile of relief. And what had happened to that marked reluctance to speak to Stefano that had led her to make one excuse after another for the last few days? Maybe she felt, I thought with sudden inspiration, that being unjustly accused of theft was going to give her back the moral high ground that she had lost in the débâcle of trying for the baby. After being proved so very wrong in this Stefano was going to have to be more careful about what he accused his wife of in future. Even if he wasn't entirely convinced James had had nothing to do with Cressida's precipitate flight, he was hardly going to be in a position to make a song and dance about it, was he? He might even try to make amends by giving James some business, I thought hopefully, wondering if that would mean that he and I would have to continue, strictly in the interests of verisimilitude of course, to be 'friends'. I enjoyed this pleasant fantasy for several miles before it occurred to me that it was unlikely Stefano ever felt he had to make amends for anything.

We had reached the suburban sprawl at the end of the motorway which officially calls itself Kent but for all intents and purposes is now part of London when Cressida came out of her reverie and said, 'I wonder how the thieves managed to work out the combination for the safe? In films they put stethoscopes to the door to listen to how the tumblers fall but I can't really believe they do it like that, can you?'

'No,' I replied absently, concentrating on trying to find a space to get on to a roundabout. It wasn't until we were going sedately down the road opposite (my car not having the youth or the acceleration to dodge in and out like a boy racer) that I repeated, 'The safe? But the china was on the shelves in Stefano's little room.'

'No, it was in the safe in his study,' Cressida said in the tone of someone explaining something to a complete idiot. 'After he went to Milan I thought I'd better do something to put him in a better mood so I decided to have the room repainted. I put the china in the safe for protection – except for my bonbonnières which I took up to my room.' She glanced guiltily at me. 'I know James said I shouldn't, but I thought it wouldn't do any harm for a little while.' She made a face. 'Then the woman who was doing the paint techniques sprained her wrist so everything was put off for at least three weeks. But I left the china in the safe to save moving it again.'

I frowned. 'I'm sure that Stefano said when he came back all the shelves in his study were bare. Not that the safe had been broken into. Does he know that you'd put it in the safe?'

'Of course! At least . . .' she hesitated '. . . it was supposed to be a surprise so I wouldn't have told him on the phone, I probably put it in my note . . . Maybe I didn't . . .'

I was so excited I could hardly speak. 'He must have seen those bare shelves and leaped instantly to a conclusion! I bet you'll find all the china is still safely locked away. It's wonderful! He's going to be thrilled! He'll welcome you back with even wider open arms. You know, the messenger who brings good tidings.'

'Yes,' she agreed in a slightly hollow voice. She didn't sound particularly delighted by the knowledge that burglars hadn't been riffling through her home after all. In fact she sounded positively put out. More than put out, more as if the bottom had dropped out of her world. I wouldn't have bet so much as 5p on her not finding some fresh reason not to speak to Stefano. I was right.

'Who are you going to ring first to say the china hasn't been stolen after all, Stefano or the police?' I asked cheerily.

'I don't know.' Her eyes were wide and innocent. 'You know, it might be best to find out first what's been stolen. I'll have to contact the police. It might take a bit of time before they agree to tell me, but you do understand that I don't want to make a complete fool of myself by calling off the whole search if it turns out there's a container load of other stuff that's gone missing.'

It's a good thing I'm not of a betting nature. As disingenuous statements go that one took a lot of beating.

'Cressida!' I cried indignantly. 'How can you keep on doing this? We're talking about *James* here, somebody you went out with for a year. Someone you're supposed to have loved, for heaven's sake! And it's *your* husband who's accusing him of dealing in hot antiques. If this goes on much longer James's livelihood could be wrecked!'

'He'll survive. Most antiques dealers have that sort of thing said about them at some time or other,' she replied casually.

I gave her a really dirty look, redolent of all that I thought of her extraordinarily cavalier attitude about the mess James was in, at least partially – mostly – because of her. She might not have *meant* Stefano to think she was eloping with her former lover, but due to her ineptitude at writing legibly and including all the relevant information

– to say nothing of indulging in some truly provocative husband baiting – that's what had happened.

She coloured. I was pleased to see that not even Cressida could manage to avoid the overripe tomato look when blushing, though it faded much more quickly than it does on normal people, leaving her merely looking becomingly flushed. 'I didn't mean it to sound like that!' she said quickly, and sighed deeply. 'OK. If you can find out which officer is dealing with the case, I'll give him a ring. That should sort out one problem at least.' And she lapsed into silence, staring morosely out of the window at the serried rows of bay-fronted Victorian terraces we passed, one after another.

Her taciturn mood was so profound that even I didn't feel I could break into it to ask where she was thinking of spending the night, still less ask her why she'd apparently changed her mind about speaking to 'darling Stefi'. I decided to take her to the flat. Doubtless she was hoping I'd offer to put her up anyway, and I supposed it was still close enough to her own flat-sharing days for her not to be totally horrified by a flat lived in by females without a full-time staff to pick up and clean after them. Revved up by James's experiences I scanned the parked cars as I found a space near the flat to see if they held suspiciously slumped figures supposedly taking a nap, hat pulled down over the nose so that the brim hid the whites of the eyes as my every movement was recorded. It all looked much the same as usual and there were no vans with revolving antennae and a sign saying 'AA Snoops' handily written on the side as a clue. Actually I hadn't really believed Stefano would bother to have my flat watched, but I was still nervous enough to make Cressida stuff that distinctive hair of hers inside her jacket and cram an old rainhat of mine on the top. I have to say that a red plastic bucket lookalike bought for two pounds at the local market didn't make a particularly felicitous combination with a burnt orange cashmere jacket from Whistles but we weren't running a fashion parade.

Horatio gave me a decidedly unenthusiastic welcome, taking one look and then expressing his disapproval of my daring to go away for nearly a week without him by turning his back and settling down to lick his stomach. He thawed slightly when I produced the chocolate sardine I'd bought him in France; among the many things which make up Horatio's unusual diet is milk chocolate as a treat (he also likes spaghetti and sucks up the strands slowly, one by one, which is not a sight for weak stomachs). He ate the head off his sardine, decided to leave the rest for later, and jumped up on to the sofa beside Cressida, making the chainsaw noise which passes for a purr.

She put out a hand to stroke him and he instantly lumbered heavily on to her lap. She winced visibly. I'd been bustling around, putting my suitcase in my room, scanning the outside of my mail to see if anything really alarming had arrived in the last week like my bank statement, jamming the kettle on for a much-needed cup of tea, trying to get my recalcitrant cat to speak to me, seeing if there were any urgent messages from Liv, checking the answer machine in case there were any loving, miss you messages from Daniel (there weren't), or any words from James (several, all rather irritable). I fast forwarded Darian's message, reckoning I'd listen to it later when I was feeling stronger, and assessed the contents of the fridge to see if, as usual, Liv had run us out of all the staples. I've never been quite sure why, when she is the one who doesn't work during normal shop opening hours, it was always me who trolled around the supermarket on Saturdays stocking up. Or maybe I am. If Liv does it she comes back with an extra large jar of black bean paste and no loo paper. I sighed. Oh, well, black sugarless tea is very good for the figure.

I hadn't taken much notice of Cressida except to be glad that, unlike so many guests, she had the sense to sit down and keep out of the way while I was having my five frantic minutes. But her intake of breath as she received Horatio's leaden weight full on her stomach penetrated even my bustle. She was leaning back her head, eyes closed, cheeks ashen white. 'Are you all right?' I asked. (Though people often pale when Horatio jumps on them.)

She grimaced faintly. 'I keep on getting a tummy ache and I'm a bit queasy too. I've been feeling sort of like this, but not quite so bad, ever since we left for Paris. I expect it's just all this stress I've been under.'

I nodded knowledgeably, though I'm the sort of disgustingly healthy person who only ever suffers a headache as a result of excessive consumption of cheap plonk so I have absolutely no idea what a stress-induced stomach ache is like. But it sounded uncomfortable. She assured me it was perfectly all right to leave her alone so I went off to see James with my slightly uneasy conscience soothed by my own nobility in making up my bed for her and tucking her up with a hot water bottle, a trashy novel and Horatio as chief weigher down of the duvet. And the phone. My initial churlish suspicion that she might be putting it on a bit to avoid being pressured was dispelled by seeing the colour of her face, no one could fake that, but sympathetic as I was she wasn't getting out of making that call. With a wan smile she promised that as soon as I rang her from James's with the number she'd be on the phone. Tell that to the Marines, I thought, quite prepared to find her conveniently asleep when I came back. Too bad. In that case I'd set the ball rolling by ringing the police myself.

The lights were on outside James's house to my slight disappointment. I'd been rather looking forward to seeing him being followed by his guard dogs. For one thing I'd love to know how they managed to find a parking space in this crowded street from where they could conveniently watch the house. The nearest one I'd been able to find was around the corner, and quite useless unless you had a very long periscope.

James answered the door on the first ring, throwing it wide and enveloping me in a bear hug. I automatically returned it, throwing my arms around him and hugging him back. Well, you do, don't you? He leaned back, keeping his hands linked around my waist, and bent forward to kiss me briefly on the lips. It took all my self-control not to respond with pennants flying. 'Are you pleased to see me or is this a show put on for the neighbours?' I asked, keeping a stern check on my hormones.

'Laura, if you'd let me I'd show you just how pleased I am to see you,' he murmured, eyes dancing, slipping his hands inside my coat. My nerve ends went into overdrive. 'But it would be more seemly inside, behind a locked door.'

'Certainly not,' I said in my best schoolmarmish manner, gently pulling myself free before I could change my mind. I picked up my tote bag, holding it in front of me like a chastity belt. 'We've got things to do, we can't afford to waste time on inessentials.'

James looked highly offended. I smiled at him placatingly. 'Have I got a lot to tell you! But first . . .' I fished in my bag and got out a couple of bottles of wine and an extremely smelly cheese which had been responsible for a lot of suspicious sniffing on the train. 'Here, I bought you a present.'

He brightened, insisting that we go into the kitchen and open one of the bottles at once. I wasn't about to refuse. I felt I needed it. Wine relieves tension, whatever the source of that tension. Even if it is six foot two and showing a disturbing tendency to act out of character. I'm not a heavy drinker – well, definitely not what you'd call alcoholic or anything – just someone who likes to have a glass of wine from time to time, or rather more often to be honest, but even I was beginning to think that once this was all over I'd better go on a liver-relieving stint for a bit. At least a few days.

The kitchen had what estate agents call 'plenty of potential'; in other words it hadn't been touched for the last thirty years apart from the modern day bachelor essentials of a microwave and a state of the art fridge with ice dispenser. When James opened the door to stow away the cheese I saw that its gleaming glass shelves held little more than half a lemon, two bottles of tonic, several bottles of white wine and a half of champagne. With its feeling of being somewhere food wasn't prepared the kitchen bore an uncanny resemblance to the one in Daniel's flat, though his had less alcohol in it. The other difference was that James's kitchen was a shining monument, despite its age, to the efficiency and hard work of his cleaning lady. Every surface shone, the windows gleamed even in the dark, the cloths had been rinsed and hung out to dry over the sink, Barker's bean bag must have been hoovered that morning since there was hardly any trace of deadly persistent black Labrador hairs over the red paw print fabric; I was sure that if I looked the wall behind the cooker would be clean and free of grease. A memo board above an empty vegetable rack held a list of messages in neat curly writing: 'Paid milk bill, £4.36', 'Gas man came to read meter', 'Out of floor polish, will buy more Monday', 'Please don't let Barker bring his bones into the house'.

I had a feeling this last was a plea from the heart made many times before. 'Where is Barker? I thought you said you were borrowing him?'

James was showing by his fancy wrist movements as he uncorked the bottle that if the antiques business failed he could always get a job as a barman. 'Back with Harry.' He looked up. There were lines around his eyes that hadn't been there when I'd left for France. 'I thought it better to have him settled elsewhere in case the police turn up and haul me off to the clink.'

'You don't really think they will, do you?'

He poured wine into two glasses and pushed one over towards me. 'I sincerely hope not. As yet they don't have enough to go on to get a search warrant – but from what I know of Stefano he's willing and able to give them all the evidence they need.' He waved his hand around vaguely. 'I don't care. They can go over this place with a fine tooth comb, but if they search the shop – well, it's like the tax people. They're going to go on looking until they find something. And they probably will,' he added gloomily.

My glass stopped halfway to my mouth. 'James, you don't really deal in hot antiques, do you?' I asked, appalled.

He stared at me long and hard in a manner worthy of Lady Bracknell. 'What do you think I am?' he asked coldly. 'A crook?'

His glare was so blighting that I almost shrivelled on the spot, but now that the doubts had been raised they had to be answered. 'You tell me,' I snapped. 'Stefano said you were. I didn't believe him.'

James's mouth relaxed fractionally. 'Thank you for those few words of support,' he muttered in a way that suggested it might be some time before I was forgiven. 'And that was a bit rich coming from Stefano since he's hardly in a position to throw stones at anyone's glass houses,' he added irritably.

'Are you afraid that he might have something planted in the shop?' I said, eager to make amends.

James ran a hand through his hair. 'It's occurred to me. But since we always watch anyone we don't know very carefully, it'd be difficult to do it without being seen. And I check what they've touched after they've gone, too. No, what I meant is that there's bound to be something, somewhere in the shop that I bought in good faith but which didn't belong to the person who sold it. Pa used to have a regular, a little old lady who'd bring in a bit of silver whenever she had a bill to pay. It turned out that every time she went to see her brother she'd go away with something or other of his in her handbag. But if the police find something a bit dodgy and they're in a bad mood – which they probably will be with Stefano breathing down their necks – they aren't going to say, "Oh, what bad luck, it happens to everyone sometimes." They're going to book me for handling stolen property. And then they'll really take me apart.'

He rested his chin on his hand, staring morosely at his wine. 'Still I suppose that might mean that the very smelly beggar who appeared on Tuesday and accosts anyone who tries to enter the shop will go away. And the man who claims in a loud voice that I sold him a desk with legs married from another piece may decide it's not worth coming in for the fourth time.' He laughed grimly. 'I think Stefano's ensuring that if he doesn't succeed in putting me behind bars, he's at least going to bankrupt me. That way he can be quite sure I won't have the dosh to keep Cressy in the very expensive style to which she's accustomed.'

I didn't know what to say. My own frustrations seemed to pale to nothing alongside this. I reached over and put a comforting hand on his. He looked up and smiled in a way that made me feel I was one of the nicest people around. Certainly his mood seemed to have lightened a bit, for he took a sip of the wine then held up the glass against the light, examining the colour with moody concentration. 'This is very good, Laura,' he said with pleased surprise. 'Where did you find it?'

'Somewhere near Bordeaux,' I said airily. (Actually it

came from a supermarket, albeit upmarket.) 'As we had a free day we spent it sightseeing. We saw some really nice places.'

'Great! Enjoying yourselves and leaving others to deal with the fallout from your near escape from death,' he said grumpily. 'Have you *any* idea of the fuss there's been? Luckily it was only Stefano who recognised you from the television – you were on for a second in the background – so I had a peaceful night. But I had Imogen on the telephone every half hour from nine o'clock in the morning demanding the latest news and my assurances that you hadn't been swept away in the swollen waters of the Garonne. When I pointed out that you'd already been rescued and according to the photograph seemed quite dry, and so presumably had never encountered any icy water, she told me that I had proved myself to be a very cold-hearted little boy when I was eight and I hadn't improved as an adult!'

'Poor James,' I said, laughing at his outraged expression. 'But what *did* you do when you were eight?'

He looked distinctly shifty. 'I can't remember,' he said in a barefaced lie. I'd get it out of him somehow. 'Imogen was a doddle compared to Aunt Jane who just wouldn't get off the phone. Then there was Katie, Pa, and seemingly every single one of your step relations who preferred to turn to me rather than spend money ringing Paris to bother your mother! It's surprising,' he added reflectively, 'how many people who claim they *never* look at the tabloids just happened to be glancing through the *Daily Mail* at the hairdresser's when they recognised your picture. Sorry, Aunt Jane buys it for her cook.'

I thanked heaven I had been safely out of touch when all this was happening. I knew only too well how intensely dramatic my family could be – all the disparate parts of it. Whoever coined the term 'British reserve' certainly didn't have their acquaintance.

James rested his elbows on the table and stared into his glass. 'But that was nothing, absolutely nothing, compared to the hullabaloo this morning when everyone saw the gossip column – which of course they hardly ever read either,' he said in heavy voice. 'You'd have thought I was personally responsible for besmirching the noble name of Lovatt.'

I could just hear Imogen and a couple of the other aunts and their views on men who messed around with married women. I was no longer surprised James had new lines around his eyes. In fact I was surprised his hair hadn't gone white. I squeezed his hand again. He smiled briefly. 'I did consider pointing out that Harry's tried just as hard as me to blacken the Lovatt name but I didn't think they'd be prepared to listen. And of course today there have been a few journalists too, wanting me to confirm or deny the story. So I told them,' he raised his head and looked at me with a touch of defiance, 'that it was complete rubbish, that in actual fact Cressy was simply taking a break abroad with my girlfriend.' I didn't need to ask which girlfriend he'd named. I also had a fair idea of the sort of possessive terms in which James would have deemed it necessary to describe his 'girlfriend' too.

'Oh, thank you, James! Couldn't you just have said that Cressida was with her friend?' I demanded in exasperation. 'What's Daniel going to think when it's splashed all over the papers that his girlfriend is actually another's?'

'I daresay he's far too literary to read the sort of papers that have gossip columns, and he says he never believes what's printed in the gutter press anyway,' James replied with infuriating accuracy. My warm sympathetic feelings were wilting rapidly. They died completely when he added reflectively, 'And he'll be able to turn his love-lorn angst into a few beautifully worded paragraphs for his next book so he'll reckon it was worth it.'

I snatched my hand away and glared at him. He took no notice. 'Have you any idea where that story came from?' I demanded coldly.

'Yup. I haven't been sitting on my hands doing nothing while you were swanning around the continent,' he said pointedly. 'Amazingly enough, the story originated with Cressy.'

My mouth fell open. '*Cressida?* She told the papers she was having an affair with you?'

'No, of course not!' he said with an impatient shrug. 'But she was banging on to her girlfriends at La Cucina about how I'm always there for her and the only one who could help her,' I noticed with a certain amount of irritation that he seemed by no means displeased that Cressida thought she could put so much trust in her ex-lover, 'and she needed to see me desperately.' He looked at me with raised brows. 'Do you know what that's about?' I shook my head. 'Arabella and the others were so worried about the state Cressy was in that they couldn't resist discussing it with all their girlfriends. Naturally by the time the story reached Serena it had been improved somewhat.'

'Serena?' I echoed.

He nodded. 'I went around to see her on Tuesday to find out exactly what she'd been up to.' He grinned evilly. 'She didn't look very happy to see me. Claimed she didn't know anything about it at first. She told me in the end.' I wondered, not without a certain amount of malicious enjoyment, exactly what methods James had used. He made a face. 'She was out for dinner, had a bit too much to drink and someone said he'd heard that I'd got a new girlfriend. It was too much for her. She said in point of fact she knew better and that I'd gone back to Cressy . . . It just so happens that Serena's friend Patrick who was there too earns his champagne money by scouting stories for the gossip columns.

'Serena claims that she rang him the next day to say that it had been the drink speaking but he hadn't believed her.' I didn't believe it either. Serena would *never* admit that she could get drunk enough to start passing on slanderous stories. James's mouth took on a particularly grim line. 'She won't do it again, I can promise you.'

If I was a nicer person I would have found it in my heart to feel a twinge of sympathy for Serena. But I'm not.

He ran his finger idly around the rim of his glass. 'I suppose I might be able to convince Stefano I haven't laid an improper finger on Cressy for over two years, but I really don't see how I can make him believe I didn't whip his china out of some form of revenge for his taking my woman.' I opened my mouth but he went on, shaking his head in bewildered fashion. 'The problem is that it's exactly the sort of thing he'd do himself so he's hardly going to believe me when I say I didn't have anything to do with it, is he?' He reached across me for the bottle and refilled our glasses. 'If this was a novel,' he said, 'I'd turn detective so that I could find out who really took that china. Unfortunately,' he pulled an expressive face, 'I don't have a clue how to go about it.'

'You don't have to. No one took it. It's in the safe at Hurstwood House.'

He choked, sending wine spluttering all over the table. I caught the glass just in time before it tipped over, and thumped his back rather ineffectually until he got his breath back. He raised his head. 'Did I hear you right?' he asked in complete disbelief. 'That Stefano has had the bloody stuff all this time? And that he hid it so he could persecute me? I'll *kill* him! I'll—'

'He doesn't know,' I said quickly before James could get too carried away. I told him all about the misunderstanding that had led me to think Cressida had the china and how I'd realised she didn't. 'I should think Stefano stormed in that evening, found Cressida's note which he couldn't read anyway, saw the empty shelves and instantly added two and two to make five. He probably didn't even stay long enough to talk to the housekeeper before dashing off to London in search of Cressida.'

'Knowing her she'll have forgotten to tell the housekeeper as well.' James twisted around and glared at me accusingly. 'Why the hell didn't you tell me this before?'

'Because you didn't give me the chance. First you were groping me, then you were talking too much for me to get a word in edgeways.'

'I don't *grope*!' he snapped back.

Quite true actually, but it still had a pretty disastrous effect on my straight thinking. I smiled apologetically. 'I'm sorry. You're right, I should have told you straight away.'

He blinked. Apologies from me were still a novel experience. I expect it took even him a bit of time to get used to them. 'Have you got any other surprise revelations for me?' he asked, though the sting had gone out of his voice.

'I don't think so, but I'll tell you everything that happened just in case I'm accused of hiding something else.' I gave him what was meant to be a saucily disarming smile, the type that Meg Ryan or Mira Sorvino use with such success in their films. You know, where the man melts and in the next scene is eating out of their hands. Mine must still have been coloured by a fleeting memory of that grope or whatever else you like to call it for James grinned and murmured, 'Hang on, Laura. Don't you think we should get the talking over first before we get on to *that*?'

I started talking very fast to try and hide my embarrassment, and then when I realised that James might think I was doing it deliberately, slowed down to the pace of a solemn funeral oration. Actually by the time I had finished he was far too absorbed in the puzzle of what it was that Cressida was firmly keeping close to her chest to bother about baiting me any further.

He tilted back in his chair, making it creak ominously as he put his hands behind his head. 'You say that she didn't seem to mind about a burglary? Odd, I remember when her car was broken into and the radio stolen. She went ballistic. I can't imagine her just accepting that her house could be broken into and the code of the safe cracked. Unless . . .' He jerked with excitement and the chair, already precariously balanced, wobbled backwards. He deftly tilted it forwards with an ease that spoke of having done this many times before and grasped the table, face alight with excitement. 'Unless there was something she hoped would have been stolen along with everything else!'

'James, you're brilliant!' He looked as if he entirely concurred with this statement. 'That must be it! Or something she could claim was stolen.'

'Good point. More likely in fact. Did she give you any hints?' We spent half an hour speculating what exactly Cressida's secret could be, with ideas that grew wilder and wilder as we finished the bottle, but in the end we had to agree the only way to find out was to ask her. From my experience of Cressida it was going to be much like prising information out of a clam. 'And then,' said James, resting his chin on his hand, 'we'll be able to concentrate on persuading her to go back to where she should be, in the arms of her husband. And I'll be able to go about my business without feeling that someone's writing everything, even the filling in my sandwich for lunch, down in some little black book. Though,' he looked at me seriously, 'if she really doesn't want to go back to him, I'm not going to make her. Whatever Stefano threatens to do.'

Really there was no need for him to get nobly back on his pedestal, I thought crossly. Cressida had quite enough men prepared to be her knight in shining armour without James polishing his as well. 'What answer you get will probably depend on the direction the wind is in!' I said sourly. 'And, incidentally, what exactly made Serena so willing to believe that Cressy would junk her marriage to go waltzing off with an ex-boyfriend?'

James cleared his throat. 'Er – she appeared to believe that Cressy and I must already have resumed our affair, otherwise I'd never have broken up with Serena herself.'

He was concentrating on his glass as if trying to work out how to blow another one like it. I'm not put off that easily and am quite capable of reading between very wide lines. 'What you – and she – mean,' I said grimly, 'is that *you* would never have let someone as gorgeous as Serena go for someone like *me*.'

He nodded unhappily and to my annoyance didn't even try to dispute the basic premise of the statement. Sometime later I was going to be able to while away a few very pleasurable hours thinking of ways to get even with Serena. 'So according to her you had a hidden agenda all the time – to get Cressida back. Is that true?'

'Of course it isn't!' he said indignantly.

Good. 'And is the rest of it true?' I asked, seizing the opportunity to ask something that had been plaguing me ever since I was propelled into this mad escapade. He glanced at me warily. 'That, given the chance, you'd take Cressida back like a shot?'

He looked at me owlishly as if he was having difficulty focusing, or understanding what I was saying. I knew James far too well to think he could become seriously addled on half a bottle of wine, but just in case he was thinking of trying for RADA I decided I might as well spell it out. 'Are you still in love with her?' I asked bluntly.

His face went completely blank for a few seconds, just long enough to make me feel that I'd blundered in to private territory, then he smiled faintly. 'No, I'm not.'

I could try for RADA too. I'm sure that my face didn't show any of the blinding relief I felt, though really it wasn't anything to do with me other than a general familial concern that James shouldn't squander his emotions on a hopeless passion. I had other fish to fry. I realised guiltily that I had forgotten to ring Daniel to tell him that I'd come back two days earlier than planned. But it would be a pleasant surprise for him when I dropped around this evening before going back to Cressida. 'That's good,' I said lightly, 'because despite everything she's potty about Stefano. But it's funny how everyone thinks you're still carrying a torch for her.' I fixed him with a pointed look.

James sighed with a certain amount of irritation. 'I suppose you're going to nag me until I'm driven into telling you! Yes, I wasn't happy when Cressy chucked me like that, especially as it was so public, but we were coming to an end anyway. She just reached it before I did,' he said wryly. I waited in expectant silence, he needn't think that a couple of pretty uninformative sentences was enough. 'I was very fond of Cressy, very fond indeed,' he said with a reminiscent look, 'but even before she met Stefano I'd realised that we'd drive each other bonkers if we lived together. So when she dumped me I was upset and my pride was hurt, but I knew it was the best thing really. Satisfied?'

Not really, I felt it left out a lot of detail, such as was this the stiff upper lip taken to extremes? But it was obviously all I was going to get. For the moment. The grandfather clock in the hall began to chime the hour, reminding me that I'd already left Cressida alone for a couple of hours when she wasn't feeling well and still had another call to make. I pushed back my chair and stood up. 'I've got to go, I promised Cressida I'd be back by nine.'

'You can't drive very fast if it takes you an hour to go less than two miles.'

'I've a call to make on my way home,' I declared airily.

'Bit early, isn't it? Wouldn't nearer midnight be better?' James asked in an innocent voice.

Honestly! He'd murder me if I kept on making cracks about his girlfriends! So why was it all right for him? I thought furiously as I strode out into the hall, snatching up my coat with a grand gesture from where I'd thrown it on the chair. A trailing arm caught a pile of letters waiting to be posted on the little side table and sent them flying to the floor. Seething with self-inflicted mortification I bent down to pick them up. At least James had managed to get the bloodstains out of his carpet I saw with relief as I straightened upright and arranged the letters back in their neat pile.

'What do they say about more haste and less speed?' murmured James as he opened the front door with a flourish. He glanced out, then his arm snaked back and caught me around my waist, drawing me to him while he took his time about giving me a goodbye kiss. I can't say I struggled overmuch. I mean, no matter how angry I was with him I couldn't punch him out, could I? There was probably someone watching and taking all this down. I froze for a moment at the thought, then mustered my acting abilities and relaxed. After a few more seconds I didn't need to act any more. James kisses as if it's the main course, not an aperitif to be got out of the way as quickly as possible before you settle down to the real business of the evening. Thinking about anything else would be a bit like reading a trashy novel while eating caviar. 'Was that a demonstration for the detective?' I asked as he finished. I should think the car windows had steamed up if so.

'No, that was just for pleasure,' he murmured against my cheek as he let me go. 'Good night, Laura, sleep well.'

Fat chance! I thought as I walked down the street with an idiotic smile on my face, my mind churning. I mean, I'm given to exotic and eventful daydreams, but what on earth were they going to be like from now on with *two* male interests? Of course I was far too sensible to really get myself involved with James, all he was doing was having a bit of fun. Besides I had a real boyfriend, didn't I? But, boy, were my fantasies going to be enjoyable!

CHAPTER 15

Chinks of light were showing through the threadbare curtains at Daniel's window so he must be home. He never bothered to leave lamps on to deter burglars – for the good reason that there was absolutely nothing worth stealing unless some rival had designs on his creative endeavours. And even then the chances of his being able to read Daniel's spider-like scrawl were virtually nil. I leaned over to the back seat and scooped up an immaculately wrapped and bowed box of extortionately expensive *sarments de Médoc* that I'd bought from a haute couture version of a *chocolatier* yesterday. No ready to wear or machine made chocolates for Daniel, he ate only the very best. Once he saw these I'd certainly be forgiven for not ringing him before I came round, I thought complacently as I rang the bell.

He took such a long time that I wondered if I was being a modern day woman from Porlock. (The last time I'd been accused of that was when I'd sneezed just as he'd been about to write down a choice phrase. I was given the impression that if this book failed to win the Booker prize the blame could be laid squarely at my feet.) The door was finally flung open and Daniel stood there, staring at me as if he'd never seen me before. He was as heartrendingly good-looking as ever, dark hair tousled, shabby sweat shirt pushed up to his elbows and long feet bare, though unusually enough he must have remembered to shave in the last couple of days for his chin was quite bare of the normal (and very scratchy) stubble. 'Laura! What a surprise!' he said finally, as he leaned forward to give me a kiss. 'I thought you weren't coming back for another couple of days.'

'Change of plan,' I said shortly. I was well aware that I was more demonstrative than Daniel, but even by his standards this greeting was pretty unenthusiastic. 'Did I disturb you in the middle of writing?'

He stared at me and said vaguely, 'No, you didn't.'

'Good,' I said and held up the box. 'I've brought you a present.'

It got the welcome I hadn't. His eyes brightened and he put out his hand with a murmured, 'Thanks, it's really kind of you.' It's incredible how someone that thin and ethereal can be so greedy about sweet things.

I moved the box out of his reach just in case he had any ideas about taking it and then shutting the door and said firmly, 'I won't stay for long, I've got a friend staying with me who isn't very well so I've got to get back to her.'

With a faint sigh he stood aside and let me in. 'Is the friend that Cressida whatsit?' he asked as he followed me up the passage to his paper-strewn sitting room. Actually it was tidier than usual; the special lined notebooks he used for his writing had been gathered off their usual places on the floor and stacked in a fairly neat pile and the wastepaper basket must have been emptied in the last few days since the crumpled pages within hadn't yet over-flowed on to the carpet.

'Yes, but how on earth do you know about her?'

'A friend of hers came around to see me. Said that you were with her and thought I might be able to help her trace you both.'

I wheeled around. 'What friend of hers?' I asked in alarm, my mind already racing to the most ridiculous and melodramatic conclusions about what Stefano could possibly be up to now.

He coughed and harumphed. 'She was called . . . Sally. No, not that. Serena!' he said with the innocent air of someone producing a rabbit out of a hat. I didn't believe it for one moment. In my experience no man, not even Daniel, forgot Serena's name. Had she come on to him? I thought, eyes narrowing. I wouldn't put it past her. In fact, I'd be almost prepared to bet on it. It would have seemed like poetic justice to her to steal my boyfriend. Was *that* why he'd shaved? He was certainly shuffling his feet in a self-conscious fashion that was quite unlike his normal behaviour, though that could be because I was staring at him in the manner of a mongoose looking at an errant snake.

'And just how did Serena know that I knew you?' I asked in a clipped voice.

He rubbed his chin thoughtfully. 'I don't know precisely. I think she said that your stepbrother had mentioned it.'

'Oh, had he?' I muttered grimly. That explained the slightly wary look on James's face when I'd said I was going around to see Daniel unannounced. He must have known perfectly well that all he had to do was drop Daniel's name in Serena's shell-like and she'd do the rest. The Machiavellian bastard! He needn't expect any help from me in future! In fact I was in half a mind to leave him and his ex-girlfriend right where they were, in a stew of their own making.

Daniel picked up one of his 'How to Write' books off the table, saying with patently assumed casualness as he closed it, 'If Cressida whatsit is ill hadn't you better get back to her?'

I smiled sweetly at him. 'She'll be all right for a bit.' I sat down on the sofa to his obvious dismay. I didn't have to sweep any crumbs off it which was unusual. Was he expecting Serena to come around this evening? 'What did she say?'

'Nothing much except to ask if I knew where you were,' he said, looking hunted. 'She also said something about you having an affair with your stepbrother, but I didn't believe that, of course.'

'Why not?' I asked, a bit offended by the tone of his voice.

'Come on, Laura, you're hardly his type, are you? I only met him the once but he's obviously the sort of bloke who likes blondes in sports cars and you're more of a home-loving bird; cooking, cleaning and all of that.' It did wonders for my self-esteem to be described as an up-to-date Mrs Mop. 'That's not to say you aren't very attractive, warm and cuddly.' So make that Mrs Mop with a dash of teddy bear thrown in since I was apparently quite useful for the occasional cuddle. 'And anyway I know you aren't interested in shallow men like him.'

I quashed an unworthy impulse to put him right on that score. 'Did Serena stay for long?' I asked idly, more as a way of preventing myself from asking the other questions that were threatening to trip off my tongue, such as didn't the suggestion that I might be having an affair with someone else worry him *at all*, than because I was actually interested.

'Er, no, of course not,' he said quickly. 'Only a few minutes in fact.'

He looked so transparently guilty that I couldn't resist teasing him. 'You mean, she didn't make a pass at you?'

His eyes widened. 'Well, no, she couldn't, could she? Um, why should she?' he added hastily. 'I mean, she didn't seem the sort of girl who would make a pass at anything in trousers—'

So much for Daniel's brilliant character observation. 'Why couldn't she?' I asked, standing up. He was so absorbed in the fascination of his own psyche that he was a terribly bad actor; he hadn't spent long enough assessing other people's reactions to him ever to have learned to be convincing. He was hiding something about last night and, I was prepared to bet, hiding something right now. That fake bout of coughing hadn't been a time-gaining exercise while he thought of a plausible story, it had been to cover a noise within the flat. 'Last time I was here I left one of my favourite hair slides on your chest of drawers,' I said over my shoulder as I crossed the room, 'I'll just go and get it.'

His mumbled protest came too late to stop me flinging open the door and exclaiming, 'Well!' in a suitably out-raged voice. The blonde agent whom I'd last seen at

Charlotte's party was standing by the bed in a pair of leggings and an inside out jumper, looking distinctly apprehensive. I had been right about the size of her bottom, the leggings were a definite mistake.

'I can explain,' said Daniel.

'I'm sure you can,' I replied. So *this* was why he wasn't worried about the possibility of my playing around elsewhere. 'Like it's not what I think and this is all perfectly innocent.' I kept an eagle eye on the blonde and she flinched backwards slightly as if I'd just threatened to come in and flatten her with a right hook. 'Like hell it is! She's promised to find you a really sympathetic publisher who understands the needs of a rising young writer like yourself,' from the blonde's expression I wasn't that wide of the mark, 'and of course such a meeting of sympathies and interests means that passion inevitably rises and you just couldn't help yourselves.' The corners of the blonde's mouth twitched. I had a feeling it was actually the two of us who had something in common; we'd both seen the most beautiful man we'd ever dreamed of, let alone actually set eyes on, outside a cheap romance and had gone all out to get him. Daniel, as I had good reason to know, was a pushover for a determined woman. Well, at least Serena didn't get him, I thought with a giggle. I smiled at the blonde. 'Good luck. I hope you've brought your Marigold gloves with you, you're going to need them.' I gathered from her grimace that she was already aware of that.

I pushed my way past Daniel who was still gaping at me like a landed fish and picked up the box of chocolates from the sofa. He made a sort of inarticulate protesting noise. I think he'd really expected me to leave them so he could share them with his new girlfriend. 'Horatio likes chocolate too,' I told his appalled face. 'I think you're more of a Milk Tray man these days, don't you?' And feeling extremely pleased with myself for being able to dream up any sort of parting quip I swept out, my exit only slightly spoiled by the lock on his front door sticking and my swearing efforts to get it to undo.

I was faintly surprised by how cool I was about the big betrayal scene. I felt stupid more than anything. My fantasies about being the sort of woman who could have two men panting after her at the same time had been well and truly shown up for the hollow sham they were. One falls straight into the arms of the first woman who asks him. The other – well, he might have woken up to the fact that I was no longer a sullen and fat teenager, but I was fooling myself disastrously if I believed he'd ever look on me as more than a temporary and amusing diversion. And now, I realised with alarm, I didn't have the protective buffer of fidelity to hide behind to protect me from James when he was in advancing mood either. Oh, hell!

What's the connection between a betting shop and a gas bill? Other than if you've lost your shirt on the horses you might be tempted to put your head in the oven ... Except that I have no idea why the betting shop opposite my car made me think of gas. Anyway I did a quick U turn (a slow one actually), much to the volubly expressed annoyance of the man behind me, and shot back towards James's house.

He stiffened defensively when he saw who it was rapping on his door so loudly. Conscience, or rather sense of self-preservation, working, I expect. 'Laura—' he began.

'Forget that!' I interrupted. 'James, why did someone come to read the gas meter today when you've only just had the bill?'

'What do you mean?' he asked in a puzzled voice as he shut the door behind me.

'One of those letters I knocked off the table was to the gas board. It's the bill, right?' He nodded. 'Your message board in the kitchen has a note from your domestic treasure that the man came to read the meter. I can't believe anyone as efficient as that would leave week-old messages on the board, so he must have been today or yesterday.'

'Today. Dolly only comes three days a week. Yes, you're right, the meter can't be due to be read again for at least two months. Well done! I saw the message but I never made the connection.'

'Well, you've had a lot on your mind, you must expect to miss a few things,' I said in a smugly kind voice.

He threw me a dirty look. 'I wonder what our gas meter friend wanted?'

'To look for something?'

He shook his head. 'Dolly would never leave anyone alone even for a minute. Her mum got her pension book stolen by a supposed council worker checking for damp, so she's very careful.'

'To leave something?' I suggested again.

James nodded gloomily. 'I'm afraid so. We'd better go and check in the cellar. She wouldn't have bothered to follow him down there and I suppose he might have used the loo too. She definitely wouldn't have gone in there!'

It didn't take long. The search was aided by the unusual tidiness of his cellar, undoubtedly the work of the inimitable Dolly. It had the usual complement of old furniture and unidentifiable bits that were too good to throw away and might come in useful someday, but instead of being chucked in higgledy-piggledy like the normal cellar, everything was arranged neatly in piles along the walls. It was the first cellar where I'd ever been able to walk from one end to the other without tripping over something. James started to search there while I did the downstairs loo, looking in all the obvious places like inside the cistern and behind the hand towels neatly stacked in a cupboard. But it wasn't until I felt down the back of the pillar that supports the basin that I felt the little package wedged between the pipes. I left whatever it was protectively encased in several layers of bubble wrap and took it to James. He had just finished running his hands along the myriad pipes that lined the walls. 'I found those,' he said, jerking his head back towards two more bubble-wrapped lumps that he'd put on the seat of a three-legged chair. He frowned as his fingers dug into a crevice made by a rotten brick. 'I think that's about it. I've looked everywhere I can think of, unless of course he buried something and then put a bit of furniture over it.' He shook his head. 'No. Too great a risk of being discovered by Dolly doing some very suspicious digging.'

'A spade isn't part of the normal meter reader's equipment either,' I pointed out.

'And you can't make much of a hole with a clipboard even in a dirt floor.' James clapped grime off his hands then wiped the residue off on the seat of his trousers in a way that would have deeply shocked his daily. We bore our finds off to the kitchen and put them down on the table.

'Should we have a look to see what they are?' I asked doubtfully. 'I mean, you'll get your fingerprints all over whatever they are.'

'*Our* fingerprints are already all over the wrapping,' he said. 'I should reckon that's quite enough to convict if anyone is so minded.'

I swallowed hard. 'Do you think that's what he's intending? To plant the stuff and then give the police "new" evidence so they'll come and search the house?'

James looked grim. 'I don't think so, or not yet anyway. I reckon that even Stefano knows if he goes too far he'll never get Cressy back. She's basically very honest.'

'So far as he knows she's dishonest enough to swipe his whole china collection,' I reminded him.

James pursed his lips. 'I'd forgotten that. Let's hope that Stefano's merely trying to frighten me into telling him where she is and not indulging in a game of tit for tat.'

I agreed heartily. 'Or,' he said, with a glance at me, 'trying to work on *you* since he knows that you *do* know where she is.'

'Frankly I'm beginning to feel like picking up the phone and telling him now!' I said grimly.

'Laura!' exclaimed James and glared at me sternly until I meekly said, 'I didn't mean it.'

He gave me one of his brilliant smiles so my heart thumped like a Labrador's tail after it's been told it's a good girl. 'Oh, well,' he said cheerfully, 'we might as well see what I'm about to be hauled off to clink for.' He carefully snipped away the pieces of Sellotape that stuck the bubble wrap together and gently unravelled the package I'd found. We looked at the enamelled snuff box in James's hand in stunned silence. 'Good God!' he said eventually. 'This can't be genuine!'

He held it up to have a closer look and the movement made the sparkling stones set around the portrait on the lid of a gentleman in a powdered wig wink in the light. 'Are those diamonds?' I asked in disbelief.

James shrugged. 'I don't have a jeweller's glass with me, but they can't be! It would be worth some astronomical amount if they were. And even if not, it'd still set you back quite a lot if you wanted to buy it.'

I craned over to have a closer look at it. 'I wouldn't. It's too flashy. I preferred the boxes Cressida was supposed to have pinched.'

'This one isn't in quite the same league,' said James with damning professional indifference. 'I don't like it much either, but that's because of the portrait. He looks very pleased with himself, doesn't he?'

I took another look. 'Mmm, he does.'

James held it up to the light. 'He reminds me of someone. I wonder who? Oh, I know. He's got a look of your Daniel,' he said with a consciously innocent expression.

'I hadn't noticed,' I said coldly. But he was right, damn him! 'Even if the stones are only paste it still looks too valuable for a game of hunt the snuff box. What happens if Stefano doesn't get it back?'

'Unless he's decided he doesn't like it any more and

doesn't care what happens to it, he must be fairly sure that he will,' James said in a quiet voice. 'Let's see what the other two are.'

They were a pair of deliciously fat painted wooden cherub candelabra, about twelve inches high. James thought he remembered seeing them on the mantelpiece of the dining room in Hurstwood House. 'Aren't they *gorgeous*?' I said in a longing voice.

'They're very pretty, but not, I think, very valuable,' he said, casting a critical eye over them. 'That one there has been restored quite heavily, and the other has broken his arm at one time and had it stuck back on again.'

'Doesn't matter, I still want them,' I said. I don't often see things I fall in love with at first sight like that, but I felt a real, covetous longing for those cherubs. I could just imagine them at either end of the mantelpiece in my bedroom or maybe in the living room . . . I couldn't make up my mind, I just knew they'd look perfect wherever they were.

James eyed the haul on the kitchen table and sighed. 'Stefano's being a bit slow off the mark. You'd have thought he'd have arranged for the police to come around with a search warrant already. But what the hell am I going to do with them? I can't leave them here and I daresay that if Stefano's detective sees me leaving with any sort of parcel he's got instructions to ring the police and say I'm carting stolen property around.'

I hoped he was exaggerating. 'I'll dispose of the cherubs for you,' I offered. 'They'd look great on my dressing table.'

'Laura!' said James in a shocked tone. 'They don't belong to you!'

'I know,' I said regretfully, 'though you could claim that Stefano had as good as given them to you by putting them in this house.'

James closed his eyes in despair. 'Female logic! I don't think the police would see it that way.'

'Neither do I,' I agreed, 'and I was only joking.' James didn't look as if he thought this any joking matter. 'But unless we put them in the post and send them back to Stefano the only thing to do is for me to take them. I'll put them in Cressida's suitcase and no one can say that *she* doesn't have a right to them.'

James brightened, then his face fell again. 'I don't know. What happens if you're found with them on you?'

I shrugged. 'Presumably even Stefano will balk at having me dragged off to jug for theft! Come on, James, it's hardly likely, is it? It's only a short trip back to my flat. Or I could put them in the bin on the corner if you'd prefer?'

'You will not!' he snapped. 'But the stakes are getting too high, I don't want you mixed up in this any more.'

I sighed in exasperation. He was being absolutely serious, but this certainly wasn't the moment for him to start developing a sense of honour and a need to protect the little woman. 'It's a bit late to start worrying about me being involved. You should have thought of that before you started blackmailing me with threats to squeal to Imogen,' I pointed out quite reasonably. James winced as if I'd just thrown an accurate but unfair punch. 'Besides,' I shrugged, 'what risk is there to me? All I'm doing is taking some of Cressida's things back to her.'

'Okay,' he said finally, still looking unhappy. 'But ring me at once if you get into any trouble.'

'I won't,' I said, rather touched by this hitherto unseen chivalrous aspect of James's character, at least so far as I was concerned. I didn't expect it to last for long. I wrapped up the snuff box and the cherubs and put them in a carrier bag.

'Oh, and by the way, did you know that Serena, of all people, went around to see Daniel yesterday?' I said as I was about to leave.

'Did she?' he asked in a casual voice.

'And do you know something else – she made a pass at him.'

'She did?' he asked with completely unconvincing astonishment.

'Oh, yes.' I smiled brilliantly. 'And he turned her down.'

This time James's surprise was absolutely genuine. 'Really? You're sure?'

'Yes, but I wonder how she knew that he was my boyfriend.'

'I can't think,' he said warily.

'You can't? I'm *so* glad. Anyway no harm was done,' I said brightly and reached up to kiss his cheek before I let myself out. Yet again I was smiling to myself as I left James's house. It seemed to be becoming quite a habit. It was great to feel he didn't have the upper hand all the time.

CHAPTER 16

Having successfully avoided arrest for possession of stolen property I let myself into the flat, looking around in very theatrical fashion to see if Cressida was about. I'd decided it would be better if she didn't find out about some of her husband's more dubious activities until after she'd made her all important telephone calls and I was quite sure she wouldn't have made them without me there to force her. The sitting room was empty so I crept in and stuffed my bag of loot under the sofa then went to see her. She was sitting up in bed looking as near to plain as it was possible for her to be. Her chalky white skin and red-rimmed eyes made her look like a B-movie victim about to be the vampire's supper for a second or third time. My initial reaction was that she was a rush off to Casualty job, but she assured me she wasn't feeling any worse, certainly didn't need a doctor, then burst into noisy tears.

'I'm never going to be able to speak to Stefano again,' she wailed. 'He'll never forgive me. Never, never, never!'

'Forgive you for what?' I asked, sitting down on the bed beside her and putting my arm around her shoulders.

'I've been so stupid!' she cried, more loudly. Horatio

gave her a disgusted look and, declining to stay in a room with someone who made more noise than he did, got up and stalked with weighty dignity out of the room. I fetched a box of man-size tissues, put them on her lap and sat down beside her again.

'What have you done that's so dreadful?' I asked. Her sobs were getting noisier and noisier. I was afraid that in a moment they'd turn into full-blown hysterics and the only cure I know for them is the old jug of water trick. I didn't want to soak my bed if I could help it so I patted her hand and said again, 'Come on, Cressida, why don't you tell me what the matter is?' As the sobs diminished a little I added soothingly, 'You know what they say about two heads being better than one. And a trouble shared is a trouble halved. I might be able to help. You probably can't see the wood for the trees.' I was beginning to sound like Darian, I thought in alarm.

'I doubt anyone can get me out of this wood,' she said in a muffled voice and blew her nose loudly. 'I'm sorry, Laura. I shouldn't have broken down like this, but you're so sympathetic.'

Was I? Curious more like. 'Is this what's been on your mind all week? I could see there was something worrying you but I didn't like to ask.'

I left a hopeful silence dangling. At long last she picked it up. 'It's all my fault, that's what makes it worse, me and my temper. And then I had to compound the error . . .'

I could have screamed with frustration. 'I'm sure you don't have a temper,' I said, hoping to move the story along.

'Oh, I do,' she assured me, eyes wide. 'I try and keep it

under control, but sometimes—' Her expression darkened and her fingers picked at a loose bit of patchwork on the bedcover. 'When Stefano went away after he discovered that letter he seemed to think everything had been settled and that from then on I'd do exactly as he wanted.' She dabbed delicately facewards with a tissue. 'Well, I'd said I was sorry and that I wouldn't deceive him again. I might even have said I really was going to try for a baby.' She lifted her eyes to mine. 'You know what Stefano's like. It's easier to agree with him when he's angry,' she said earnestly. I could vouch for that.

Cressida sniffed pointedly. 'But he didn't believe me!' she said with what seemed like genuine indignation. 'He rang me from Milan and said he'd decided I should go back to live in Italy. When I said I wouldn't go, he said in that case his sister or his mother would come to live with me in England to teach me my family responsibilities! I said I wouldn't have them, he said it was his house and he would invite whom he liked to stay.'

'Oh,' I said inadequately.

It seemed to satisfy Cressida as a sympathetic response for she nodded. 'He wouldn't *listen*! He knows I don't like Lucrezia or his sisters and they don't like me but he just said I'd forfeited any right to be treated with consideration. He went on and on in a horribly cold voice, no thought for what I was feeling at all.' Her eyes filled with tears again. 'I know it wasn't right to deceive him but he didn't seem to believe that I was sorry. I got so *angry*!' she added with what sounded like massive understatement. 'He's never, ever spoken to me like that before, as if I was one of his staff who hadn't done the filing right! He said that, whether I liked it or not, Lucrezia was on her way and then put the phone down.'

She pushed her hair back off her forehead impatiently. 'I'd been taking the little bronze of the dancing faun to the safe when the telephone went. I was so cross I couldn't think straight except that I wanted to do something that would upset Stefano.' I began to get a nasty feeling. She bit her lip and looked at me through tear-filled eyes. 'I picked up the faun and threw it at the fireplace! And, oh, Laura,' she choked on a sob, 'I didn't think I'd do it any harm, not really, because it's a bronze but the metal must have been thinner than I thought and it caught the edge of the fireplace. I dented it all down one side!'

I could see why she wasn't keen to tell Stefano this, but surely all was not yet lost? 'Couldn't you have it repaired? Tell him you had a bit of an accident with it and not let him see the extent of the damage?'

'Not letting him see it was the problem! At first I couldn't believe what I'd done, I couldn't think straight, I thought Stefano would *kill* me when he found out!' she declared tragically. 'When Arabella rang, banging on about the seminar, it seemed the ideal solution. I had an excuse to go to London and could take the faun to James, because he'd always help me and would know what to do. And with luck Stefano would think it was in the safe with the china and I might even be able to get it back without his knowing it had ever been damaged.'

From the sound of it she'd been pretty hopeful. Didn't that sort of skilled repair take some time? Stefano would certainly have begun to smell a rat if his precious things had stayed in the safe for too long. 'So poor Arabella didn't make the convert she thought she had,' I said irrelevantly.

Cressida smiled faintly. 'I thought it would be quite useful to learn how to stand up to Stefano, but a lightning course in casting bronze would have been more to the point.'

Too true. 'So what went wrong?' I asked.

'James wasn't there!' she said crossly as if he'd deliberately let her down. 'And his staff said he'd be away for two days so I had to go to a couple of places myself. I asked about repairs and they both refused to touch it. One said he didn't do that sort of thing and the other said he had a backlog of about six months for repairs. So to while away the time until James got back I went off to Folkestone to do those follow up seminars.' She looked up and grinned with a trace of the old Cressida. 'At least they got me out of London and Stefano's reach – so much for standing up to him! The faun came with me, of course. I stayed with Sam.'

'But Arabella said he never had any of his graduates in his house?'

Cressida sniffed derisively. 'That's quite true normally, but he invites certain favoured female graduates.'

She let the rest of her sentence hang in the air for a moment. I stared at her incredulously. 'Oh, don't tell me the great Sam suggested you stand up to Stefano in a really definite way by having a one or several night stand?'

Cressida giggled. 'More or less. Except Sam likes sandwiches.'

I frowned, at a loss, and she giggled again. 'Three in a bed, the other party being his wife.'

'Crippen!' I exclaimed. 'So what did you do, beat it?'

She nodded. 'I didn't need that sort of complication. Not then. Have you ever tried it?'

'Certainly not!' I said quickly.

'Me neither. I wonder what it's like,' she said thoughtfully, then to my relief returned to the subject. 'I moved straight into Bosun's View. It was very peaceful, I rather liked it there. After a couple of pretty fraught weeks with Stefano it was bliss to be somewhere where the most tension-inducing thing was persuading Mrs Jessop to give you a second cup of coffee, and to go along to follow up seminars where you got ordered around and told what to think. I just drifted for a couple of days, didn't bother to think about what I was going to do. Can you understand that?' she asked anxiously.

'Of course,' I assured her.

'Then when you turned up and said Stefano was after my blood for taking the china, I knew he'd found out that the faun had gone but wasn't saying.' She looked straight at me. 'Incidentally, I do know his father almost certainly didn't find it in a shop in Milan but "liberated" it during the war. All I can say is that if it's the real one, the old Count's sticky fingers saved it from going to Moscow with the Russian army to disappear into a vault somewhere, so maybe it was better off with Stefano.' I was tempted to point out that if it had been lying in a vault in Moscow it wouldn't have been hurled at the wall, but decided it wasn't too tactful. Cressida smiled wistfully. 'Stefano really believes I'm so naive I've never noticed the way he steers anyone who might know too much away from that faun.'

I stared hard at my interlaced fingers. So Stefano believed that Cressida, with James's connivance, had helped herself to his favourite object in the world as well as his china collection. Of course in Stefano's mind it would have been James who'd pointed out to Cressida that what they had was no minor copy but a major work of art and one that couldn't be reported as missing to boot. Even sold through the criminal underworld for a fraction of its true value it would provide Cressida with the ample dowry Stefano claimed she had taken with her. Add to this murky scenario a good dollop of spiteful innuendo from Serena via a so-called journalist which had given it a spurious air of veracity and perhaps it wasn't so surprising that a man of Stefano's volatile temperament had gone completely off the deep end.

'But surely if you 'fess up to Stefano, maybe tell a few little white lies . . . you know, you fell over while carrying it and dented it. Leave out the bit about hurling it at high speed into the fire . . . he'll be so pleased that, firstly you haven't been nicking all his things, and secondly you haven't been having it off with James, he'll forgive all.' Her eyes began to brim with tears again and I said flippantly, 'What's the problem? Have you lost it or something?'

'Yes!' she exclaimed and burst into tears.

It took quite five minutes to calm her down again. What she'd done was one of those classic stupid mistakes you can see coming a mile away when someone else makes it but with a sinking feeling in the stomach acknowledge you'd be quite likely to make yourself. Sam had taken his rejection in apparent good part and offered to lend her some things, stuff she'd forgotten to bring which is useful for the seaside: wellington boots, a heavy raincoat, a selection of books, his wife's spare hairdryer. They were all in the two large carrier bags she had returned to his house on our way to Ashford with a message that she'd included a few of her own books which she didn't want to take to Paris and Sam was welcome to them. I guessed it before she even told me. She'd wrapped the faun in newspaper and another plastic bag and put it at the bottom of one of the carrier bags. And forgotten it was there. It wasn't until she was in Paris that she realised that she had inadvertently given it away but consoled herself that, basically being a nice bloke, Sam would give it back as soon as he realised it was a mistake. As she'd discovered this evening she'd been wrong.

'He says,' she said, sniffing into her tissue, 'that we don't make mistakes, that everything we do is because we want it to happen that way.'

'So if I run over my cat in the car it's because I really want my cat dead?' I asked sceptically.

'Exactly. It sounded a bit funny at the time. Now I don't think it's true at all.'

'It's complete hogwash!'

'I told him my husband would never forgive me if he discovered I'd lost his faun in that way but he said that deep down I must want to provoke a confrontation with Stefano – I mean, I've done that already without having to resort to giving away one of his favourite things, haven't I?' she asked quite reasonably. 'So it *is* rubbish! And Sam says that one of the most important lessons to be learned from Lifesigns is that you have to take responsibility for your own actions no matter what the consequences.'

'Of course you do, but I don't see why that means he is refusing to return something you didn't mean him to have in the first place!' I retorted. I thought it was far more likely that this Sam reckoned he'd got his hands on something that might be worth a fair amount of money, even if he didn't know exactly what it was he had, than that he actually believed all this sanctimonious cant he'd been spouting to Cressida.

'Neither do I, but he's absolutely adamant.' Her face hardened with a flash of temper. 'Do you know, he even said he couldn't give it back to me because it would be bad for my personal development!'

'The bastard!'

'He's worse than that,' she muttered. 'When I think of how much I looked up to him . . . I'm going to finish him. I'll tell everyone what a fake he is, what a dirty greedy hypocrite, how he can't keep his octopus-like hands off the women in his seminars . . .'

Loath as I was to drag her away from her empowering fantasies of revenge, I had to say, 'We'd better get the faun back first.'

Her face fell immediately. 'We can't, unless we break into his house and steal it back.' She looked hopefully at me.

'That might be going a bit too far,' I said firmly, trying to plan on the hoof so to speak, or rather to come up with some better idea on the spur of the moment. There was enough of a risk of a police presence in my life just now without positively inviting it. She shifted back against the pillows, looking absurdly young for a married woman with a husband like Stefano. The simplest ideas are often the best. 'I'll tell you what,' I said. 'Tomorrow, you and I'll go down to Folkestone and demand the faun back in person from this Sam. It's much more difficult to come out with all that choosing your own destiny and meaning all your mistakes rubbish when you're face to face with a sceptical audience. I bet he thinks he can push you around because you're pretty and look young and have a gentle manner. He imagines he can pat you on the head and treat you like some dizzy little blonde. He won't try that with two of us. The last man who tried to do it to me couldn't walk straight for a week.' Not true unfortunately, but another black mark in the lie book which is being kept on me in heaven was worth it for the smile that replaced some of the bleak desperation on Cressida's face.

'But what do we do if he refuses?'

I gritted my teeth for a moment. Honestly it wasn't surprising this Sam bloke thought he could pull a fast one and lay claim to an artistic treasure. Sometimes Cressida behaved like a complete wimp! She always expected someone else to come up with the answers. The most she did to help herself was to allow her eyes to fill with tears and then some man would rush in. Maybe she couldn't help it. Pretty people always have others eager to do things for them, and if you never do anything how can you learn to be independent? Whatever, I found it pretty exhausting. 'If he refuses we move to Plan B,' I said importantly.

'What's Plan B?'

Good question. 'It's . . . it's . . . you tell Stefano and let *him* go down and get it back.' Simple, obvious and very effective.

Of course Cressida didn't see it that way. Her eyes widened in horror. 'I couldn't!' she squeaked. 'He'd be furious.'

'Nothing like as furious as he will be if he thinks you really did go off with the faun,' I pointed out. 'He's going to be beside himself with joy that he's got you back and, I'll bet, in a mellow mood too. Tell him a few little porkies about how you came to damage the faun, explain truthfully how you came to give it to Sam, and I can almost guarantee that though Stefano might get cross, if you play your cards right he'll think it's the sort of mistake anyone could make. Especially his very pretty, contrite and much adored wife. At the very least he'll realise you didn't deliberately give it away.' She nodded thoughtfully as if it had at last occurred to her what a powerful weapon she had in her ability to wheedle prettily. 'Then leave the rest to Stefano. He'll make Sam hand it back. You can be sure of that,' I said with grim relish. I was rather sorry I wouldn't be there if it ever came to a confrontation between Stefano and the patronising head of Lifesigns. 'But, Cressida,' I fixed her with a stern eye, 'you really will have to talk to Stefano this time! No more saying you can only get through to his answering machine.'

She looked away. 'I was frightened to speak to him,' she said, not bothering to deny it. 'I told you rows make me feel ill, and I know he'd never really do anything to James. He may have a dreadful temper but he's not a *wicked* man. I know he accused James of stealing the china but he really believes that, doesn't he?'

About as much as he believes pigs are supersonic, I thought, and decided that in the interests of everybody

I'd keep quiet for a bit longer about what we'd found in James's house courtesy of Cressida's good as gold husband. If she got a sudden *crise de conscience* and decided she couldn't possibly live with somebody who was prepared actively to err on the shady side of the law we'd all be in the soup. At least I managed to make her ring the number James had given me for the police officer who had questioned him about the whereabouts of a large collection of missing china. Inspector Lambert kept sensible hours and had gone home but she left a message for him to ring her back first thing in the morning. And I wouldn't let her get away with fudging the issue this time, I thought firmly as I left her to go to sleep.

I was thinking that a bit of sleep for myself would be no bad thing when Liv came roaring in, desperate to catch up on absolutely everything that had been happening. The telephone calls I'd made weren't nearly enough, she said firmly, especially as I'd seemed more interested in enquiring about the welfare of my cat than in passing on news. So we ended up by sharing one of the presents I'd brought back for her while she lay stretched out on the sofa with her feet comfortably propped up on the arms listening to me Tell All. I had to repeat myself in several places as she quite understandably got confused. She slopped some more of Intermarché's best into her glass and said thoughtfully, 'I don't know why it is that things always seem to happen to you, Laura.'

'I certainly don't invite it,' I said a bit huffily.

'No, but you seem to be a sort of magnet for trouble,' she pointed out. It was depressingly like the sort of thing Darian was inclined to mutter in my presence, though her voice didn't contain Liv's note of indulgence. 'Still,' she went on cheerfully, 'if this Sam fellow doesn't give the faun back I know William's got a whole lot of pig slurry he wants to get rid of. I'm sure he'd be very happy to leave it in Sam's garden.'

I thought about it for one glorious moment. 'I wish,' I said, plumping up the cushion behind me. 'It's just what the bloke deserves. But even for you and your lovely blue eyes I can't see William driving the slurry tanker from Swindon to Folkestone.'

Liv wrinkled her nose. 'Well, he might if it was the EC commissioner who had the bright idea of cutting his subsidy, but I suppose you're right about Sam. Are you going to take Daniel down for moral support when you go to Folkestone?'

'Er, no,' I said in a strangled sort of tone.

Liv looked up quickly. Sadly she knows me too well, and realised long before I got the chance to make up a face-saving excuse that something was up. 'Have you dumped him?'

She needn't sound so enthusiastic about it, I thought crossly as I filled her in. And she needn't find it so funny either. There was absolutely nothing amusing about Daniel's taking up with someone who was both fatter and older than me, even if said someone did have a more artistic sensibility. But frankly the early start, the events of the last week and the best part of a bottle of wine meant I couldn't rustle up the energy to be offended by her misplaced sense of humour. I'd get even later.

'I shouldn't worry about it if I were you,' Liv finally said in a sympathetic voice, obviously thinking my numbly tired expression was masking deep anguish. 'From what you've said about her she won't have your skill with a washing machine. He'll be back as soon as he realises his socks don't make the journey to the laundry of their own accord.' The slightly sarcastic note was a bit rich coming from her. Until she persuaded William to get a daily to do it she used to do all his washing and ironing. I don't do ironing. I have enough trouble coping with my own.

I half heartedly threw a cushion at her and yawned hugely. 'Daniel can come back with his twin brother if he likes, and the local rugby team – especially the local rugby team – but not until I've managed to have some sleep.'

Surprisingly enough Liv took this incredibly subtle hint and even helped me wrestle with putting up the sofa bed, an operation which usually requires circus strong man muscles. We don't use it much. After five minutes of lying on it I realised why friends who have stayed overnight never seem to be very keen to repeat the experience. It's not only staggeringly uncomfortable, but due to the amount of wine that has been spilled over it at one time or another – I sniffed at the arm, some this evening by Liv – it smells like a bar at the end of a long day. Thoroughly put out by my moving resting places Horatio signified his disapproval by walking round and round the bed, so that every time I did manage to drop off to sleep I was soon woken up by leaden-footed steps going up my legs and a heavy weight crashing down on my middle. He finally settled at about three-thirty, comfortably establishing himself in the middle of the bed with the duvet immovably anchored under him, so that I was both short of space and cold. I didn't dare shift him over in case he started his marathon again.

I was so deeply asleep when Cressida shook my shoulder to wake me that I couldn't think who she was or what she was doing here. 'Laura, I'm sorry,' she whispered, holding a hand to her stomach, 'I think I need to see a doctor.'

I sat up blearily, blinking back the focus into my eyes. It was still dark outside. 'What time is it?' I yawned.

'Six o'clock. I've been trying to hold on until surgery hours but,' her face creased, 'the pain's *awful*, and it's getting worse. I think there really is something the matter with me.'

I took in her lank hair and cheesy pallor. 'Well, you certainly don't look the full quid,' I said frankly. 'Where does it hurt?' She pointed to her right side and winced, staggering slightly. I was getting alarmed. My knowledge of first aid is limited to applying a plaster, but even I could see that she should have consulted a doctor hours ago. 'Come on, I'm going to take you straight to hospital,' I said, getting out of bed.

'You won't leave me there, will you?' she asked, looking very frightened. 'I hate hospitals.'

I smiled reassuringly. 'Sure, I was planning to chuck you out of the car at the doors to the Emergency Department and leave you to look after yourself! But I suppose if you insist I'll stay for at least five minutes before I roar off to have a much better time.'

I scrambled into my clothes and threw a few things into a bag for her in case she had to stay. By the look of her it was a near certainty. Luckily, so early in the morning the roads were nearly deserted. My hands were shaking so much I'm sure I'd have wobbled into the oncoming traffic if there had been any. They were incredibly efficient in Casualty; it took hardly any time for a doctor to see her, just as quickly he had her admitted to the wards as a case of suspected acute appendicitis. Within half an hour she was lying in bed in a small side ward looking young and very scared. She clung to my hand and refused point blank to let me leave, even though the staff nurse said rather frigidly that hospital policy didn't allow friends to stay while the doctor was examining a patient.

Cressida's grip tightened as if she was afraid I was about to be removed by force. I wondered if any blood was reaching my hand at all. 'In that case I won't be examined!' she declared tearfully.

Staff Nurse's capacious bosom rose indignantly while the doctor who, judging by the shadows under his eyes, was nearing the end of a very long shift wiped his hands on his coat. 'There, there, don't get upset,' he said before the nurse could launch into a speech about spoiled young girls who didn't care for proper hospital routine. 'I'm sure we can stretch a point just this once.'

'Thank you, doctor,' said Cressida with one of her blinding smiles. He beamed back, looking less tired by the second. From his bemused expression he would have been prepared to examine her while wearing a gorilla suit if it would make her happy. He poked, prodded, declared he was fairly sure she needed to have her appendix out promptly but said that he'd like her to have a scan just to make sure it wasn't an inflamed ovary. I had to indulge in an orgy of form-filling on her behalf while she was wheeled off to have it. I was still trying to remember where I'd put the piece of paper with her doctor's address when she came back. 'The ovary's absolutely fine,' she reported gloomily. 'So it must be the appendix. Laura, I'm so frightened!'

I patted her hand, saying what you always do: that it's a common operation, doesn't even hurt much, nothing to it, she'd be out of hospital within days. But it didn't seem to console her much. 'Would you like me to ring Stefano?' I asked at last.

'Yes, please!' she breathed, looking as if all her problems were about to be solved for her, but then her face fell. 'We haven't done anything about the faun yet.'

'I expect that'll be the last thing on his mind when he hears you're about to be operated on. And if he asks, you can always pretend you're still woozy from the anaesthetic.'

She nodded slowly. 'And I do want him here so much,' she wailed, eyes filling with tears. 'I'm sorry, Laura, you're being tremendous, but you aren't *him*!'

'Don't worry, I'm not at all offended. The card with all his numbers on it is still in my purse, I'll go and ring him straight away.'

'Do you think he'll come?' she whispered.

I smiled at her. 'Of course he will, you dolt!' If he didn't I'd go around there and fetch him myself.

The fates must have been smiling on me. The pay phone at the end of the ward wasn't being used and I actually had enough change for it without making the usual embarrassing journey down to the newspaper shop in the lobby and offering a five-pound note in payment for a packet of Polos. Except that when I rang the flat a female voice said sharply, '*Pronto.*'

'May I speak to Stefano, please?'

'Who is it who is on the telephone?' asked the voice I guessed belonged to one of Stefano's sisters. Even if I hadn't heard Cressida's descriptions of her sisters-in-law I would still have taken an instant dislike to her on the basis of the cold arrogance of her tone. Mentally I begged Cressida's pardon for thinking she'd exaggerated.

'Laura Moreton.'

'My brother has no wish to speak to you.' And the telephone was slammed down.

I took a deep breath. I resisted hitting the telephone or shouting abuse at it. After all it was quite innocent of any crime. I made a couple of mental wax images of rude, poisonous Italian witches and spent an enjoyable minute sticking imaginary pins into them. Then I took another deep breath and redialled. When that haughty voice answered I said in a broad London accent, 'Count Stefano Buonotti, if you please, missus. This is Sergeant Caldwell from Kennington Police Station. At once, missus. This is urgent.'

Much to my surprise it worked. Being Italian she wasn't able to tell quite how unconvincing my South London accent is. Stefano was on the line within thirty seconds. 'What is the matter, Sergeant?'

'The matter is that Cressida's in hospital and your sister won't let me talk to you!' I snapped.

'Laura!' he said harshly. 'How dare you—' Then, 'What do you mean, *hospital*? What has happened to her?

Where is she?' There was a satisfying degree of panic in his voice which augured well for a reconciliation.

'Can you get here as quickly as possible? Adelaide Ward, Queen Anne's Hospital. She's asking for you, Stefano.'

'I am leaving now,' he said. I presume he really was for I heard a clunk as if the telephone was hitting the floor, followed shortly by the sound of a door slamming.

I walked back to Cressida smiling. 'He's on his way, I hope he was already dressed when he answered the phone. If he wasn't, judging by the speed at which he seemed to leave, he'll be turning up in his pyjamas.'

'He'd better have been dressed. He doesn't wear pyjamas!'

She looked up as the Staff Nurse approached with her clipboard. 'Doctor's confirmed you'll have to be operated on for your appendix, Mrs Buonotti. A nurse will be along in a few minutes to start prepping you.' She smiled kindly as Cressida's eyes grew wider and wider. 'Don't be afraid, dear. It's quite a commonplace operation these days and I can promise you there's really very little risk to your baby at all.'

CHAPTER 17

I sat down heavily on the side of the bed. Cressida stared at the nurse, open-mouthed, looking like a fish in shock. 'Baby?' she said at last, sounding as if she was talking from the bottom of the bath. 'Risk to the *baby*?'

'Really, dear, as I said, there'll hardly be any,' said the nurse comfortingly. 'Of course we prefer not to operate on a pregnant mother if we can, but frankly we don't have the option where you're concerned.'

'You've made a mistake,' said Cressida faintly. '*I'm* not having a baby. You must have mixed up the test with someone else's.'

'Didn't you know?' asked the nurse in surprise. 'Oh, my dear, I hope it hasn't been too much of a shock for you? No, it's you all right. Doctor could feel it when he was examining your tummy and then it showed up on the scan, clear as anything. About eight weeks, he says.'

Cressida put one hand gently on her stomach. 'But how . . .?' she began, then giggled faintly. 'Well, I suppose that's obvious, isn't it? The normal time-honoured way. You know that famous letter from my gynae, Laura? It said I should go and see him because,' she put on a snotty doctorly voice, 'my "form of contraception had proved itself to be sometimes unsatisfactory and the failure rate to be unacceptably high". Bit late for the warning, wasn't it?' She giggled again and shook her head disbelievingly. 'Now I look back I should have known, I had *all* the signs, but I was so tied up with other things I never noticed. Well, I've never been pregnant before so I didn't know what to expect. No wonder I was knackered all the time! Stefano said it was too many late nights. He was wrong, wasn't he?' she said in a satisfied tone. 'That doesn't happen often.'

'So it's good news, dear?' the nurse asked anxiously, voicing my worries exactly.

'Oh, yes!' Cressida smiled brilliantly. 'It's the best news in the world! My husband is going to be so pleased.' She looked at me. 'Do you think he'll believe it was intentional?' she asked in a low voice.

I shook my head firmly. 'Don't even try it!' I hissed back.

The nurse hadn't heard and was beaming. 'Well, don't be surprised if you have a few mixed feelings, my dear. It takes a bit of getting used to even when you've been trying for one and are expecting the news. I've had six myself and you could have knocked me over with a feather each time I discovered I was pregnant.' It was difficult to imagine anything less substantial than a fork lift truck having much effect on Staff Nurse Rogers. Her voice dropped confidentially. 'And to be frank, to start off with I wasn't too pleased about the last two, but that soon passed. It's difficult to be unhappy about a baby. I just love them,' she declared in a blinding statement of the obvious. She went all soggy and misty-eyed as she con-templated the baby-powder-scented future for Cressida, then shook herself back into starch and thermometer mode. 'So don't you go worrying yourself about the operation. It'll go right as rain and we'll have you up and about in one shake of a lamb's tail, just you see.'

'Operation?' Cressida said blankly. 'Oh, I can't have that until I've talked it over with my husband. He might not agree. It's the risk to the baby, you see.'

The nurse's bosom swelled out like a turkeycock's. 'I trust your husband's primary concern is with *your* health, Mrs Buonotti,' she said coldly. If it wasn't I got the distinct impression Staff Nurse Rogers would soon be putting him right.

'Isn't there more risk to the baby if you *don't* have the operation?' I ventured.

'Absolutely,' said the nurse, looking at me with approval for the first time. Maybe there were some advantages to having visitors cluttering up her ward at nine in the morning.

Cressida stuck out her bottom lip, looking both obsti-nate and childish. 'I'm not agreeing to anything until I've spoken to Stefano.'

She was absolutely immovable. Both Nurse Rogers and I tried to make her change her mind, with no success, and the nurse was beginning to mutter about the dire neces-sity of having to call the consultant to come and explain to Cressida exactly why she must have the operation. I gathered one did not disturb this august being lightly. She fixed me with an eagle glare as if I was equally culpable in Cressida's decision and said coldly, 'I'll leave you for five minutes to see if you can talk some sense into your friend,' then stalked off with her ramrod straight back exuding disapproval to the nurses' station at the other end of the ward.

Cressida looked at me with a guilty expression. 'Do you think I'm being very silly, Laura?'

'Yes,' I said bluntly.

She pouted and chewed delicately on the end of her nail. I noticed she never actually bit it or made the end ragged and unsightly, just sort of sucked the end as if it was a grown-up version of a baby's rusk. 'You see,' she said in a serious voice, 'I know how Stefano's mind works. If he believes I'm prepared to put the baby at risk he might think I don't care for it.' Personally I would have thought that even Stefano would see that the baby was going to be at far more risk if Cressida got peritonitis but she didn't look receptive to ideas like that. She pushed herself up in bed, frowning slightly. 'He seems to think that I'm capable of doing anything at the moment: steal, run off with James . . . he might work himself up to a point where he began to think it might not even be his baby.'

'Why on earth should he think that?' I asked, astonished. 'I mean, I know he's jealous of you, but surely he can't really believe . . .' My voice trailed off as I saw her expression. Was she thinking she might have thrown her arms around James's neck once too many times and given Stefano *real* cause for suspicion? 'It *is* Stefano's baby, isn't it?' I asked directly.

To my horror she had to think for a moment before she said brightly, 'Yes, it is.' After a pause. 'Definitely.'

I sank down limply, my stomach churning unpleasantly as I thought of her baby being born with moss green eyes. 'Who . . .?' I asked, swallowing a lump in my throat. 'Could it possibly have been James's?'

'James?' she echoed. 'Heavens, no! He says he's got very few scruples but messing around with married women is one of them.' My heart appeared to start beating again. 'More's the pity,' she added with an impish grin that left me wondering whether she was being serious or not. She looked away, twirling a lock of hair absently around her finger. 'I had a brief fling with someone else. It didn't mean anything and it was only a couple of times.' She shrugged. 'I was angry with Stefano, I did it to get back at him.'

'You choose some pretty high-risk methods of showing your disapproval with him, don't you?' I said at last. 'In future don't you think you'd better find ways which don't have such potentially disastrous repercussions?'

She nodded thoughtfully. Nurse Rogers advanced towards us, clipboard in hand. 'Well, Mrs Buonotti, are you prepared to sign the consent form or must I call the doctor?' she enquired in arctic tones. The swing doors at the end of the ward crashed open and Stefano tore in, looking around frantically for someone to help him. In deference to his sister's presence in the flat he must have pulled on his trousers before he answered the phone but there was precious little evidence of his doing any other dressing. His bare feet had been pushed into Docksiders, his navy blue blazer was buttoned over nothing more than a hairy chest, his chin was dark with stubble and even his short hair looked in need of a good brush.

Nurse Roger's eyebrows shot skywards as she surveyed this disreputable figure. Cressida's head whipped around as he careered to a halt at the nurses' station and she leaned forward, calling, 'Stefano, Stefano!'

Nurse's mutter for her to keep her voice down as this was a hospital and not a bawdy house was lost in the answering cry of '*Cara mia!*' as he bolted down the ward with his arms wide open. He seized Cressida in his arms, hugging her tight and raining kisses on her hair and upturned face. 'My darling! My loved one! I have been so unhappy without you, I have not known what to do,' he declared in a loud voice, quite oblivious to the fact that he had company, a lot of company, who could hear every word and were listening eagerly. 'Don't ever leave me again, please, please. Without you I am nothing, life is not worth living—'

Feeling decidedly *de trop* I got up from my chair and backed off a little. I didn't want to make it too obvious that I was eagerly attending to every word of this reunion. Judging by the line of interested faces turned towards us the rest of the ward was enjoying it too; one patient had drawn back her curtains so that she could hear better.

Cressida was returning Stefano's embraces with enthusiasm – too much enthusiasm for Nurse Rogers's outraged sense of propriety. With a flick of her starched cuff she began to draw the curtains around them, much to everyone's disappointment. But her eyes were twinkling as she whispered to me, 'Had a quarrel, did they?'

I nodded. 'I'll say!'

'The making up is always the best part,' she said with a fond smile.

Annoyingly the drawn curtains muffled the voices within quite effectively, though by straining hard I could catch the occasional phrase such as, '... so sorry', '... never again', 'I promise never ...', 'whatever you want', which seemed to be fairly equally divided between the two voices. It sounded as if they were making up most satisfactorily. But the incredulous cry of '*You're pregnant!*' echoed right around the ward. As did the smacking kiss that followed the news.

'Someone's pleased!' whispered the nurse complacently.

There was more muffled mumbling and then a clatter of feet as Stefano ripped open the curtains and marched up to Nurse Rogers, eyeballing her furiously. 'What do you mean by telling my wife there is any question of her not having this operation?' he demanded. 'That she should put the baby before herself? Call yourself a nurse! You should be torn off your list! You are supposed to care for people, not tell them they should give themselves up for others!'

Poor Nurse Rogers looked very taken aback at this completely unjustified attack. 'But I—' she began, all her starch and vinegar dissolving in the face of Stefano's anger.

He swept on regardless. 'How *dare* you suggest to my wife that I would care more about the baby than for her?'

'I didn't,' said the nurse, beginning to recover herself.

'You must operate at once! At once, do you hear? My wife is worth more to me than one thousand babies ever could be. Do you understand?'

'Perfectly,' said Nurse Rogers acidly, 'as does the whole ward and most of the hospital now! We've been waiting this last half-hour for Mrs Buonotti to sign the consent form for the operation but she wouldn't unless you agreed to it.'

To my surprise Stefano flushed slightly under his villainous stubble. 'My apologies, Signora. I misunderstood what my wife told me,' he said quietly. He turned around and twitched back the curtain. 'Cressida, you are having this operation. Now. No further discussion about it.' He took the clipboard and form from the nurse's hand. 'Sign this. Don't argue.' Thirty seconds later he handed the form back with Cressida's rounded scrawl at the bottom. 'Here you are.'

Nurse Rogers beamed. 'I do like a masterful man,' she said to me in a low voice. All was forgiven. The bustle came back into her stride as she summoned a student nurse to start getting Cressida ready and announced she was going to inform the surgeon at last that his patient would definitely be ready for him this morning. I hung around feeling like a complete spare part but didn't think I could slip away without saying goodbye to Cressida. My tummy gave an embarrassingly loud rumble, pointing out I'd been up for hours with no breakfast. It also served to remind Stefano of my presence. He turned his head and looked at me with eyes that were fractionally warmer than a mountain stream, but not much. 'Laura, thank you for calling me,' he said punctiliously.

I shrugged. 'It was nothing.'

'It is a shame you did not think to telephone me before,' he said in a hard voice, 'then my wife's life would not have been endangered by your dragging her away on this unnecessary escapade.' My mouth dropped open in astonishment. 'She was quite healthy when I left her,' he added with sublime unreasonableness.

'Hey, hang on a moment!' I gasped. 'An inflamed appendix isn't something you *catch*! And even if it was, mine's in perfect order so she certainly couldn't have got anything off *me*!' Just in time I managed to bite my tongue on a resounding, 'So there!'

The student nurse put her head around the curtains and made shushing noises at us, threatening to have us banished from the ward if we didn't shut up. Stefano's jaw went rigid. I couldn't bear to think of the damage he must be doing to his teeth with all that grinding. His nose went up and he stared at me down it with centuries of ingrained aristocratic hauteur. 'I do not see any need to discuss this further with you!' It nearly worked. Unfortunately for him I'm not sure that even Prince Philip could carry off a supercilious pose like that when he was (a) very hairy, and (b) not wearing anything under his jacket.

I stared pointedly at his chest, then his feet, then his stubble. 'Don't you, indeed?' I asked acidly. 'Bit late to take that attitude, Stefano. If you didn't want me involved you shouldn't have started threatening James!'

Oh, dear, I'd forgotten that he wasn't the type of man to appreciate being answered back by a woman, and one more than twenty years younger than himself to boot. It looked as if an iron bar had just been rammed under the shoulders of his jacket. Steam was metaphorically coming from his nostrils. Tact, sadly, is not my middle name.

The more sensible part of me, the bit I tend not to listen to very often because its advice is so boring, told me it would be more productive to conciliate Stefano than to drive him into a corner. But my head was too fuzzy from lack of sleep and food and I was frankly too fed up with his belligerence to bother. Fortunately, before he could give in to his baser nature and throttle me as he obviously wanted to, the student stuck her head out between the curtains again and said, 'Miss Moreton, Mrs Buonotti wants to speak to you. She's very insistent,' she added with an expression that indicated she thought Cressida was being thoroughly unreasonable. 'Could you spare a moment?'

Stefano made an odd noise from behind me. For a moment I thought he was going to forbid me to take my contaminating presence anywhere near his wife but even he must have realised that he wasn't going to get very far with that. Cressida turned her head towards me as I slipped behind her curtains and hissed, 'Laura! What are we going to do about the faun?' The faun? I'd completely forgotten about it. And what was this 'we'? In my present mood I didn't see why she shouldn't tell Stefano she'd had the blessed thing melted down for scrap and let him put *that* in his pipe and smoke it.

'I shouldn't worry about it,' I said in a heartily reassuring voice. 'Stefano's so happy to have you back he's going to forgive you anything.'

'Shsh!' She pointed towards the ward. 'We must get it back, Laura! It would ruin everything if he were ever to know I'd given it away!' *Given* it away? That wasn't what she'd said to me last night.

I gave her a severe look and she turned her head, not meeting my eyes. 'I didn't exactly *give* it away, but I didn't exactly not know that it was in the carrier bag when I told Sam he could have everything in it. I was angry with Stefano,' she mumbled. And you wanted to get back at him without taking full responsibility for it, I thought. Honestly, in many ways she had the morality of a six year old. And like a six year old she expected other people to get her out of trouble.

'Is Laura tiring you, *cara*?' called Stefano in a voice stiff with disapproval.

Cressida started and turned apprehensive eyes towards the shadow thrown on to her curtains. 'No, of course not, darling,' she quavered, then returned her pleading gaze to my face. I was somehow given the impression that if I refused her now I was going to be personally responsible for ruining the rest of her life. And that it would weigh heavily on my conscience. Well, perhaps it wasn't a good idea if she went down to her operation worried sick, even if I did think that her worries were a bit exaggerated by now. As the means of soothing the angry breast of an enraged husband an operation and a surprise first baby come well into the double whammy stakes. I reckon he'd have forgiven her anything. Well, perhaps not eloping with James. I sighed heavily and said gracelessly, 'I'll go down to Folkestone myself and get it then.'

'Oh, will you? Laura, you *are* kind,' she exclaimed happily. 'You'll do it today, won't you?'

All I wanted to do was eat breakfast and go to bed. The last thing I needed was another long journey and then a scene at journey's end while I tried to wrest the faun out of Sam's greedy grasp. And then if I did manage to get it back, I was prepared to bet Stefano would accuse *me* of stealing the bloody thing. Cressida fixed me with her expectant puppy look. 'All right, today,' I said grumpily and then decided that she could jolly well do something for me too. 'On one condition, Cressida, and only that.'

'What?' She eyed me warily.

'You tell Stefano the moment I leave your bedside about the china being in the safe.' As she opened her mouth to protest, I said firmly, 'Come on, he's hardly going to go rushing off to Hurstwood to check what's actually in the safe while you're being operated on, is he? And I'll bring the faun back to you tomorrow.' I touched my head in lieu of a handy piece of wood, praying this was actually going to be true.

'All right,' she said reluctantly.

'Promise?' I demanded.

She seemed on the verge of making some excuse again, then sighed. 'If I don't promise you won't go, will you?'

'No.' Actually I didn't put too heavy a reliance on Cressida's promises either but it was worth a shot.

'OK, I promise,' she said heavily, as if I was being totally unreasonable I noted with some indignation. 'Sam's address is in my diary in the top drawer of my bedside cabinet.'

'Won't he be doing one of his seminars this weekend?' I asked hopefully as I scribbled it down.

Cressida shook her head. 'Only the first weekend of every month and you'll definitely find him at home today. It's his son's birthday party and he's a devoted father.'

Your average devoted father didn't, in my experience, try to arrange three in a bed sessions under the same roof as his child, but maybe I was unfairly prejudiced. Sam could have sent his son out to overnight with a friend in anticipation of adult fun.

'OK, I'll do my best,' I said, standing up as the nurse came back in.

'I'm going to have to turn you out, our patients aren't allowed to have visitors before their operations,' she said with a professionally insincere smile. She cast an expert eye over Cressida and smiled, more genuinely this time. 'Well, you look much happier, Mrs Buonotti. Sorted out what was worrying you, did you?'

'Completely. We were due to go to the seaside today, and Cressida was worried I wouldn't want to go without her,' I said. She shot me a reproachful look. I grinned. 'I suppose as we're in hospital it would be the height of bad taste to tell you to break a leg, but you know what I mean! I'll come and visit you tomorrow, Cressida, and I might even bring you a souvenir!'

Nurses were bustling around the beds, twitching sheets and straightening corners in preparation for the morning round. Stefano was being shooed into the waiting area by one of the students who was officiously telling him he'd be allowed to see his wife for a minute before she went down to theatre but he couldn't disturb the ward routine any further. Judging by the surreptitious looks she kept on giving his eccentrically clothed figure she was actually more worried that the doctors might think she was giving house room to someone better accustomed to the squats opposite. He stood listlessly, staring blankly at a poster telling patients to 'Give Nurse a Smile', his face a mask of worry. Despite myself (I can be quite nice sometimes), I stopped.

Touching him on the wrist, I said, 'She'll be all right, Stefano, honestly.'

He swung around, his face savage with shock. Well, I hoped it was just because he was startled. I smiled nervously. 'I'm sure that if it was really urgent they wouldn't have sent her for those tests and things. Fragile-looking people like Cressida are always the strongest.'

Heavy eyelids were lowered to shield his eyes. 'It is kind of you to be concerned but I will take care of my wife from now on,' he said coldly.

So it was like that, was it? I gave him a meaningless smile and walked off without bothering to say goodbye.

CHAPTER 18

I went straight back to the flat for copious amounts of coffee and a plate of toast and scrambled eggs shared with Horatio. I hadn't been intending to share it, but I was no proof against the cat equivalent of ram raiding. I poured myself another cup of coffee and spread the last piece of toast with raspberry jam, cats don't like fruit fortunately, and took it off to eat in the bath – an unusual habit, I'll admit, but at least it means you don't make a mess when you spill jam down your front. Washed hair, twenty minutes of soaking in hot water with liberal dashings of Liv's Mary Chess bath oil and a chapter of my book (finally I was able to discover if the heroine was ever rescued from her grim plight), and I was almost human again. I was guiltily relieved to be alone. As Darian complains so often, I might like to waste half the day gossiping with my friends but I do like my own space too. And it has to be admitted that a week in Cressida's company isn't good for any woman's self-esteem. So, I'm not in the top ranks of the world's high flyers looks wise, but never before have I gone for so long without even being *noticed*. As I got dressed I enjoyed the feeling that I could contemplate wearing my black jeans without the dispiriting reflection that my entire outfit probably cost less than my companion's underwear. Whatever they say about cheap and cheerful, cheap is hardly ever as cheerful as expensive. Gosh, the black jeans fitted! I could do up the zip easily. Well, fairly easily! Just suck my tummy in a bit and pull hard ... All this stress has had some good repercussions, I thought, beaming, as I swung round to admire my reduced *derrière* in the mirror.

Energised as one is by the thought of a few lost pounds I put on the green jumper that Imogen and Dad gave me for Christmas and which brings out the red lights in my hair, slapped on some make up and decided that if I had to go to Folkestone I would jolly well take some company. Ten minutes later I was knocking on James's door.

He opened it, yawning hugely, wearing a short silk dressing gown and so far as I could judge nothing else. His hair was standing on end, his chin was bristly and his red-rimmed eyes were having difficulty coping with even the light of this cloudy day. In short he wasn't a pretty sight. 'What are you doing here at this unearthly hour?' he asked.

'It's half-past ten and I've been up for hours,' I replied primly, and for once truthfully.

'Can't think why,' he mumbled. 'I was up until three-thirty checking that our mysterious friend hadn't left any other surprises for me around the house.' And seeing the bottom of more than one glass of whisky by the look of him. He yawned again. 'It's always very nice to see you, Laura.' His expression sharpened a little. 'Particularly nice this morning – that colour suits you. But do you want something or is this a social call? Because if it's the latter could you come back in about three hours?'

'It's no social call. We're off on a trip to the seaside.'

He blinked. 'A what? To where?'

'Folkestone.'

'Folkestone!' he exclaimed, waking up a bit, and glared at me suspiciously. 'You aren't planning to go on one of these ridiculous seminars, are you?' he demanded. 'Because I can tell you now,' he wagged his finger at me to emphasise his point, 'I'm not accompanying you.'

'No, we aren't going on a seminar,' I said. 'But unless you want to give whichever of Stefano's detectives is on duty today the opportunity of taking some *very* interesting photographs, I'd avoid making too many violent gestures on the doorstep if I were you.'

He looked down and hastily drew the edges of his dressing gown together. 'I suppose there's some good reason for your wanting to go to Folkestone,' he said in a sour tone that indicated he doubted it very much. 'You'd better come in and tell me what it is.'

He still looked as if he'd left his brains behind in bed. I didn't feel he could cope with the latest revelations until he'd got himself together a bit. 'Why don't you go and get dressed and I'll make some coffee?' I suggested. 'A large glass of Alka Seltzer might be a good idea too.'

'Some breakfast?' he asked hopefully in the eternal fashion of a male confronted with a gullible female who might be willing to undertake domestic tasks.

'I don't do breakfast,' I told him severely. Then remembering that I wanted him to come with me, added grudgingly, 'I'll see what I can find, just this once.'

'Laura, you're a heaven-sent angel!' he exclaimed, putting an arm around my shoulders and dropping a kiss on my mouth. He'd brushed his teeth so it was very pleasant. He stayed where he was for a few seconds then stepped back. 'Time for a cold shower,' he said regretfully, and went up the stairs.

The kitchen seemed almost completely devoid of food but I was sure that by breakfast James didn't mean a gin and tonic with an olive chaser, so I started searching in the back of cupboards. By the time he appeared, wearing a pair of jeans so old that the fabric was almost white at the knees, and looking remarkably alert considering what he'd been like ten minutes before, I'd found half a loaf of fairly ancient bread to toast and just enough butter to grease it. Showing that he had a truly iron constitution James loaded the toast with the last of a tub of coleslaw and three pieces of salami, pointing out when I protested that the Swedes have pickled herring for breakfast, and come to think of it, he thought he might have some marinated kippers in there somewhere . . .

I was interested to see that even he lost his appetite for a moment and had to put his laden bit of toast down when I began to explain why we were going to Folkestone and how Cressida had hurled the faun at a brick wall. He looked as if he would have forgiven her almost anything else – adultery, fiddling her taxes, highway robbery, you name it. Despite what he'd said the night before I wasn't at all certain his long infatuation with Cressida really had come to an end so I helpfully pointed out that she'd as good as admitted that she'd actually given the thing away and now it was being left to us to get it back. I could have throttled him when he murmured with an indulgent smile, 'Cressy's always needed someone to help her along and it's hardly her fault she's landed up in hospital, is it?'

He got up and wandered around the kitchen hoovering up the last of anything edible and remarking that he supposed it really was time he went out and did some food shopping. 'And I suppose that if we're going to the seaside it would be unfair not to give Barker a walk on the beach,' he added thoughtfully and rang up Harry, arranging to meet him in the car park of the local shopping centre in twenty minutes.

'Why there?' I asked as James put on a dark jacket and wrapped a red scarf around his neck.

'Wait and see,' he said with an infuriating air of superiority, picking up a pile of clothes for the dry cleaner's which he threw into the back seat of his car. He glanced in the mirror as we drew out. 'Keep an eye on the red Fiesta, the one that's just pulled out at the end of the road. I think that must be today's bloodhound.'

Feeling wonderfully cloak and daggerish I kept looking over my shoulder at the innocuous-looking little car that did indeed appear to be following us, unless, like James, the driver enjoyed the scenic and circuitous route to the supermarket. 'Aren't you going to whizz around all these streets and shake him off?' I asked.

He shrugged. 'Can't be bothered. He's welcome to follow us to Sainsbury's if he wants.' Then he grinned. 'I tried it earlier in the week and had no luck at all. The blighter knows these back roads better than I do. I did what I thought were a couple of really crafty turns and he was waiting for me at the crossroads. He must have done the knowledge at some time.'

As usual on a Saturday morning there was a slow-moving queue of cars waiting for one and a half hours of free parking in the multi-storey car park next to the shopping centre. We tagged on the end. Was James planning to do his grocery shopping now? I wondered as we inched slowly forward. Otherwise surely it would have been more sensible to meet Harry outside? Certainly quicker. 'What's he doing now?' asked James.

I looked back. 'He's drawn into the side, opposite the entrance.'

He grinned. 'Excellent! Probably thinks we're planning to nip around and go straight out again while he's stuck waiting to get through the barrier.' He leaned out, got the ticket, the barrier opened and we shot through up to the first level where a blue BMW convertible was drawn up by a pillar. A large black head hung out of the window, long pink tongue lolling. Harry, recognisably James's brother but taller and with matinee idol looks, was leaning against the car and waved idly at us as we stopped behind him.

Two girls in their twenties drove slowly past, heads swivelling as they passed him. Sadly they were wasting their time and their lustful thoughts. The love of Harry's life is a rugby player called Arthur. The greatest loss to womankind since the death of Rudolph Valentino came over and gave me a rib-cracking hug. I returned it. 'Lovely to see you, Laura. You're looking great,' he said, running an expert eye over me. Harry has an acute appreciation of looks in both sexes. 'But what on earth are you doing mixing yourself up with that tiresome woman Cressida?'

'Ask James. It's all his fault!'

'It's not. I didn't tell you to take her to Paris!' he said indignantly as he fished a dark yellow blouson jacket out of the dry cleaning pile and put it on.

'I couldn't understand that either,' said Harry. 'Nor why you tried to set her adrift in turbulent flood waters. Can't blame you, though. Personally I wouldn't have bothered to rescue her. When all this is over you must both come round and have dinner and tell me all about it.'

'Sure thing, bro,' said James, 'but when that'll be God only knows. We don't know what new bombshell Cressy's going to spring on us next and expect us to sort out for her.'

Both of us looked up at his rather sour tone. Was James finally becoming disenchanted with her? I wondered, finding that the grey sky outside suddenly looked as if it held a promise of sun.

'Let's go, Laura,' he said, looking a bit uncomfortable under our combined gazes. 'I'll bring it back this evening,' he called as he got into Harry's car and leaned over to open the passenger door for me. 'Thanks.'

Harry gazed anxiously after us. 'Look after it!' he called. 'And I'll have your guts for garters if it's got so much as a scratch on it. Do you hear?'

James waved one hand lazily out of the window in answer as he reversed at a speed that brought a pained expression to Harry's face.

'Oh, I see,' I said as I fended off an enthusiastic licking from the back seat with only moderate success. 'It won't occur to the detective that you might have switched cars. What a brilliant idea.'

'It was, wasn't it?' agreed James.

I pushed Barker down and said, 'Did you just think of it this morning?'

'No, Harry and I thought up several ruses to use if necessary earlier on in the week,' he said a bit absently as he tried to get something out of a pocket that was confined under the seat belt. I bet they'd had enormous fun in the planning too. It was a good thing for Harry's peace of mind that he wasn't there to see the car wobble violently as James finally got at what he was feeling for and pulled out a striped woolly hat. He put it on, bringing the bottom right down to the level of his eyebrows, making himself look alarmingly like a trainspotter. 'Won't recognise me now, will he? Even if he suspects we might have changed cars and is watching all of those coming out.'

'I doubt your own father would recognise you,' I answered faintly. The ensemble didn't make him look his best. Men with noses like that shouldn't wear tea cosies.

'I've decided to spare you a hat,' he remarked as we approached the exit. 'Girls always make such a fuss about their hair being messed up, but bend down so he can't see you.' I obediently cramped myself into the footwell so the only visible occupants of the car were a nerd and his dog. I wondered if the detective would think there was something odd about a nerd driving such an expensive car, then realised he'd decide this was just another rich nerd. Albeit with an unusually gaudy taste in head gear.

'Okay, you can get up now,' said James five minutes later, taking the hat off and throwing it behind him on the back seat.

I sat up, rubbing a stiff neck and feeling the blood drain from my head back to its normal habitat. Barker decided I needed a reviving licking. 'Did it work?' I asked.

'Of course.'

I halted my involuntary bath by clasping Barker firmly around the muzzle. 'Um, would it actually have mattered if we were followed to Folkestone and the detective saw us going to Sam's house?'

'I shouldn't think so,' said James cheerfully, 'but it was fun throwing him off, wasn't it?'

'Great fun,' I muttered, and no doubt it was even more fun having a chance to get his mitts on Harry's new car. I rubbed my shoulder where over-enthusiastic cornering had probably produced an enormous bruise.

He laughed when I complained. Typical, I thought, closing my eyes and trying to pretend I didn't know exactly how fast we were going.

'I doubt it'll make Sam Elliot any more accommodating if we disturb him in the middle of his lunch so we might as well get something to eat ourselves,' said James as we reached the outskirts of Folkestone sometime after one o'clock. That was fine by me. I was starving. 'But we can't leave Barker alone while we eat in a restaurant, so shall we get a picnic and eat it on the beach? Now the sun's come out it shouldn't be too cold,' he said, drawing into a parking space outside a delicatessen.

'Am I being given a choice?'

'Of course,' he said promptly. 'If you want I'll willingly take you for a greasy hamburger and soggy chips and cola, sitting on a metal chair at a too-small table. Then Barker and I will leave you there while we go for wine and sandwiches on the beach. I'd rather you came with me, though, I have to share the bottle with someone and too much wine isn't good for Barker. He starts making vulgar suggestions to poodles.'

I laughed. 'Then I suppose I owe it to him to protect him from the perils of alcohol.'

Manlike, James insisted on walking for what seemed like miles along the promenade before he found a spot he declared exactly right. Frankly, this particular bit of shingle beach, where we could sit with our backs against the promenade wall with the warmth of the sun in our faces and watch the sea, looked much like the other twenty or so similar spots he had considered and rejected but I decided it would be politic not to say so. I'd had to stay in the car and protect it from a ferocious-looking warden while he chose what we ate and I hadn't forgotten his eclectic choice of food for breakfast so I was a bit suspicious of what might be in the carrier bag he'd been swinging from one hand. But what he produced from his Aladdin's bag was just perfect for the beach: sandwiches with tangy fillings, a couple of still warm small pies, a bunch of grapes and some suitably rough red wine that wasn't overpowered by ozone and sea spray. Naturally he'd remembered to buy a corkscrew. Much more surprising were the napkins to wipe our fingers on.

'I love the sea in winter,' said James idly as he watched a pair of gulls squabbling over a bit of seaweed. Barker was also watching them intently, torn by the need to go and chase them off *his* beach and the equally pressing necessity of staying by us in case we should happen to drop one of our sandwiches.

'Me too, it's so nice and empty.' I took a swig of wine out of my plastic glass and leaned back against the wall, my eyes shut against the sun. 'Do you know, this is the first time for over a week that I've been able to just sit down and *do* nothing? I've either been chasing around after Cressida, or travelling, or working. I did have that time with Mum, but Cressida was there and Mum isn't exactly a rest cure at the best of times!'

'Mmm,' James agreed. 'But you don't think I'm going to let you sit and do nothing for long, do you? We've got a job to do and Barker needs a walk first.'

'I was afraid of that,' I said gloomily.

'It'll do you good.' He shovelled the rubbish back into the bag and handed the last unwanted sandwich to a grateful dog. 'You can walk off lunch.'

'You're a real boost to a girl's ego, James!' I grumbled as I scrambled to my feet. 'I take it you mean that someone my size needs all the exercise they can get.'

He stopped for a moment and looked at me with raised eyebrows. 'Stop fishing for compliments, Laura,' he said in the dismissive voice he used to employ with me ten years ago. 'You know perfectly well that while you don't look like a coat hanger, you've got the sort of figure most men fantasise about.' Then he turned back to what he was doing. I stood there open-mouthed, wondering if I'd heard right.

I couldn't have, I decided as we walked along the beach and skimmed stones along the water for an ecstatically barking Barker to try and retrieve. Or rather I threw stones which, to his disgust, often didn't even reach the water's edge, or if they did, fell with a disappointing plop.

James, with infuriating competence, managed to get some of his to do three bounces before they went under. But to my intense pleasure Barker decided he who threw the stone was also going to have the privilege of having Barker shake himself dry all over him. We had to extend our walk by another twenty minutes so that James's trousers could dry off, not that any of us minded. It had turned into a glorious afternoon with the sun glinting off the sea and a wind that was just cool enough to refresh but not so cold as to chill extremities and turn one's nose an unflattering colour. In fact I would have been quite happy to go on for much longer, strolling past old-fashioned wooden beach huts, now closed up until the summer, throwing bits of driftwood for a delighted dog and chatting to James about nothing very much. And it wasn't simply because I felt that I'd enjoyed the last hour and a half more than anything I'd done in the last few months. I was now getting distinctly cold feet about seeing Sam Elliot at all. There might be a horribly embarrassing scene and, while James relished a fight, I most definitely didn't.

I was so preoccupied with my worries I wasn't too clever about the directions to Sam's house which led to a common driver/passenger conversation. 'What do you mean, you can't remember what the road looks like? You drove here, for God's sake!' And, 'Trust a woman not to be able to read some simple directions!' And, 'If you're so bloody clever find it yourself and don't ask me!'

Needless to say we couldn't find a single passer-by in the whole of Folkestone who had ever *heard* of Chintlesham Road, let alone knew where it was. After ten minutes of acrimonious discussion and driving around streets that all looked depressingly like the last we turned into a side road and I saw a familiar-looking large house with balloons tied to the gate and a van parked outside with 'Funny Bunny Children's Entertainments' painted along the side. Just in time. James was muttering that I should thank my lucky stars we weren't in France since he'd be able to claim throttling me was a *crime passionelle*, and would undoubtedly already have taken advantage of it.

'Remember to leave the talking to me,' he said as he pressed the bell in the large brick porch.

'*Ja wohl*, boss!' I said smartly and saluted.

He looked down his nose at me in an expressive manner but before he could do anything was forestalled by the sound of pounding feet and the door being flung open. The sounds of shrieking and general mayhem drifted towards us from the other end of a hallway with raspberry pink walls and over-polished parquet. A very small person, with large blue eyes nearly obscured by a long fringe, stared up at us. 'Are you coming to Barnaby's party? 'Cos if you are, you're late,' it said. 'We've started. We've played Pass the Parcel. Isabelle won.' Due to an extremely modish blouson jacket and jeans outfit it was difficult to tell what sex it was. I would have hazarded a guess at feminine but didn't dare say in case I caused irreparable offence.

James bent down. 'I'm afraid we haven't been invited to Barnaby's party,' he said gravely. 'We'd like to see Daddy.'

The small person hesitated, obviously unsure what to do, and was saved by a dark-haired man in his thirties coming through a door at the end of the hall. 'Who is it,

Max?' he called. Lucky I *hadn't* said anything.

Max turned on his heel and belted back to the party, calling as he went past, 'For you, Daddy.'

'Sam Elliot?' asked James as the man approached.

He nodded, dark eyes watching us warily. He was dressed conventionally enough in the middle-class male yuppie uniform for weekends of jeans and V-necked pullover over a striped shirt, though it was easy enough to see he didn't buy his clothes at Marks and Spencer's, and also that if he wasn't careful good living was going to give him quite a substantial paunch in the near future. The planes of his conventionally good-looking face were already a bit blurred, though his skin glowed a healthy brown, no doubt gained from a ski slope somewhere.

'We'd like to have a word with you,' said James breezily.

I suppose you don't get to head up an outfit like Lifesigns without learning something about how to read body language. Sam certainly caught on to ours quickly enough. He stiffened and said immediately, 'I'm very busy and as you can see there's a party going on for my son. I don't have the time . . .' and began to shut the door.

'This won't take long.' James put his foot forward before the door could be closed in such an adroit manner that I wondered if he'd had practice.

'Look here!' said Sam. 'If you don't let me close the door immediately I'm calling the police.'

James left his foot exactly where it was. 'I'm sure you don't want to do that. It might lead to some awkward questions being asked.' Sam Elliot's eyes flickered uneasily as James gave him a singularly unpleasant smile. 'Wouldn't it be better if we discussed this inside rather than on the doorstep? I'm sure you wouldn't want your son's guests to take back a garbled version of what we have to say to you.'

I had no idea that James could give such an immaculate imitation of an enforcer from the more sinister sort of debt collection agency. It certainly had the required effect on Sam for he stepped back grudgingly and opened the door wide, though he tried to retrieve a little lost ground by saying aggressively, 'I can only give you five minutes.'

'That should be fine.' James stepped back with exaggerated courtesy and waved me to go on in front of him and into a small sitting room done up to the nines in rag rolling, marbling and swagged and ruched curtains. The over-stuffed sofas were so plumped up that it was difficult to imagine anyone had ever dared ruck up their smooth line. Too bad, I thought, leaning back against a serried row of cushions in co-ordinating colours set on their corners with mathematical precision.

James sat down in an arm chair with frilled covers and stretched out his legs comfortably in front of him while Sam took what he must have hoped was a commanding position in front of the fireplace, his feet spread out and hands linked behind his back like a colonel of the old school. James didn't look in the least intimidated. He smiled benignly and said, 'As I'm sure you've guessed we're friends of Cressida's. She would be here herself but she's in hospital, so we've come instead to collect the statuette she accidentally left in the carrier bag she returned to you.'

Sam's mouth set into a thin line. 'She gave it to me.'

'It wasn't hers to give away,' James said, not bothering

to argue the point. 'It belongs to her husband.'

Sam shrugged. 'She'll have to explain herself to him then, won't she? Cressida put me to a lot of inconvenience with all her fits and starts – I had a lot of difficulty finding someone at such short notice to fill her place as helper at last weekend's seminar just because she decided to go off jaunting to Paris,' he glared at me, 'not to mention putting her up and then having to find her a hotel.'

'Not to mention her turning you down,' I interrupted. 'That must have been *very* inconvenient.' I looked meaningfully at James. 'Sam doesn't usually have graduates of his courses to stay in his house, but he made a special exception for Cressida. Then he made her a *very* interesting proposition, one that involved his wife too – or was it someone else's?'

James rested his chin on his fingers and appeared to be studying something in his lap very intently while flags of colour appeared along the blurred lines of Sam's cheekbones. 'I don't know what you mean!' he stammered while I looked at him without saying anything. Wisely he didn't go on trying to deny it but cleared his throat. 'Cressida put me to a lot of trouble, I altered a lot of my arrangements to suit her and look how she repaid me!' he said, deliberately avoiding my gaze and shifting his feet from side to side. 'One of the most important things you learn from a Lifesigns course is that you have to shape your own life and not blame others for your mistakes.' He was gaining confidence as he got underway with a spiel that had doubtless been used many times before. 'That's why I don't blame *her* at all for *my* mistake in inviting her to come and stay in my house,' he said with spurious generosity. 'But it wouldn't be helping Cressida at all if I were to give her the message that she can do what she likes in a temper because she can always put it right again afterwards. So that is why I'm keeping that statuette,' he said virtuously. 'It will be a valuable lesson for her.'

'And a valuable possession for you,' murmured James. 'I'm sure you wouldn't be quite so keen to keep it if it were merely something that had been picked up from a tourist shop in Florence.'

Sam did the soft shoe shuffle again. 'That's got nothing to do with it!' he said with patent insincerity. 'As I said, my mind is made up. The statuette is mine now and I have no intention of giving it to Cressida. I'm sorry you've had a wasted journey. Now if you don't mind, the entertainment will be over in a minute—'

James didn't move. He stared at Sam levelly over the top of his linked fingers. Sam shoved his hands into his pockets and leaned forwards. 'I've said all I'm going to. Leave now before I call the police. There's nothing more to discuss.'

'Yes, there is,' said James softly. 'If you call the police I shall have to inform them that you have in your possession one of only two bronzes in existence by the Florentine master Giacomo Farelli. A statue that happens to be on the International Register of Stolen Works of Art.'

Sam's eyes bulged slightly in their sockets. 'That can't be true! Cressida said her husband's father had bought it.' He took a handkerchief out of his pocket, looked at it vaguely and put it back again, regaining a little poise.

'Even if it is stolen, as you claim, it wouldn't make any difference. I'd say I had no idea that it was.'

'But that's not true!' said James. 'I've just told you. And you're still insisting you won't give it up. Laura will be my witness that you are knowingly keeping a stolen art treasure, won't you?' I nodded vigorously. 'At the very least you'd be done for possession of a stolen object even if you managed to escape extradition to Italy. You might, I suppose, just get away with probation for a first offence,' he mused, 'though frankly I think I'd rather be safely locked away in prison than facing whatever Stefano would do to me once he found out I was the one responsible for his losing his beloved possession permanently.'

'Are you saying that Cressida's husband is some sort of criminal thug?' asked Sam with a brave attempt at a contemptuous laugh.

'Oh, Stefano's not a *thug*, not personally,' said James airily. Sam's ski slope brown complexion acquired a greenish tinge. 'He's charming to meet socially, very cultured and hospitable – unless you've done something to offend him or made a pass at his wife. He's very protective about her.' Sam went a little paler. 'And it's quite true he doesn't surround himself with men who look like gorillas in white suits and dark glasses. But he is Italian,' James began ticking off points on his fingers, 'it's widely known that his present fortune is based on his father's black market activities during the war and that it's best not to enquire too closely exactly what it is that Stefano does, where his money comes from or ask who his associates in Italy are. I've heard that they come from

Palermo.' He paused for a moment and looked at Sam. 'That's in Sicily, in case you didn't know. And you might ask why he wants to sink millions of pounds into a luxury hotel unless it's because when the money comes out again it'll have been through the financial equivalent of the hot wash. I'll leave you to draw your own conclusions.'

Sam's jaw sagged. 'You don't have any proof,' he said finally, tugging at the collar of his shirt with one finger as if he needed air.

'With people like that I don't *want* any!' said James meaningfully. 'I know what I believe. And right now Stefano thinks *I'm* the one who has the statuette. Since he's already given me a very effective demonstration of how he'll frame me and ruin my business if he doesn't get it back, I'm sure you'll understand why if I can't return it myself I'll have to let him know where it really is.'

'I thought you said it *wasn't* his?' protested Sam.

James smiled faintly. 'Stefano *thinks* it's his, and with people like that it's best to let them have their way.'

The door burst open letting in a wave of high-pitched laughter and a blonde woman in her thirties. She gave us a single harassed look and then addressed herself to Sam. 'There you are! Look, I *cannot* cope with feeding twenty-three five year olds on my own and that *useless* entertainer says he's not paid to help during tea!' she said in the voice of one who has just reached the end of her tether. 'That little . . . so and so Damien has already thrown jelly at Alice and made her cry, and Joshua offered to show his willy to Venetia if she gave him her mini Mars bar . . .'

Children's parties had certainly got a lot more interesting since my day. Sam said hastily, 'I'll only be another minute, Susie, I promise, and then I'll be there to give you a hand.'

'You'd better be!' she declared desperately as a piercing scream rent the air. With an apologetic look towards James and me she shut the door.

'You heard my wife, she needs me. I can't stay and listen to any more of this ridiculous farrago of lies about Cressida's husband being connected to the Mafia,' blustered Sam. 'Please go now.'

'No,' said James flatly. Sam stared at him nonplussed.

James stood up, his lazy air dissipating like smoke in the wind. 'You've got a simple choice,' he said in a level voice. 'You can either give the faun to us and we'll return it to Stefano, saying we collected it for Cressy after she accidentally left it behind. Or,' he put his hand in his pocket and drew out a mobile phone, 'I ring Stefano and tell him that it's here and you refuse to return it.' Sam's eyes were fixed in fascinated horror on the phone as if he'd never seen one before. 'I'll leave him to deal with you in his own way, all I care about is getting him off my back. Then you really will have the chance to follow your Lifesigns precepts and discover what it's like to accept the consequences of your own mistakes. There's one thing you needn't worry about. Stefano's old-fashioned. I don't believe he'd do anything to harm your wife or your children.'

'You bastard!' said Sam in a shaking voice.

'No,' said James coldly. 'You're the one who's greedily hanging on to something that doesn't belong to you.' As Sam havered, seemingly rooted to the spot, James continued in a harsh voice, 'Make your decision. What's it to be?' and began punching in numbers.

'Stop!' gasped Sam. 'You can have the bloody thing back if it's that important!'

James's fingers stayed in the air, still poised above the phone. 'You've seen reason at last, what a relief. Why don't you go and get it and then you can rejoin the party before your wife brings an action for divorce.'

Sam cast him a look of loathing as he stumped out of the room.

'You were brilliant!' I whispered. 'I never thought you could sound so sinister.'

'I quite surprised myself,' he admitted. 'But I'm glad he didn't call my bluff about calling Stefano. I forgot to recharge the battery.'

Sam clumped back in carrying a large bag which he almost threw at James. 'Here you are!'

'Careful, we don't want to cause any more damage,' said James as he looked in the bag.

'Will you just get out of my house?'

'Nothing would give me greater pleasure,' James said affably, 'but I'll just check the faun first, if you don't mind?' He drew out an untidily wrapped parcel and laid it on the sofa, gently removing the layers. His breath hissed in distress as the last came off. 'Oh, Cressy, how *could* you do this?' he murmured.

I peered over his shoulder. One leg and the arm which held the flute were bent sideways, a split almost severed the other arm in two at the elbow and there was a marked dent in the faun's shoulder where it had hit the corner brick edge on. Cressida must have a strength belied by her apparent fragility to do that much damage. 'Is it repairable?' I asked.

James frowned as he examined it carefully. 'Luckily the face isn't damaged at all so it shouldn't be too much of a problem,' he said, running his fingers over it as if it was the finest silk, 'but no matter how clever the restorer is, it always takes a little bit away from the original. It isn't just the maker's work of art any longer, it's his and someone else's. Still,' he straightened up and started rewrapping it, 'I suppose we should be thankful that it wasn't worse.'

'Or that the fire wasn't alight when she threw it in the fireplace!'

He shuddered and grinned. 'Thank you for putting things into their proper perspective, Laura!'

Sam was almost visibly hopping from foot to foot in his impatience to see us go. 'Come on, haven't you seen enough?' he demanded.

'Leaving now,' said James promptly, putting the statuette back in the carrier bag and picking it up. Sam followed us as we made our way to the front door and James turned back to look at him. 'Just one question before we go to satisfy my curiosity. What were you actually planning to *do* with it? Have it repaired and display it somewhere?'

'God, no!' said Sam. 'I don't even like it. My wife wants a new conservatory. We were going to do it on the proceeds of selling the faun.'

'She must be after quite some conservatory,' said James mildly.

Sam protested indignantly, 'We're hardly the idle rich, if that's what you mean! We've *earned* all our money. Unlike some.' He threw a pointed glance at James. 'We don't have ancestral acres to draw upon when we need the odd ten thousand pounds or so for improvements to the house.'

James stared at him like an ant about to be squashed. 'So you intended to pay for your improvements by what was effectively theft? And justified what you were doing by spouting mumbo-jumbo rubbish about spiritual growth! You're not only greedy, duplicitous and amoral, my friend, you're incredibly stupid as well!' he said with withering contempt. His arms tightened around the parcel containing the faun. 'This isn't worth anything like ten thousand pounds.'

'I had it valued by my brother-in-law,' Sam said with a superior look on his face. 'He said ten thou, even fifteen if I was lucky. And since he runs an antiques shop I think he should know, don't you?'

'He doesn't know his whatever from his elbow if he thinks that,' murmured James as he opened the door and waved me through. 'A Farelli bronze is practically priceless. This one, even damaged, sold legally, would start at about half a million pounds. Since it's stolen, you might have to settle for about two hundred thousand. Now perhaps you'll understand why Stefano Buonotti is so keen to have it back?' He smiled nastily at Sam's stunned expression. 'And it sounds to me as if your brother-in-law has the same attitude to ripping people off as you do!'

CHAPTER 19

'Was that true?' I asked James as he carefully stowed the package away in the boot of the car under the glowering gaze of Sam Elliot, standing guard in his porch to make sure that we were really going. James looked up questioningly. 'About the faun.'

'Absolutely. If anything a bit on the low side.'

'Wow!' I said, seriously impressed. And to think Cressida had picked up something worth a cool *half a million* and flung it into the fireplace with the force of an England bowler trying to save the match. It didn't bear thinking about.

James came around to my side of the car and unlocked the door. He put his arm around my shoulders, giving me a hug. There was a resounding bang as Sam's front door slammed shut.

'What's that for?' I asked in surprise.

'Do I have to have a reason?' I met his eyes, feeling my heartbeat suddenly accelerate, then he shifted his gaze to the top of my head and dropped a distinctly brotherly kiss on my forehead. 'Thanks,' he said, letting me go.

'What for?' I asked again, feeling bewildered and rather let down.

'For helping me when it was nothing to do with you.'

'Well, what are families for?' I asked lightly, though I could feel a curious flatness come over me. 'Besides, I didn't have much choice, did I? You were blackmailing me!'

'Only the once, and you don't really think I'm enough of a snake to split on you to Imogen, do you?' he asked, eyes twinkling.

'Now you tell me!'

'I was hardly going to do it before, was I?' he pointed out, reasonably enough by his standards, I presume.

I got into the car as huffily as I could, which was a difficult procedure since Barker was enthusiastically expressing his pleasure at having company again. 'Do you think Sam will come after us and try to hi-jack the car or something now he knows what the thing is worth?' I asked, glancing towards the house. 'He didn't look very happy.'

'About as sick as the proverbial parrot!' James on the other hand looked extremely happy. 'He could try and see if he can catch me,' he said with a gleam of anticipation. Then added in a regretful voice, 'But he won't have the chance to do anything bar gnash his teeth. He'll be too busy refereeing fights over who gets the last chocolate biscuit, and being lambasted by his wife for leaving her in the lurch with twenty kamikaze five year olds, to do anything except think longingly of the money he let slip through his sticky fingers. That's when he's in between bouts of quivering with fear that big bad Stefano is going to come after him as a punishment for holding on to the thing at all.'

I pushed Barker off my lap. He has the misguided notion that passengers in the front of cars enjoy having a large, hairy, hot lump sitting on them. With a reproachful expression he clambered on to the back seat and breathed heavily down my neck. 'I don't think I'm going to be able to face Stefano in future, now I know that he's connected to the Mafia.'

James glanced over at me with one of his haughty expressions. 'You don't seriously think I'd have allowed you anywhere near Stefano Buonotti if he was really involved in organised crime, do you?'

I looked at him doubtfully. In the past I would have said without hesitation that he wouldn't have thought twice about it. Now I was beginning to wonder if I hadn't occasionally been rather unfair. I must have been too slow with coming out with a reassuring denial because he said in freezing tones, 'I can promise you I'd *never* have put you in that sort of danger.'

He looked so offended I found myself almost stammering out apologies. 'I thought the Mafia didn't harm women?' I said by way of appeasement.

'Ideas like that belong back in the days when the good guys always wore white hats and the fallen woman repented of her sins before expiring in the arms of the hero,' he said dismissively, but the brief flare of temper seemed to have disappeared. 'Come on, I wouldn't even let Cressy give me a kiss on the cheek if I thought her husband was in the Mafia! It'd be concrete boots under the nearest motorway bridge in no time at all.'

'But if he's basically quite honest, what's he doing planting stuff in your house?' I asked, confused.

'Of course he's not honest!' said James scornfully as we drove off. 'He didn't steal the faun himself but he sure as hell hung on to it! And I'd bet anything you like that his pad in Italy has a few other pieces that he "inherited" from Papa and is none too keen for experts to examine. Does Cressy know it's the original?' he asked as an afterthought.

Surprised, I said, 'She suspects it is.'

'How humiliating she didn't think highly enough of my expertise to worry I'd recognise it for what it was. At least Stefano did, which is some consolation.' He laughed shortly. 'Though to be honest I might not have been suspicious at all if he hadn't made it so obvious he didn't want me near it. I doubt he makes mistakes like that often.'

'I think he thought you were going to be some sort of dilettante and found it a bit of a shock when you turned out to be quite so knowledgeable,' I said, remembering Stefano's absorbed expression as he and James had briefly found common ground in antiques.

'Perhaps,' he said, accepting the implied compliment as no more than his due. 'According to Pa, who likes to keep his ear *very* close to the ground, Stefano's "consultancy" services run along the lines of passing large amounts of money under the table between two sides – but just because he's Italian and bribes people to get contracts doesn't mean he's in the Mafia! Even so,' he added thoughtfully, 'he's not someone I'd advise getting on the wrong side of.'

'What a shame you don't take your own advice then,' I said pointedly.

His face took on a depressingly familiar shuttered look. 'That's not entirely my fault,' he protested.

'Well, if you hadn't given Stefano the impression you'd be only too happy to take his wife off his hands, he might not feel quite so violent towards you,' I said sourly.

'I don't behave any differently with her than I do with the rest of my ex-girlfriends,' he said mildly. But did his other ex-girlfriends behave differently with *him*? 'I can't help it if she's got a manically jealous husband.'

You could stop looking at her as if she's the last chocolate in the box, I thought crossly, aware that whatever I said was going to make me sound like a shrew, and a jealous one to boot. I stared out of the window instead, my good mood over the successful completion of our mission completely evaporated. Oh, well, as soon as we gave the faun back to Stefano I could stop running around at James's beck and call and it would be another three years before we saw each other. This conclusion wasn't as consoling as I'd hoped. Why should it matter whether he still thought wistfully of Cressida? He was far too fond of his own skin to risk it by actually fooling around with her, or I hoped he was, and besides I was nursing wistful thoughts of my own, wasn't I? I should be anyway. Actually I had been too busy to spend any time at all thinking about Daniel. I'd better have a quick wallow now, I decided, summoning up some sad thoughts. After all I had just broken up with my boyfriend of a year and was entitled to them. I sighed soulfully.

'Are you feeling all right?' asked James. 'You look a bit funny.'

Barker sat up and licked my ear.

In view of the general insensitivity of the male occupants of the car I decided to give up on wistful thoughts. Besides gentle yearning didn't at all suit the fizzy edginess that was inexplicably churning up my insides. I sat in restless silence for some miles while it occurred to me that I was being rather unfair to James. It was hardly his fault he was still hung up on a pretty flibbertigibbet who'd given him the elbow two years ago. So I was still angry with him about it, but at least I *knew* I was being unfair. Another few miles and I'd unbent enough to say, 'You were brilliant with Sam! I'd never have believed you could be so menacing.'

James flicked me a sideways glance as if to check whether I was about to start having a go at him again, then smiled. 'I haven't had so much fun in ages!' he declared with relish. 'It beats outbidding Geoffrey Simpson for a set of library chairs into a cocked hat – which was the most exciting event of the week before last.' But his voice held a distinct note of dissatisfaction. Perhaps aware of it he went on, 'I couldn't bear to be shut up in an office like Harry, no matter how much he earns, and there's a tremendous buzz when you've made a good sale or discovered something fantastic. But sometimes,' he sighed, 'I wish that what I was doing was less *middle-aged*.'

I looked at him in alarm. James used to have a marked streak of wildness, which was one of the reasons he created such havoc amongst all the local females (and aroused such distrust in their fathers), but since he had taken over the business he had seemed to become a relatively sober citizen. It sounded as if the change in him was barely surface deep. Well, if he had to break out occasionally I hoped he would choose to do something safe like mountaineering without ropes or lion taming and not get his kicks by baiting a notoriously jealous and vindictive Italian about his wife. Or even having an affair with her.

'If I were you I'd drive in a slightly more middle-aged fashion,' I said after a glance at the speedometer. 'You're going to have a really exciting time explaining if the police stop you for speeding and discover half a million quid's worth of stolen property in the boot.'

'Your average traffic policeman wouldn't know a Florentine bronze if it hit him on the head!' said James with a laugh as he slowed down fractionally. 'But point taken. You don't realise how fast you're going in this car.'

'Of course not!' I said derisively. 'Try telling that to the driver of the car with the flashing blue light behind you!'

'Blast!' snapped James, foot moving down sharply on the brake, and looked in the mirror. 'You *cow*, Laura!' he said after a moment. He kept to the speed limit after that even though it was another five miles before he'd speak to me again.

We agreed – well, we did eventually – that I would keep the faun at my flat with the rest of Cressida's stuff until I could give it all back to her. James had got back on to his protect-the-weak-little-woman soap box again and was banging on about not wanting me to be involved in this any further. I had to point out I was already storing, with his agreement, three items almost certainly recorded with the police as being stolen and that another item on the International Register of Stolen Art Treasures was nothing much extra. The resulting argument did much to dispel the lingering traces of my former bad mood, especially after I won it. James isn't a bad loser; he merely grumbled about pig-headed women who were too strong-minded for their own good, all the way from Catford to Dulwich which I reckoned was quite moderate, given the heat of our discussion. The South Circular was unusually clear for once too.

'Are you sure about keeping it with you?' he asked anxiously as I picked up the carrier bag with the faun in it. We were standing on the pavement near his house, while we went back over the subject that I considered had been aired at least five times too often already. Barker had been dropped off at Harry's. James had made a sterling effort to keep the car on the grounds that it would be very useful to have a vehicle unknown to the local Philip Marlowes, but this ingenious attempt to hold on to a fast toy for a bit longer had been firmly overruled by his sapient elder brother. For once no other car pulled out behind us as James drove me to get my own rust bucket from where I'd left it that morning. We couldn't decide if Stefano had called off the watchdogs or merely given them the night off. James looked a bit disappointed; he'd been thinking of something clever to shake off a pursuer involving an underpass and a private road through an exclusive development of flats. It looked like he wasn't going to get the chance.

'Look, there's nothing to worry about,' I said patiently. 'Stefano's hardly going to break into my flat to get back his own property, is he?'

'Depends if he thinks you really are going to return it,' said James stubbornly. 'He may well be blackening you with his own brush.'

I rubbed my hands together to warm them up. If James didn't stop dithering about I was going to be a candidate for frostbite. 'I'll tell you what,' he said, brightening, 'I'll get Barker back off Harry. He can be your guard dog.'

'No way!' I said. 'Firstly I wouldn't dream of spoiling Barker's trip to Harry's friends. He likes swimming in that river. Secondly, he'd be no ruddy use at all as a guard dog unless he just happened to knock the intruder over in his haste to stand up and lick his face!'

'But the result would still be the same,' protested James.

'And then he'd give the intruder a nice reviving bath so he was back on his feet again in no time,' I pointed out. 'But the last and most important point is that I am *not* giving house room to Barker and Horatio at the same time!'

James had already had the privilege of meeting Horatio and had left the encounter with a lot more respect for cats, or some of them. 'I hadn't thought of that. But I don't want you to be on your own,' he persisted, stuffing his hands into his pockets and rocking backwards on his heels. He had a very determined expression on his face, the sort that one of his Norman ancestors would have worn when he'd made up his mind to capture a castle or two and didn't feel like listening to his wife when she said they'd got enough already. We were going to be here all night at this rate.

'Protect me yourself then, if you're so worried,' I said

crossly, wondering why he hadn't suggested it.

He gave me a sideways look. 'I wouldn't want to tread on the heels of Dracula's assistant.'

I swallowed hard and said, 'He's busy.' The last thing I was going to do was let James know of my farcical discovery of last night. I couldn't bear the thought of his mockery.

If James noticed I didn't leap instantly to Daniel's defence he didn't say, but murmured that it wasn't a bad idea to come around in a way that made me think he had been waiting for *me* to suggest it. Why? I'd never before known him be backwards in coming forwards about something he wanted to do. Perhaps he was being unusually tactful.

'Good, that's settled,' I said briskly, moving towards my car and shelter from the wind. 'And if you're a good bodyguard I'll even make you some dinner.'

He looked exaggeratedly apprehensive. '*Can* you cook now? Your chilli powder casserole is etched indelibly in my memory.'

'That was years ago,' I said with dignity. 'And I didn't realise the top had fallen off the chilli powder until it was too late.'

'You still served it!' he said with a grimace. 'We all had third-degree burns in our mouths!'

'I haven't put anyone in hospital for at least a month!' I said in hurt tones. 'But if you're worried your indigestion pills won't be strong enough to cope, we can get a takeaway.'

He laughed. 'I'll take your word for it I won't need them. Joking apart, you look tired and I'm not surprised with all you've been up to recently. The last thing you must feel like is racing around a kitchen.' His finger traced a line under my eye, presumably the outline of a bag. I was torn three ways, feeling soggy inside at his unexpected consideration, suspicious that he was trying to weasel out of having to try my cooking, though with more diplomacy than usual, and complete despair at the implication that I looked like a hag. The Sta-put range of make up that I'd nicked from the Rainbow Cosmetics samples at work obviously didn't stay put as much as was claimed. 'Why don't we go to that little Italian place around the corner from your flat?' he asked.

Part of me would have liked to demonstrate to James just how much my cooking had improved in the last ten years. I don't want to blow my own trumpet – well, actually I do – but it's generally admitted that my chocolate soufflés are wicked. Isn't it extraordinary how after decades of feminist teaching the average woman still has an instinct to retreat straight back into the kitchen the moment she wants to impress a man? But cooking makes me flushed (and frequently bad-tempered) and Alfredo's garlic bread is something to die for, so we arranged that James would come around in an hour or so once I'd had time to have a bath and change (and make up, scent myself, go through the entire contents of my wardrobe, throw same on the floor in despair, etc).

If I hadn't known better I'd have sworn James had been doing much the same. His hair was still damp from the shower and he'd changed into a soft blue shirt and cord trousers with a dark jacket on top, but I doubted he'd had as much trouble as me in finding something that didn't make his waist look as if the measurement had got mixed up with his hips. He also smelled very nice, I realised, sniffing appreciatively as he kissed me on coming in. He never used to kiss me this much, I thought. I couldn't say that I objected.

'You look good enough to eat and I'm starving so we'd better go out soon,' he said, smiling at me in a way that made my stomach do cartwheels. He looked over my shoulder. 'What have you done with the faun? Is it somewhere safe?'

Trust him to concentrate on the important things, I thought crossly. 'I put it with Cressida's suitcase, and shoved the whole lot under my bed.' Considering that half my clothes and most of my shoes were also under the bed it wasn't likely any intruder would ever be able to disinter the case even if he was brave enough to risk the monster dustballs that lurked there. 'And Horatio's asleep on top of the bed.'

'Horatio's breath at twenty paces is enough to stun even the most determined burglar,' James agreed in the voice of experience.

'I couldn't bear it if anything happened to him,' I said worriedly. 'I thought you were just getting the wind up before, but you don't really think someone is likely to break in, do you?'

'Of course I don't! I just wanted an excuse to spend the evening with you.'

I looked at him for a moment, trying to work out if he was being serious or not. I still didn't know at the end of it. 'A simple request would have done,' I said lightly, fetching my coat.

'But I don't like being simple, it's boring.' Now I knew he hadn't been serious, and felt a distinct twinge of disappointment.

Alfredo's was as ever hot, steamy, noisy and full of cooking smells. I took a deep appreciative breath as we went in, my mouth already watering from the pungent scent of tomatoes and garlic rising from a plate of *spaghetti puttanesca* being carried past us. We were placed at a rickety corner table romantically lit by a candle in a bulbous Chianti bottle that had been almost completely obscured by the multi-coloured drips from dozens of previous candles. Another two straw-covered bottles were suspended from the ceiling above our heads and a large, brightly coloured fresco of Santa Lucia covered the wall behind James's back. Alfredo doesn't believe in letting a good cliché go to waste. You should see the things he gets up to with the giant pepper grinder.

There was a lovely end-of-term feeling as we nibbled the famous garlic bread and began a bottle of Lambrusco. The end was in sight but I didn't yet have to get down to the mundane things in life like doing a week's backlog of washing and worrying over how I was going to explain myself to Darian on Monday morning. Naturally enough, I suppose, the conversation over the antipasti and the spaghetti drifted towards Stefano, Cressida and what I'd done while I was toting her around France. I was decent enough to emphasise the more sensible things Cressida had done, like blandly assuring the vegetarians that of course the *pommes frites* had been cooked in vegetable oil and it was their imagination that they'd just heard Alexandre declare he did all his frying in goose fat.

I slid over the inference that it showed what an excellent liar she was. I did have a brief battle with my conscience about some of the things I said about her, but it was only a brief tussle. James found the story about how she'd driven my credit card up to near implosion point much funnier than I did. And it wasn't as if I was portraying her as being *bad*, just rather feather-brained at times and always ready to leap into something without any regard for the consequences to anybody else, but I think he had already realised that.

'What a silly girl she is,' he said, shaking his head. The indulgent note in his voice scraped my nerves like a saw, and it was only with difficulty that I stopped myself from pointing out that perhaps at twenty-eight Cressida should start growing up a little. I didn't want to sound like a complete and utter bitch.

I was rewarded when he added thoughtfully, 'She runs poor old Stefano ragged, I don't envy him.' And smiled maliciously. 'He's going to have a wonderful time refereeing the fights between Cressy and his mother about who has the care of the baby! I'd put my money on Cressy. I don't reckon he'll risk her running away again – or trashing another of his treasures.'

It would be a long time before James forgave her that. All to the good, I thought, as I absently forked my spaghetti around my plate. Despite my previous hunger I didn't seem to have much appetite. The tension I'd felt in the car was mounting again and it didn't go well with Alfredo's clam sauce. Frankly I was getting a bit fed up of talking about Cressida and Stefano all the time, I thought, as I took another swig of wine. I wouldn't have minded talking about something else, such as myself or James – or James and me. But all he wanted to do was discuss *her*, it seemed.

And it would have been nice if he'd looked at me a bit too. I didn't know why I'd bothered to raid Liv's wardrobe after all of mine hit the floor, rejected, to pinch her mauve angora off the shoulder sweater which kept sliding off to one side in the most alluring way. (Even if I say so myself, I've got nice shoulders.) From the way James kept his eyes firmly on his plate and not on how one of my better features kept revealing itself, you'd have thought I was sharing a table with a newly ordained monk who feared damnation if he so much as caught a glimpse of a naked collarbone.

James's normal ready conversation seemed to have run out, perhaps there was a limit to how much even *he* wanted to say about Cressida, and we finished the meal in near silence. 'Coffee?' he asked as Alfredo cleared our plates and gave a disapproving sniff that mine hadn't been completely licked clean.

'Why don't you come back and have coffee at my place?' I asked. 'I promise it won't have chilli powder in it!'

James smiled in a rather perfunctory manner and shook his head. 'You should have an early night. I'd better not.'

I didn't *want* an early night. At least not the type I was sure he meant, I thought crossly, as he signalled for Alfredo to bring him the bill.

We walked slowly back to the flat. I stopped outside, looking up at our darkened windows while James fidgeted beside me as if he couldn't wait to get going. 'I wish you hadn't put the wind up me about intruders. I get bad enough heeby-jeebies about being alone in the flat these days as it is,' I said with a reasonable amount of truth. I actually had the wind up far more about the probability that I was about to say goodbye to James and he was going to walk out of my life again for God knows how long.

'But Liv'll be back soon from work and then you'll have company.'

I shook my head. 'It's Saturday. She'll already be on her way to Wiltshire and true love among the pigs for the weekend.' I laid my hand on his arm and looked up appealingly. 'Won't you come up and check there aren't any bogeymen up there?'

To my chagrin he hesitated perceptibly for a moment then said, 'All right.' What had happened to the chivalrous male who had been worrying about all the risks to me earlier on in the evening? I thought in irritation as we walked the two floors up to our door in silence. He looked briefly around, which didn't take long in a flat of this size, and came to find me in the kitchen as I was ladling coffee grounds into the filter. 'It's fine, no one's here,' he said curtly, standing in the doorway as if poised for flight. 'Nor any spooks, boggarts or snoopers.'

'You're going to have a cup of coffee at least, aren't you?' I asked. Well, he could hardly refuse now I was actually in the middle of making it, could he?

One of his quick smiles lit his face. 'You sound just like Aunt Jane. "James, you must have just *one* more piece of cake before you go," ' he said in a quavering falsetto that took her off perfectly.

'Well, I certainly won't be offering you anything to eat, not after you finished my plateful as well as yours.'

'Shame to let it go to waste, and I was hungry.'

'You're always hungry. How you don't get fat with the amount you eat, I'll never know!' I said with a burning sense of injustice as I eyed his flat stomach. A fat-burning metabolism and obscenely long eyelashes as well. It wasn't fair. And not particularly good for my blood pressure to consider either of those attributes. 'And don't tell me it's all in the genes. It makes it even worse that I don't have them!' I declared crossly.

James leaned against the door frame, his arms folded. 'The difference between you and me, Laura, apart from the obvious, is that I wouldn't be improved by soft bits whereas you,' he looked me up and down very slowly, making a quiver start from the top of my spine and go all the way down into my legs, 'look just fantastic with every one of them.'

If any other man had said that to me and looked at me in that way I would have known exactly what he was on about, but just as I was about to give James a real come hither from under my eyelashes and wait for what happened next, the coffee machine, with immaculate timing, gave its customary burping to indicate it was finished with the job. James flicked his eyes away casually and stood up straight as if we hadn't just been in a smouldering scenario worthy of three fire engines.

'Shall I carry those for you?'

'Thanks,' I mumbled, sure that if I did it I'd spill coffee everywhere, probably over James's head as I threw the cup at him in sheer frustration. By the time I was halfway through drinking it depression had replaced frustration. Flirting with every female under fifty and most of those over it was as natural as breathing to James. I *knew* that. He'd shown often enough what his type was: blonde, slim, beautiful, delicate Dresden-like figures. I couldn't claim a passing acquaintance with even one of those attributes, I thought gloomily. So what a fool I was to imagine even for a minute that his attitude to me was anything more than brotherly. Except brothers don't normally enfold their sisters in X-rated clinches on doorsteps. Well, not the ones I know anyway. If I were a truly modern woman, the one I profess myself to be after several glasses of wine with my girlfriends, I'd put my hand invitingly on his knee with my most seductive smile and see where we went from there. But the very thought of the cool look of surprise he might, and probably would, cast at me knocked that notion on its head and turned me back into a truly modern wimp. It's a good thing I'm not a man. The fear of rejection would stop me from ever getting a kiss, let alone laid. Besides it was glaringly obvious he had no interest in me. He wasn't even trying to sit near me on the sofa, he was at the other end, coffee untouched while he concentrated on talking to Horatio. He even preferred the attractions of an overweight cat with half an ear and villainous personal habits to me. That showed me.

About five minutes later, without having addressed a single word to me, he stood up and announced he'd better get going and let me have some sleep. Sleep was the last thing I wanted, I thought rebelliously. 'Do you have to?' I asked. 'I'm still a bit nervous about possible intruders.' I dropped my eyes a little and shuddered theatrically.

He stared at me suspiciously, as well he might. He was probably remembering how singularly unmoved I'd been earlier in the evening. He sighed deeply and ran his hand through his hair. 'I don't know,' he began.

I wriggled back against the sofa cushions so the neck of the jumper slipped off one shoulder again. James's eyes seemed to be fixed on Horatio as he waddled towards his cat flap. Probably worried his chaperone was leaving. But did his glance flicker sideways? 'Or are you afraid that now it's the witching hour your diabolical charms will begin to have their customary effect on all unattached females near you?'

James didn't smile. 'You aren't unattached,' he said shortly. 'You've got Daniel.'

I shook my head. 'Not any longer.' James turned his head towards me sharply. 'Serena failed with Daniel because he'd already shacked up with a literary agent with a very large posterior.' At least he was looking at me now. There was a distinct question in his newly attentive eyes. 'I found her there last night. Her jumper was on inside out,' I added irrelevantly.

He laughed. 'You do seem to make a habit of bursting in on men at the most inappropriate times, don't you?'

'It seems so, doesn't it?' I agreed. 'And before you ask, I've been trying hard to feel depressed about it all day and I haven't succeeded.'

He laughed again, looking quite pleased about the news. I hoped it wasn't just fraternal pleasure. Well, the way his eyes were fixed on my legs as I stretched them out in front of me didn't seem very fraternal to me. The stockings had obviously been a good move. 'Even so, boyfriendless as I am, I do know how to behave. You needn't worry that I'm going to pounce on you and rip all your clothes off,' I said teasingly, moving around a bit more so that the neck of the jumper fell to near indecency level.

At that he strode over to me and stood over me, one leg on either side of my outstretched ones, his hands on the sofa above my shoulders. I felt pleasurably trapped. He bent his head towards me. 'Listen, you idiot woman!' he said tersely. 'I'm not in the *least* worried about that! What worries me is that I won't be able to resist doing what I've been wanting to do all evening – rip *yours* off.'

There was silence as our eyes met. I took in a shaky breath. He smelled faintly of wine, food, a lingering waft of aftershave. Intoxicating. 'Well, why don't you?' I asked. 'And let's see what happens.'

CHAPTER 20

Rather late the next morning I was wandering around the flat in the sort of happy daze that comes from an active night with not much sleep in it, still a bit bemused by the revelation that James wanted to do more than cheat at cards with me. And very nice it was too, I thought with a smug smile, as I picked an elderly newspaper off the floor. The inevitable pangs of hunger had driven him out to forage for ingredients for a proper breakfast and the Sunday papers, saying that if he left it to me I'd probably come back with a small loaf and a low-fat yogurt. He was wrong. It would have been a fat-free yogurt. I have to make some gestures towards keeping my figure in control, and besides it gives you the same virtuous feeling that you get in the sales. Save now, spend (more) later. I was trying to make the sitting room look reasonably respectable before he came back. (Three thousand years ago I would doubtless have been picking mammoth bones up off the floor of the cave before he came back with a nice wild boar for me to roast. So much for the liberation of womankind.) But a burst of my rarely encountered housewifely energy is not to be ignored so I waved a duster in the direction of the table and retrieved various miscellaneous items from behind the sofa cushions before plumping them up. I stood back and looked at them sadly; I didn't mind that they lacked the military precision of Sam's sofa but it would have been nice if there had been enough stuffing for them to do anything other than sag.

Dreamily I laid the table, choosing the best pieces out of Liv's and my mismatched china, i.e. the stuff without cracks in it and not the faded Bunnikins plates from Liv's nursery days. Horatio made a dash for the table and I caught him in mid-leap just as the bell went. It's not for nothing that my last birthday present from Emma was a butter dish with 'Don't Let The Cat Get The Butter' written around the sides. I went to answer the door, thinking that James must have forgotten to take the key I gave him, my attention on the wriggling, indignant cat under my arm. 'Look, if you don't behave I'm going to throw you out!' I said sternly as I opened it.

'*Che?*' asked a startled voice. I looked up and dropped Horatio in shock. Instead of James, laden with bags and papers, there was Stefano, looking with his heavily shadowed chin and belted camelhair coat more like an Italian gangster than I'd ever seen him before. All he needed was a black shirt and a white tie.

His eyebrows snapped together as I gasped, with surprise, not with guilt or displeasure or whatever it was he evidently thought I was feeling. 'You are busy. I will come another time,' he said coldly.

'No, I was talking to the cat, not to you,' I said in confusion. 'I'm sorry, I was surprised. Come in.'

He looked pointedly at my dressing gown and bare

feet. From his expression of extreme disapproval you'd have thought he was the vicar and I was offering to entertain him in my most diaphanous negligee, not an extremely proper tartan flannelette floor-length job from Marks and Sparks. Maybe he was merely objecting to people who aren't dressed by midday, but men who haven't shaved when they have that much beard, I thought with a glance at his chin, aren't really in any position to cast aspersions. Designer stubble didn't work on Stefano, there was just too much of it. Finally he appeared to make up his mind that I wasn't about to do a flannelette version of the dance of the seven veils and, inclining his head slightly, came in.

'I expect you've come for Cressida's things, haven't you?' I asked as he looked around the small living room with the vague air of someone who isn't really used to being in places like this. Thank heavens I'd already cleared away the worst of the clutter. 'Sit down for a moment while I get some proper clothes on,' the fashion in which he was pointedly averting his eyes from my bare feet was making me feel uncomfortably underdressed, 'and I'll find them for you.'

He took off his coat and sat down gingerly on the sofa, casting a wary glance at Horatio who was glaring at him balefully, probably blaming him for his precipitate trip to the floor. I had a feeling that Stefano was about to get the treatment that any self-respecting cat will dole out to someone they sense doesn't like them. Since he had just gone to the top of my personal list of the ten rudest men in London I reckoned I'd leave Horatio to it.

More haste, less speed. The sort of infuriating thing

Imogen says, but true nonetheless. I put my finger through my tights in a place that was going to show and had to search desperately for a clean pair in the rubble that counts as 'putting things away' in my drawers. After that I decided it wouldn't hurt Stefano to wait, he had Horatio to look after him and James would be back soon, so I took my time over choosing which jumper suited me best (I didn't have much choice, there were only two that were clean and without holes under the arms) and putting on confidence-boosting make up. Five minutes later I stepped out, dressed, groomed, coiffed and displaying a lot more of myself than I had when I'd answered the door. Stefano stood up promptly as I came in. I felt this had less to do with formal *politesse* than an urgent desire to get Horatio off his knee.

He was making me nervous, just being there. It was too easy to believe every word of what James had told Sam yesterday about someone who was staring at me with black brows drawn together in a straight line, mouth grim and unsmiling. I said uncertainly, 'You'll have some coffee, won't you?' and headed straight for the kitchen to make it without waiting for an answer. I needed some sort of stiffener, and I'd already made a bad enough impression without adding to it by hitting what was left in the gin bottle before midday. So it would have to be a hefty dose of caffeine, just the thing to get my nerves *really* jangling. Stefano followed me and stood watching me in brooding silence as I ladled coffee into the filter paper. His unwavering gaze was making me even more edgy. 'How's Cressida?' I asked to break the hush. 'Did the operation go well?'

'Perfectly. She is a bit sore, of course, but she has already had a walk down the corridor.'

My heart gave a nasty little tumble. He sounded so severe I wondered if there had been another row or, God forbid, if there was something else which Cressida had done and hidden from me? I ploughed on, 'And the baby? You must be so thrilled.'

His sombre expression instantly faded and he took on the beaming look of the intensely proud expectant father. 'Yes, I am. I am still not quite used to it.'

The frank delight in his voice made me feel all gooey and sentimental inside. He sounded like a changed man, reformed by impending fatherhood, I thought mistily. 'You should have seen Cressida's face when the nurse told her! She was completely over the moon!' No need to mention that she probably saw it as the best timed marriage saver ever.

His dark eyes flashed. 'I was afraid she didn't want children.'

'She seems to have got her wires in a bit of a twist,' I said carefully, wondering how pleased he would be if he knew exactly how much Cressida had confided in me. I was absolutely sure he wasn't the sort of man who would appreciate someone knowing that he'd been driven to slipping off quietly to a fertility clinic to get himself tested. 'She was worried you wouldn't find her attractive once she was pregnant.'

'Impossible!' he exclaimed incredulously. It could never have occurred to Stefano that there were *any* circumstances in which he wouldn't find his wife attractive. Well, I approved of men like that, I decided, thinking that perhaps he did have the makings of a good egg or whatever the Italian equivalent was. A *buon uovo*, presumably.

'What are the visiting hours for the ward? I'll go along and see her this evening.'

The mood of bonhomie vanished like hail in a micro-wave. 'I am not sure—'

'Oh, I won't stay for ages and exhaust her, I promise you.'

He bent down and brushed cat hair off his immaculately pressed dark trousers. 'The truth is, Laura, that I would prefer it if you didn't go to see Cressida.'

'Might I ask why?' I said after a moment.

He straightened up to look at me. 'While I realise it isn't actually your fault that she had appendicitis—'

'How kind of you to acknowledge that!'

His jaw tightened. I'd forgotten that Stefano didn't care to be interrupted. He glared at me and went on, 'I think your influence on her is not good.' This statement was so outrageous I could only stare at him, no doubt with my mouth open in very unflattering fashion. 'Of course I should have known that anyone associated with James Lovatt would not be reliable, but you have – what do you call it? – an honest face. I believed I could trust you.'

'What have I done to deceive you?' I asked, finding my voice.

'To start with, you were not honest about your other boyfriend.'

I raised my eyebrows. 'What makes you believe I'm obliged to tell you *anything* about my love life?'

Our eyes locked, then vaguely to my surprise his dropped. He must have conceded that point. 'And you promised me you would tell where she was.'

'All I promised was to tell you if she was with James, and she wasn't!' I corrected him.

Stefano sighed impatiently. 'You know perfectly well that you broke – how do you English put it? – the spirit of our agreement, if not the letter. You should have told me you had found her. You, of all people, knew how worried I was about her.' He shot me a pugnacious glance but I didn't say anything. I couldn't. A guilty little voice was telling me I could at least have sent him a message as soon as I realised Cressida wasn't being entirely honest about her efforts to get in touch with him, but I could hardly tell him that at that point I was still not completely sure he hadn't been doing something horrible to her. 'And then to be irresponsible enough to persuade her to go to France with you, and put her in danger by insisting she come to that ridiculous conference! How stupid are you to book a riverside hotel in this season?' He shuddered dramatically. 'When I think that my precious girl could have drowned because of you, I feel like killing you!' His hands flexed on the counter top.

My mouth snapped shut at last and I slammed the tin of coffee in my hand down on the chopping board. Stefano stopped in mid-denunciation and looked at me in mild surprise.

'I've had just about *enough* of this!' I said in a tight voice. 'I refuse to carry the can because your wife doesn't appear to be able to behave like an adult. None of this would have happened if she didn't throw temper tantrums like a toddler!' I glanced at him sharply and demanded, 'She's told you the truth, hasn't she? About how she flings antiques around like building bricks?' I saw him wince slightly and it made me even more annoyed that he felt he could lay any responsibility at my door. 'Do you really think I wanted Cressida tagging along when I was making my first trip to see my mother in nine months? Or to put myself fathoms deep in debt paying nearly all her expenses because she went on buying clothes even after she knew her Gold Card wouldn't work?'

'She told me she'd borrowed some money off you. If you are so worried about it I can give you a cheque now,' he said in a bored voice, patting his pocket, 'or cash if you prefer. How much is it? About a hundred pounds?'

'More like five or six hundred!' I said coldly. His eyebrows shot upwards. 'I'll work it out accurately and give you an account. I'd hate you to feel that besides deliberately endangering your wife I was making a profit out of you as well!'

He sucked in breath through gritted teeth. 'I do not believe it was deliberate,' he declared as if he was generously conceding a point. 'You may have meant well, but you did not think far enough ahead.'

'Well, *thank you*!' I snapped. 'And did *you* think ahead when you told Cressida she was being put under the jailership of your mother?' I was pleased to see he looked as if I'd just hit him. 'Or did you bother to think that your and Cressida's shenanigans were probably going to cost me my job?'

He started. 'I do not understand. What have Cressida and I to do with your job?'

I glared at him bitterly. 'To start with, my boss wasn't impressed by your bursting in to the office and creating a row. Still less by my taking a friend along to a client's sales conference, no matter how useful her language skills turned out to be. I've got to explain myself to her tomorrow morning, and I've a jolly good idea what she's going to say. The chop. Push off. Finito.' I took a deep breath, absolutely determined I wasn't going to let this horrible man see how worried I was about my future. 'And the basic reason I'm going to get the sack is because you and Cressida prefer throwing dramatic scenes to talking to each other!' I said, punctuating each word by jabbing a finger towards him. 'So how *dare* you blame me for *anything*, you . . . you ungrateful *toad*!'

Judging from his stupefied expression Stefano had been called many things in his life but never that. He opened his mouth to speak but before he could say anything I pushed past him roughly, not trusting myself to stay in the same room as him. 'I'll go and get Cressida's case from my bedroom. I won't keep you more than a minute so perhaps you'll be good enough not to add unreasonable delay to the list of my sins you're compiling!'

The case was dumped unceremoniously in the middle of the living-room floor. Horatio had made himself a comfortable nest on the coat Stefano had flung across one of the chairs. I didn't remove him. I hoped Stefano was allergic to cat hair. I marched back to the kitchen. Stefano still hadn't moved. Hands shaking with temper, I placed three packages in front of him. 'Your property, I believe.'

He glanced down vaguely. 'Are these something to do with Cressida?' He looked at one curiously and pulled at the wrappings. A cherub's head appeared. 'Oh,' he said, for once apparently lost for words.

'I'm beginning to regret not telling her about the interesting things we found in James's house, but at the time I didn't want her to think badly of you.'

He lifted his head; to my amazement he was flushing brick red beneath the olive tone of his skin. 'Thank you,' he said quietly. Stefano was many things but at least he wasn't a hypocrite. 'How did you find them?'

I told him and he nodded. 'I knew you were clever.'

He needn't think he could get around me by paying me compliments now. 'I was only going to use them to threaten James, make him tell me where Cressida was,' he said absently as he finished unwrapping the cherub and laid it down.

I raised my eyebrows sceptically. 'Like hell you were! You were trying to teach him a lesson. Show him how powerful you are, how you can skirt around the law, plant evidence of a crime, do what you like. Let him know that people who cross you are never safe.'

Stefano stared at me. 'You are very acute, Laura.'

'Not really. I'm only just beginning to appreciate the sewer-like paths of your mind.' He looked really annoyed at that. I cast a wistful glance at the coffee machine and wondered if I could pour myself a cup. I was damned if I was going to offer him one now, he didn't deserve my hospitality. I decided I could quite easily ignore the manners carefully driven into me by Mum and Imogen. I got my mug out of the cupboard, saying over my shoulder, 'And if you hadn't been able to persuade the police to have the house searched? I doubt Dolly the domestic treasure could have been tricked into letting your man in a second time so your lesson would have been a very expensive waste of time.'

Stefano shrugged in the manner of a man who can afford to lose a few thousand without it hurting too much. 'It would not have mattered, they aren't pieces I care about very much.'

'If you don't care for those cherubs you have no soul!' I retorted. I filled my mug and took a reviving gulp. His mouth tightened as he noted the omission of a cup for himself. I leaned back against the cooker and looked at him. 'But surely you know that James just gets more and more stubborn if he's threatened? He'd never have told you where Cressida was, whatever you did, even if he knew.'

He shook his head. 'I didn't expect he would. He is no weakling. I was merely starting my revenge. For his stealing my wife from me. And my china.' His eyes narrowed reflectively. 'And if he had taken either he would have been a lot safer in prison than anywhere I could reach him.'

Funny how he and James were in complete agreement on that point.

He was so direct, so straightforward in his belief that what he'd done was at the very least understandable, if not absolutely justified, that I almost laughed. It was that or give way to fear. What had he been planning to move on to next? And in their capacity to find an excuse for whatever they did he and Cressida were well matched, I thought, annoyance mounting again and vanquishing the collywobbles.

'So you set James up for his own sake, to avoid being tempted to do him over?' I said derisively. 'How very noble of you!' Stefano's jaw tightened aggressively. 'And it was a complete waste of time too. For heaven's sake, he certainly didn't want to take her—'

Stefano shook his head disbelievingly, as if it were impossible that any man wouldn't want to run off with Cressida if he had the chance.

'And she's never had any intention of going back to him, no matter what she might taunt you with when she's annoyed!' His face wore the blank mask of someone who is hearing, but not listening to what is being said to them. 'I've just spent a solid week in Cressida's company and I can swear that it was *you* she was thinking about all the time, *you* she referred everything back to, *you* she talked about until I was about to *scream* at the sound of your name!'

The exasperation in my voice caught his attention. The aggressive set of his cashmere-covered shoulders relaxed. 'This is true?'

I bared my teeth in a smile. 'Right now I'm not in the mood to make up nice little lies to make you feel better. So if I tell you Cressida would no more dream of leaving you for another man than fly to the moon, you'd better believe it, buster!'

He was silent, fingers running absently over the face of the cherub, tracing the little upturned nose, the curve of the smiling mouth. 'And the way they were during the hunt ball?' he asked at last. 'They never stopped embracing!'

'A bit of an exaggeration. I don't know what Cressida thought she was up to. Maybe playing power games, showing that if you didn't do what she wanted she had other fish she could fry if necessary.' The sharp look I got indicated that perhaps I'd hit a chord. 'A dangerous game,' I added, and got a nod in response. 'And as for James, I think he just enjoyed yanking your chain a little.'

Stefano stared at me, puzzled.

'You ground his face in the proverbial dirt when you took Cressida from him – did it publicly too. I expect he couldn't resist dealing out a bit of the same when he got the opportunity. That's all.'

Stefano inclined his head as if he totally understood this macho way of thinking. 'But he is still in love with her. Everyone knows that!'

'Who says so?' I asked scornfully. 'Cressida?' Bet I was right there. 'It's not true, and I wouldn't hang around him if it were. I'm not into three in a bed, even if one of the three is a figment of wistful imagination! But I'm not going to say anything more about it. You're too pig-headed to see that the most James feels for Cressida is fondness and that all she wants to do is flirt with him. You must positively *enjoy* being jealous!'

Somewhat to my surprise he didn't fly into a rage, merely took a deep breath and said slowly, 'You are very sure.'

'I am.'

'Good, I am glad for you. It is not pleasant to doubt the one you love – I don't do it through choice. Maybe now I can be easier.' He looked at me out of those dark eyes and smiled. 'I can believe that if you really are James's girl-friend he has no need to look at other women.' The look he gave me spoke volumes. I wondered if he had known about the deception right from the very beginning, before James ever took me to the hunt ball. 'Certainly not at my wife,' he added pointedly. Then, as if the atmosphere hadn't recently heated to about a thousand degrees, he pulled down the cuffs of his shirt, adjusted them just so, and casually shoved the cherub back into its wrappings. 'Thank you for the offer of a cup of coffee,' not by the flicker of an eyelid did he indicate that I'd pointedly not given him one, 'but I must return to my sister who will be awaiting news. Cressida has been moved to room 8 in the private wing of the hospital,' he said, tucking the three packages under one arm. 'I know she will be pleased to see you.'

So I was reinstated as *persona grata*, with presumably this being all the apology I or James was ever going to get. I really didn't know whether to laugh or weep with frustration.

Stefano looked with displeasure at Horatio who was comfortably curled up with one paw, rather sweetly I thought, tucked into the sleeve of the coat, and removed him at arm's length as if he were something particularly noxious. He shook the coat out vigorously before he put it on and picked up the suitcase. 'This is everything?' he asked.

I was about to say yes, go, and good riddance when I realised that the faun was still wrapped up in its bag under my bed. I opened my mouth to say so when Horatio, quite unperturbed by being dropped on to the floor again, sidled up to Stefano and began to rub himself against his trouser leg. Impatiently Stefano pushed him away with his foot, not very hard but roughly enough to make me see red. *Nobody* kicks my cat. Stefano stared at my open mouth coldly and repeated in the tone of a potentate addressing a particularly stupid shoe shine boy, 'Is that all?'

'No,' I said finally. 'It isn't. You owe us, Stefano. What are you going to do about it?'

I stopped, appalled by my own daring as his face set in forbidding lines. 'What do you mean?' he hissed. 'Do you wish me to repay you your money now?'

He said it with such contempt I got annoyed again. 'I said I'd give you an account and I will. I'd like to be repaid by the end of the week. It's James I'm talking about, not me.'

'What?' asked Stefano in bewilderment.

'For the last two weeks you've been harassing him with private detectives, trying to pin crimes on him, sending stinking so-called tramps to sit outside his shop and bogus former buyers to put off customers inside. And I daresay you've been passing round the word that what he sells is complete junk too.' Stefano's eyelids flickered so I reckoned I wasn't far wrong there. 'Generally making his life hell for no good reason. You need to make it up to him.'

Stefano's eyes narrowed. 'And if I don't?'

I took a deep breath. 'You don't get the faun back,' I said in a rush before I could wimp out.

In the long silence that followed I almost did several times. It was only the thought of the odious satisfaction Stefano would feel when I obediently presented him with the bronze that stopped me from scuttling into my bedroom and digging it out. He looked at me incredulously. 'Laura, are you trying to *blackmail* me?'

I shrugged weakly. 'Yes, I suppose I am.'

To my immense surprise he began to laugh. 'Do you have any idea what a – as you English say – can of worms you are opening?'

'Probably,' I admitted.

'So what do you want?'

I didn't know precisely. I hadn't got that far. 'Do what he was hoping for in the first place,' I said at last. 'Give him a commission to find the furniture for your new hotel.' Stefano's eyebrows went up and I said placatingly, 'It's not as if it's going to cost you very much. You know yourself that he has a good eye and once word gets around that you've employed him it'll offset all that bad-mouthing you've been doing.'

'That is all?'

'I think so.' I frantically tried to work out from Stefano's impassive expression whether I'd asked for too much or too little. I began to quail under his considering look and was inwardly pleased when I heard the muffled sounds of someone trying to insert a key and open the door while not bothering to put down what they're holding. I smiled apologetically at Stefano and sidled over to open the door before James's curses became audible to the old lady down the corridor.

'Thanks, sweetheart,' he said putting down three carrier bags and clasping me around the waist. 'Mmm, nice skirt. Did I tell you what good legs you've got?'

'Several times,' I muttered in acute embarrassment. From where he was standing Stefano had a direct view to the front door. '*James!* Stop that!' I hissed as he showed signs of investigating to see if there were tights or stockings under the skirt. 'We've got a visitor!'

James looked up, let me go and stalked stiff-legged like a bristling dog into the sitting room. 'Good morning, Stefano,' he said with a marked lack of enthusiasm. 'How's Cressy?'

'Very well,' said Stefano with equal warmth.

'I suppose you've come to collect her luggage,' said James, stating the blindingly obvious. 'Don't let me delay you.'

'I will not, I promise,' Stefano assured him, 'but I have some business to finish with Laura first.'

James moved swiftly to my side, putting his arm around my shoulders. 'I won't have you bullying her, Stefano! Do you hear?'

His eyes glinted with amusement. 'Perfectly, but I think you have it wrong. I have not the chance, it is *she* who is bullying *me*!'

I squirmed uneasily under James's questioning look. I didn't think he'd approve of my amateurish blackmail attempts. Stefano smiled and said, 'Laura tells me she will not give me back the faun unless I do as she wishes.'

I was right. '*Laura!*' James exclaimed in an appalled voice.

'She wants me to give you a contract to supply furniture for the hotel.' Stefano's dark eyes flicked to James's arm, still draped possessively around me. 'I cannot see that my partners will object. After all, it is not your *professional* expertise I have ever objected to.' Their eyes met in complete accord. 'And what else, Laura?' Stefano continued, still looking amused.

I couldn't think. 'You could call the detectives off.'

'I have already done that. I got bored of reading about

you kissing on doorsteps.' I felt myself begin to blush. James chuckled. 'Besides they were not efficient. Only fools would have allowed themselves to be shaken off as they were yesterday. And you, Laura, what do you want for yourself? A new job? With the hotel?'

'No,' I said without hesitation, unable to think of anything worse than working for Stefano. Actually I didn't want to lose the job I'd already got. I enjoyed it. I'd miss it, even Darian. 'But if someone from the hotel were to contact the agency, saying they'd like to talk about us doing your PR and insisting I was involved, they wouldn't dare sack me in case they lost a potential big client. And by the time they discover they aren't going to get it all the fuss about Cressida's going to the conference will have died down.'

Stefano nodded in agreement, then waved his hand imperiously. 'No. It is better you have the account. One agency is much like another, I find.' I choked, imagining Darian's horrified reaction to this piece of heresy. He smiled evilly. 'I shall, of course, insist you are our account executive. I look forward to working with you.'

I was speechless, envisaging a future where Stefano would be going over my press releases with a fine-toothed comb. What had I got myself into? I thought, appalled. Maybe the dole queue had its attractions after all. Then I realised that Darian, as my director, would have to be involved on an account this big and began to think of client meetings with both her and Stefano present. They had got on *so* well before . . . Maybe my prospects for a happy working life weren't so dark after all.

Stefano pushed up his sleeve to look at his watch and

said, 'I do not like to hurry you, Laura, but I must leave. May I have my bronze now?' I hesitated for just a moment and a faint shadow crossed his face. 'I assure you, I will keep my word. You have heard the expression "Honour amongst thieves"?'

It wouldn't have occurred to me to call Stefano anything so straightforward as a thief, but I got his point. Anyway, there wasn't going to be much I could do if he decided not to keep his word, so I went and fished amongst the dustballs for a masterpiece of Florentine bronze sculpture.

Stefano turned the package over and over in his hands as if he didn't dare open it and look inside. 'How badly is it damaged?' he asked quietly.

'Less badly than the Carvello bronze,' James said, referring to a statue of Mercury that had been attacked by a lunatic with a hammer the year before, 'but it's bad enough. Your problem is going to be finding someone sufficiently discreet with the skill to do the repairs.'

A long look passed between the two of them. 'You know someone?' asked Stefano.

'Possibly,' James said guardedly.

He did? I thought in surprise. How come? There seemed to be a lot I needed to find out about James. Was it normal for antiques dealers to know who the dodgy restorers were?

Stefano finally left after flamboyantly kissing my hand and telling me he was particularly looking forward to our future association, something which made James put one arm pointedly around my waist. Stefano kissed my hand again. To stop James doing something provocative like telling Stefano to give his dearest love to Cressida I handed him the carrier bags and told him to go and unpack them in the kitchen while I saw our visitor to the door.

Stefano stopped by the open door and said quietly, 'My partner will ring James tomorrow. But do not expect me to become friends with him. That is too much. He was with my wife before me, and I am old-fashioned and jealous enough to mind about that very much.'

'Fair enough. I'm not sure James really wants to be *your* friend either,' I said. 'Business acquaintance will do him fine.'

'And Cressida would be sorry to lose touch with you.'

'Yes, I'd miss her too,' I replied. 'I look forward to lots of long, gossipy girls' lunches.'

Stefano's eyes met mine. 'I think we understand each other,' he said with one of his sudden charming smiles. 'I do have a soul, Laura, and I think these should be where they are most appreciated. I am not ungrateful for what you did. Thank you.' He placed the parcels containing the cherubs in my hands, kissed me on both cheeks and was off down the corridor before I could find the voice to thank him.

James was standing in prime viewing position, arms folded. 'And what was all that about?' he asked severely after I had shut the door.

I grinned at him. 'Nothing important. Stefano's just given me a present.'

'You know what they say about Greeks bearing gifts? The same applies to certain Italians.' He looked at me suspiciously then sighed. 'Honestly, Laura, I don't know what came over you. You must have been mad!'

'You'd have done the same, given the chance,' I pointed out, reasonably enough.

'Yes, but it's all right for me to take risks,' he said with that weird male logic so prevalent in the species. 'I don't know whether to throttle you for being so stupid and foolhardy, or kiss you for being so clever.'

I tilted my face towards him. 'May I suggest the latter?' I said hopefully.

'Good idea,' he said, taking the cherubs away and putting them on the table.

'What about breakfast?' I asked a few minutes later.

'Bother breakfast,' said James. 'This is much more important.'